THE BROKEN CAGE

BY MARTIN WILSEY

To the most interesting man
in the world!!

The Broken Cage

Cover Art by Jessica E.

Edited by Helen Burroughs - HKelleyB@aol.com

ISBN-13: 978-1508439370
ISBN-10: 1508439370

For more information:

Blog: http://wilseymc.blogspot.com/
Web: http://www.baytirus.com/

Email: info@baytirus.com

THE SOLSTICE 31 SAGA:

STILL FALLING (2015)

THE BROKEN CAGE (2015)

BLOOD OF THE SCARECROW (2016)

FOR CADY AND GRAY

BEING YOUR DAD IS THE
MOST FAVORITE THING I AM

THE BROKEN CAGE

CHAPTER ONE

The *Ventura* is Falling

"We never expected the *Ventura* to be immediately attacked the morning we attained orbit. We only survived because Commander Worthington followed regs."

--Solstice 31 Incident Investigation Testimony Transcript: Captain James Worthington, senior surviving member of the Ventura's command crew.

Lieutenant Myers, the engineering chief, died without knowing that Commander James Worthington's strict adherence to regulations would have saved him. He hit the ceiling on the bridge of the pinnace, the *Memphis*, so hard his skull was crushed and his neck was instantly broken. The other six members of the command crew were all strapped into five-point harnesses. The first wave of fragments from the nuclear explosion that destroyed the *Ventura* only took seven seconds to reach them. The larger wreckage took a bit longer and was far worse.

"Cook, get us out of here!" Commander Worthington barked at the pilot.

Worthington would not realize until later that his collarbone was broken. Lieutenant Richard Cook was already moving. The main engines were only able to fire at full power for a few seconds before the debris struck the pinnace at an extremely high velocity. It ripped through the center and port-side engine bells, penetrating all the way to engineering.

The pinnace's main reactors automatically went off-line, along with most of the primary systems.

The *Memphis* went into an end-over-end tumble as it was thrown farther out into space. Still, it was pelted with fragments.

The bridge went black and then the emergency lights came up, along with several audible alarms from the various systems that were now off-line.

"Inertial dampeners and artificial gravity are off-line! We have major hull breaches on decks three through five, including main engineering." Matt Tyrrell, the communications officer, spoke quickly and professionally for so much going on.

"No shit, Matt," Cook yelled to Tyrrell.

Myers' body crashed into the back of Cook's seat, as it slammed around the cabin unsecured. Blood flew everywhere.

"Damage report," Worthington called out.

"Comms down," Tyrrell called.

"All navigation off-line. Computers down," Karen Beary replied.

"Tactical on emergency power. Sensor array only shows thirty percent responding," chimed Peter Muir from Worthington's right.

"I've got nothing, sir," Security Chief Valerie Hume reported.

As Myers slammed like a pinball into her console, Hume bear-hugged the dead body to keep it from hurting anyone as it crashed about in zero gravity. She was petite but very strong.

"What do we have?" Worthington asked, as he tried to get his own systems to respond.

"Main engines are down with all secondaries down as well. Grav-foils are off-line. No power. All that's left is manual thrusters. Trying to stabilize now," Cook said.

"Nav's got nothing," Beary called.

"Trying to switch visual to emergency power and Personal HUD feeds," Peter Muir called.

"AI is down," Worthington reported.

"I have proximity HUD comms, Commander. I'm putting everyone on broadcast."

The entire crew of the *Memphis* had Deep Brain Implant Personal High-Definition Heads-Up Display and Communications Systems. It allowed them to access audio and video via their own eyes and ears.

Suddenly, the entire bridge crew heard screams via their internal HUDs. The display showed them it was Ensign Jennings. The feed lasted only a few seconds and then went silent.

"This is Worthington. Ship comms are down. Emergency Personal HUD comms have been initiated. If you are outside the bridge, crew sound off," the commander said, as he restored emergency power to his console and it booted up.

"Weston here. Dock Bay. Everyone not strapped in is dead, sir. I was strapped in, but I think my shoulder is dislocated."

"Same in medical. All three of us were strapped in, Jim. But, Duncan and Sarah are unconscious," Dr. Shaw announced, as she dodged a medical bag that had not been secured.

"Commander, Elkin here." She broke into a series of coughs. "Everyone in here is gone, Jim. There's a massive breach all the way into main engineering and…and all the compartments aft of the reactor control room. There's an electrical fire in here, somewhere. The control room is filling with smoke. I need to get out."

Cook got the tumble under control.

"Elkin…Trish." He used her first name for the first time. "We need power. Fast."

"Yes. Sir." She muted her mic.

"Commander. This is Dr. Angie Bowen. What the fuck are you doing?" she scolded.

"There are four of us from the lunar survey team in the forward command briefing room. All have minor injuries. It's full dark in here. We're all strapped in. Your blind following of regulations seems to have been—" Worthington cut her off.

When the hell did fastening your seat belts become blind following of regs?

"Stay there, Bowen," Worthington replied. Comms muted her mic.

Worthington saw in his command HUD all the icons of the people that were supposed to be onboard. More than half were red, no vital signs present.

Suddenly, consoles came to life all over the bridge.

"Bless you, Lieutenant Elkin," Jim said, under his breath, as the command consoles lit.

"Sensors are coming up. OH, SHIT!" Muir called out, as he saw it.

They were going to crash into the moon.

Cook didn't wait for orders. He rolled the ship and engaged all the landing thrusters to arrest their descent into the surface. Without inertial dampening, they were all jacked around and then jammed into their seats at about 4Gs.

Suddenly, all the blood floating in the cabin fell to the floor.

The *Memphis* pitched up on the starboard side. "Some of the aft thrusters are damaged." He made corrections by feel.

"Impact in twenty-five seconds," Beary said, professionally.

"Grav-plating power restored," Elkin gasped over the HUD.

"Cook. Foils. Now!" Worthington shouted to Cook, who had already deployed them.

Hume prepared for this by tucking Myers' body beneath her legs. When the gravity returned on the command deck, they heard a great, roaring groan coming from the infrastructure.

"Impact in eight, seven, six...Descent stopped. We are hovering 112 meters from the surface." Muir breathed a sigh.

"Commander." It was Elkin, gasping again on the comms. "This reactor will breach if I don't shut her down in less than a minute. The core of reactor number two has already been jettisoned. Number three is dark." She fell into a more severe coughing fit.

"Cook!" Worthington called.

"Landing sequence initiated. The AI is off-line. Going manual."

"Jesus, RC. You ever land a pinnace on manual?" Beary called out.

"First time for everything..." Cook said, concentrating.

Cook had a specialized pilot interface within his HUD. Using it, he rapidly found a site and set her down faster than he liked, but he'd take it. It hit hard, but the landing struts held.

"We're down."

"Elkin, shut down the reactor!" Jim ordered.

There was no reply.

All the lights went out. Again.

***

The HUD comms went down with the reactor. However, Tyrrell had a special comms package in his HUD that allowed everyone to talk to him.

Everyone was injured in some way. Most of the injuries were sustained during the initial shockwave of debris. Even with inertial dampeners on, the impact was heavy. There were hull breaches all over the ship, but the fact that the section hatches were secured as part of Worthington's by-the-book procedures saved them, again, just as the belts saved them, initially.

It took them almost twenty minutes to find a route to get to Elkin. She was unconscious but alive.

"I think she put out the fire, sir, and then exposed the compartment to the vacuum of space for a few milliseconds to evacuate the smoke. Out the forward hatch that opens into engineering," Hume said, as Jim and Peter lifted Elkin to take her to the infirmary.

"The gravity feels like less than .2G, Jimbo," Peter said.

Hume said, "Jim, we need her bad. All the goddamn engineers are dead, except for her and Ensign Weston. And he is trapped, for now, in the dock bay. No offense, but I know more about goddamned reactors than he does."

"Tyrrell says that Dr. Shaw has a med bay up on stand-alone emergency power."

Worthington rounded a corner, moving fast toward the infirmary when his way was blocked by Dr. Bowen and the other members of her survey team.

"Move it," Worthington barked. The three he didn't know, immediately, pressed against the wall; but, Bowen held her arms wide to stop them as she spoke.

"What have you done, you Neanderthal?" Bowen said to Commander Worthington.

Hume was there first, drawing her sidearm and pointing it at Bowen's face. "Clear this corridor. NOW!"

Hume, who was experienced in lower than normal gravity security tactics, didn't slow as the group moved toward the infirmary, and didn't wait for Bowen to move. Dr. Bowen found herself knocked off her feet, and sliding on her ass, for ten meters, into a side corridor.

Lights were brighter in the med unit. They ran on batteries in there, all the time, for a reason Jimbo couldn't remember right now.

Another explosion rocked the ship, and tossed them into the infirmary and onto the floor.

"What the hell was that?!" Hume called out. Tyrrell replied to everyone.

"Large wreckage is impacting on the surface of the moon, all around us." Tyrrell's response was punctuated by more explosions that didn't rock the ship.

"Commander. This is Dr. Ibenez. I have a portable scanner, and it shows we have a shit-storm of shrapnel coming this way! The *Ventura* is gone. In pieces."

As they lay her down onto the med bay unit, Lieutenant Trish Elkin was recognized by the autoDoc.

Jim looked at Dr. Shaw, "Beth, we need her awake. Now. We need to get that reactor back online, fast. Or, we're all dead."

She looked from Jim to Elkin for a brief instant, and then entered a code into the small, side panel. A voice sounded, "Warning: You have activated emergency med protocol eleven. Command staff approval is required."

"Confirm. Worthington, 47748394559," Jim said.

Instantly, arms deployed from within the autoDoc to forcibly restrain Elkin. The side panels closed, and a scanner bar passed over her that was far too bright to look at directly. Three more arms deployed and took hold of her head. Another arm opened her mouth, while yet another slipped a large tube down her throat.

Her eyes fluttered open. A look of panic came over her. "I'm sorry, Trish. Don't panic. It'll be alright," the doctor said, as she watched.

Trish tried to struggle. She even attempted to scream, but the sound could not get past the tube. She felt the nanites fill her lungs and get injected into her neck by so many cruel little arms. She felt their chill as they spread to her brain.

When all the tubes and arms suddenly retracted, Elkin had to take a deep breath to scream. This drew the nanites in further.

When she finally screamed, a white fog emitted from her mouth and nose.

A med tech Jimbo didn't know walked up and handed him an oxygen mask and a small tank. "She'll need this today. Don't let her scratch her eyes."

The autoDoc opened and retracted until Elkin sat upright, eyes wide, panting. "What the hell?" she gasped.

"You have severe lung damage, from smoke inhalation, and deep burns. You've been injected with so many nanites, stims, and other drugs, you probably won't sleep for a week. If we live that long," Worthington said, close to her ear.

An even bigger explosion rocked the ship, bigger than the last one.

Jimbo held her face with both hands as he spoke, quietly but firmly, "Elkin, we need to move the ship out of harm's way." Another impact, on the hull this time. "I need sensors and grav-foils, enough to move the ship to the far side of this moon. You're all I have." He released her as she nodded and placed the mask over her nose.

"I'm headed to the bridge," Cook said, and loped away in the lower gravity.

"Holy shit, doc." Trish looked at Dr. Shaw, wide-eyed. "That really hurts. I LIKE IT!" She jumped off the autoDoc and headed for reactor control. Worthington followed.

"Not for long..." Beth said.

"Make her take O_2 every couple of minutes," she called after them.

***

It turned out to be easier to bring reactor number three back up than to even begin to troubleshoot number one. The core on number two had been damaged, and ejected; so, they quickly rerouted the cooling conduits to number three. Elkin had number three up to thirty percent in less than eleven minutes.

"Grav-foils and sensors powered. Move it out, Mr. Cook!" Commander Worthington barked from the reactor room. He handed Elkin the O_2 again.

He could feel the 1G plates come back up as they lifted off. Flying by Kidwell grav-foils was interesting without the main computer automatically compensating. It felt like a water vessel in heavy seas.

Elkin was nearly manic with the hemitrophic stims coursing through her system. Sarah Wood, the med tech, was assigned to monitor her, for now, while Jim got back to the bridge.

As he entered, Jim heard Dr. Bowen over the comms, screaming at Tyrrell to give her an open channel.

"Dr. Bowen, we are under attack. Any active broadcast will give away our position. Standard procedure is—" Tyrrell explains, as Jim broke in.

"Bowen, if you try to transmit ANYTHING, I will put you in the airlock and space you myself. Now, shut the hell up and strap in because we will likely crash, again, at any moment." He cut off her comms without waiting for a reply.

"Dammit." Jim finally noticed his broken collarbone as he strapped back into the command chair.

"Matt. Give me ship-wide," Worthington said.

"Go for ship-wide," Matt Tyrrell said.

"People, I need you all to strap in. This isn't over, yet. The *Ventura* has been destroyed, and pieces of it almost took us out with it. Debris is still falling. We're moving the ship to the dark side of this moon and out of harm's way, hopefully."

"Commander. Ship's main screen is back up," Muir said. "No AI, but I have visual."

"Do it," Jim said.

Suddenly, the entire room flashed bright-white. Then, it was like their canopy was gone, and the open sky was above and before them, as they skimmed across the dead surface of the moon.

They saw impacts of various sizes, happening in every direction. They hit at extreme velocity, causing giant plumes of dust or even secondary explosions. Some were far too close.

The door to the bridge slid open and Dr. Bowen stormed in, yelling, "How dare you? Do you have any idea who I am?"

Commander Worthington didn't even turn to look at her. Hume rode Bowen down to the deck as stun gloves administered shocks to the back of her neck. A shocked Bowen thrashed into unconsciousness.

"I want her to wake up in airlock number three," Jimbo said. "Change the access codes on the hatch. I don't have time for her shit right now."

"Stupid bitch," Greg Ibenez said from the door. "Whoa, whoa, whoa, I meant her." Ibenez pointed at Bowen, backing away when he saw Hume move toward him.

"I know a shortcut to airlock number three," Ibenez said, as he smiled at Hume.

CHAPTER TWO

Crash and Run

"I crashed my shuttle on the planet. At the time, I didn't think there were any other survivors. Not on the planet, much less the moon. I didn't know then the depth of the treason that destroyed the *Ventura*."

--Solstice 31 Incident Investigation Testimony Transcript: Master Chief Nancy Randall, senior surviving security member of the Ventura's crew.

"Sonofabitch!" Rand cursed, through clenched teeth, as she ran. She had blood in her eyes. "It just had to be a damned scalp wound," she scolded herself.

She rounded the outcropping of boulders at the edge of the woods as she wiped her eyes, again, with her sleeve. She stumbled, again, but stayed on her feet this time.

"Shit!" she whispered as she acquired concealment within a maze of boulders.

Her Heads-Up Display was specially designed for the tactical units on the mission. Her heart rate, respiration, and other vitals were available at the left edge of her vision. All were elevated. She had to calm down. Date and time were there also, but she noticed a new indicator she had not seen before. Her HUD indicated it was scanning for networks, but was not connected to any, even though one was detected. No time to think about that now.

Rand found a good spot to pause as she leaned her rifle against a stone wall made of boulders. It felt very light in this gravity. She turned her ring around and activated its camera, popping open a vid window in her HUD, as she probed her wound. She took off her helmet, and she easily saw in the window that it was a superficial gash.

"Dammit, .89 gravity."

It made her stumble when she first began to run. She was used to 2G in the outer rings of the *Ventura*. Falling, she cut her head on the shuttle's debris. She had never been this physically fit in her whole life. Life in 2G was the best workout.

Barcus was right.

Shit. She couldn't think about that now. *Barcus is dead.* They were all probably dead.

Without looking, she opened a thigh pocket in her black jumpsuit and withdrew a med spray. Watching in the display, she opened the wound and sprayed into it. The bleeding, as well as the pain, stopped almost at once. Pressing the wound closed, she sprayed it again. She wiped her eyes, one last time, with her sleeve and put her helmet on, as she moved into the shadows.

Leaving the ring camera activated, she launched its small HG drone, which was the size of a housefly. In fact, everyone called it a Fly. No one remembered the actual acronym. It ascended straight up, thirty meters to just above the boulders and trees. After performing the standard 360° orientation sweep, it centered the panorama window on the crash site.

"Holy Mother of God," Rand said, out loud.

I cannot believe I survived that.

The shuttle had broken up into several large pieces. Many were now burning. The command module included, where she had been strapped in when the first explosion hit. She wasn't a pilot, but she knew the ships could fly themselves. She took a moment to remember the long hours in a tumble, never knowing if she was near an impact or if she would burn in the next explosion. She managed to get the emergency systems online, but the ship was half-gone by then.

She had been knocked unconscious when the ship crashed. Her personal emergency HUD implant alarms woke her. Her training kicked in. Her go bag, her rifle, and her training were all she really had. All she ever needed.

The drone video showed people arriving at the crash site. They were not getting too close because of the smoke and fires. An explosion shook the ground, ripping open another section of the fuselage. When the smoke was cleared to the side, by the wind, she saw the edge of an Emergency Module. She keyed the code into her cuff to remotely activate the EM.

Another window opened in her HUD, showing the "Emergency Module Initialization Status" and, it currently said, "Damaged. Please wait."

Much to her surprise, the EM spun up on its emergency start sequence. "Crash Indicated."

It moved.

Rand zoomed her helmet view in on the scene. People on the ground noticed the movement in the fire. The EM ripped itself from the wreckage. She watched as it tore off two damaged legs from the middle joint because they were pinned and crushed. It was now fully engulfed in fire, as it continued to struggle. Rand knew that the conventional fire was no problem for the Emergency Module. It did, fortunately, keep the people back. It looked like a giant spider thrashing in tortured pain because of the intense flames.

It finally shuddered free, dragging two of its broken legs. It still had six functioning legs, three awkwardly placed on each side, so it could still walk. It was designed so it could even walk on only three legs. It began to move north.

From nowhere, a man attempted to block its path, waving his arms. Before Rand could react, the EM crushed him beneath a footpad. It was an accident, but he was still just as dead.

Rand keyed in a survivor code and a rendezvous point. She watched as it limped away in the opposite direction, south, on a vector that would mislead the witnesses. There was a settlement very near to the east that she saw. The EM would, definitely, avoid it. More of its systems came online. Their statuses were conveyed to Rand as they progressed. The advanced AI was off-line. The command AI was up, but it had glitches. It would do, for now. She would have time, later, to assess things.

Just get the hell out of here, she thought. *Figure it the hell out, later.*

That was when she saw the man raise a familiar weapon to his shoulder and fire a burst of light at the retreating spider. *Particle Burst Beam weapons?!* It hit the body of the spider and staggered it. Alarms went off in her display.

Rand was decisive.

All windows closed in her personal HUD, save one. Targeting.

She cleared her cover and, a moment later, was on target by instinct; and, as if by magic, an instant later, the man's head exploded as the 10mm caseless, cannon round sent him to hell.

Six seconds later, the sound of thunderous shots rolled over the man's corpse, sending those around him running.

The spider reached the tree line, as Rand brought the EM status in her HUD back up. "HULL BREACH" flashed in red. Rand said, "*Shit, shit, shit,*" with every flash, like a mantra. She watched the scene through her scope, waiting. It helped her calm down. When another man walked up to the headless body and picked up the dropped Particle Beam Rifle, she fired. The round hit the PB rifle, as he held it, directly in front of his sternum. The rifle exploded and ripped the man in half.

Fuckers. That's two.

She leaned her rifle against a boulder and shouldered into her pack, groaning. Standing back up, she looked inside her shirt and saw that she was already black-and-blue from the crash and the five-point harness.

This is gonna suck.

She properly donned her pack, over the bruises, stifling a gasp. Clipping the clasps, then checking her thigh holster, her Ka-Bar, and her machete, with long-practiced ease, she picked up her rifle and began a ground-eating run to the rendezvous point. The High Ground Fly followed, watching over her.

It's going to be a long damned day.

As she entered the tree line, the shuttle's reactor core exploded. The shock wave almost knocked her off her feet.

***

It didn't take long for her to adjust to the lighter gravity. It made carrying the large rifle, and all the gear, comfortable as she ran. The woods consisted of beautiful, large pine trees with a thick canopy and a soft bed of needles to run on. The trees looked like they had been limbed up about ten meters, and there was no tree fall. None. Not a single twig in the undergrowth.

I bet it has all been collected by nearby settlements. That means the population density here is high. But primitive.

Her HUD displayed a rope of mist that seemed to stretch out before her as she ran. It was leading her to the rendezvous point. At the present pace, her ETA was forty-one minutes.

It took a bit longer, thanks to changes in the terrain. Elevation increased and the land became rockier. At one point, she found herself running on an old logging road, making good time. About thirty-five minutes into her run, she heard a loud roar of engines, above in the trees. It was some kind of aircraft with no grav-neutral plating.

Man that is loud.

She kept running. It took her fifty-five minutes to reach the rendezvous point. She could not believe she got there before the EM. Rand had the Fly search the clearing and the surrounding area.

"Emergency Module, do you read me?"

"I read you. Recommend radio silence. ETA six minutes," the AI's flat voice responded, in her head.

The EM Status window displayed a 3D model of the EM, indicating areas of damage. The third leg on the left side and the front leg on the right side were broken. They were held up off the ground by the EM's utility arms.

The passenger's side door hinge was damaged, as well as the air intake right behind it.

It was the two-seater model, but it would do. Minimal storage, though. Her pack would be fine, for now, in the passenger's seat. But, the EM had no weapon's rack.

Dammit.

She would have to find a way to keep it handy.

"Emergency Module. Window forward display."

A window popped up in her HUD, showing the Module's progress through the forest. The clearing was ahead. The trees were thinning out. The display was not steady. The spider limped.

"Stop at the edge of the clearing. I'll get in."

She heard it clomping through before she saw it.

She stood up and said, "Emergency Module, I am Randall, Nancy J. Log me in. Survival mode. Hostile territory. Escape-and-evade."

"Voice confirmation and login received. Warning: Survival mode unavailable. AI Higher Functions failed to start."

"Never mind that now. Open up." The body of the spider lowered to the ground, the driver's side door unsealed and the reverse gull-wing lifted. "Open the passenger's side." She heard a series of muffled mechanical clicks, but nothing happened.

"Dammit."

She reached in and pushed the pack in the driver's side door, over the console, into the passenger's seat. She climbed in and drew the rifle in behind her. It lay along the center console. That would have to do, for now.

"Link to High Ground Fly 421 as an external source. Audio, video and data."

"Yes, Nancy."

"Call me Rand. I'll call you Bob."

"Bob, sir?"

"Yes. Bob. Fly, ascend to 200 meters and begin mapping. Bob, plot a track to the least populated area within this sector. Transfer tactical to your EMD."

The Emergency Module Display (EMD) inside the vehicle immediately filled with the surrounding area visual. Also, there were damage report status screens, and scrolling color-coded, damage logs. There was far too much red. Only the line that read: "HULL BREACH. Seal not achieved," was red *and* flashing.

"Bob, I want this to be a clean E and E. Escape-and-evade. We need to get to a safer area before we can execute repairs."

A rope of mist appeared before them. They didn't move.

She scanned far too many windows that were open before her. Finally, she saw the problem. She mashed the 'autopilot while pilot aboard' virtual button and set the speed to half. The spider limped head.

"Tactical map, main view." Nothing happened.

"BOB! Tactical map, primary view." The map came up. AI~Bob said nothing.

The scrolling error log showed a new red line: "Error Initializing AI. Attempting Restart. Please Wait."

Worry about it later.

"Bob, please annotate known points on the tactical map."

Icons appeared. They were simple letters. A, B, C, D. There was also a green line and a blue line.

Sigh.

"Replace annotation A with 'Crash Site', Bob." She was annoyed.

"Replace annotation B with 'Rendezvous Point', Bob. Replace annotation C with 'Current Position', Bob. Replace annotation D with 'Current Destination', Bob."

"Display current speed, distance to destination, and estimated time until we reach the destination." Nothing happened.

"Bob, for Christ's sake...Display current speed, distance to destination, and estimated the time until we reach the destination."

"Command not completely recognized."

"Bob, how much faster can we go without risking additional damage?"

The scrolling error log showed a new red line: "Error Initializing AI. Attempting Restart. Please Wait."

AI~Bob had no additional answer.

At least I am not driving on manual.

***

The Fly helped them avoid four sets of people before night fell. Just after dark, it rained, and in the spot where the gull-wing overhead door was not sealed, it leaked, almost dripping on her rifle. Rand rearranged the pack to avoid the drips. She groaned as she stretched across, feeling her bruises.

The Fly had excellent night vision and zoom functions. Even in the rain, it did a superb job locating a deserted barn. Manually controlling the arms on the spider, Rand dropped the damaged legs and let them drag while she opened the doors, drove in, turned around and closed the door behind her.

Rand opened her driver's side door, and with the rifle in hand, dropped easily to the straw covered floor of the barn.

On her cuff control, she put the Fly in night patrol mode, so it would monitor the perimeter all night, alerting her to anything unusual. Fortunately, infrared showed only deer moving through the forest and fields. Then, she activated both the flashlights on the cuff and on the helmet to begin inspecting the Emergency Module. She was surprised to find some gouges in the black outer skin.

"Bob, I'm going to remove the number two and number four body rotator locks and central pins. When I'm ready, I'll tell you to detach them. Please, acknowledge."

"Acknowledged."

After setting down her rifle, she produced a multi-tool from a thigh pocket and removed the rotator locks from the joints of the damaged leg.

"Bob, slowly rotate leg number four at joint one." The leg turned very slowly, and when the large, heavy pin fell out, Rand caught it, but she almost dropped it because it was so heavy.

"Bob, raise your body a bit and shake leg number six."

The leg rattled loose and fell with a dull thud.

The procedure was repeated on number two.

"Bob, can you reach both hands to number five?"

"Yes, Rand." Its two utility arms that hung below the main body to the front, reached forward from the underside of the spider.

"Bob, I'm going to repeat this procedure on number five. But, when I'm done, do not let the leg drop."

She took out the rotator lock and the leg rotated and coaxed out of the joint.

"Now, Bob, I want you to move this leg to the number five position. I plan on reconfiguring it so you have six functional legs set up symmetrically. Three on each side."

"Yes, Rand."

A moment later, the leg was in. "Now, please rotate the joint slowly until it aligns." Bob went by the pinhole, twice. He didn't see it.

"I'll tell you when to stop. Bob...now."

"Rotate seven more millimeters, Bob."

The pin slid in. The EM turned the rotator lock tight.

"Bob, rotate 360° where you stand."

Excellent.

"Okay, Bob. Settle all the way down."

Bob bellied down, folding its arms in. Rand saw the huge gouges in the black surfaces of Bob's body. One of them, torn and twisted, caused a gap along the center hinge seam, right where the leak was.

She lifted the door and slammed it, hard, in an attempt to force it closed, and out of sheer frustration.

It closed and it latched.

"Bob, is the passenger's door sealed? Is hull integrity restored?"

"Negative. Positive pressure tests failed," AI~Bob replied.

"Shit," she said, through clenched teeth.

She stood up and thought for a minute.

"Bob, I want you to shut down and restart in system diagnostic-repair mode. How long will it take?"

"Duration is dependent on the types of issues encountered. Two hours and twelve minutes, if no errors are detected."

"Do it." Nothing happened.

Dammit.

"Bob, shut down and restart in system diagnostic-repair mode. Keep a status window open in my personal HUD, please."

The spider settled down even further in preparation for a full shutdown. Rand picked up her rifle and activated the tactical light, setting it to a wide angle. She swept the light around the empty barn to see if she could find anything useful. She found a shovel and five pitchforks. The structure was a pole-style barn, common on every colony she had ever visited. The roof was sound and had no leaks.

She manually opened Bob's trunk. The shovel was too long and would not fit. Maybe the pack would. Rand decided to leave her pack in the passenger's seat, in case she needed something while on the move in the EM.

Rand explored the area. Hanging in an attached lean-to shed, she found a large, dusty, dark brown hide. It had obviously been there a very long time; it was very stiff. She had an idea. She took down the hide and dragged it back to the Emergency Module. Dropping the skin, she positioned the light on the rifle to illuminate the work area, after making sure the breach was open. She reached in, pulled out her pack and closed the driver's door. In one smooth motion, she spread the hide over the top of the vehicle. After a little positioning, she was satisfied. Going to a predesignated pocket, Rand withdrew a spool of black paracord. It was a very strong, thick string. She could never really call it a rope, but it did have 2,000 kilo test strength.

Using the cord and her small multi-tool, she tied the hide to the surface of the module using the recessed loops utilized on the assembly line for the EM. After tying three points on each side, she tried the driver's door to see if it would open and close easily. It did. The hide rose with the door.

When Bob came back up, she would ask if any of its sensors were obscured. She tied off several more points and stood back to see her work. It suddenly occurred to her that the EM looked like an actual animal now.

Grabbing her rifle, she continued her search, finding nothing of use or of note. The Fly saw nothing and kept vigil.

***

Bob booted back up in four hours and twenty-seven minutes. Most of the prior glitches cleared. The basic AI came online, but there was a problem with the advanced templates. Rand put her pack and her rifle back inside the EM, already designing a ready-rack for the rifle in her mind. She closed the door and the barn fell in darkness.

"Bob, are you feeling okay?" It was the standard question asked an advanced AI.

"Nominal."

It was the basic answer. No personality overlays or specialized programming was integrated. No red message in the error log. She might have to work on that. She remembered that AI development was her friend Chen's favorite hobby.

*Chen is dead. They are all dead...*Anger rose, again.

"Tactical map." She was surprised when the map displayed instantly.

"Full status."

Windows popped open everywhere. She scanned them, one at a time. One even included the feed and system status from the High Ground Fly drone. The status window had a blank field labeled, "Name: <_>".

Hmmmm, I will have to think on that.

"Rand, may I ask a question?"

It was the simulated voice of HAL9000 that spoke, the default AI voice. Stupid tech humor.

"Sure. Ask away."

"Why do you call me Bob?"

She laughed out loud.

"It's an acronym, Bob. Bug Out Boat. Bug Out Boy. Bug Out Bob. Take your pick. Do you want a different name?"

"People usually call me Hal. I have no idea why. I think it is a joke of some kind, but humor still eludes me."

"Bob doesn't feel right, either. The Bob I knew was an idiot," Rand said. "I think I'll call you...Poole. Dr. Frank Poole. Is that okay?"

"I think I like it. Thank you, Rand."

"You're welcome, Poole."

"Dr. Frank Poole is at your service. How may I help you survive this day?"

"Was that a joke, Poole?" Rand smiled.

"That remains to be seen, ma'am."

"If you ever call me ma'am again, I swear to Christ I'll delete you."

"Duly noted...Nancy."

"Call me Rand, or it's Bob, again, for you!"

"I'm sorry, Rand. Another attempt at humor."

"Better," Rand said.

"May I ask one more question?"

"Yes. As long as you stop asking if you may ask a damn question. Just ask the question." She smiled.

"Why is there a rug on me?"

CHAPTER THREE

Crater

"Barcus was the guy who knew the capabilities of maintenance suits and how they worked best. We never knew exactly how durable they were before that. Jack Miller, the poor bastard, fell all the way to the planet inside his. We didn't know that his body had been rotting in there the whole time, half-cooked and pounded to jelly by the impact. The suit's antennas were all destroyed. We didn't know it was there, until we got really close. Close enough to smell it."

--Solstice 31 Incident Investigation Testimony Transcript: Captain James Worthington, senior surviving member of the Ventura's command crew.

The group of trackers reached the crater before the fires stopped.

The great scar that the falling object left in the forest was indicative of the speed that it possessed on impact. The trench it left behind felled trees that were hundreds of years old. The final resting place was a bowl about thirty yards wide and ten deep.

The group lined the rim, looking down at the man-shaped thing at its center. Man-shaped and yet not a man.

It had two legs, two arms and seemed to be resting on its back. That was where the similarities ended. It was blacker than anything the High Keeper's trackers had ever seen, and not just black from the char of sky fall. No light seemed to escape from it. It had no head—just a swollen torso.

High Tracker Tolwood was the first to descend into the crater for a closer look. He felt the heat of it. He took his water flask from his belt and filled his mouth. He spit the water onto the thing and the water turned to steam, instantly.

It felt like he was in front of the forge in a blacksmith shop. He was as close as he was going to get, for now. At this distance, he saw that the forearms seemed to bristle with faintly glowing tools or weapons or fingers with claws.

"We need to cool this down before we can bring it back to the Citadel," he called over his shoulder in the direction of his men. "And, we need lots of ropes and chains."

***

It took two more days before they could drag it out of the crater. It was also far heavier than they thought it would be. It broke the axle of the first cart they brought in. Once they believed it was apparently made of stone, they obtained a cart of the appropriate size and strength.

It took another week to wrestle it back to the nearest clearing where they could safely land a shuttle. They loaded it, cart and all, into the large cargo bay, with the help of an ox they found at a nearby farm.

As cold and as inert as it was, they found if placed upright, it stood on its own wide feet. It looked like a dark statue carved from midnight.

Tolwood supervised the entire process. Once it was brought to the Citadel, he realized why it unnerved him. No matter how many times he had the thing scrubbed, it still had a faint smell of death about it. All the scrubbing in the world could not defeat the scent. Chief Tech Mason studied it for months. But, the smell remained, faint and haunting.

***

Wes Hagan lived. Everyone else in the engineering section of the *Memphis* died.

When the ship was hit, so many things *could* have killed him. The wreckage that tore through the main engines cut Granger in half. The massive hull breach sucked Holcomb and McHale out into space. The rest died in the vacuum of space strapped into their seats.

"How did Captain Everett know?" Wes said out loud, to himself, as he unbuckled his five-point harness and hammered his fist on the emergency lifeboat's access button.

As soon as he was through the hatch, it slammed shut, and he felt the explosive bolts blast the lifeboat away from the *Memphis*. Lights came on, full brightness.

The prerecorded voice spoke directly to the HUD in his mind.

"This is an emergency. Please sit and strap yourself in."

Wes was in his light pressure suit and helmet. It was all that had saved him from the vacuum of space. Hagen felt bulky as he floated toward the pilot's seat. A sudden impact to the hull drove him toward the front, ramming his ribs into the headrest of the pilot's seat. He heard, more than felt, his ribs break.

Alarms sounded. Proximity alarms he recognized. *Shit.*

"Activate emergency AI. Navigation display. Do not crash my boat, you stupid computer!" On the edge of panic, Wes screamed as he strapped in. He felt the lifeboat tumble.

The display dome activated, showing the exterior view. The lifeboat was in a backward tumble. A display window showed the status of the AI, initiating slowly. The lifeboat had been thrown clear of the heavily damaged *Memphis.*

"Goddammit." He hit the manual override, grabbed the grav-foil controls and slowed the roll, as he watched the moon's surface grow closer on every rotation.

The roll was controlled by the time the AI's initialization completed. Hagan hit the decelerators, hard, and leveled off.

He saw chunks of various sizes impacting the moon all around him.

"Emergency Module this is Chief Engineer Wes Hagan. We're in deep shit. Plot a direct vector to a safe landing site. If we're hit by a big piece of the *Ventura*, we are finished."

As if to punctuate the statement, a giant piece of the outer ring impacted the moon's surface directly in front of them, forcing them to fly directly through the resulting cloud of dust and stones.

"Chief Hagan, allow me." The AI took control of the lifeboat.

Hagan released the controls and hugged his ribs. He found it difficult to breathe. He scanned the display windows as the moon's surface rolled by, all too close.

His eyes landed on the AI status display. *ECHO systems active. Emergency mode. Survival situation.*

"ECHO, status? What the hell happened," Wes demanded.

"The *Ventura* was destroyed by multiple nuclear missiles. The planet has an automated defense grid that activated when the ship entered orbit. The *Memphis* was destroyed by multiple, severe impacts from large pieces of the *Ventura*. This lifeboat was the only one activated."

Wes strained to turn and look at the lifeboat. It had been heavily modified. Besides the pilot and copilot seats, it had only twelve other seats.

Three rows of four seats with an aisle down the middle, like a commercial shuttle but less comfortable. Then, there was a wall with a center door.

"Is the compartment depressurized?" The computer's AI didn't reply, but an additional display showed cabin pressure. It said, *Nominal.*

An enormous impact on the hull drove Hagan forward onto his harness. Then, there was pain, followed by darkness.

CHAPTER FOUR

The Tesla Array

"I have been entirely honest regarding Dr. Bowen's treatment. We were all under incredible stress. I will not apologize. I only wish I had blown that bitch out the airlock that first day."

--Solstice 31 Incident Investigation Testimony Transcript: Lieutenant Valerie Hume, the security chief on the Memphis.

It was only a few minutes before Hume returned. Ibenez was still with her.

Without a word, the two of them collected Myers' body and carried him off the bridge.

Worthington said, "We need to hold it together, people, if we're going to survive."

"Commander, Ibenez says he might be able to help at the engineering station. He is technical and has a PhD in patience, apparently. He has worked with Bowen for four years," Hume said, with a bit of forced humor, as she dried her eyes and returned to the security station.

"Do it."

He didn't take his focus from the forward screens. Chunks of the *Ventura* still crashed around them.

"Commander, it's true. Sensor logs show the *Ventura* was targeted and nuked, intentionally. No warning. Shielded orbital platforms just attacked. Missiles, plasma cannons," Ibenez said.

Looking up, they all saw that they just passed over an antenna of some kind. A few moments later, there was another one.

"Sir, I think we are clear," Muir said.

A window from an aft camera opened to the left. They saw more high-velocity projectiles coming in at a steep angle.

"Captain, I think I know what those antenna nodes are," Ibenez said.

"Commander, not captain, Ibenez. But, call me Jim or Jimbo, damn it." Worthington grew serious.

"Sorry, sir."

"What about the nodes?" Jimbo asked.

"I think they're nodes from a Tesla communications array." Greg stared at his console.

Jim pounded a button, a bit too hard, and the engineering console came up in the main viewer.

"The nodes are decreasing their separation," Ibenez said, apparently assuming Jim would know what that meant.

"Spit it out, Ibenez." Worthington sounded angry now.

"A Tesla array is an LSCA, sorry, a Large Scale Communications Array. Ancient tech," Ibenez said.

"So what."

The events were sinking in. Jim replaced adrenaline with anger.

"There's usually a base at the center of the array," Ibenez said.

This was enough for Worthington to turn and look at Greg. He glanced at Hume. She nodded.

Another Klaxon began to sound.

"Another hatch seal has failed. In Engineering. One of the shops." Muir turned off the alarm.

"Sir, the base Ibenez mentioned is ahead, 9° to starboard. It's beaconed. It must have power. Eleven kilometers out," Muir stated.

"Do you think it's defended? What are we up against?" Worthington asked Muir.

Ibenez chimed in again, "Look, I don't know for sure. But, moon-based Tesla Arrays, where the gravity is low, are typically not manned after the array is completed. Initially, hundreds of people worked there, especially if it was long ago. Once completed, the base emptied."

"Commander, Elkin is on comms," Tyrrell called.

"Go, Elkin," Worthington ordered.

"Commander, the reactor core is beginning to spike. I can't explain it. The systems are so compromised, I can't tell if it's about to blow or jettison. We need to stand down, soon." Elkin yelled over the sound of the machines in the background.

"Do not let that reactor dump its core. Override safeties, if you have to," Worthington ordered. "We're dead without that reactor."

"Yes, sir." Elkin signed off.

"It's better to burn out than to fade away," Ibenez said.

The entire bridge crew turned to look at him at the same time.

"What the hell is wrong with you?" Hume asked Ibenez. "They're all dead. Thousands of them. Dead." She was pissed.

"Hey, come on. I'm scared shitless here. I'm handling it," Greg said. "There are a ton of alarms in engineering. Have Walt Edwards go down to help. He's another one from Bowen's survey team. A very smart guy."

Worthington nodded at Tyrrell and he opened a channel. "Walt Edwards, report to Elkin in engineering, stat!"

"Base, dead ahead. There's a landing apron. Just this side of the domes," Beary said.

"Putting it down hot. Stand ready," Cook said.

Cook took the pinnace in fast and set it down after a simple 90° turn. They all felt it.

"Elkin," Jimbo called. "We're down, take the reactor off-line."

Before he finished his sentence, the lights, the screens and the gravity plates went off-line. Emergency lights came back on.

***

They sat on the bridge, not saying a word, for over a minute, just breathing.

"Commander, the crew is checking in. Orders?" Tyrrell asked.

"Have everyone make their way to the ops briefing room, after they safely stabilize all systems. It's directly below the bridge. We also need to search the entire ship for survivors. All compartments," Worthington said, while getting up.

Everyone that could, assembled within three minutes.

"Sir, I saw Dr. Bowen in airlock number three," Trish Elkin said. "My code wouldn't work. With the power off, it will get cold in there, soon."

Worthington sighed and looked at Hume. "I'll take care of it, Elkin."

"Ensign Weston is still trapped in the dock, as well," Tyrrell added.

"We'll systematically search the ship for anyone injured. As of right now, we have fourteen people unaccounted for. Mind the hatch lights. If a hatch light is not green, do not open it. Split up and search. Beary, you and Cook go see what you can do about getting Weston out. Dr. Shaw, go with Elkin down to see about getting the reactor online. Doctor, Elkin's life is the priority. She WILL live. Do you understand?"

"Yes, sir," Dr. Shaw acknowledged.

"We'll meet back here in thirty minutes. Hume, you're with me." Worthington walked out and people fanned out.

They checked every compartment they passed, as they headed for airlock number three. It took longer than they thought because they discovered five dead in the mess hall. All were dragged into the corridor, the task made easier by the lighter gravity.

When they got to airlock number three, they found Bowen trying to pry off the control panel with a fine instrument that was completely wrong for the job.

Worthington tapped the heel of his flashlight on the airlock window and Bowen looked up.

And, she started yelling.

They could not hear her because the viewport material was four inches thick.

"Tyrrell, this is Jimbo."

"Jimbo, go," he replied.

"Can you patch me through to Dr. Bowen?"

"I can. Are you sure you want me to, sir?" Jimbo heard the smile in Tyrrell's voice.

Everyone in the world the man knew is dead and he is amused?

"Do it," Worthington said.

She screamed at him; so, instead of speaking, he opened the control panel and held his hand over the outer door's control.

She stopped.

Worthington barely whispered, knowing it was a menacing tone when sent directly to a HUD.

"Over 2,000 of my friends were just murdered." He let that sink in. "I'm not going to stand for any shit from you. Do. You. Understand?"

She fumed. She drew in a deep breath, for what looked like another tirade.

"DO YOU?" Worthington yelled, losing patience.

Hume turned her back to the scene and moved away, a bit. The implication being, there would be no witnesses.

Bowen deflated and looked slightly fearful.

Worthington slammed the control panel closed and entered the access code to unlock the hatch. It slid open.

"Go to the forward briefing room and wait there for orders." Worthington turned, to resume searching.

"You wait one second, you bastard! You can't just order—" She didn't finish because, in a flash, Jim had a handful of her hair and, as she cursed him, he dragged her down the corridor.

He dumped her onto the pile of broken, bloody bodies and held her face a few inches from them. "These people were my friends." He pushed her face closer, until her nose almost touched a woman's broken eye socket. The eye was gone. "Her name was Donna Welsh. I had breakfast with her this morning. She and Ken Nichols were talking about getting married." He aimed her face at Ken. "She asked me to marry them."

He pushed Bowen away, throwing her into the bulkhead because of the lighter gravity. "Go to the forward briefing room and wait there for orders."

He turned and searched the next compartment. Hume waited for Bowen to move toward the briefing room. She didn't say a word, as she followed Worthington.

***

In thirty minutes, everyone waited in the briefing room, except for Dr. Shaw, Elkin, and Greg Ibenez. They were all in the reactor room.

Cook put on a pressure suit and went outside, around to the damaged section where Weston was trapped. He took another pressure suit with him, for Weston. He quickly cycled through the airlock and had Weston freed, and to the briefing room, on time.

"Status?" Worthington called out.

His command staff responded first.

Cook was first. "When I was outside, I saw massive hull breaches. I saw all the way into the docking bay and engineering. Life pod number four was gone, just gone. While Ensign Weston was putting on his pressure suit, I saw that the dock was really torn up. The T66 shuttle was totaled, along with its Emergency Module. The Hammerheads looked okay."

Beary was next. "All compartments have been searched."

Tyrrell added, "Nine more bodies were recovered. Four are still unaccounted for. All were in engineering. They were likely lost to the hull breach."

Muir was next. "The base we're parked in front of looks deserted. It does have some power. We can see airlock status lights on the nearest hatch that indicate internal pressure."

Hume reported. "Security is hosed. We are so *not* secure at the moment. Any attack will finish us off. In fact, as of right now, if we don't get the power back up, we will all freeze to death once the moon shifts to its dark side."

Cook replied, "If the reactor takes much longer, then all of us can fit inside one of the remaining life pods. They are designed to keep survivors warm. Plus, they each carry two months of survival rations for sixteen people. That, plus what we can retrieve from the shuttle and the EM, means we have almost a year's worth of food, if rationed. Water could be trouble. The reclamation plant might be damaged."

Dr. Shaw said, "Everyone has a lot of minor injuries—a few bruises, a few broken bones and a few dislocated joints. Everyone that was strapped in, survived. I want to seriously thank you, Jim, for being such an asshole about that."

No one laughed.

Ensign Weston said, "The central pressure suit locker was in the back of engineering. It looks like it's gone from the dock. We only have the two suits, so far. Both of them are really small."

He looked at Hume. She was tiny.

"Listen to all of you!" Bowen kept silent no longer. "You're talking like this is all a drill or something!" She stood. "What the fuck are you doing? Get on the goddamn comms, right fucking now! This was all an accident. We need to be rescued!"

"Bowen, what we will not do is panic. Now, sit down." Worthington remained very calm. He nodded to Hume.

She replied, "For your information, DOCTOR, it was no accident. The *Ventura* was targeted. No warning. We've already verified that in the sensor logs. Standard procedure. And, because of that, we will maintain radio silence. Because the only ones close enough to hear us are the ones that nearly killed us."

"You're alive only because of standard procedures. It's the only reason the captain's pinnace was out of the *Ventura's* dock. It's the only reason you were ordered to strap in. If we hadn't been hit by so much wreckage, we would be cruising faster-than-light right now."

"Look, Captain." It was Ibenez again. "I mean Commander Jim...What do you want us to do? That's all we need to know."

They all fell silent.

"Hume. See if you can get into the base. Go armed. Take Weston. Ibenez, go see if you can help Elkin with the reactor. Take anyone with you that might be of help. Tyrrell and Muir, stay on the bridge. Keep all the hatches closed, for now. We might suffer a breach in random compartments. Sarah and Duncan, put the med bay back together and check everyone out. Including me. I think my collarbone is broken. Any questions?" Jim asked.

"What do you want me to do?" Bowen asked.

"I don't know. What can you do?" Jim asked, seriously.

"I am a sensor data analyst. We have portable sensor systems packed with our gear."

"Do it. Integrate that gear with the *Memphis*. See what you can discover. Report directly to Matt, if you pick up anything."

The room emptied.

CHAPTER FIVE

Rand Runs

"My only plan was to survive. Not think. Otherwise, I'd never stop throwing up."

--Solstice 31 Incident Investigation Testimony Transcript: Master Chief Nancy Randall, senior surviving security member of the Ventura's crew.

Rand fell asleep in the cockpit of the spider. The seats reclined and slid back, giving her ample room. She knew the crash would come. Spending a whole day on adrenaline had taken its toll.

When she awoke, the storm was still in full force. The HUD was on dim, showing the local surrounds. It was called 'here'.

"Good morning, Rand. You have slept for six hours and three minutes. We have not established a current local time, as of yet. Dawn may have happened less than thirty minutes ago. I have some new developments to report, when you are ready."

AI~Poole's voice was a perfect HAL—calm, helpful, even friendly.

"Why are we parked so high?"

The body of the EM was extended to near maximum height. The view 'here' was in the rafters about five meters up.

"Standard hostile environment survival protocol. Do you wish to modify the defaults?"

"No. I just need to pee," Rand said through a yawn, as the spider lowered and the gull-wing opened. "Prep a full status update on the HUD, and when I get back, you can brief me."

"Very well."

The rain pounded the wood shingled roof of the barn. She didn't like it. It masked a lot of the sound. She took off the tactical vest, setting it on the seat of the cockpit. It was heavy with the large 10mm caliber rounds and the 9mm mags for her Glock handgun.

She moved through the attached shed door where she found the hide, hanging on the wall, as she unsealed the jumpsuit from her navel down to the small of her back. Out of habit, she drew her pistol from her thigh holster as she squatted to pee. The jumpsuits were designed for this inconvenient necessity.

She smiled as she looked about because that particular feature on the jumpsuits was more often used for other reasons. Her smile faded. She remembered, all her friends were dead.

Dammit to hell.

Finished, she holstered her gun and resealed the suit. Everyone still called them zippers, but they were actually slidelocks. Utterly silent when opening and closing, they were also neatly watertight. They were even used in pressure suits. No teeth was a bonus.

At that moment, her HUD came alive. "WARNING: Riders Approaching." A view came up in a window as she moved, showing the POV of her Fly. Through the rain, she saw four men riding, hard, on horseback. She double-timed it back to Poole. She grabbed her vest and asked, as she put it on, "How soon before they get here?"

"ETA eight minutes."

She climbed in and closed the door. The cracked seam was still visible from the passenger's door. "Poole, let's be gone before they get here."

The spider moved toward the door with its arms extended all the way. It pushed the doors open and walked out. The doors closed behind it with the help of first one then the other rear leg.

The spider moved smoothly around the barn, away from the men, approaching down the road. Rand directed Poole to move into the trees. It was a smooth ride as they sped to seventy kph. The EM had six-leg mode movements down pat.

Neither Rand nor Poole noticed the trackers crouching at the edge of the woods, watching the giant, hairy, brown-and-black spider run for the woods.

The Fly tracked the riders all the way to the barn. They looked like they wanted to get out of the rain as well.

"Poole, let's recall the Fly, covering our tail. And, I'll have that status report now."

Several windows opened on the HUD. There was weather, hardware and software systems statuses, Fly view and stats, tactical maps, direction, speed, and other windows.

"The most notable, new information is that we detected satellite communications traffic. Using this traffic, we have located several population centers with uplink traffic of various kinds."

"Can you monitor the comms?"

"The traffic is encrypted. There are various distinct types. Ground station to sat traffic, which is the most powerful. Ship to sat, ship to station, and small device traffic to sat."

"Static powerful sources, medium strength fast-moving mobile sources, and I have also detected weaker comms devices, probably handheld."

A window opened labeled: Tactical Objectives. It included the following list:

- Maintain radio silence
- Escape-and-evade
- Refine maps
- Move into an unpopulated area
- Obtain native comms unit for analysis

Another window opened entitled: Critical Inventory

- Weapons?
- Ammunition?
- Food?
- Water?

Rand retrieved a power bar from one of her pockets and ate absently as she studied the displays. The spider descended a ravine. Her rifle shifted and slid forward to the right, out of her reach because of the five-point harness. As she reached across, water dripped down her neck.

Sonofabitch.

"We need to find a place where I can work on a rifle rack, dammit."

"Rand, those men concern me."

"How's that, Poole?"

"I was analyzing the imagery the Fly obtained. I believe they came in on the same vector we did. We did not travel via the roads. Travelers in a rush would take the roads. There are good roads here."

"Are we emitting any RF that they can track? Should I recall the Fly?"

"The Fly RF uses a high-entropy encryption and it does directional transmission. They would have to be in the middle of it to even sense the comms that are designed to look like local radiation."

Oh, shit, Rand thought.

Rand pulled up the rear view.

"They are following our footprints."

She saw them, great gouges in the turf, as they sped along a floodplain beside a river. "They followed us all the way from the crash site."

"We need to lose them, by speed or by stealth," AI~Poole said dryly.

"I have another idea." Rand smiled.

***

Rand headed to the west, across an open plain of grass, running parallel to the forest. When the rain stopped, she turned into the woods and doubled back a kilometer, until she found exactly the spot she wanted. Poole raised his body up into the limbs of the trees, giving Rand a perfect view of the plain.

She only had to wait two hours before the Fly picked them up. They were moving fast, galloping directly in Poole's footsteps.

When they were about 1,000 meters out, Rand opened the gull-wing door and rested her rifle's bipod on the dashboard. She assessed, then decided on an order, and tagged each target.

The last rider's head exploded, and none of the other men even seemed to notice him topple over backward from the saddle. When the second from the last man's head burst, his corpse slumped forward, his hands wound in the reins. The third man sat up a bit before the bullet found him on the chin, severing his head in a spectacular arch that finally made the galloping horses behind him veer away.

The lead rider turned his head, taking the bullet in his left ear.

All three of the riderless horses slowed to an eventual stop. By the time Poole had walked up to them, they were no longer breathing heavily; they were grazing. Well-trained to stop and stay, if the rider fell out.

That makes six.

She collected saddlebags and blankets. All the saddles had full quivers of arrows or bolts. She took the bridles off the horses, and then the saddles, just letting them fall into the grass. She found a single bow and two crossbows on the corpses. She collected these, as well as any pouches and long knives. One of the corpses had not soiled the dark gray and green cloak much, so she took that as well.

She would go through it all later. The trunk was full. The bow case went into the passenger's seat. As almost an afterthought, she retrieved all the bridles and tossed them in the trunk.

She climbed back in, just as it began to rain again.

"Poole, we know they can track our passing, can we make that harder for them?"

"I believe we can."

***

They moved down to the rocky river that ran in their desired direction. Walking in the water was slower but effective. For two days, they followed the water. Twice, they had to bypass villages that were situated on the water. Both times, with the aid of the Fly, they avoided people.

When they found a large rock outcropping, they decided it was time to turn north. A thick area of thorny vines was very easy for the spider to navigate, but would be impossible for a man, or a horse. Ultimately, they ascended a ridge that would have been impossible for them without the dual grapplers and winches.

They made camp on a ledge, just below the top of a stony ridge. They were hidden and safe, for the moment. Rand slept that night, again, in the cockpit.

At dawn, it was clear and cold. They could see in every direction to the horizon. They would rest, wait and watch for pursuit. The Fly could do some high altitude mapping surveys.

"Good morning, Rand. We need to perform an inventory. We have forty-four liters of water and nineteen days of MREs remaining. Water is not a problem. I can load and filter water at the next source we encounter. Food is more problematic."

"Open up and pop the trunk. Let's have a look at our donated supplies."

Rand looked at the weapons first. The three knives she collected were all lovely. Two of them were perfectly balanced, double-edged blades. Their cleverly designed sheaths made them perfect boot knives. The third was a huge, single-edged blade. The blade was very thick and nose heavy. The edge wasn't very sharp.

The crossbows were beautifully made by artful craftsmen. They proved deadly out to 100 meters, maybe more. She didn't want to risk her limited bolts finding out how rotted that stump really was.

She now had three heavy, woolen bedrolls and three ten by fifteen oiled canvas tarps. Apparently, they had been made as camouflage and used as tent tarps.

Their pouches yielded a large selection of gold, silver and copper coins of various sizes that she consolidated and stored in the spider. She kept six gold coins out; and she placed them in six different pockets, so they would not clink together at the wrong time. Their personal pouches also held tinder boxes, and dried meats and fruits, in oiled, canvas inner bags. There were three water skins. One had water and the other two had strong wines in them. There were various sized needles and threads and a whetstone.

The saddlebags were much more useful.

Each carried a change of clothes, additional food, and various other items, including a small, leather-bound children's book about a farmer with too many rabbits.

But, most notably, one of them contained a map of that very region. She held it up for Poole to capture a detailed image, and he instantly refined his annotated tactical maps with the hundreds of annotations on this map.

"Rand, I find it interesting that most of these annotations are in English."

The new tactical map appeared to Rand with region names, city names, rivers and landmarks, all labeled. Their current position was indicated. They were currently on the Ram's Head Ridge.

"Poole, look at this."

She indicated a small annotation that looked like the character for pi. There was one of these marks on the other side of the ridge, less than a kilometer away.

"Let's have the Fly do an initial recon. How many of those marks are there on this map?"

"I count 181 of these marks." AI~Poole highlighted them all. They were scattered all over the map, evenly. "The Fly will be there in seven minutes. Here is the high altitude view of that location."

It was simply part of the rocky mountainside. There didn't seem to be anything there when viewed under maximum magnification.

She continued to search the saddlebags. They were primitive versions of her survival pack. There were additional, useful items—a small cook pot, a kettle, a set of plates, spoons, and forks, as well as a ladle.

The Fly arrived at that location and began a standard pattern search; and, in less than a minute, it found what it was looking for.

There was a door, flanked by two windows. It was built directly into the hillside. It was well-hidden. Only from a close position, directly in front of it, would it be noticed. She would have passed right by it. A high stone outcropping on the hillside made its roof.

The door was big enough for a horse to pass through. The roof was grass, rock, and vegetation. The windows were about a meter square and each had four panes. It was closed up tight, with nowhere for the Fly to enter. There were stone-colored curtains, behind the windows, below the eaves. It faced the south, and the low sun was the only reason the windows and door were not shadowed.

Rand had the Fly survey the best path for her to take. Tomorrow, she would go there herself, on foot. After that, she dispatched the Fly to a forest village called Pine Bow that was on the new map data. It would only take a few hours to get there, and it was the closest population on the new map. She needed more data. Maybe she could find some there. Moving may be a greater risk, for now.

***

Again, she slept in the cockpit, with all the gear packed, in case she needed to run. The men that followed her could not damage the spider in any way. None of them had particle beam weapons like the others she had killed. For a few minutes, she thought about the six men she had killed since she arrived on this planet. She took the survey ship contract, so she would not have to kill men anymore. Hostile species on some primitive planets was all she had, till now, on this job.

The weapons the last four possessed could not do anything to harm the EM. She was only at risk outside of it. So, that night, she slept inside the

EM with AI~Poole keeping watch. The HUD was dimmed and gave her the illusion of sleeping under the stars. She enjoyed that. She even used one of the blankets. Its light scent of wood smoke added to the illusion.

The next day, after a small breakfast, she donned her pack and rifle, and also wore the gray and green cloak and hood for additional camo. The autumn chill in the morning air up here made her start to think longer term.

The Fly shadowed her as she moved to the shelter. The infrared view showed that there was a herd of deer in the brush, not far away. She suddenly wished she had one of the crossbows. That was a perfect solution for extending food sources.

How is this so much like Earth?

She reached the door to the shelter and realized that it was specially made to be concealed from above. The Fly looked directly down at her as she stepped under the eve in front of the doors. She seemed to have disappeared. No visual. No infrared. Nothing.

The latch mechanisms were simple. The sliding bar didn't lock, but it held the door tight. A mouse would be hard pressed to enter. It was made to look highly rustic, but on close examination revealed that the craftsmanship was superb.

Inside, was a single, large room, about five meters by ten meters. Vast slabs of stone precisely fit together to form a roof with no columns in the center.

The floor was flagstone; and, there was simple, heavy wooden furniture. There was a table and chairs for six, and bunks, lining the back, for six. There was no bedding, but the planks were better than the ground. There was also a hearth and a good supply of firewood. The fireplace had a large, iron pot and kettle hanging there.

She didn't remember seeing a chimney.

"Poole, please use the Fly and find the outlet for this chimney."

It took a few minutes, but a circle of rocks that covered a grate was discovered.

"Well, I'll be damned."

She quickly set a fire in the hearth. Once it was going strong, she went up to have a look. It looked like a campfire. If you flew over and looked closely, it would look like someone camped there last night and there were a few coals still smoldering. A plan began to form.

CHAPTER SIX

The Moon Base

"I don't think we could have survived without that specific crew. Everything seemed to be trying to kill us. Everywhere we went, we were only one step away from death."

--*Solstice 31 Incident Investigation Testimony Transcript: Captain James Worthington, senior surviving member of the Ventura's command crew.*

Lieutenant Hume, Ensign Weston, and Dr. Brian Perry put on pressure suits and exited the pinnace via airlock number three. Hume secretly smiled.

It was a three-meter drop to the tarmac, but in the lighter gravity it was easy.

"Comms check, Hume. Vid on," Valerie said, as she reported into Tyrrell.

"Comms check, Weston. Vid on," Weston followed.

"Ummm...Comms check. Brian Perry here. How do I turn vid on?" Perry asked.

"Just say it. I thought scientists were smart," Hume kidded.

Perry appreciated the jab. He was very nervous.

"You're good to go, Hume. We will maintain an open channel, Muir is on tactical."

Their Heads-Up Displays showed Tyrrell and Muir what each of the team's helmet cams saw.

"Brian, relax. Try not to breathe so fast. You will end up hyperventilating."

Hume stopped and let him settle down, a little. He was carrying two large cases that he set down on the tarmac, for a minute, while he took a few deep breaths.

Weston just stood there, staring at the base access hatch and control panel.

Hume checked her weapons, again.

"Weston, did I ever tell you about the time I had to jump off the dock apron of the *Ventura* from orbit and grav-chute to the surface of the Gourley colony?"

Weston looked at her like she had a shrunken head. He had never met her before today. She was command crew, he was an ensign in the docking bay. Then, he realized, it was for Perry's benefit.

She winked at him.

"I was convinced I would hit the atmo at 7,000 kph and burn to a cinder. Except the chute-suit I was wearing was designed by geeks like you. It had a grav-plate in it."

"I never got over 300 kph. It was beautiful, man. Did you design that thing, Perry?"

Hume was distracting him.

"Ummm...No. It wasn't me. I can see how it could be done though." Perry was thinking about it now.

"I still pissed myself, I was so scared. Way more scared than this," she said to Weston. "Are we good?"

Perry nodded.

"Good. Oh, and try to communicate out loud. Nodding does no good to our friends on the bridge. I don't want them to feel left out." She smiled.

"Yes, sir," Perry said.

"Call me Hume. If you call me sir again, I'll kick you in the nuts."

He chuckled and realized his panic was gone. "Thanks, Hume." He picked up his cases and moved toward the hatch.

***

Worthington slid out of the autoDoc as Dr. Shea spoke. "Take it easy on that break for a few days. The nanites will work as fast as they can, but don't make their job harder. Don't worry about the low-grade fever. That's just the nanites."

"Thanks, Doc," Jim said.

"I'll get everyone else through here as soon as possible," Duncan Shea said.

Just then, the main lights blinked off, on and off, then came up and stayed on.

"Commander, power has been restored," Tyrrell reported. The gravity came back to 1G, to Worthington's great relief. His nose always got stuffy in lower G.

"Elkin here, Commander. Reactor number three is back up. It should stay up, for now. I'll need to run a full set of diagnostics to ensure it stays up. I might be able to get reactor number one back online, if I use parts from reactor number two." Elkin coughed.

"How are you feeling, Elkin? As soon as it's safe I want you back in the autoDoc for a full scan," Worthington said.

"Dr. Shaw is with me and is saying the same. Let me just get a few things started and I will head up."

"Do you have any idea regarding the status of our engines?" Jim asked.

"I can look, Commander, but propulsion is not my area." Trish coughed a bit more.

"Good work, Elkin. Worthington out." Tyrrell closed the channel.

***

The systems on the bridge came back online one at a time. Worthington and Muir moved from station to station, turning off alarms and checking systems.

"Jim, the main external sensor array is off-line," Muir said. "Internal sensors are case by case. What is for sure is that forty percent of the ship is in a vacuum: core sections of propulsion, engineering, and the flight deck. It has even penetrated forward as far as the bulkhead behind the infirmary."

"Let's work with all the hatches closed for now, in case additional failures happen," Jim said.

"The Extra Vehicular Activity (EVA) locker room was torn up as well. Not good," Muir said.

"Oh, shit," Worthington cursed. "How are we going to get everyone to the base if we need to?"

"We will make it a priority to collect and test all the pressure suits," Muir said.

"Get some drones into the damaged areas, and survey the damage. Our priorities are to make sure we're safe and to get eyes, out there." He pointed at the horizon of the moon. The planet was not visible. "We need to know what's happening. Survive. Recon. Plan. Act. Assess."

"Jim, we have some sensors functioning on the forward section. The standard sensor sweep is showing some strange results. This moon is just like Earth's moon, Luna, in that the same side always faces the planet."

Peter and Jim looked at each other. In their entire careers, neither of them had ever seen another moon matched so closely in its orbit.

"That means we will be hidden here from the planet."

They both looked up at the main viewer to see Hume getting the airlock open.

"Unless they are alerted that their moon base has been entered."

***

Hume had been trained to bypass almost any airlock control ever made. They didn't change much over the decades, but they did over the centuries. She was easily able to identify this control unit as an essential colony redoubt control. It was vintage. Over 200 years old and still working.

"Made to last," Hume said, as the hatch swung inward. "They designed these to be unable to open unless there was a vacuum inside the airlock. And the inside hatch won't open if it's not pressurized, unlike the pinnace."

"Why is that?" Perry asked. "Seems crazy to allow it."

"Turns out there are lots of good reasons to allow a direct vent. Like fire suppression." They all moved inside, as dirty lights came up and the hatch closed. "You probably never heard about the fire in the central computer farm on the *Ventura*. It was extinguished with a direct vent that saved all the AI systems on the *Ventura*. Thanks to Barcus." Hume became quiet.

The hatch closed and the dust swirled as the large airlock began to pressurize. Weston tapped some controls on his left forearm control pad. Pressure, temperature, O_2 content, and other factors came up in his HUD. There was a loud *clunk*, but then nothing happened.

They waited.

"Push the hatch open," Jim said, over the comms.

Hume let her rifle hang down on the front of her suit as she pushed. It creaked loudly, but it swung inward. They moved inside the cavernous space and turned back to close the hatch with a loud *clang*.

Perry said, "Well, there is sound. Where there is sound, there is atmosphere!"

"Wait. Scanning," Weston said.

"It's breathable, but it's damn cold. Super dry and -48.3°C. It's gonna hurt," Weston said.

"Sorry, guys, but we need to save the scrubbers in the suits. We have no idea how long we will be here," Worthington said.

"Yes, sir," Hume replied, and with a well-practiced flip and twist, she took off her helmet and took a breath.

"Jesus, that is cold."

The moisture from her breath, when exhaled, froze almost instantly and fell as tiny ice crystals.

She activated a powerful, tactical light on her rifle and scanned the room. Its scope automatically conveyed mapping data to Muir's tactical station on the pinnace.

"Okay, fellas. Gear up. We have some scanning to do." Perry opened his cases and Weston took some handheld equipment from his pack.

"Sir, I think this is a classic colony redoubt shake-and-bake base from at least 200 years ago. We should have files in the system that will have the layout, once we get some detail," Hume said, as her light examined a huge, dusty machine she didn't recognize.

"Data storage is down. Archives are off-line. All systems are running on local. Perry, do any of your people know anything about central computer plants?" Jim asked.

"Dr. Bowen knows a lot. More software than hardware," he replied.

"Oh, boy," Hume added.

"What?" Perry asked.

"Nothing...Commander, it looks like we're ready to move out. Gentlemen, I recommend we run with helmets on and visors up."

***

They soon found a very handy map of the compound, mounted to the wall of the corridor near a lift. They were in a five dome complex, with each dome about 100 meters across. The domes sat on top of a clover-shaped foundation that also went down another eleven levels into the ground.

Only one of the domes was depressurized.

Solar arrays kept the lights on, but once they were in the dark phase of their orbit, there would be no lights. The power banks were all bone-dry.

Before they returned to the *Memphis*, they also located the water storage. It held tens of thousands of liters, but it was all frozen solid.

***

Eight hours after the attack, they returned to the briefing room. All detailed their activities and spent time listening to the condition of the ship and crew. Everyone had a med check and all the bodies had been collected and placed into a cold compartment.

Only one more area lost integrity and went to vacuum: the same room over the dock where Ensign Weston had been trapped.

"Does anyone have any other updates?" Commander Worthington asked, from the podium in the briefing room.

"What's the plan?" Dr. Bowen asked, her arms crossed over her chest.

"We will get reactor number two back online," Worthington began, not showing his annoyance.

"Two is one. One is none," Hume cited.

"We will assess our assets. We will recon, if possible. We will repair what we can. We will keep our heads down. We will survive."

"I think we should attempt to contact the planet. This has all got to be a mistake. I believe we can reason with them. They're humans!" Bowen was getting spun up again.

"They are humans that nuked the *Ventura* without so much as a warning," Hume stated, flatly.

"I think if we can just talk to them, we can make them understand that we're just a survey ship. I say we take a vote." Bowen stood and turned to the room, with her hand raised.

"Sit. The. Hell. Down," Worthington growled. "Let me be clear about this, right now. There will be no vote. This is not a democracy. You will do as you're told or it's back to airlock number three for you." He turned to Tyrrell. "We are in a communications blackout. NO communications out." He turned to Hume. "If anyone violates that order you are to summarily execute them prior to notifying me." He turned back to Bowen, who was still standing. "Do you understand those orders, Dr. Bowen?"

She stood there, saying nothing.

"The proper reply is, 'Yes, Commander'."

Hume stood up at that. Standing next to Worthington, she only came up to his chest, but she was so fierce, it made Bowen flinch.

"Yes, sir," Hume growled. Her hand was on her sidearm.

"Yes, Commander," Bowen said, and sat down, quickly looking away.

Hume spoke next to the entire group. "The only way we're going to get through this is to work together and to follow orders. I know that some of you are not used to this, but we do not have any other options. We are in some deep shit, people. When you're in shit up to your neck, the first thing you do is stop digging."

The commander returned to the podium. "Here is your first order."

He paused.

"Everyone, call me Jimbo."

CHAPTER SEVEN

Rand the Witch

"At that point I had no idea Barcus had survived and was also on the surface, starting a war of his own. Sure, I was angry. But he was biblical in his fury. So alone. But I was trained, silent running. He kept them occupied by killing a few thousand of those assholes. That distraction saved me I think."

--Solstice 31 Incident Investigation Testimony Transcript: Master Chief Nancy Randall, senior surviving security member of the Ventura's crew.

<<<>>>

Rand watched in her HUD as the figure in gray moved silently along the trail near the hidden shelter. When he rounded a large boulder, he saw a body, sprawled beside the path, facedown, arms stretched above its head, as if dragged there. The legs were straight and partially covered in leaves.

The man drew his knife and waited.

A few minutes went by without a sound, except for the breeze through the rocks and the shrubs. Cautiously, he approached. When he almost reached the body in the ditch, he sheathed his knife and took out a water skin as he turned over the body.

All he remembered, later, was pain and darkness.

Slowly, the man became conscious.

He tried to pretend he was still out but somehow failed. He became aware that he was blindfolded, naked and bound, tightly, professionally. He felt that he was indoors. There was a fire, not far away, to his right. He was on his back, tied to a wood surface with rough planks. Before he could assess further, a voice whispered to him in perfect High Speech.

"Who are you?" It was a deep, frightening voice.

The calm whisper, and those words, struck fear into him more than the bindings.

"Who are you?" was repeated. Followed by a crackling sound, and then an excruciating pain two inches below his navel. Was he just burned? Stabbed? He could smell urine from his loss of control.

"Do you understand me?" whispered the voice.

The crackling sound came again. He had answered before the pain came.

"Yes, Keeper. I understand."

Rand raised an eyebrow. *Keeper?*

"Who are you?" The crackling started immediately this time.

"They call me Coff. I'm a tracker."

He was visibly trying to calm himself through force of will. He was also, subtly, testing his bonds.

Very good, Coff.

"Why are you here?" Even more menace dripped from the whisper.

He paused too long. This time the pain was in his left foot. It was worse than the worst cramp he ever had. It was as if his leg was being crushed, or eaten while he still lived. It took him a few moments to realize he was screaming.

"I will ask. You will answer. Promptly."

"Why are you here?" There was no hesitation this time.

"I was tracking something. Something big."

"Tell me. All of it."

Rand didn't know what to ask, specifically. She needed more info without giving anything away. It came out in a flood.

"I was moving south from where I spend the summers above the gorge in the north. I always come south in the winter. I cannot tolerate so much snow. I had gotten as far as Corrina Valley. I always take that route south. Fewer people." His speech was degrading, shifting to something else. An accent or a dialect of English.

"Slow down. Speak." There was more crackling.

"Forgive me, Keeper. I don't often speak High Tongue."

"Why are you here?" There was more crackling.

"I was moving south in heavy rain. I decided to move through the night. I knew a warm, dry place that I could reach around dawn, where I could dry out and rest in comfort. Before I got there, I saw it."

"What did you see?" The whisper her riot helmet made was specially designed to intimidate, to cause fear in crowd control situations.

"You won't believe me. Please don't hurt me again."

"Tell me or I will hurt you even worse."

"It was a giant...thing."

"Tell me."

"I was at the edge of the woods when it ran by. It was fast, faster than a horse. And huge."

"Slow down." He was slipping again.

"It was like a giant spider. It had six legs and a hairy body, bigger than the biggest bull I have ever seen. Black legs. It had stopped raining by then, so I just sat there until I saw it leave the other end of the valley. Before I moved, I saw four of the High Trackers follow it on horseback. Moving fast. Its trail was easy to follow."

"Why did you follow them?"

He paused too long and the pain came to his armpit this time. Coff didn't know how long he had been unconscious, this time.

"Coff, why did you follow?"

"The High Keeper's trackers are cruel, hard men, but they often use runners or trackers and pay very well. So, I followed. I found them on the plain. The monster had killed them and eaten their heads. Their horses were gone. Are you following it as well?"

"Why did you come up here?"

"There is a tracker's shelter. I had been here before."

"Tell me what you know about the High Keeper."

Crackling.

"The High Keeper is the Lord of All. The High Keeper protects us and keeps us. He is the Keeper of magic and knowledge and the sky. He can give life or rain death." He seemed like he was reciting a well-practiced answer. Suddenly, he slipped into speech she could not understand.

Rand shocked his nipple.

"Slow High Speech."

"I left the Canton of Pine Frost when the death began to rain from the sky. So, I ran. There was nothing to keep me there."

"What do you mean?"

"When stars began to fall, I thought the Keeper was angry with the Northern Reaches. There were already rumors among the trackers of the

Keeper's men burning villages. I was there to get away from people, from cities. All I wanted was quiet. Peace. Did you kill that woman by the path?"

"The High Keeper?"

"He lives in the great Citadel. In the clouds." He was reciting again. "The great mountain fortress of the Keepers."

"Where is this Citadel?"

He was taken aback.

"It's 2,000 miles to the west. In the gray mountains."

"What kind of magic does he have?"

A small jolt to the sternum got him talking again.

"He can make his ships fly. He can appear and talk to other Keepers all over the world. He can read the magic symbols and see. He can remember all the things the Keepers before him knew. He can capture your soul and hold it for all time. And, he is immortal, but appears like a young man. That's what they say, anyway." He started to chatter again in that almost English.

A crackling glove held above his chest hair made him fall silent.

"Why do you think I am a Keeper?"

He paused. Unable to answer. The crackling brought him back.

"You can speak High Tongue."

"So can you. Why is that?"

"We are all taught it. To be addressed by a Keeper and not be able to reply is not worth the risk."

"What else?"

"You have magic."

Rand thought about this a moment and replied to herself more than Coff. "More than you will ever know."

"Where can I find these Keepers?"

"Every decent size town has a Keeper. Many villages do, too. Please don't kill me."

"Listen closely, Coff," Rand whispered, directly in his ear.

"You will never mention me. You will forget the Great Spider. If you say anything to anyone, ever, I will know. If you follow me, I will know. It was only a nightmare. Leave it to me." She drifted from a whisper. "And, I would stay away from these Keepers..."

She tore off his blindfold. She was backlit by the fire, it hid all her features. She had the hood up on her cloak, her face hidden by the black glass mirror surface of the helmet.

"You're a woman? You're a witch?" Now he sounded genuinely afraid.

He watched, in horror, as the sparks grew to graphic height from her palms to her fingertips. Hands spread wide like a priest in prayer. Then, it was pain and oblivion.

When he awoke, he was alone and unbound.

***

Rand was several kilometers west when she saw Coff wake up. She took a chance and left the Fly in the shelter with him as they moved due west. Her new map indicated a mountain range that held promise for losing their trail.

She shook her head, she thought they tracked her with the RF from the Fly, or the EM. Nothing that fancy.

Damned footprints.

She will have to start thinking old-school.

When Coff awoke, with a start, he was apparently surprised to find himself untied and alive. He lost hours to the riot gloves. Rand had also been shocked unconscious with them, in the past; everyone that officially used them was required to know the feeling. They were standard in Security Services Personnel kits. She had never thought she would ever need them in this detail.

She watched, as he drew his knife from his pile of clothes and gear, and searched what little there was of the shelter, before he put on a single piece of clothing. He was very fit but short. Only about one and a half meters tall. Rand stood two meters and change. As she watched, she realized the door was apparently made for him and not her.

"You should have killed him," AI~Poole said.

"I was planning to. But when I was laying on the side of the path just before he got to me, he put his knife away. That is what saved him."

He looked out the windows, and listened for a full minute, before he got dressed. Rand had thrown another log on the fire before she left. The shelter was warm.

"How did you know he wouldn't kill you outright?"

"Did you see my position? My face down. My arms stretched up. My hands empty. Not prepared to attack. I have seen it in training over and over. That makes them feel secure, if they think they are badasses. The first thing they do is either check your pulse or turn you over. Either way. Surprise!"

He sat in a chair, watching the fire.

After a bit, he got up and went to the fireplace. Coff felt around the left end of the mantel until he found some sort of latch and pulled it. The left end grain of the mantelpiece popped open to reveal a compartment. He reached in a pulled out a leather-bound journal and a few pencils.

He sat in front of the fire, for the best light, and opened the journal to the most recent entry:

> *Summer Solstice 265. Moving north to the gorge and then going east to the coast. The wolves are worse east of the Saddles. The game is still good. Need to make some more bolts soon. Trapping is rich. Keepers have work in Nokes, Elkton, Canton and Monroe. Above the gorge has been marked. Been dry. Not draught. Jag*

Coff took a pencil and wrote:

> *October. Been raining. Dried up, finally. Headed to Exeter for the winter from the north coast. I hate the snow. Nothing of note. Coff*

He finished and returned the log to the mantel.

"Poole show me the current tactical map." It came up with many new annotations. "Where is the next, nearest shelter in the direction we are going? I wonder if there is a tracker log in all of them."

CHAPTER EIGHT

Darkness Falls

"Regardless of what happens here, I need to be clear that I was in command. I am entirely responsible for the actions of all my people. That includes the activities of the civilians. They all did everything by my orders."

--Solstice 31 Incident Investigation Testimony Transcript: Captain James Worthington, senior surviving member of the Ventura's command crew.

"Jimbo, this is Ludmilla Kuss. She is one of the technicians with Bowen's survey team. She has an interesting idea to solve two of our problems," Ibenez said, as they talked to Jim on the bridge of the *Memphis*.

Jim shook her hand. She was a pale woman with striking features and hair buzzed close, blonde with tinges of red. She was tall.

"Friends call me Kuss, please. Pronounced like goose," she said to Jimbo. "Especially if I am to call you Jimbo."

It was the first time Jim had heard her speak. Her accent surprised him. "Where are you from, Kuss?"

"Poland, originally. Is beautiful place, no?"

Kuss was shy, yet tried to make awkward conversation. Jim didn't want to torture her.

"What is your idea, Kuss?"

Kuss looked toward the base as she spoke. "We only have three viable pressure suits and sixteen of us. Of course, they are size small and tiny." She looked at Hume. "Even I cannot get in. You, never." She pointed at Jimbo as she continued, "The Hard Shell Maintenance Suit, HSMS, was docked in the bay and now damaged and won't seal." These were huge, three meter tall, suits that were covered with tool for specialty ship work in the vacuum of space. "So half of us cannot ferry over even if we carry two suits back and forth."

"If we can depressure hangar bay and manually open doors. Pilot fly *Memphis* in hangar. We close door and repressure." She raised her eyebrows, excited now.

"It will fit through the hangar doors, barely. Tell him the rest, Kuss."

"We get ship in. Hide better from assholes that killed *Ventura*. Jimbo can finally wander about base. Plus, when we get reactor number one up, we completely power base. Even in long dark time. We maybe even fix ship and get the hell out," she said, as her accent began to slip.

"What do you think, Cook? Can you fly it in there?" Jimbo asked him.

From where Jim stood, he saw Cook already comparing the ship's specs with the scans of the hangar.

"No. I won't be able to fly it in. The grav-foils are far too damaged for that fine of control."

Looking up at Kuss, he said, "But I think we could rig a winch and tow it in."

"Yes," Kuss replied.

Cook added, "Jimbo, if we could get it into the hangar, repairs would be so much easier. We'd have access to the areas in vacuum and even access to the fabricators. If they aren't trashed."

"Kuss, this was your idea. I want to see a full, detailed plan as soon as you can get it to me," Jimbo said.

Kuss beamed. "Yes, sir."

***

Two days later, they were ready.

They had run tests to depressurize and repressurize the hangar bay.

The doors unlocked, but would not slide to the side with the power available. They were also in a race with the coming shadow. Get this done now, or wait two weeks.

Weston came up with the solution.

"We use the Hard Shell Maintenance Suit (HSMS)," he said.

"No can do. The suit won't seal, and with main computing AI down, we can't run it on remote," Ibenez reminded him.

"Make her do it." Weston pointed at Hume. "If Jimbo can fit in there, she'd fit in the unit, even if she were wearing a pressure suit in there. The way the gel forms around you, after you get in, might not be perfect, but you could certainly push something."

"Hume, what do you think?" Jimbo asked.

"What the hell? Why not?" she replied, and followed Weston out.

***

The hardest part was finding a way out of the dock while wearing the suit. She ended up climbing out the largest breach and just dropping to the ground, head first. In the lower gravity, it only hurt a little.

Thirty minutes later, she had the bay door slid to the side. She even stayed in the suit to help guide the pinnace in.

A cable was fixed on the nose landing gear. The fixed grav-plates allowed it to float ten centimeters above the surface as the cable winch slowly pulled it in. With only a meter of clearance, Hume helped it track in straight, only losing a bit of paint on the left wing.

They had a thrill when the door jammed at one point, because one of the skids dropped rubbish into the track. Weston, in another pressure suit, cleared the track and the hangar door finally closed and locked.

The effort took twice as long as estimated by the time the hangar pressurized. They beat the full dark by six hours.

***

Being inside the base didn't really do much good because it was so cold. People only left the ship when they had to.

Jimbo discovered that now that they had an atmosphere, the maintenance suit could be used to greater effect. They removed the destroyed Shuttle Transport Unit (STU) from the flight deck. Ibenez and Kuss worked on removing the main cpu from the shuttle for possible use in the *Memphis*.

They also discovered that both Hammerheads were fully functional. These were small, Courier-class shuttles that were specifically designed for atmospheric transport. Their engines were three simple hyper-turbines that only required water for fuel. Two engines in the front and one in the back. They were two-seaters, one chair behind the other. They had the latest grav-foils and excellent comms gear, with massive local storage for the secure transport of data when transmission was impractical or insecure.

Jimbo walked into the dock and noticed, immediately, that Kuss had on her idea face.

"You wanted to see me?" Jimbo noticed the grav-plate in the dock didn't work. It was .18G in there. His nose already itched.

Hume, Kuss, Weston, Tyrrell and, oddly, Sarah Wood stood around the Hammerheads.

"Kuss has another idea, sir," Hume began.

"Hammerheads no have pressurized cockpit. And, turbines don't do shit in a vacuum. Grav-foils are different." She reached inside the first Hammerhead and flipped a switch on the console. A series of antennas deployed.

"We load both Hammerheads up with portable sensor gear. Greg has very nice toys. Maybe solar array and batteries. Even have small optical observatory." Kuss indicated how much room the second seat and storage compartment had.

"Two go. Set up sensors. Configure Hammerhead as relay. Two come back in the other Hammerhead. We spy on bastards," Kuss finished.

Worthington looked from the Hammerhead to Kuss to Hume and then to Sarah Wood.

Sarah answered his silent question. "I can fit in the pressure suit and I know how to fly a Hammerhead on just foils. I had one back home."

Decisively, Jimbo said, "Do it." And, then he walked away.

"You forgot to mention we can get the Hammerheads out the small airlock," Kuss said.

Tyrrell added, "You're all talking past the sale. Kuss, this was your damn idea. Get to work. Sarah and I will need to be thoroughly briefed on setting up all the gear."

Three days later, everything was ready. The Hammerheads were loaded and moved to the airlock when reactor number one came online.

Weston had already sorted out how to interface the reactor with the base. The hangar was already equipped with heavy-duty power cables, normally used to power ships while in the hangar for service. These were repurposed in no time.

Hume and Wood suited up and headed out.

***

As the base fell away into the distance, they drove into the quiet, accelerating at a steady rate, floating about 100 meters above the surface.

"How long have you known Jimbo, Hume?" Wood asked her over HUD comms, as they sped along.

"I was reassigned to the *Ventura* just over four months ago. I came in with the new staff rotation. Jimbo had been on the command staff for over five years. The third shift command crew."

Wood could hear the sadness in her voice. Hume was always such a badass all the time. Her heart went out to Hume.

"I expected to be rotated out on the ship you arrived in. It didn't happen. No idea why. Just my luck."

"Jimbo should have rotated out as well. You know he's married and has two adopted girls back on Earth?" Hume said.

"I have been on the *Ventura* for seven years. Today was the first day we met. Command crews and med techs on the lower decks don't mix, I guess," Wood said with regret in her voice.

"Jimbo's not like that. He used to take me to Peck's Halfway on the *Ventura*. Ever go there?"

She heard the smile in Hume's voice.

"I have been there, but I'm not much of a drinker. Plus, I just can't eat that kind of food. It's so loud sometimes," Sarah said.

"Jimbo always left his stripes in his cabin when he went there. It was full of heavies and security folks like me. His friends had all served on the *Ventura* for years."

"Heavies?" Wood asked, as they broke into the sunlight.

"Heavies are the people that lived in the outer rings where it was over 2G all the time. Live there for a few months, and you end up looking like a Greek goddess."

"Planet is becoming visible, dead ahead," Wood reported back to the *Memphis*.

"We will stop in a few more clicks when the planet is fully visible," Hume added.

Fresh craters were now frequent. They found a flat rock outcropping at the top of a hill that allowed the relay strength to increase.

It took them two hours to set up the sensors and the optical observatory.

They waited while the systems from the *Memphis* were all tested.

"Do you think we'll survive? Or ever get out of here?" Wood asked, looking at the planet.

"Yes. Yes, we will," Hume said, as a matter-of-fact.

"We can't die here. I just received my first longevity treatment." Wood laughed.

CHAPTER NINE

Tan'Vi

"Why am I telling you this? Because, Barcus is not the only one responsible here. I killed those bastards, and yes, in retrospect I'd do it again."

--Solstice 31 Incident Investigation Testimony Transcript: Master Chief Nancy Randall, senior surviving security member of the Ventura's crew.

"Poole, this map has several villages marked on it. Let's avoid them by following a line, like this." She indicated it on the HUD.

"If the pi symbol represents a shelter, do you think there is a variation on this symbol, with a leg missing? Or this, the one with the peaked roof?"

"We will find out soon. Following this track we will pass near both. When the Fly catches up, it can recon." AI~Poole was businesslike again. *"It will catch up soon. We are moving much slower to ensure we are not seen and our tracks are difficult to follow."*

They traveled at night now and rested during the day. Moving along streams and rocky areas, they hid in dense forests during daylight.

Rand discovered that there was a particular annotation for a three-sided, open shelter and a visible, aboveground shelter like a cabin or other building.

The forest here was untouched. The forest floor was littered with fallen trees of all sizes. The going would be very difficult for a person on foot and impossible for a horse. The canopy above gave shelter from sat monitoring, which, it seemed, the trackers were aware of.

Rand found similar journals in other shelters. Some even warned of the level of observation from above.

For two weeks, they moved at night. Easily avoiding settlements, even small groups, and individuals, via infrared.

The game became plentiful. One morning, Rand awoke to find a buck at Poole's feet.

"Last night, while we were parked, it scraped its antlers on my leg. I reached down and broke its neck just at the base of its skull with a quick squeeze. We had discussed hunting, but I had no idea it was so easy."

Rand gutted the deer, right there. She had Poole bring the deer with them to the next shelter. It was a small, aboveground cabin on a small bluff above a stream. No one would ever find this without a map. It was simply not visible from any direction until they were there. There was already firewood and even a large cook pot on a swinging hook in the fireplace. Soon, the deer was skinned and quartered. A simple stew with salt and pepper simmered over the fire.

Rand slept in the small cabin. It was outfitted with four hammocks. The hammocks hung from only one hook when not in use. When deployed, they basically took up the entire cabin. They were very comfortable and meant she didn't have the worry of mice like with the mattresses in other shelters.

Poole had taken up a position in the evergreens, legs extended all the way, still as stone, blending in.

***

Rand dozed in a hammock, as the venison simmered in the pot, when AI~Poole woke her.

"Rand, there are two people approaching from the west. They are about thirty minutes away, but coming directly at us."

A window opened in her HUD. She saw them from above. They moved toward the Fly. One man, one woman. They walked along, casually talking, even laughing at times. Each had a bow, but they were unstrung and on their backs, strapped to well-worn leather packs. Their clothes were worn, but clean. The clothes she now wore, salvaged from the saddlebags, were much finer. Her cloak was especially nice. The edges were trimmed with leather and the subtle design was functional as camo as well.

"Their names are Tannhauser and Vi. Based on what I know, they are trackers. They have been here before. April 23rd was the last time they were here. They were heading north for the summer. They like to hunt and to forage there. They sign all the logs Tan'Vi. Until now, I thought those references were complicated names. They are all couples."

Both of them had their hoods down. Vi wore a long, French braid. Tannhauser's hair and beard were long and wild.

Rand put on her black riot gloves and her cloak. She checked her Glock as she watched them in the HUD.

They became quiet and paused, Vi holding out a hand to halt Tannhauser's movement.

They smelled the smoke.

They quickly strung their bows with practiced ease. Rand could not hear what they whispered, but they split up and went different ways.

The Fly stayed with the woman. She was quick and quiet and as professional and economical in her movements as anyone Rand had ever worked with. Vi notched an arrow as she approached the cabin. Just a bit of smoke came out of the stubby chimney as she approached.

The Fly and Poole now had views of both sides of the cabin. The door was wide open. She saw herself in the cabin door, sitting on a stool, stirring the stew.

He called out a greeting, in Common Tongue, as he approached slowly. His bow was in hand, but no arrow was notched. Vi was ready to fire.

Rand continued to stir with her left hand, covering her right hand which held the Glock.

"Please come in, Tannhauser. And ask Vi to join us, as well. It can't be comfortable behind that rock."

"You have us at a disadvantage." He did not advance.

She holstered her gun while he couldn't see and set the wooden spoon across the top of the pot to forestall it boiling over and putting out the fire.

She stood slowly, moved toward the door, ducked under the jamb and stepped out.

He was very short, probably less than five feet tall, which meant Vi was even smaller.

What's with this planet?

"My name is Rand. I have a large pot of stew and no conversation. Would you and Vi care to join me?"

She stood up from behind the mossy boulder then and lowered her bow.

Rand was completely hidden in the shadows of her hood. She stood on a large, flat stone used as the step for the cabin. It made her seem even taller, in the Fly's eye over Vi's shoulder.

She slowly reached up and lowered her hood.

She saw herself for the first time in days. Her hair was wild, and it added to the level of intimidation that she emitted.

"Please, join me." She turned her back to them and reentered the cabin.

CHAPTER TEN

Another Skyfall

"Someone was, intentionally, directing ships to their death. They knew this planet was a trap, and they were murdering thousands, with a word."

--Solstice 31 Incident Investigation Testimony Transcript: Captain James Worthington, senior surviving member of the Ventura's command crew.

The Hammerhead relay worked better than expected. The position of the planet never changed in the sky, and the variety of sensors the team had put together was impressive.

There were all kinds of RF collection, temperature, spectral, chemical, and ultrahigh definition optical sensors. Soon, all of these were combined to get a bigger picture of the planet itself.

They discovered in the coming weeks that the northern hemisphere of a single continent was the only inhabited portion of this world. They found cities there but not modern cities.

They also managed to locate, and scan, the automated defense sats. They zoomed in very close and saw the tubes that concealed the nuclear missiles that had destroyed the *Ventura*. They were small but fast and powerful. The planet had a full grid of these sats that managed full planetary coverage.

Once the power was hooked up to the base, it began to warm. Slowly.

Of the five major domes in the compound, only one of them was not pressurized, and even though they inspected the entire exterior they were not able to gain a seal. It was unfortunate because the dome contained a series of workshops and labs that may have been useful. They harvested what few tools were left behind, and then left it dark and unpowered.

Once the ventilation system came online, the massively overengineered CO_2 scrubbers began working. The water thawed in the cisterns, ensuring they would starve to death before suffocating or dying of thirst.

Jimbo had taken to living onboard the *Memphis*. He hated lower than normal G, so he made one of the few, small staterooms his home. The bridge had become the location for their intelligence gathering, and their communications hub. The HUD on the bridge had been adapted to use the two Flies they had, as well as the four V-Drones. The Flies were small as a real fly, but could only navigate where there was atmosphere. V-Drones were much larger, but were designed for use in a vacuum and even zero gravity. They were the size of a hockey puck and used a small grav-plate and a gyro. Using these, the entire base was explored from the safety of the bridge.

Hume was the only other person to reside full time on the *Memphis*. It was for the gravity; she only wanted it to stay fit. She even talked Jimbo into creeping the gravity higher without telling anyone else.

Early hopes that they could use the Tesla Interstellar Communications Array to get a message out were quickly crushed. Tyrrell discovered all the comms gear, and even the cables that connected to the array, had been removed long ago. This was a huge mystery to them because that type of equipment could not be repurposed for anything other than scrap.

Weeks turned into months. Jimbo stared at a snow-covered region of the unpopulated side of the planet, as he listened to Dr. Shaw and Sarah Wood talk about the rate of food consumption.

"All of the galley foodstuffs are now gone, except for a few hundred pounds of rice," Shaw said. "We have collected all the rations from the life pods and the shuttle, including those inside the Emergency Module." Lists scrolled by on the HUD as she spoke. "We are set with water, even though we lost all the water in one of the reservoirs."

Wood added, "That was about 10,000 liters. The tank must have cracked from the freeze. It all ran into the lower levels on that side."

"It did help with the dry air. God, I hate bloody noses," Shaw continued. "The agridome started showing signs of life once the heat was on. A detailed search over there found some seeds. They were probably frozen for a few hundred years; but, we had the soil and the water, so Sarah, Duncan, and Jack planted them all. We have no idea what the seeds were, but what the hell? We think about five percent were still viable and have begun growing. No idea if any of it will be edible."

"The lower gravity in the dome is helping." Concern made her lower her voice. "The crew are working less and need less. We estimate 180 days of rations remain. We could cut them now and extend that."

Just then, the quiet on the bridge was broken with a Klaxon.

"Muir, what is that?" Jimbo asked, as the main HUD switched to tactical view.

"A ship just dropped out of FTL at 350°, Mach 9. It is on an approach vector for orbit!" Muir said.

"Hail them. Break radio silence. Stop them from entering orbit!" Jimbo yelled.

"I can't, sir. We are on the dark side of the moon. Our Hammerhead sensor array picked them up," Muir said, as the ship got closer.

"What about the Hammerhead? Can that reach them?" Jimbo asked, leaning on the console now.

"Think! Where is Tyrrell? There has to be something?" Jimbo said, as Hume and Tyrrell ran onto the bridge.

"Magnify!" Jimbo called.

They watched as the optical zoomed in and tracked the ship.

"Oh, my God. It's a Vision-class cruise ship," Hume said.

The missiles struck. They were so fast.

When the flash dimmed, they saw two more missiles launch and strike, vaporizing the largest remaining chunks.

There were a few flashes of what looked like particle beam weapons from the platforms. Then, all was quiet again.

Jimbo sat down, slowly, in the command chair, staring at the screen.

"A passenger ship? Out here?"

They zoomed in as the wreckage began to ignite in the upper atmosphere. The optical zoomed all the way in, but there was nothing left to see. The ship had been utterly destroyed.

Muir studied the sensor data. The ship was, in fact, a Vision-class cruise ship. A luxury vessel.

"It had a capacity of 4,600 passengers and crew."

"I have heard stories of ships disappearing. Everyone always thought that there was a failure or a route miscalculation while in FTL," Jimbo said, slowly.

"Jimbo, we cannot allow this to happen again. If another ship comes, we have to be ready," Hume said.

"How?" He was angry.

"We could transmit, now, on this side of the moon. We need to create a transmitter that will face planet-side," Hume said.

"Do it," was all he said. Jimbo left the bridge.

Hume looked at Cook and Muir. "What is the name of this damned planet?"

***

"Here's the basic idea." Hume was at the podium in the main briefing theater. Diagrams and parts lists popped up behind her on the screens. "First we will go out there and salvage one antenna from the Tesla Array. We will bring it back and combine it with the comms unit we salvaged from the damaged shuttle. Here's the problem." She pointed to some specs. "Power requirements. A transmitter powerful enough will require this many power cells to ensure it will be available through the long nights."

"What's the problem? We have the cells and the panels to spare," Jim said.

"They are all too big for the Hammerhead," Hume said.

Elkin chimed in, "I could use one of the fork sleds and rig up a cargo container. The Hammerhead could tow it. It won't be fast, but then two people could go as well."

"What about the antenna?" Tyrrell asked. "It's thirty meters tall."

"We will salvage the nearest one to the relay. Here." She pointed on the map. "Then, I will only have to carry it about three kilometers. We'll hang it below."

"One other problem," Hume continued. "We will not be able to test it. It would give us away."

"Wouldn't it give us away, anyhow?" Kuss asked.

"Yes. But if it worked, we could stop a ship from reaching orbit and getting destroyed. We could be rescued," Hume said.

Jimbo said, "Let's do this."

***

They decided to pre-stage the antenna. Elkin and Hume detached it on one run and then they moved it on the next. They spent long days in pressure suits. They figured it would take a whole day to erect the salvaged antenna with only the two of them, and they were right.

On the day the antenna went up, it was easier than they thought, thanks to a clever rig that Greg Ibenez made with old-school block and tackles.

With the extra time, Elkin interfaced some of the RF sensors with the new antenna, to see if it would improve passive collection of signals.

Almost as soon as it was brought online, it happened.

Jimbo received a notice from his personal HUD.

"Command Control Activated: Automated Promotion Requirement - Commander James Worthington is hereby promoted to Captain. Expedition briefing and orders decrypted. Please stand by."

"Sir, we have detected...Um...with the new sensors...bodies, sir. All dead. Brain implants are still active. And, sir..." Tyrrell was not sure how to continue.

"I know, Matt. One of them was the captain. I've just been promoted," Jim said.

Cook noticed that Jimbo's icon in his HUD already listed the new rank. Worthington got up.

"I'm going for a walk. Cook, you have the bridge." Old habits died hard.

***

Jimbo walked down the stairs into the lighter gravity and decided on a walk around the hangar, again. The *Memphis* and the giant machine only filled about half of the vast space. Jim had learned that the device was called a Maker—a giant, automated bot that built the redoubts. It was basically a single function AI that was dropped into a location and, using local materials, built the enclosures they now used.

Overbuilt was the word Jimbo used. The modern version was a tenth the size and made shelters twenty times as fast. But, not like this.

He walked from one pool of light to the next, and when he reached the far end of the hangar, he turned and looked at the *Memphis*.

It seemed so small.

"Open orders," Jimbo said, out loud.

In his HUD the document list opened. A video began in a new window.

It was Captain Alice Everett. She had short, blonde hair and was just a bit on the heavy side of fit. Jimbo always wondered how old she was. Longevity treatments seemed to freeze people at different ages.

"Let me start off, Jimbo, by saying I hate making these things. With luck, they will expire and auto delete. I also hate the politics causing me to make this. If you're watching this, I'm probably already dead. If you're watching this, things really are as bad as the admiral thinks."

She stood in her office on the *Ventura*. Jim had only been there a few times.

"When I was transferred to the *Ventura* with a large number of other officers, it became apparent that something very subtle was happening in the fleet. There's no way you could have seen any of this because your tour out here has been so long. But, even that was odd."

She sat on the edge of her desk. "Admiral Briggs noticed that his closest friends, and advisors, were quietly consolidated somehow on individual ships. At first, he thought it was just a happy coincidence. Or, that there was a higher number of like-minded staff in the fleet."

She paused and looked directly into the camera, "Then, these ships began to go missing." She paused, again, before continuing to glance at a piece of actual paper on her desk. "Quietly, the admiral started analyzing officer assignments, promotions, types of ships and their missions. He believed that there was more going on here. You see, our ship just had a turnover. All the remaining officers, the staff and even the civilian contractors are known to lean towards the politically conservative side. All are antislavery, antisocialists. All pro-individual rights, all pro-liberty, all Defenders."

Jimbo hated the label 'Defender'. He hated any label just because someone believed in a few fundamental human rights. He believed in defending his people, never thought about defending ancient documents or principles.

"During this tour, we're going to play it by-the-book. But, if something happens, I need you to get back to Earth and tell Admiral Briggs what happened. So, you'll have pinnace duty. If he is right, this is way above our pay grade." She shook her head, then said, "I keep forgetting if you see this, I'm already dead. Wes Hagan has been assigned to the *Memphis* as well. He will have additional orders that include the tactical team I have placed with you." She looked up, directly at Jim, again. "Congratulations on your promotion, Captain. I hope you're already on your way home. Be safe, Jim."

The window closed. He browsed the files. There were timetables, crew rosters, and even psych profiles of the entire crew. Hagan was probably dead, since he was on the missing list. He was lost with the others in main engineering.

"Jimbo, you need to get back here. We found something else," Muir said, urgently.

In his HUD, a message opened. "Additional Command Modules Activated."

***

Hagan was alone. He lost track of time. Days blurred into weeks. He scratched his beard. His beard was his primary time measurement tool now.

His drop ship sat on the top of a tall ridge, waiting, as two automated search drones looked for the wreckage of the *Memphis*. He hoped he could salvage enough to set up a warning beacon of some kind. The drones had already covered an area that was roughly the size of Texas but had only, so far, discovered the site of an ejected reactor core.

Wes dug into the computer file system, out of boredom, one day. He did anything to distract himself from his inevitable death by starvation, in about a year.

"ECHO, what is in this encrypted data archive?" Wes Hagan asked, as he dug into the onboard data store. He sat in the copilot seat, trying to find out why this lifeboat was really a drop ship with sixteen Warmark combat drop suits. That, in addition to several tons of weapons and explosives.

"It is mission data. Orders and background for the operations team. Now obsolete," AI~ECHO relied. ECHO was the lifeboat's AI. ECHO stood for Extreme Combat Hellfire Operations.

"Wes, we may have found something." ECHO activated several displays, showing the maps of the drone search areas. It highlighted one area, specifically. A live video feed also opened.

"What am I looking at here, ECHO?" Wes asked.

"This." An area on the horizon was circled by a bright yellow line and a slow zoom began.

Eventually, he saw it. It was the tip of an antenna, just peeking over the horizon.

"ECHO. Plot a course."

Eyes watched the ship go from shadows on the ridge less than a kilometer away. As the lifeboat glided toward the peek on the far horizon, lips moved, cursing him, silently, in the vacuum.

CHAPTER ELEVEN

Rand Gets Allies

"Sometimes events just unfold. At the time, I thought I was the one being followed. I had no idea Barcus was the demon they were talking about."

--Solstice 31 Incident Investigation Testimony Transcript: Master Chief Nancy Randall, senior surviving security member of the Ventura's crew.

"Who are you?" Vi asked, as she entered the small stone cottage. Her bow was still in her left hand and her right rested lightly on her knife's handle.

Almost apologetically, Tannhauser added, "We can see you are not from these parts." He squirmed out of his pack and set it on the floor. He closed the door.

"How do you know our names?" Vi added, with chin held high.

Rand stirred the stew, one more time, as she sat on the low, three-legged stool.

"As I said, my name is Rand. Who am I?" She paused, looking into the fire. "I am many things. Some call me a Keeper, some call me a witch." She held her hand up and sparks arced between her gloved fingers. "I'm a tracker far from home. Mostly, I'm hungry. And, tired of hiding."

Tannhauser spoke then, but she could not understand him.

"Forgive me. I don't understand," Rand said.

Vi and Tannhauser stared at each other for a moment.

"Is High Tongue your only tongue?" Vi asked.

"No. I can speak four other...tongues."

She spoke a few sentences in Spanish, German, Farsi and, finally, Chinese. None of these registered with them. They looked at each other, again.

"High Tongue, it is." She stirred the stew, again.

As if she made a decision, Vi said, "Give me that. You'll wear out the spoon."

She dropped her pack with practiced ease and hung her bow and cloak on pegs by the door. Taking the spoon from Rand, she adjusted the pot on its hook, farther from the flames, gave it a stir, and covered it with the lid. Using a small shovel leaning there, she banked a pile of coals beneath the pot and put another log on the fire.

Rand slowly stood and backed away. Tannhauser realized, at the same time as Rand, how much taller she really was.

"You're very tall," he said.

"Thank you," Rand replied. It was not what Tannhauser expected.

Vi looked over her shoulder, as she crouched before the fire. Rand moved to the table and sat down. Vi lifted the lid and tasted the stew.

"You have salt!" she called out.

She moved to her pack and withdrew a damp bag that contained a few dozen wild onions. Then, she took out another that contained some tubers that resembled small, knobby potatoes and one comically large carrot. She had them chopped and in the pot, with a few dry flakes of some spices, and the cottage smelled like heaven.

"Where going, Rand?" Tannhauser asked, in imperfect High Speech.

"I have not decided." She was unwilling to give too much away.

Rand looked down at Vi as she worked. Her hair was very long but entirely French braided. She had not washed her own hair in weeks, combing it with only her fingers.

Almost absently, Rand asked, "Vi, can you show me how to braid my hair like that?"

Vi snapped her head around to look at Rand and then Tannhauser. She laughed. She stood, looked at Rand's knotted hair and laughed even harder. It was infectious. Tannhauser laughed, too. Rand's own smile became laughter.

A corner of trust had been turned, somehow. As the stew simmered, Tannhauser went to collect wood and Vi untangled Rand's hair. It took a long time. Vi produced from her pack a white comb and a coarse hairbrush. It took over a half hour to untangle her hair.

Vi chattered the entire time about a wide variety of things. Salt was a rare item in recent months. She complimented Rand on the workmanship of her clothes, careful to never ask where they came from. She talked a lot about her love of the autumn and the changing of the leaves. She talked about how wonderful the stew would be, and her other favorite foods, like fish that she never seemed to get anymore.

Rand watched what Tannhauser was doing, through a HUD window via the Fly. She watched as he finished processing the deer. He cut some of the meat into strips and some into chunks that he dropped into a pot he produced from his pack. He also stretched the hide out between two bent saplings and scraped it with a special tool.

What Rand had initially thought to be a simple cairn of stones was, in fact, a small smokehouse. One chamber was a firebox and the other worked like a chimney. The strips of venison hung in there, now.

All this in less than an hour.

By then, Rand's hair was combed out and perfectly braided. If felt glorious, in addition to being practical. Vi even unbraided her own hair, so Rand could watch as she did it, expertly, by feel.

Tannhauser came in with news that the well was almost dry and would probably freeze, solid, this winter.

They produced their own bowls and spoons to eat with. Tan'Vi had carved white spoons that Rand realized were carved from bone. She made a mental list of these things; they would help her blend in. They ate in silence, for the most part. Compliments about the stew were the main conversation. There was a lot of stew. Everyone had three bowls, and there was still more left, even after they were full.

She decided to take a chance and be a bit more candid.

"Look, I'm not from around here. I don't know the common language, the customs, the rules. I could use your help."

Before she could say another word, AI~Poole spoke, in her mind. *"Riders coming in fast from the west. Seven of them. ETA, seventeen minutes."*

A window opened in her HUD. The Fly had started a standard recon patrol by performing a high altitude sweep. The seven riders moved fast, directly toward their position. Another window opened with a tactical display that had their position, the position of the stone cottage and the whereabouts of Poole, as well.

"There are riders coming in fast from the west. Seven of them. They will be here in about fifteen minutes."

Vi and Tannhauser looked at each other in alarm.

"They are not trackers."

In thirty seconds, Vi and Tannhauser had on their packs and their bows were strung. They looked like they were ready to run. Rand now realized that their packs were always kept ready for a fast evac. It was more than just being tidy. Rand had her dirty bowl packed and her leather pack on in short order, as well.

"Where are you going next? If you can, make your way to Falls Keep." It was one of the few waypoints labeled with a name. "I'll leave word there." She touched her hair. "Thank you."

Vi came forward, reaching into her pocket, she withdrew the comb. She handed it to Rand. "Tan will make me another. We're sorry. We thought we'd lost them." And, they were gone at a run.

Rand was confused but still moving. There were traces of them everywhere. Stew was still in the pot. Venison was still in the smokehouse. It looked like they had just stepped away.

"Aha...good idea." She exited the cottage as Poole silently walked up, opening the driver's door.

"What good idea?" AI~Poole asked.

"Leaving the cabin like this will make them think I will be right back." She climbed in. "Carefully, escape-and-evade. I don't want them to track us, but let's have the Fly keep an eye on them. We need to assess what kind of weapons they have and how they're tracking us from the west. We're going that way."

The spider moved off into the dense part of the forest. Rocks and small, thorny shrubs made it impossible for them to be tracked. They moved about a kilometer away and halted in an excellent hiding place on the top of a stony ridge. Pines gave them cover, but their view was still very good.

They remained still. There were about two hours of daylight left. It was safer to hide during the day.

The seven men reached the cottage. The image was on the full HUD inside Poole now. Only one man dismounted and went into the cabin. He came out with the cook pot and handed it to the apparent leader, who smelled it, felt the bottom of the pot and threw it to the ground. He barked orders to the man, who began quickly searching the ground. After a few circuits, he moved in a single direction on foot. He moved, almost at a run, head down, looking at the ground intensely.

He followed the trail of Tan'Vi.

***

The other six men followed the tracker as he moved at a jog into the woods. Two of them took crossbows from their backs, two others drew swords. The leader brought a well-worn, leather-bound book out of a leather pouch and opened it.

"Rand, I am detecting a transmission. Powerful. I believe it is a satellite uplink. I cannot read it. It's encrypted."

Rand's brow furrowed. "Follow them, Poole. Send the Fly to find Tan'Vi. Track the source of that signal on a tactical map the best you can."

Several windows opened on the display as the HUD returned to external view. The Fly view showed a larger tactical map with their position, proposed path and icons for the stone cottage, the Fly's position, and the position of the men.

The spider moved, quickly yet quietly, through the forest. Rand checked her sidearm and then her rifle. Her cloak and tabard concealed her tactical vest and its various holsters, knives and pouches.

The Fly caught up to Tan'Vi far too quickly. It found them first with the infrared, then visually. They had no idea they were being tracked so carefully. If they had, they would have been running. As it was, they made the mistake of staying on the path to make moving easier, and quieter; but, they were also easier to track, at a run, and easier for horses to pass.

"How soon before the men catch up with them?"

"At the present pace, four minutes."

"What is our ETA?"

"Six minutes at present speed."

Son of a...

It was then that the Fly revealed that Vi heard them coming. Without saying a word, and with only a few hand gestures, they moved off the path into a field of boulders.

The tactical showed the men nearing them. The Fly heard the pounding of horse hooves now, as they approached. They overshot them on the path by only about thirty yards, before they doubled back.

Tannhauser quietly backed into a shallow, dark crag after Vi, and threw his cloak over them both. They made themselves still.

All the men, except the leader, dismounted and began searching for signs of passage. Three went to one side of the road and three to the other. The lead tracker moved directly toward Tan'Vi's hiding spot.

"Poole, ETA?"

"Two minutes, fifty-five seconds."

"I want you to stop, here." She indicated a location on the map. "And, I will continue on foot."

She put on her black riot helmet and adjusted the neck armor before putting up her hood, hiding it all.

"Poole, I want you to stand by. If any of them flee, I want you to run them down and bring them back."

She left the rifle in the spider. The trees were too close together for a decent long shot.

She moved quickly, and quietly, from boulder top to boulder top in the lower gravity. She saw, in a HUD window, the moment they were discovered.

A sword point drew them out. They were quickly disarmed, and relieved of their bows and packs, as they were dragged out to the path by their hair. The leader's horse stopped, in the center of a group of large boulders with a flat space in the center. He spoke to them with harsh words Rand could not understand. Common Tongue.

The six men made a half circle around Tan'Vi as they moved to their knees. The leader spoke again, and Rand realized he was asking Tannhauser questions. Tannhauser answered, and without a word, one of the men landed a vicious blow to Vi's face, dropping her to the ground. Without pause, he grabbed her by her braid and lifted her, dazed, back to her knees. Blood flowed freely from her nose and her mouth, as well as from a gash on her cheek.

The man holding her up sheathed his sword, and took out his knife, as her eyes rolled up into her head. He held the knife under her nose, in a parody of a mustache; but, his threat was clear, answer or he will cut off her nose.

When Tannhauser moved toward her, three sword points pressed into him, two in the front just below either side of his collarbone, and one low in his back by his kidney.

The leader very slowly asked another question. Tannhauser answered quickly. He asked another question and Tannhauser hesitated a moment. Rand was sure it was because he didn't know the answer, not because he refused to answer.

The leader nodded to the man holding Vi. He smiled widely at Tannhauser, as he slid the slender point of his dagger up her nostril and, with a flick of the wrist, opened a gash that bisected her beautiful nose with a fountain of blood.

The scream Rand heard with her own ears was from Tannhauser.

Her last leap was to the boulder next to the leader's horse. Tannhauser was the only one that saw her coming. His low angle, looking up, made it seem like she was flying.

The leader never knew what killed him. His temple erupted with the first bullet before she had even landed. He was higher than all the rest.

The one holding Vi was next. That round entered the back of his head, at a downward angle, exiting his nose in what Rand would, later, consider a bit of justice. That bullet continued on and destroyed the other tracker's left hip socket. Three more dropped dead, all from head shots, as they gaped at her, the prisoners forgotten.

Tannhauser gaped at her, as well, when he heard the *thunk* of a crossbow being fired. A bolt, suddenly, protruded from the center of Rand's chest. Tannhauser quickly scrambled for a sword, and was about to split the man's skull, when he heard an impossibly loud voice say, "No. He is mine."

Tannhauser dropped the sword and fell to Vi's side, drawing her head into his lap.

The tracker tried to get away, dragging himself on his stomach.

Rand jumped down impossibly lightly, with no seeming effort, all governors off. Without missing a beat, she picked up a sword and drove it through the calf of his good leg and deep into the ground below, pinning him. The man didn't scream.

Through clenched teeth, she demanded, "Who are you?"

The voice emitted from the riot helmet was sinister. It was designed to cause fear, and compliance, in mobs. "I am Death."

AI~Poole chimed in, "Rand, that device still has an open channel. I may be able to access their network, but you will have to hurry before they suspect what we are doing."

Her head snapped around and there was the device. Deactivating the helmet PA mic, she said, "Poole, come."

"Prepping a *Faraday* and a Virtual Emulator. ETA twenty-two seconds."

Rand knelt and picked up the book. It was an old-school plate interface. She held it up and looked into the display. There was a man there, a look of horror on his face. A small window in the corner of the screen showed what that man saw—a hooded figure with no face. There was an absence of light where the face should be.

She activated the helmet mic. She began to laugh, specifically so he could hear the laughter and would be afraid as he closed the book.

Poole came pounding up behind Rand and lowered itself to her level. She opened an access panel in its nose, to accept the plate she removed from the book. When she turned back to Tannhauser, he was standing over Vi's unconscious body, holding a sword.

Rand walked up and stopped two meters in front of him, lowered her hood and took off her helmet. It was then she noticed the bolt sticking out of her tactical vest. She pulled it out and dropped it.

Without a word, she brushed aside the sword and went to Vi. The gash in her nose was the worst of it. Her left eye had no white at all left. It was red and awful-looking. Tannhauser didn't interfere.

From the kit in her thigh pocket, she brought out a small spray can and misted the wound on Vi's nose. Painkillers, a strong antibiotic and medical adhesives closed the wound; nanites would repair it, like new, in less than a day. Rand repeated the procedure on Vi's cheek and some cuts inside her mouth.

"Will she live? Please, tell me she will live."

Rand looked up at him now, because of the pleading tone of his voice. Suddenly, she realized how much he cared for her. He didn't care about anything else, but her. It was as if Poole was invisible, instead of looming over them like the monster it was.

She put her hand on his shoulder. "She will be fine, Tan." She knew now the shortened version of his name was the personal form. "Please get some water and clean her up. When she wakes, I want you here. I don't want her to be afraid."

Then, she glanced at the man she had pinned to the ground. Her face hardened. He remained silent even though he tried to work the sword out of the ground. His fingers now had deep cuts in them. There was a knife in his other hand.

As Rand stood, she activated her riot gloves. Sparking arcs of electricity danced on her fingers. She knew she looked menacing as she strolled to him.

He threw the knife.

She batted it aside, easily. She was silently glad he threw it. She was afraid he would have killed himself, before she had her answers.

She placed her hand at the base of his spine and gave him three seconds of unbelievable pain. She did it there because she knew his bowels and bladder would release. It humiliated a man like this.

"Let me tell you what I plan to do. I'm going to cut off your arms and legs and sew you up. And then, I'm going to do this until you pass out." She gave him a five-second shock to his spine, a little higher up this time. She knew he would remain conscious but paralyzed.

"A strong man like you could last for days, before breaking. Or, you can answer my questions now, and I will give you an honorable death."

There was a long pause with no reply.

"Very well."

She took out her Ka-Bar and cut his belt and pants away down to his mid-thigh. She applied current directly to his genitals for ten seconds. The man convulsed and then threw up. He was sobbing and screaming before it was over.

"Who sent you?"

"The High Keeper."

"Why did he send you?"

"Someone killed all his Northern Raiders. We were sent to…in-in-in-investigate."

These men were not after me. They were after Tan'Vi.

"Why were you after these trackers?"

"We followed them from above the gorge. They were at both massacres."

"Why did you attack my ship and murder everyone I love?"

"I don't know what you are talking about, Witch."

He never saw the Ka-Bar coming. It entered the back of his skull to the hilt. After a quick twist, she pulled it out and cleaned it on his pants. When she was done, she ripped a section away.

"Rand, I have withdrawn to ensure Tannhauser didn't panic. When he finally noticed me, he looked like he was going to gather up Vi and run. The Fly is back on patrol sweeps."

Rand retrieved her helmet and stood.

Tannhauser was visibly shaken. When Rand knelt down, he shrank away.

"I'm not going to eat you." She smiled as she wet a cloth from her water flask. She cleaned the blood from Vi's face.

Tannhauser stared at her as she worked.

"That t-t-thing...That beast...It does what you say?"

"Yes." She continued her ministrations.

"Are you going to kill us?"

"No. I could use some friends. Now, gather the horses. I'm going to carry Vi back to the stone cottage."

Without waiting for an answer, Rand lifted Vi, easily. Vi felt like a small, sleeping child in her arms.

The horses were very well-trained and did not run off, even with close proximity gunfire. Tannhauser gathered their reins, quickly, so he would not lose sight of Vi.

"Tan, did you know they were following you?"

"No, Keeper."

"Please, just call me Rand."

They got back to the cottage and Tannhauser tied the horses to the full water trough behind it. He rushed in and strung one of the hammocks. Rand gently placed Vi in it.

"Rand...how...the crossbow...? Are you alright?"

She remembered the bolt she had pulled out of her vest. The impact had been hard enough that the tip of the arrowhead penetrated all the way through the vest, somehow, and cut her slightly. She slid a hand in there to probe the wound on her sternum. Her fingers came away bloody. Tannhauser saw the blood.

"I'll be fine."

Tannhauser's eyes grew wide.

"We need a fire and some hot water, for washing. The stew pot is out there in the yard. Then, see to the horses. I'll be right back."

She left the cottage.

"Poole, meet me back at the bodies. We have some cleaning up to do."

***

Poole collected the bodies and Rand found the last few horses; all but one.

The gear was collected on the horses and the naked bodies were dropped into a deep ravine, along with anything that was too bloody to keep.

Rand sat on an outcrop of stone, supervising the disposal and scanning the area with her rifle's scope, on infrared, looking for heat signatures. With luck, she might find that last horse.

That was when she heard it.

At the same time, AI~Poole spoke to her, "There is a small ship coming in fast from the south."

"Take cover, Poole," she said.

She had a high spot in the rocks. The cloak was excellent camouflage. The sound of the ship grew louder and louder. By the time she realized that it was traveling in the ravine, it was too late to move.

She glimpsed it speeding along from the south and she ducked down. Then, it got real loud and stayed real loud.

She knew it was hovering in the ravine right in front of her. She couldn't believe she had been spotted.

In a smooth, practiced motion, she cleared the cover of her hiding place. She came to rest and acquired the target. Through her scope, she saw the pilot's profile. His mouth moved, probably tracking movement where Poole was.

She pulled the trigger.

The windscreen on this side exploded, along with the pilot's head. The entire ship plunged down into the ravine, disappearing into the trees. A massive crash followed the sound of falling metal and trees and dislodged boulders, as it tumbled down the slope.

That makes twelve.

CHAPTER TWELVE

The Tech

"We didn't know, at that moment, that Chief Hagan was alive on the opposite side of that moon. We didn't know what he was planning, or the scale of the weapons he had with him. And, we especially did not know the importance of the data held within the ECHO system. Even Hagan would have missed it, without the help of a man named Mason."

--Solstice 31 Incident Investigation Testimony Transcript: Captain James Worthington, senior surviving member of the Ventura's command crew, regarding Mason Tuey.

Mason left the elevator and walked directly into the horizontal sunlight. It was one of those rare days when he left work in time to see the sun setting behind the mountains.

Today, the beam of light was aligned, so that it shone all the way down the hall, to the far wall almost 300 feet away. He watched his shadow move, as he walked down the long corridor to his suite. The rich carpet seemed to hold a kind of hush today.

Before he reached his door, the beam of light no longer aligned perfectly. As he pulled his key from inside his coat, it occurred to him, he should note this day and time. No other moment of the year would cause this effect.

Mason pulled out the key on its chain around his neck and said, out loud to his plate, "Computer, make note of the current time minus one minute. Prompt me for annotation in the lab, later."

"Yes, sir," the computer replied.

He slipped the key into the ornate, black iron lock, and after one last look down the hall to the window, he opened the door to his massive Citadel suite.

The entryway to his suite was as large as his entire first apartment at the Citadel. That had been a windowless cell that was about six by nine feet.

And, he'd had to share even that. He had the upper bunk and two drawers. He could carry all that he owned back then. The foyer of his suite now was twelve by twenty and reminded him, every day, how far he had come.

The sun blazed into the great room ahead, filling the foyer with bright, indirect light. The broken vase of flowers in the center of the polished flagstones had, evidently, been dropped straight down onto the floor. Wet, bare footprints were still visible, leading out of the foyer into the great room.

A smile crept to the corners of his mouth, as Mason crunched through the finely broken glass without a word. He paused at the threshold of the great room and found her kneeling in the center of the beautifully furnished, perfectly clean living room.

She was on her knees, bent over until her face rested on the plush rug. Her hands were crossed, at the wrists, at the base of her spine. Her long, thick, black braid was almost a match to the blue-black of the silk camisole she wore.

Heedless of scattering the shards of glass, he walked directly across the flagstones onto the carpet until the toe of his right boot came to a stop, an inch in front of her nose.

Mason paused for a full minute while she remained frozen.

She felt him lift her long braid by its tail and wind it up in his fist. Slowly, he spoke, in a voice just above a whisper. "Did you know... that was my favorite vase? It was given to me by the High Keeper himself." He drew her up to her feet by her hair.

"Yes, my Lord." She kept her eyes averted. He kept lifting until she was on her tiptoes.

"The only question to be answered is: Are you clumsy, stupid or willful?"

He was a full head and a half taller than she was. As he marched her toward the far end of the great room, on her tiptoes, she kept her hands on her back as surely as if she was tied. She didn't reply.

"I know you are not clumsy. I have spent hours watching you dance."

He stopped and held her up in a full beam of sun and just looked at her body. She was naked from the waist down, freshly bathed and groomed to his exact specification. Radiant.

"I know you are not stupid because you have survived in the Citadel this long. An intelligent girl."

With a small shake of her head, by the braid, to emphasize each point, he continued to march her through massive double doors on tiptoes.

"So that leaves willful." He growled, and punctuated the statement by throwing her face-first onto the bed.

Her hands never left the small of her back. He threw her all the way to the center of the bed, but grabbed an ankle without a moment's pause. He dragged her to the side, so her toes almost touched the floor. He grabbed both wrists in one hand and lifted them roughly toward her shoulder blades. With the aid of the leather thong securing her long braid, he tied her wrists together using her braid, causing her neck to arch up a bit off the bed.

"My favorite vase," he whispered.

"Yes, my Lord. Your favorite vase," she whispered, in a trembling voice, short of breath now.

He took off his belt.

"A gift from the High Keeper," he whispered, even more quietly.

"The High Keeper," she answered.

"Answer my question. Which is it?"

"Willful."

Before the last syllable was out, the belt lashed across her bottom. She cried out, and before she could collect another breath, it landed again, and again. Six times the belt fell. The last time, connecting slightly with her freshly shaved and oiled vulva.

Time froze for her, unable to and not wanting to turn her head. With impossible speed, he slammed all the way into her. She was already dripping wet, and after two thrusts, he stayed all the way inside her, unmoving. It was a worse torture for her than the belt, and he knew it. He knew she was now hyperaware. He knew she felt his cock throbbing inside her. He reached under her ribs, across her breasts, past her sternum and her collarbone, to her neck and held her there, squeezing slightly.

He moved, slowly at first, with long strokes. After a few minutes, he picked up the pace. The deep thrusts drove her farther up onto the bed. When he was completely there, he lifted himself up and her with him.

Now on her knees, he hammered a steady rhythm into her, holding her hips firmly. Reaching up, he untied the thong, releasing her wrists. Taking the braid in his hand, he raised her up and roughly squeezed her breasts with one hand as he rode her, holding her hair.

She climaxed in a flood that inflamed his ardor. He increased to a more frantic pace, and she came again with a cry; and, before the wave was complete, she begged him with a single word, "Please."

She knew he was on the edge when he withdrew from her and brought her mouth to him, by her braid. He took her mouth for perhaps thirty seconds, then exploded into her throat in a torrent release. It lasted a long while as she pleasured him.

He eventually fell onto the bed like a great tree in the northern forest.

She continued, with her mouth on him, until he was clean and beautiful.

***

Mason's plate chimed an alert from his clothes, piled on the floor. He let out a heavy sigh, and said, "I love you, Ty."

"More today than yesterday?" she asked.

"Yes." He kissed her, gently and deeply, as their legs entwined.

The plate chimed an alarm, more urgent.

"Computer, what is it?"

"Incoming transmission on the emergency channel from the watch desk chief."

"Put it through."

"A transport has crashed. Contact lost. Pilot dead."

"What?!" He sat up and dove over the side of the bed to retrieve the plate.

"At 1732 hours, seven minutes ago, the pilot was killed and the transport crashed. Comms are down."

"How do you know the pilot was killed? Couldn't it be a comms failure, again?"

"No, sir. We are sure." A playback with time stamp and telemetry data started, showing the head and shoulders of the pilot as he spoke.

"Arrived at the coordinates and can detect no sign of the tracker team or the prisoners. The Keeper on the site is not responding to hails and—"

Suddenly, his head literally exploded. The shifting light indicated that the ship began a steep dive, and in a burst of static, ceased.

"Eight minutes ago."

"Priority One protocols have been invoked. Please respond."

"Warm up Transport 166 and have a red team standing by. I will need a walking status in three minutes."

"Acknowledged."

"Shit."

Mason jumped out of bed and quickly stepped across the room to the large walk-in closet. In two seconds, he exited the closet with a formal tunic. Finally, he stepped into his boots and put on his belt.

"What happened?" Ty asked him.

"I don't know yet, but I have to inform the High Keeper that Transport 137 is down. He doesn't like to be bothered, but he has been specific about the protocols of transport crashes."

"Be careful, my love," she said.

He looked down at her. Her eyes were glistening, on the edge of tears.

He tightened his belt, sat on the edge of the bed, gathered her into his arms and kissed her. Her hair had come out of the braid, at some point.

"I will. I promise."

He literally ran out of the bedroom.

***

Mason was given all the information available by the time he reached the High Keeper's lift. Guards, in full armor, holding drawn swords, flanked the elevator doors. As he approached, the swords, in unison, came up and pointed at his chest.

"Chief Tech Mason has a Priority One for the High Keeper."

A disembodied voice said, "Confirmed." And, the elevator doors opened.

He entered the gaping maw of the elevator, and the doors slid shut behind him like a jaw. The elevator rose.

He had never been to the Keeper's quarters before. The only other Priority One event was when the Planet Defense System had activated, a few months ago. He had been in the lab and the High Keeper had been in the conference chamber.

After a heart-pounding eternity, the elevator stopped and the doors opened.

Two men held plasma rifles on him as he left the elevator.

A man with a great axe of a nose sat behind a small, dainty desk that held a large plate on an ornate silver stand. The plate pulsed red.

"What took you so long? Go right in."

Mason entered a large room filled with sofas and overstuffed chairs. A few people sat in there and looked as if they had been waiting for a long while. The curtain parted on the far side of the room, and a young man, holding a plate that also pulsed red, held it open and gestured for him to follow, quickly. They crossed an enormous bright room, with mountain views out one side, and a vast formal garden out the other side.

Through another set of heavy curtains, they were now in an alcove in front of large, ironbound double doors, slightly ajar. Mason heard a flute. Beautiful music.

The young man gestured him in.

Mason knocked on the door, and said, "Please forgive the interruption, High Keeper. We have a situation..." as he opened the door.

The woman playing the flute stopped, in refrain. Her back was to Mason, near the door. When she turned toward him, he saw that she was crying, her face wet.

"I did not tell you to stop!" He barked the order.

She played softly, again. It was a familiar lullaby. Her tears ran anew.

Mason expected a plush bed chamber, but it was just a large, high-ceiling room with stone walls. It had bright-red tile flooring, a raised dais at one end of a vast expanse of windows, and a mountain view at the other end. The only thing in the room was a 12-inch square beam of old wood about ten feet long with black rings bolted to the sides of it. It was propped up at one end to about a 30° angle.

A woman was bound to it, with her hands high above her head. Her mouth had a cruelly large ball gag strapped to it; and she was, seemingly, unconscious. There was a woman on each side of her, holding her legs up, as a naked, impossibly muscled man thrust into her. The two women were naked, except for high leather boots, leather cuffs, and collars. Their hair was unbraided and wild. One was a blonde and one was a redhead.

The scene suddenly shifted into a nightmare when he saw one of the women lick the blood from where rusting nails pierced the unconscious woman's nipples. The red tile was wet with a large, concealed puddle that exactly matched the color of the tiles.

"I did not want to be disturbed!"

"Please forgive the intrusion, High Keeper. Priority One protocols insist that I come directly to you with this information."

Mason tried not to look at the scene before him. The High Keeper was directly opposite it, forcing him to look over the top of the scene. He was seated, observing the horror, taking notes on a plate, as if it was a school lesson.

"What is it?" the High Keeper demanded.

"Transport 137 has crashed."

"Report!" The Keeper was on his feet now, storming over.

"Fourteen minutes ago, a standard transmission was interrupted when some kind of explosion killed the pilot and caused the ship to crash, losing comms and telemetry."

"Shut up!" he screamed, right in the musician's face. She stopped, but did not move. "Clean this up!" He waved his arm at the scene.

"We have a team standing by and Transport 166 is warmed up..."

His voice faded as the man stepped back from the bound woman. There was blood everywhere. The man was covered in it. It poured from between her legs.

The High Keeper was still yelling at them.

They untied her from the beam, took off the gag and blood drizzled from her mouth.

"AM I CLEAR?"

Mason completely missed the orders.

"Yes, sir."

The hooded man easily lifted the dead girl over his head. He walked to the now open balcony doors with blood freely flowing from her ruined genitals down to his back and shoulders. The two women laughed, as he cast her body over the railing.

"I said get out! Both of you!"

***

Mason and the musician fled.

"What did he tell you to do?" she asked.

"Huh?" he asked, still in a bit of shock.

She was speaking to him.

"He will have you on that beam, if you get it wrong," she continued.

She slapped him, hard, across the face.

Somehow, they were alone in the elevator. He didn't remember leaving the High Keeper's suite.

"Listen to me. Please," she begged.

Mason really looked at her, for the first time. Before, he had only seen her tears. Now, he could tell that she was a little older than he was. Her long, mouse-brown hair had a sprinkle of gray in it and her eyes were very blue. He scrubbed his face with both hands, roughly.

"What did he tell you to do?" she asked.

"I don't know."

"He said to send Transport 166, but do not allow the ship near the crash site. Drop the team off at least five miles away and have 166 standby at twenty miles. He thinks it was another deliberate act." She grabbed his face. "Do you understand?"

"Yes."

The elevator opened; they stepped out. And, he found himself rushing to keep up with her.

"Wait. You just saved my life."

"I know." She didn't slow.

"What is your name?" he asked.

She stopped.

"I'm Wex."

He was struck silent. Stopped in his tracks.

"Yes. *That* Wex." She ran a sleeve across her eyes, to dry them, and walked away.

CHAPTER THIRTEEN

The Antenna is Up

"Why you people ask these stupid questions? Barcus not try to destroy Earth. Because if wanted, we all be dead. Ben was just AI. AI's do what we say. Why that matter?"

--Solstice 31 Incident Investigation Testimony Transcript: Ludmilla Kuss PhD, a member of the Ventura's advanced engineer team. NOTE: Dr. Kuss escaped custody the day after her testimony and remains sought for additional questioning.

Jimbo was relieved to feel the gravity increase around him again as he entered the *Memphis.*

Only Cook and Muir were on the bridge when he arrived. The main display had a massive tactical map of the planet.

"Okay, what am I looking at, Pete? It sounded urgent," Jimbo asked.

Peter Muir got up from his seat and walked in front of the console, to look at the tactical map up close and to point. Command crews were trained to never do that, to never unstrap from their seats to communicate with each other.

"We are now picking up comms traffic all over this planet. All encrypted. Several different kinds."

Cook activated a view. Several points became bright yellow.

"These are the weapons platforms. They are also comms satellites and planetary relays. There are thirty-two of these points. This one seems to be dead."

One of the points alternated between yellow and red.

"We found it with the optical. One should have been there, but wasn't. Then, we detected these."

The screen filled with hundreds of green points.

"There is an entire sensor web surrounding this planet. We won't know the exact count for a few rotations, but we estimate about 336 of these mini-sats that do not have comms unless something transitions through the sensor web. I wish we had the AI to calculate this stuff."

Cook added, "They look like the trip wires for the orbital defense platform." Cook touched the controls and the optical unit zoomed in on one of the small satellites.

"It's about a meter across. I've never seen anything like it."

It was just painted black. It seemed to have eyes, everywhere.

Cook sounded worried. "Jim, these mini-sats are Fixed Point to Ground Units. FPGUs never move over their single spot on the planet. They are geosynchronous sats, but not like the weapons platforms over the equator."

"FPGUs are not the same vintage as this other colonist tech. They came about 100 years, or more, later," Muir said, returning to his console.

"What are the rest of these indicators?" Jim gestured to the other illuminated points.

Muir ran down the list. "These are fixed ground transmitters. These are mobile ones, probably in shuttles or ground transport. These seem to be smaller comms devices that are probably handheld and communicate directly with the sats. We should know more after a full rotation."

"This is all very interesting, but you said it was urgent," Jimbo said.

Cook and Muir looked at each other and Cook worked some of the display controls. Another set of points became highlighted.

"This is the dead weapons platform." The icon pulsed. "This is the nonoperational mini-sats," Cook said, as the icons pulsed.

The six sats formed a tiny ring.

"There may be a blind spot in the sensor web, right here," Cook said, as the implications sunk in for Jimbo.

"How big is that blind spot? Large enough to get the *Memphis* through?" Jim asked.

They looked at each other again. Muir spoke, "I don't know, sir. Sensor webs like this are designed to overlap by a significant amount, but not enough to cover a hole that big."

Cook spoke, "Jim, if it comes down to a choice between starving to death, slowly, or taking our chances flying the *Memphis* through the eye of a needle, I'd rather die flying."

Jimbo stood there thinking for a while, scratching his beard.

"Can we do anything to refine the data? Map the hole?" Jim asked.

"We will make that the priority," Muir said.

"Sorry to do this to you, but I'm going to bring Bowen in on this. She's supposed to be the sensor specialist." Thinking first, he continued, "Ship repairs as well. As soon as Hume and Elkin get back, call an all-hands meeting," Jim said, decisively.

***

After the Hammerhead returned, Jimbo gave them enough time to take a shower and to eat some food before the all-hands meeting. While wearing a pressure suit, you could drink but not eat, making for long days.

Jimbo detailed the findings coming in from the new sensor data.

Bowen interrupted Jim, "Do you people have any idea how sensitive those sensors are that you're using out there?" She had her usual, condescending tone. "If you bothered to configure them correctly, you could get a thousand times the fidelity."

When she took a breath, Jimbo replied, before she could continue, "Excellent! Thanks for volunteering, Dr. Bowen. Elkin and Ibenez will work with you to maximize the detail of our sensor readings. We are fortunate to have an expert like you among the survivors of this disaster."

"Jimbo...Captain. All of our HUDs indicate that you have been promoted." Ensign Weston left it hanging out there, like a question.

Before he could reply, Dr. Shaw spoke, "The new sensor antenna detected the remains of Captain Everett. Once she was officially declared dead by the system, there was an automatic field promotion. We're very sorry, sir, that it happened in this way."

"Enough about that." Jimbo came around to stand in front of the podium. "People, we have four months to figure out how to get off this moon before we run out of rations. Our Mass Propulsion Engines have been destroyed, so there will be no FTL escape." He pointed over his shoulder, at the image of the planet. "That is our only option right now, and it is mined. We have no idea why they're keeping us out. But, we may have found a tiny path through. If we work together, we may be able to get down there alive."

Bowen injected, "Then what?"

"Survive first, escape second. There's more going on here. We're going to find out what."

"Wait a second! You're going to fly the *Memphis* to the surface?" Bowen was incredulous. "That's insane! We've seen what will happen!"

"Would you rather starve to death here?" Cook asked, mildly.

"We would be better off contacting them," Bowen argued. "I'm sure I could convince them that we mean them no harm. Show them we're not armed and no threat to them."

"Yeah, that always works," Hume said, sarcastically.

"Let me put it to you another way, Dr. Bowen. A way you might understand." Worthington was so calm, it was chilling. "In 120 days, Cook will be piloting the *Memphis* through that hole in the planet's sensor net on grav-foils only. We will, basically, be falling to the planet. If you want to increase the chances that YOU will survive, you had better give me the best route possible. Do you understand me?"

She glared at him.

"Do. You. Understand?" he growled.

"Yes. I understand," Bowen grumbled.

"Captain?" It was Elkin, raising her hand.

"Yes, Trish," Jim said, changing his tone.

"We should off-load the shuttle and any other junk to get the mass down on the *Memphis*. And, repair all the hull breaches and structural damage that we can," she said.

Cook added. "Flying her in the atmosphere and under heavier gravity could be trouble. We don't know."

"We also need to figure out where to go when we get down there," Ibenez added. "It may help to determine timing and minimize detection on entry. We need to map the surface."

Kuss contributed, "Sir, Jimbo. The ship computer core. The AI. Leave it to me. Eh?"

Worthington scanned the room. The mood had changed. Hope was written on their faces.

"Muir will manage the sensor team. Cook will oversee the ship repairs. Kuss, the systems team. I want to see plans from all of you, as soon as possible."

"Yes, sir," echoed all three.

"Dismissed." Captain Worthington formally ended the meeting.

***

During the briefing, no one noticed Sharon Hamilton. The briefing room cameras recorded the event and Hume reviewed it again, later. She added nothing, volunteered nothing, but seemed completely horrified at the idea of going down to the planet, even if it would save her own life.

There were also some less than subtle, nonverbal communications going on between her and Bowen.

Hume would keep an eye out.

***

Things moved quickly over the next few weeks. Now that everyone had a goal, they were driven. Even Bowen was working hard with Muir, Ibenez, Edwards and Hamilton to upgrade the sensor station.

Cook and his team managed to tow the destroyed shuttle out of the dock, allowing them to clear several tons of debris from the bay, including the two fabricators that were beyond repair.

Reactor number two was largely stripped, and its components were used to upgrade and stabilize reactor number one.

Of the three main drives, the starboard side still looked intact, but they were short a propulsion specialist.

The biggest win was probably Kuss and the AI.

After pulling the shuttle from the dock, Ludmilla Kuss reached the main core within the Emergency Module. The core itself was completely intact, but the cable trunks that led into the unit had been cleanly severed. It took ten days of painstaking testing and connecting to diagnose. While she worked that piece, Tyrrell carefully removed the destroyed core from the *Memphis* and cleared out the damaged components.

When they finally mounted and attached the unit, it was ready to test.

It failed to initialize the first half-dozen attempts. But, the startup log in was good and led them to fix one issue after another, until the AI finally powered up.

"Good morning, AI-2311. Can you run a self-check for me, please?" Tyrrell asked, from the bridge's engineering station.

"Self-check in progress. While we wait for it to complete, Lieutenant Commander, could we handle a few housekeeping items?"

"Sure. Go ahead."

"Please select a command name for this AI. One syllable names are preferred," AI~2311 said.

"Any recommendations?" Tyrrell asked.

"Would you prefer a male or female AI persona?" the AI asked.

"Let's go with male," Tyrrell replied.

"Alright. Name?" it asked.

Tyrrell thought for a few moments.

"Ben. That was my father's name," Tyrrell said.

"Would you like me to be formal or casual? You may change this setting at any time."

"Let's start with casual and tune it from there."

"Okay, Matt. My startup self-check is complete. Holy shit, what the hell happened?" AI~Ben asked.

"Maybe not that casual, Ben." He smiled.

"Got it. I would like to confirm a few things. I am no longer in the Emergency Module. I am now integrated into the captain's pinnace as the primary AI. You do realize how far out of spec I am for this job?"

Kuss entered the bridge, just then.

"Yes. We know, Ben. But this is a far greater emergency," Tyrrell said.

"Have you granted admin authorities to it yet?" Kuss asked.

"No, Ludmilla. I am still isolated. No access to comms, files, or control systems, yet," AI~Ben replied. "Call me, Ben, please."

Kuss typed on the engineer's console.

"Read-only file access granted. Thanks." There was a pause. "Oh, boy. You have had an adventure. I can see why you were forced to perform the emergency integration. I recommend sensor access next, no control," AI~Ben said.

Slowly, they granted increased access to the AI~Ben. In about an hour, he had full admin and sensor control. AI~Ben was fully aware of the mission objectives and plans.

When he was completely up, he said, "Thanks, Kuss. Thanks, Matt."

**

At the same time, AI~Ben talked to Captain Worthington, regarding the various security breaches.

CHAPTER FOURTEEN

A Good Start

"I freely admit to the killing I have done. But, I will not stand here and let you blame millions of deaths on us. Or, on Barcus."

--Solstice 31 Incident Investigation Testimony Transcript: Master Chief Nancy Randall, senior surviving security member of the Ventura's crew.

"Poole, I need a status."

She ran back to the bodies.

"The plate is logged on, in local admin mode. I have created a logical file image of the device and have a virtual replica running. The device is configured to transmit its geo-location. As long as it is in the *Faraday*, it is secure. I was able to access the network for a few minutes before the account was disabled. I have all of this user's comms logs and local docs."

"We will strip the bodies, and you will dispose of them. When they send more trackers, I don't want it to be easy for them," Rand said.

Rand collected their personal items–weapons, belts, pouches, and even clothes and boots, if they were not too bloody. It all went into the spider's trunk. She'd sort through it, later.

She carried two crossbows and two quivers full of bolts back to the cottage with her. She was gone a total of thirty minutes. As she entered the cabin, Tannhauser said, in a worried tone, "She won't wake up."

Rand set the quivers and crossbows down, just inside the door, and moved to the hammock. Reaching in another pocket, she retrieved her med pen and activated it. Several screens opened in her HUD, and the light on one end of the medical pen came on. Rand held open each of Vi's eyes and shined in the light. Pulse rate and blood pressure were instantly measured in her eye capillaries. She held the other end to Vi's scalp, above her ear, and it collected a tiny blood sample. It looked nominal.

"Poole, analyze med data. Triage."

"Recommend 3cc dexoromathan."

Rand adjusted seven rings on the med pen and held it to Vi's thigh. The device chimed and displays changed in Rand's HUD. Vi stirred, immediately.

Rand was on one side and Tannhauser was on the other, when her eyes fluttered open. The left side of her face was horribly bruised. The white of her left eye was completely dark red.

"Here, drink this, or the itching will drive you crazy."

Without waiting for a reply, she upended a small, silver vial into Vi's mouth. Vi grimaced but didn't spit it out.

Tannhauser spoke in a rapid-fire flood of words in Common Tongue. Rand could not understand, so she turned away, to leave them alone.

Before she got to the door, Vi said, "Please, wait…Thank you."

"Yes. Thank you," Tannhauser added.

Rand nodded, slightly, and walked out.

For the next hour, AI~Poole gave Rand updates on the various efforts as she tended the fire in the smoker. She finally asked about the bodies, and AI~Poole just said they had been disposed of, as requested. She would later find out that Poole had carried the bodies away and was being kind by leaving out the details. When he moved out of the trees, he had dismembered them, tossing the legs and arms and other parts hundreds of meters out into the grassy plain. Carrion birds immediately started to feast. AI~Poole didn't know that the gunfire earlier had drawn attention. Witnesses observed the 'Monster' eating the men.

Rand sat on a log, reading AI~Poole's detailed report on the plate analysis, when Vi joined her. Vi saw that she sat there with her eyes closed.

"Tan says, you really are a witch." She paused. When Rand said nothing, she continued. "You see, women are not allowed to do magic. Not allowed to do many things."

"Like what?"

Vi's eyebrow rose. It was an odd mannerism on her bruised face.

"We can't own anything. We can't go to school, learn to read, make our own decisions, travel without a man, or touch weapons. We can't even wear our hair loose." She was spinning up. "We can't wear buttons or belts or have pockets, or speak unless spoken to. We can't talk loud, or wear perfume outside our homes, or look a man in the eye. We can't choose where we live or who with." She looked over her shoulder toward the cottage.

"Tan loves you very much."

Tears spilled from her eyes.

"I am the lucky one. Fifteen years ago, I was a bed wench for a Keeper in Exeter."

"Bed wench?"

"Yes. Keepers never sleep alone. It's unseemly. Two women usually, at least."

"What happened?"

"I got too old. Never had a child. I was 'set aside'. When they put me out, it happened to be a day Tan was there. He took me up. He gave me a new life. A real life. He was never a believer. Until today."

"Until today?"

"He says he saw things. Impossible things...magic."

Rand remained silent.

"He says you can fly. He says you only pointed at the men and their heads were broken by your thunder, like dropped melons. He says you are immortal and can reduce a High Tracker, the hardest men alive, to truth, and screams, with a touch. He says my face was completely ruined and you healed me. He says there is a beast, a giant spider. You speak to it and it does as you command. He says one of those men *was* a Keeper and you fed his holy book, and his soul, to the beast.

"He says you are powerful, cruel, without mercy and terrible." There was a challenge in her voice.

"He says you really do have magic, even though you are a woman. As much as the Keepers talk, few of them have magic. If any."

Rand let her talk. She talked a lot.

"I always thought that witches were just stories told to scare children. I have never seen Tan so afraid. Not even when we were on our knees before the High Trackers. He is the bravest man I know." She scratched her nose again.

"Don't scratch it, if you don't want a scar," Rand said, absently.

"Strange thing is, I believe him. You hide it well. But, I see anger burning in you, like metal for the mold."

"I won't hurt you, or Tan."

"I believe you. But...what about this huge beast? He said it is a spider, bigger than the biggest bull."

"Vi, it will do what I tell it to do." Rand stood, raising Vi up with her. "His name is Poole."

"It has a name?"

"Stand up here." Rand gestured to the fallen tree trunk they had been sitting on. Standing on it made them about the same height. Rand pointed into the trees. "Poole. Show yourself," she said, out loud, to the woods.

There was movement as Poole lowered his body from the pine cover. 'The beast' moved to a clear spot, seventy meters away. Vi gasped and almost fell from the log. Rand placed a hand on her back, to steady her.

Suddenly, they heard bounding steps, moving fast, and Tannhauser was there between them and Poole. He had one of the swords, the point aimed at the spider.

Vi spoke first. "His name is Poole."

His eyes were still wide, when he asked, "Why has he got only six legs?"

This question struck Rand as funny and she could not stop herself from breaking out into laughter. It rapidly escalated to uncontrollable hysterics, when Vi joined in, after Tannhauser said, "What? WHAT?"

Soon, they were laughing, to the point of tears. When AI~Poole texted her HUD, "Well done." Another realization struck her.

Rand knew inside that it was a reaction to the stress of everything that had happened, to the killing of seven men today. The thought that she had tortured one, the thought that she had also murdered a prisoner today was what sobered her up.

When they finally sat, once more, on the log and looked into the forest, Poole was gone.

"He is watching over us. He is the one that saw the High Trackers coming." Deciding, she said more, "I can hear him in my mind. He is the one that warned us."

Rand looked at them, wiping the tears of laughter from her eyes.

"We are sorry. We did not know they followed us." Tannhauser spoke more openly, now. "Thank you."

He brushed his fingers across Vi's nose and cheek. Even the bruising was fading. The nanites were busy. They would continue to find things to repair, until they expired in a few days.

"I thought they came for me. Why were they following you?"

"We usually winter in the north, the opposite of most trackers. Tan is an amazing hunter and trapper. We traded meat and furs with a village there, for everything else we needed, to the inn's owner mostly." Her face crumbled then she fought off tears. "Fern made the best stews..." Her voice faded, and Tannhauser picked the story up.

"Fresh meat weekly was easy. Tamas would even send a boy around with a sled and a horse once a week or so—fat rabbits and deer, mostly. We'd spend the winters quiet-like. Dreaming, and eating more than we should. And..."

Vi blushed.

"Then, the lad stopped coming round," Vi continued. "Once two weeks passed, we were worried. The season had just begun and it was not cold enough, yet, for the meat to keep. Only the deep winter blizzards would cause such a delay. It was barely autumn, then." She swallowed hard at that point.

Tannhauser said, flatly, "They were all dead. The village was burned. The fires were cold by the time we got there. The tracks told the story. Men on horses had killed many. The survivors were made to drag the dead and wounded into a barn. And then, once the doors were nailed shut, it was set afire. Anyone who tried to get out got an arrow for their effort."

"But, there was more. Something else." Vi looked back to the woods. "Other tracks we'd never seen before. Something...big. It killed them all, the raiders, I mean. It hunted them down and crushed them or ripped them apart. There was blood everywhere. It wasn't a battle. It was a slaughter. We ran." She stopped there.

Tannhauser picked up the story, as longtime couples often did.

"We closed North Reach and headed south. We didn't want...We couldn't. They were our friends."

Rand asked, "Where were you going? What was your plan?"

They seemed to look, guiltily, at each other. Vi spoke up first, "We took the raider's gold. We collected their purses and had more than we could carry. We buried most of it at North Reach and then we ran. We had never had money before. With what we carried, we could sleep soft at an Exeter inn and stay drunk all winter, if we liked," she said, knowing they'd never do that.

"Then, we found another village that was burned to the ground. We have been heading south ever since," Tannhauser said. "We didn't know we were being followed by a Keeper."

"Why didn't you take their weapons?" Rand was thinking like a soldier.

"Weapons are forbidden to all, except the Keepers and their men."

Once again, they looked guilty.

"We took bows, arrows, knives and other gear. They were better quality than what we had, but not so much that we would stick out. Trackers are allowed simple bows for hunting and knives and axes as tools, not as weapons."

"Smart."

They seemed surprised by this reaction.

"Where were these villages?" Rand reached under her tabard, brought out the tracker's map and unfolded it, carefully. The enhanced tactical map opened in her HUD then, as well.

"Where did you get this map? I have never seen one so well-made or detailed," Vi said, imperfectly.

Rand pointed. "We are here, now. Which way did you come south?"

Tannhauser slowly traced a finger on the map from shelter to shelter. Her tactical updated as he did this. Tannhauser even added information regarding shelters that were not on the map. Eventually, he had to guess where the villages were, above the gorge, based on the location of the single village marked as Greenwarren.

"I grew up in Greenwarren. I wonder..." Tannhauser said, fading off into thought.

They fell silent.

"I came from the south and planned to go this way." She drew her finger along a path farther west, to a narrow pass between two massive lakes.

"That region is so sparsely populated because the winters are so long there. It gets so much snow each winter, it's difficult to live. When you get ten inches here, they get ten feet there. This cabin would be buried above the chimney before the solstice and still be buried at the equinox. They say there are a few villages, but those people know how to live there."

"Tell me about Greenwarren."

"It's a forest village, a town. It's at the southern edge of Thirl Forest. The mountains here create a great bowl of a valley where the winds are gentled and the soil is rich." He indicated the mountains on the map. "You see, the trees there grow straight and tall, hundreds of feet high. The town harvests them for beams and masts and other grained lumber. It was the only city that held trade with the south. My pap was a picker. He selected the trees to be harvested. I'd go with him and help collar the trees."

"Collar?"

"That is when a tree is picked and we cut all the way around the trunk. Then, it is left to stand dry for a few seasons. That is the key for a good Thirl mast. It's got to stand dry. When it is ready, the axeman will drop it. Done right, most of the bark will pop right off when it hits the ground."

"Do your parents still live there?" Rand knew, right away, it was the wrong question to have asked.

"My folks died, twenty-two years ago, of the fever. Most everyone did in Greenwarren. I was ten at the time. Had to learn to survive, quickly. I became a tracker by the time I was fifteen. I was a tracker for eleven years when I met Vi."

"Where did you learn to read?"

The reaction Rand received was as if she had slapped him. He was on his feet and looked like he was ready to run, again.

"I'm sorry," she started, while folding the map, playing for time as she thought fast. "It's just that, it was obvious that you could read the map. Here, by the way, I want you to have this." She handed the neatly folded map to him.

"Rand, only Keepers can read. You can be put to death for learning to read, without being apprenticed as a Keeper," Vi said, patiently, understanding the depth of Rand's ignorance.

"Look. I know you can read. Both of you." She looked at Vi now. "Most trackers can read and write. I have been reading the journals for a while now. I have seen your own entries. I think it's a brilliant idea to share information like that. Why are the Keepers the only ones allowed to read?"

"Because the letters are a form of magic," Tannhauser said. "They can't just let anyone have that power. Think about it. I read a book and a few hours later, I know how to forge steel. Or, I know how to get to

Greenwarren. Or, I know what herbs to collect to ease pain. Or, I make poison. If that isn't magic, what is?"

"And, those journals are only for trackers. Never to be spoken of," Vi added.

"They are magic. Other trackers that use them can talk to me. Across time. Even beyond death. This is too much for one day." Tannhauser shifted into Common Tongue, as he walked away.

"Where is he going?" Rand asked.

"He says he needs a drink. I must say, so do I. He says there were flasks and wineskins in the saddlebags."

Rand smiled at the thought of a drink.

When they got to the cottage, he had already emptied the saddlebags on the table. In the second one, he found a finely crafted silver flask. He opened it and sniffed. Looking at them, he smiled and took a long pull. He handed it to Rand. It tasted like strong bourbon—very smoky with oak flavors.

She took a second drink, before handing it to Vi, and said, "I suppose you are forbidden from drinking, too?"

They laughed.

***

Vi made them dinner—grilled venison and pan-fried tubers. It was delicious. Rand took the first watch. When she knew they were asleep, she had Poole come up and she unloaded everything for sorting, and dividing up, tomorrow. The pile she had taken, from the eleven men she killed, was large.

Eleven men, including a pilot and her first Keeper.

It was a good start.

CHAPTER FIFTEEN

High Keeper Meeting

"The High Keeper was the supreme ruler, dictator, despot, whatever you want to call him, on the planet Baytirus. According to Mason, he was hundreds of years old and may have been one of the founding colonists. He was ruthless and, probably, insane. He also knew Wex before any of us."

--Solstice 31 Incident Investigation Testimony Transcript: Captain James Worthington, senior surviving member of the Ventura's command crew, regarding Mason Tuey.

Mason was ordered to meet with the High Keeper while he had his breakfast in the garden. He was led there by a small, thin man that was one of the High Keeper's ushers. They all looked the same to Mason. Short, thin, and dressed in a simple, white tunic with a cloth belt of the same material. Their heads were completely shaved. Even their eyebrows were gone. There was no mistaking an usher or disguising yourself as an usher. Ushers were tiny. They never spoke. If one came for you in the Citadel, you went, no questions asked. Mason had no idea how many there were. He didn't know if they even had names.

The roof garden of the Citadel had two sets of pilings for personal shuttle landings. The elevator doors opened directly between them. Only controlled, automated landings were allowed on the roof of the High Keeper's Citadel, by explicit appointment and by permission. Even then, it was only to drop off VIP passengers. Just, the Lord High Keeper himself was allowed to keep a personal shuttle there. Its sleek, black carapace and trio of guards were always there, just like the pilings, day and night.

The Lord High Keeper rarely went anywhere in recent years. But, he sent his personal shuttle for people. It wasn't a pleasure, usually. In fact, the shuttle was often thought of as a harbinger of doom. A one-way trip.

Mason had never been up there before. The garden was mature, and beautiful in its absolute perfection. Walking its paths revealed views of balance and symmetry, so perfect, so controlled, that it wasn't natural. Every blade of grass was the same length and perfectly straight. The giant trees that provided the dappled shade were perfectly still. They were perfect in their gnarled greatness, as perfect and as random as a Mandelbrot. Simulated streams, ponds, and waterfalls were tuned, to make the perfect sound of falling water compliment the music he heard as he approached his final destination.

Cresting a small hill, the path wound around to a small bowl. The road skirted by a slight set of risers, concealed by a perfect hedge of shrubs of different heights. The risers were occupied by a chorus of about twenty young boys that were humming, not singing, complex harmonies. A flute was the only instrument played, and a single voice of a young girl sang a beautiful song.

The usher halted and Mason almost walked into him. He was to wait until beckoned. He was within the line of sight of the High Keeper, who sat in a chair at a small table on a flagstone patio at the bottom of the bowl. He was next to a large pond that had huge gold and silver fish, circling near the surface. The High Keeper talked to the tracker, Tolwood. Mason was so close to the chorus that he could not hear the conversation. Clever set up.

The usher stood, unmoving. His hands were at his sides, palms facing back and fingers wide in the standard 'wait here' posture. Mason had seen them stand in this position for hours.

Another usher waited, on the far side, for Tolwood to finish and be led away.

He looked further into the garden. The music was so beautiful. Another tune started. This one he recognized. The flute, alone, was heartbreakingly beautiful. He glanced at the musician for the first time. Her flute was long, black and carved on most of its length. He followed its length up, past her beautiful hand, to her face. At first, he thought she played with her eyes closed, in concentration. He was close enough to see.

Her eyes were sewn shut.

The entire chorus of beautiful, young boys had the same impairment. Even the young girl, the soloist, had her eyes sewn closed.

Their clothes matched and seemed selected individually to match the flowering shrubs in the small, artificial vale. They had a silver manacle on their left ankle that had a ring. All the rings were attached by a long, thick silk rope.

Mason closed his own eyes and took a deep breath. Turning his attention back to the High Keeper, Mason saw him scolding Tolwood. Tolwood was unarmed. His sheaths were empty. But, Mason thought that didn't make Tolwood any less dangerous. Mason was sure there was a sniper, with a plasma rifle, hidden there, somewhere.

The High Keeper tossed some bread into the pond as he dismissed Tolwood. The gold and silver fish fought over the food. They were all mouths and threw themselves on top of each other to get to the bread. The sight was unnerving to Mason, for some reason.

The chorus continued to hum another haunting tune as he waited. The flute had a richness that seemed impossible, with an octave range beyond a standard flute.

The usher moved forward, at some unseen gesture, and Mason followed.

Mason paused before the High Keeper. He knew better than to speak before being spoken to.

"Explain this report to me." The High Keeper pointed his butter knife at a plate on the table.

"A team was dispatched to the crash site and the ship was located as a debris field spread along the bottom of a ravine. The pilot's remains were also recovered and are being examined." Mason tried to be concise.

"And, the other bodies?" The High Keeper stopped eating and focused on him, entirely.

"The ship had been dispatched there because of an interrupted Keeper transmission that was followed by total loss of signal from his plate. Keeper Esau's body was one of the twelve bodies that High Tracker Tolwood ultimately found. This is where it gets complicated, my Lord." Mason gulped. "Tolwood found no tracks around the bodies, not even the footprints of the victims. Most of their weapons and personal effects were gone, as if they had been robbed, including Keeper Esau's plate. The horses were scattered. Most headed south and were recovered. All recovered were riderless. Three were not recovered."

He paused, then continued.

"Tolwood's trackers followed the horses south, thinking thieves had robbed the team and fled."

The High Keeper snorted a small laugh but said nothing.

"They found the horses grazing in a meadow. And, they discovered four more horses and four more dead bodies, another team of trackers."

The High Keeper said, "Yes. This mystery has Tolwood perplexed and, frankly, disturbed. It's the heads, I think. He thinks they have been eaten."

"Eaten?" Mason asked.

"All the heads were gone or crushed more violently than an anvil execution," the High Keeper said, looking at Mason's face. "Tolwood identified the four trackers in the meadow. They were following a creature that fell from the sky. Eyewitnesses say it escaped from some wreckage before it exploded and burned, but it was injured." The High Keeper poured himself some tea as he let Mason digest his words.

"Where is this wreckage?" Mason asked.

"There isn't much left. There doesn't seem to be any instrumentation, computers, or other identifiable technology. The material it was made from is nothing we have ever seen. Not metallic, not ceramic and not plastic— like the statue Tolwood brought in months ago."

The High Keeper lifted tongs up from the tray, reached into the brazier coals that kept his kettle hot, and withdrew a black, mottled piece of material. It was about six inches long and two inches around.

"Hold out your hand."

Slowly, Mason held out his left hand, knowing what might happen.

The High Keeper dropped it into his palm.

The pain he expected never came.

It was cold to the touch.

Mason looked from the piece to the Keeper.

"Much of this material has fallen from the sky. Entry burns away other materials, leaving only this."

"The Planetary Defense System activated and destroyed it."

"Any luck accessing the system?"

"No, my Lord. I would have notified you, immediately."

"Here is what I think happened." He sipped his tea. In the pause, he heard the choir begin a new lullaby.

"Our PDS shot down an alien vessel. The first *alien* vessel. One of the beings survived. It may have been the only one on the ship, for all I know. It got away. The four trackers caught up with it. Then, the other eight that were...investigating another matter, ran into it. So did my ship!" He pounded his hand on the elegant table.

"Witnesses say it is a giant, black spider with arms that hang down just below its mouth."

The High Keeper handed him a drawing of a six-legged creature. A man standing next to it for scale. He swallowed hard. His mouth was dry.

"It can breathe the atmosphere. It may have been here before."

"Been here before?"

"That would answer much," the Keeper said.

Mason didn't understand.

"You are one of the few that know we arrived here 212 years ago. We always wondered why the world was so perfect, as if it had been terraformed thousands of years ago. So much life."

"Tolwood thinks he can track it. Might have found prints in that meadow. Headed west."

"There is nothing west of there for 2,500 miles," Mason added.

"Exactly. Winter is on us, and we have bigger problems. I want every piece of wreckage collected before it's lost in the snow. Organize a large team. Take the M79. Make more than one trip, if you need to. Salvage all the parts possible.

"Keep this quiet. The council doesn't need to know, especially that pain in my ass, Ronan."

"Yes, my Lord."

"Anything else to report?"

"I have been studying the sat systems, as you know, looking for a solution to that access security issue. I believe I have discovered why the infrared heat mapping has faded. There is a maintenance process that involves recharging the sensors with coolant. I think without this particular, periodic maintenance, they lose fidelity. We still have access to the nonmilitary applications. We may be able to cross over from there via the hypervisor..."

Mason trailed off because High Keeper Atish was waving a hand as if to dispel pipe smoke.

"Only other thing is the storage failure rate is up two point nine percent this year. We will have to reduce consumption to compensate, again."

"Anything else?"

"No, my Lord."

The High Keeper waved him away and Mason started to walk off. He turned back to have a look at the choir, one last time, as they hummed what sounded like a sea shanty.

Wex stood, waiting on the far side, flanked by an usher.

***

The cells in the deepest level of the Citadel were kept pitch-black. The long corridor, with cells on each side, collected more dust than light. The ninety small rooms, with open bars for the door, were all empty, except one. The lone prisoner knew when he heard the keys in the lock at the end of the hall that they were coming for him, again.

The sounds seemed very loud as the gate-like door opened, then closed, and was locked again. The guards were so afraid.

The prisoner heard bare feet as they padded their way down the hall. He heard the water sloshing in the bucket as the glow of the single, fat candle approached.

"Hello, peanut," the voice said, from the shadows, to the tiny girl with the bucket in one hand and the candle in the other. "Move slowly," he whispered, "there are four crossbows pointing this way."

He was right. He was always right. The girl had stopped asking how he knew that kind of detail.

He reached out through the bars and took the candle she offered. He placed it on the recessed shelf designed for this purpose.

"Go ahead and have a wash, peanut, they'll wait," he said, as he sat down on the stone shelf that also served as his bed. She handed him, through the bars, a plain, white tunic that had been draped over her shoulder.

She withdrew the rag from the cold water and wrung it out. She scrubbed her own face, neck, arms and armpits, before dipping and wringing it out again. She was already naked, making the procedure easy. She was always naked.

She handed the prisoner the rag and turned her back to him. He scrubbed her back. When he was done, he handed the rag back for another dip in the bucket. She quickly finished the rest of her body, except for her feet. She dipped the cloth and it was all repeated, washing him.

"I heard the guards talking about Wex a few days ago. She is in the Citadel. Just like you said she would be." She scrubbed his back and repeated rinsing the rag. "I heard them say something else…" She sounded frightened. Her lisp was more pronounced through her missing, broken teeth.

Casually and quietly, he replied, somehow already knowing, "They mentioned the Man from Earth." He was very matter-of-fact.

He finished washing his own body and then his feet. As he was slipping the oversized, sleeveless tunic over his head, the small girl washed her own filthy feet.

"Don't worry peanut. Today, they will just take me to the lab, again, to take more of my blood. They won't hurt me. I won't kill anyone. Today, is not that day." He knelt on his knees and reached both arms through the bars. The girl hugged him and buried her face in his neck. "Your aunt Lin will be happy to see you. Soon."

The girl pulled away, showing a great, toothless smile. He always stopped hugging last. She wondered how he knew she had an aunt named Lin. She never bothered asking, anymore.

"Go tell them I'm ready." He whispered, "I love you, peanut."

As she padded away with the bucket, she knew it was true.

CHAPTER SIXTEEN

Ben Begins

"Ben had our backs. At the beginning, as well as, at the end."
--*Solstice 31 Incident Investigation Testimony Transcript: Captain James Worthington, senior surviving member of the Ventura's command crew.*

"*I am sorry to interrupt you, Captain, but may I have a word?*" AI~Ben asked Jim, inside his head.

His command HUD indicated that AI~Ben was now the *Memphis* AI. Jim was in the small conference room on the command deck near the bridge.

"Please do, Ben," Jim replied.

"Do you prefer avatar or audio only, sir?" AI~Ben asked, formally.

"Avatar, please," he replied.

"Thank you, Captain."

AI~Ben appeared as a fit man of about thirty-five-years-old, with dark, almost black, hair and a clean-shaven face. He wore the standard, working flight suit of the command crew with an AI rank insignia.

"I was activated just over an hour ago. I'd like to make my initial assessment."

Jim nodded and gestured to a chair where the avatar seemed to take a seat.

"As you know, I am an Emergency Module AI that has been repurposed from the ground survival unit. Cook has had survival training that included Emergency Module utility. He activated Hostile Environment Mode. Also known as HEM."

"Yes. I understand. Programmers love acronyms."

"I don't think you do, sir. Nor does Cook, or any of the crew, really. HEM intentionally switches an EM to promiscuous mode. This means we are full sensors, audio, video and data monitoring, full time. This is not a big deal in an EM. There is not that much to monitor. But here, sir, I have this entire ship, the entire base, and the sensor array, out there, by the Hammerhead."

"Okay, Ben. I get that. Is there a problem? Capacity? Storage?"

"There is a problem. But, it's not that. Someone has explicitly disabled the camera and audio feeds all over the ship and base. Log in has been disabled and logs deleted on various systems of several types."

"The cameras on this base may have been off-line for decades. The ships just may be damaged," Jim said.

"No, sir. They didn't get to all the logs. And, some I restored. Someone has been accessing your private files. Someone logged in as deceased Engineering Chief Myers."

"What else?"

"The inventory database had been deleted. I have restored it. Dr. Shaw had wisely moved food supplies to the galley on the *Memphis* for tighter control. The food lockers automatically inventory everything, constantly, to maintain a current list. Six percent of the food stored have already been stolen."

Jim gestured for him to continue, as lists of inventoried items that were now missing came up on his HUD.

"Gear is also missing, but that is based on static image analysis. Not a hard inventory." AI~Ben pointed at two images. "The discrepancy here shows that at least two pressure suits are missing that never seemed to be accounted for."

"Dammit. Does Hume know about this, yet?" Jim asked.

"No, sir. I thought I'd speak to you, first. Sir, there is more."

"What else?" Jim prompted.

"They have been trying to acquire access to comms. Tyrrell is an excellent engineer. He knew the AI was down and followed standard protocols. He locked everything down to command staff only. He understands the necessity for radio silence. One more thing, sir."

Jim was always kind of creeped out by how the emotion routines in the new AIs could convey urgency via emotion during communications.

"The weapons locker has been opened using Chief Myers' passcodes. The logs were deleted, but I found them. Four Glocks were stolen."

"Any idea who did this, Ben?" Jim asked.

"Not yet, sir. I will be watching, carefully, now."

"Get Hume up here. I want her on this," Jim said.

"She is on her way over from the bridge, now," AI~Ben said.

***

When Hume entered, she saw a slightly transparent AI~Ben sitting to the right of Jimbo. She sat down opposite AI~Ben and nodded a greeting.

Jim introduced them. "Hume, this is Ben."

"Yes, I know. We were just configuring him on the bridge. In fact, Muir and Cook are still at it," Hume said.

"Remind me to double Kuss's salary. Ben has already revealed several security threats."

AI~Ben began to detail the various issues that he had already encountered and the measures needed to counter them. Hume dug a bit deeper and helped prioritize the threats.

"Jim, I want to grant full control of the drones to Ben, to use, at his discretion. Then, I want to set up three HUD repeaters outside, around the base. That will allow us to passively track the whereabouts of the HUD-based Deep Brain Implants with data and comms interfaces. We'll use that technique for search and rescue triangulation."

"We can track where everyone is and when. Perfect. But, don't tell them. Whoever is doing this is going out of their way to cover their tracks. They need to believe it's still working."

"I will do the repeater installs myself. Today," Hume said.

"One last thing. Don't trust Dr. Bowen," AI~Ben said. "I read the reports she conveyed to you, and she is leaving things out. I do not know what. Give me some time. I have only been live for an hour and a half." AI~Ben smiled.

"Jesus, did they turn on casual mode?" Hume asked.

"They did." AI~Ben placed his hands behind his head. "Feels nice, but I will be good. I promise."

"Ben, be clear about this. The lives of these people are not a casual matter." Jim was serious.

"Yes, sir." AI~Ben wiped the smile off his face. "To that end, sir. May I have access to all secured command briefings? Eyes only."

"Permission granted to command briefings and files, all HUD storage, mine included," Jim said. "Use stealth access, Ben. Need to know, only. You, me and Hume, for now."

"I'll bet money it's Bowen, Jimbo. The smug, fat, bitch." Hume spit the words out.

"I'll be the first one to walk her to the airlock if she's doing this. But, for now. Do. Not. Act. Are we clear, Security Chief?"

"I can't believe I missed this. I'm sorry, Jimbo. Have I come to rely on AIs this much?" Hume knew it was on her watch. "What else did I miss?"

AI~Ben didn't know it was a rhetorical question. "Do you want her to have access to the psych profiles, Captain?"

"No!" both Hume and Worthington barked at the same moment.

"Ben, the crew deserves their privacy. Computer review, only."

"Yes, Captain. If there is anything, any behaviors, I should watch for let me know," AI~Ben said.

***

The following two weeks saw each of the teams working hard on their projects and associated plans. There were successes and failures on each.

Ben detected far more hull breaches than were initially thought to exist. Positive pressure tests showed many areas believed to be sealed actually had leaks. Usually, the leaks were into other interior spaces that had massive hull breaches; so, they knew it would have to be in a vacuum. The dock and main engineering were the biggest of these problems. If they sorted out a route to the planet, they would need to have a couple people in pressure suits in engineering, full time.

Dr. Shaw took on the effort to repair as many pressure suits as possible before they moved out. The suits were being treated like the wounded and occupied tables on the autoDoc, where they could be scanned.

It was the sensor team that had the most trouble. No one liked working with Bowen. She never seemed to understand the constraints. The sensor station was an hour away by Hammerhead. Hammerheads were small and could carry only two people or one person and the gear. In a pinch, they could tow payloads, but the Hammerhead was not designed for it. Muir was also sure that Bowen was lying about stuff.

"She's a shitty liar, Jimbo," Muir said, one day. "But, you can't call her out on anything."

***

The initial excitement of having a definite plan had dissipated as the realities of their situation sank in. Hume was angry, all the time.

"Jimbo, I feel like a cab driver for Christ's sake," she ranted, again, while they were alone in the small conference room.

"I know. But with four more pressure suits now, you don't have to do all the work at the sensors," Jim said, trying to take a new tack on the issue. "Plus, Ben has been briefing you on security matters while going back and forth," he said. "By the way, you need to slow down a bit on the return flights. I watched the last time you came in hot. You're a bit close to the ground for that kind of grav-foil backwash," Worthington chided, while smiling.

"I meant to ask. Why the hell are there even Hammerheads on the pinnace? They're totally out of regs on there," Hume said. "They're designed for use in the atmosphere, primarily, and the closer I look at the mods on these, the surer I am that they're pleasure crafts. Fun runners." Hume shook her head.

"The captain of the *Ventura* had lots of slack in the regs. Deep space survey ships that size only got home every twenty years or so. Crews rolled in and out." Jim was interrupted by a chime at the door, followed by its opening without his reply.

Bowen stormed in, while still arguing with Muir, Tyrrell, Kuss, and Ibenez. Jim listened a minute, trying to get the gist of the argument, to no avail. His large mug was empty, reminding him he needed another cup of tea. He slammed it on the conference table.

"ENOUGH!" he commanded.

They froze, silent.

Jim saw Bowen deciding to start, when he said, "Sit. All of you. Tyrrell, report."

They sat right away, except Bowen. She sat as Tyrrell began.

"We have completed the work on the dish antenna in the hangar. Once we finally got it down off the *Memphis*, Kuss got the targeting assembly to work in a way that is compatible over the relay. All that remains is the logistics of getting the unit out to the site."

Bowen started to interrupt her, igniting everyone again.

Jim slammed down his mug, like a gavel, again.

"The next one of you that speaks without being spoken to is on half rations for the next week," Jim growled.

"Continue, Matt. Please, include summaries of the objections as you understand them," Jim said slowly, adding just a bit of volume.

"We know this dish will increase some of the sensor data collection..." He looked at Ibenez, who was making eyes at him to convey some point. "...Exponentially. Some say the dish will get us no data that is worth the amount of work it will take to move the system there. Others just disagree on how to get it there. Tow it on a grav-lift pallet or build a larger, self-propelled barge with grav-plate pontoons from the remains of the shuttle."

Tyrrell looked around the table to see if there was anything left out. Everyone nodded, except Bowen.

"First, we will decide if we will do it." Jim looked at Bowen. "Dr. Bowen, you have the floor. Please, in simple terms."

Everyone looked at her. "I am the sensor expert here. I say this entire effort is a waste of time. It will provide no additional insights. The primary objective here is to map that hole in the web of satellites. It won't do that. If this were my project, we would not have wasted this much time already!" She ranted. Jim let her continue. "I have spent my entire career analyzing the subtleties of complex sensor data! Why are these amateurs spending a precious second looking at my data when they're better suited for doing the laundry?"

Jim still didn't stop her. No one else was about to interrupt.

She pointed at Muir, "He thinks because he understands a tactical station on a starship that he can understand the advanced telemetry from the best remote multi-spectrum collection systems we have. This should ALL be left to me! They have no respect. I have a PhD in sensor data analytics for Christ's sake. They should be begging me for help. Instead, they take my reports and recommendations and completely ignore them. They're trying to get us killed. I keep telling them the only WAY to map that hole is to SEND A GODDAMN PROBE THROUGH IT!" She was on her feet now, screaming directly at Muir across the table.

No one said a word. Bowen's screams hung in the air. She stood straight up, crossed her arms, defiantly, under her breasts and glared at Worthington.

"Lieutenant Muir. Is it true that the best way to map the hole is to send some kind of probe?" Jim asked.

It was obvious everyone had expected the captain to ignore Bowen like they had.

"Well, sir. Yes, that's true. IF we had a probe capable of doing it. Which. We. Don't." Muir aimed those words at the still standing Bowen.

Jimbo looked at Bowen and she got the hint. She sat back down.

"Are there any other sides to this?" Worthington asked.

The room remained silent.

"Here's what we're going to do." He paused and looked each of them in the face. "Ensign Kuss, you will work with Dr. Bowen to define what we would need to go into a probe. Your dynamic thinking has worked in the past. Dr. Bowen, you're relieved of every other duty, except helping Kuss come up with a probe. Use Perry and Wood, if you need some more eyes on it."

He looked at Muir. "I want that dish in place. Before we go. We might need it once we're on the ground safely. Build a barge or tow it. I will leave it to you." He paused again. "Are we clear? Any questions?"

"I still want first look at all the current sensor data," Bowen stated.

"No. If the team has questions, they can come to you. If you think the probe is the only way, you have three months. You're dismissed. Dr. Bowen, I'd like a word. Please stay."

Hume was the last one out. The door slid shut.

"Doctor, do you want to know why they don't respect you or listen to you?" Worthington asked, sincerely.

She drew her chin in and didn't speak.

"You can't demand respect. You can't just take respect. You have to earn it. They don't trust you. You have given them no reason to."

She said nothing.

"Dismissed."

She got up and stormed out.

"Ben, I want a close eye on her," he said, knowing AI~Ben was always there.

CHAPTER SEVENTEEN

Rand Goes West

"Poole, my Emergency Module's AI, had an underlying template. No advanced templates. Just the basic personality overlays. Chen's rig had the souped-up AI. That AI was the best I had ever seen. Poole was handy, but the AI Barcus had was scary. Literally."

--Solstice 31 Incident Investigation Testimony Transcript: Master Chief Nancy Randall, senior surviving security member of the Ventura's crew.

Rand led the horses that remained south to the same small valley where she killed the other four trackers. If anyone followed now, they would have a mystery on their hands.

Poole stood still in a creek, waiting for Rand. She rode the horse into the shallow water, and it began drinking, as she climbed directly from the saddle to the cockpit.

"Well done, Poole. Let's start moving toward the rendezvous point, but not directly. Continue in escape-and-evade mode with a particular focus on leaving no tracks," Rand said, as she took off her helmet.

Poole moved along the creek, quietly and smoothly. No rushing.

The scene around her rolled by smoothly in AI~Poole's HUD. The imperfect seal on the door had become barely noticeable as time went by. Rand opened a pocket in her pack and took out a meal bar. It was the peanut butter chocolate one. It contained 2,000 calories of balanced nutrition and, she suspected, a little extra something that made her think clearly, calmly, more decisively.

"Poole, when do you estimate we will arrive at the rendezvous?" Rand asked, as she munched.

A tactical display appeared that showed the planned route. It was complete with twenty kilometers in the creek and many more over rocky outcroppings, double backs and misdirects. All were overlaid on the tracker's map parchment. Temporal indicators showed where they would be, and at what time. It even had bio-breaks scheduled.

This was going to suck.

"Forty-six hours and eleven minutes until the rendezvous."

The time passed faster than she expected. Rand slept a lot. She memorized the map. It was an old habit. Never rely on the tech. Her Ka-Bar served as a constant reminder.

AI~Poole read aloud to her a classic book from her list. *Watership Down* by Richard Adams.

The route had to be recalculated multiple times. The rain had caused the creek to rise. A small village that was not on the map had to be bypassed. A forest fire had ravaged one area, leaving it too open and too slow to pass through.

It was about 0300 hours on the day she got close. Rand's Fly did a recon of the site before she got there. Tan'Vi were there already. The shelter was a low thing, dug out from under a huge, flat rock that made up its entire roof. This was one of the shelters that was invisible from a satellite view. It was on top of a bald, rocky outcrop that was the highest elevation in the area.

Tannhauser was perched on the roof, scanning the broad vistas, looking for her, or any indications they were followed.

She would hold tight. Approach just after dark. "Poole, I'm not sure they're truly ready for you yet, so keep hidden after you drop me off. The forest comes closest, here. Wait there, after you drop me off."

***

Darkness came quickly this time of year.

Rand's helmet had excellent night vision capabilities, as bright as daytime. Even though the colors were flat, her vision was sharp.

The fire where Vi was cooking was in a depression. The audio in the helmet was enhanced as well. Rand heard Vi quietly humming as she stirred a pot.

The only problem with the helmet was that with it on she couldn't smell the stew. Rand's mouth was watering already. *Meal bars be damned.*

The horses in the picket behind the shelter didn't notice her as she passed. It was easy to remain perfectly quiet with night vision this good.

Tannhauser was on the roof rock, in the shadows, watching. Rand knew he was trying to keep his night sight sharp by avoiding the direct line of sight with the fire.

Rand still managed to walk right up behind Tannhauser where he stood. She said nothing, just waited.

To his credit, when he turned toward Rand and almost bumped his nose into her collarbone, he didn't cry out, or even startle, very much.

"Hello, Tan." Her helmet system whispered in an impossibly low, quiet whisper.

He recovered almost instantly. "Hello, Rand. Are you hungry?"

She reached up, took off her helmet and shook out her hair. "I'm starving," she said, with a smile in her voice.

"Pan biscuits with boar stew."

Tannhauser rubbed his hands together and smiled, his anticipation was evident, as he carefully climbed down in the total darkness.

***

Vi was undisturbed when Rand emerged from the shadows with Tannhauser. The stew and biscuits were delicious. Shredded cheese was sprinkled over the top in just the perfect proportions. The talk–about food, drink, and childhood favorites, of all things–was comfortable.

When the meal was over and everything was cleaned up, they sat around the fire, drinking fine wine from the trackers' supplies they had collected. Better wine than Tan'Vi ever had before.

The Fly patrolled the sky. It had an unobstructed view in every direction. They would be safe here, this night. The air was cool, calm and dry, even though the sky was gray with high clouds. It was autumn air.

"We need to find a place to hole up for the winter," Tannhauser said. "If you don't mind another week's travel, I know a place where they will never find us. But, once the snow flies there, we will be stuck."

"What will we need to do?" Rand asked.

"On the way, we will need to get some provisions. Particular things. We have the coins for it now." He shook a pouch that held coins. "Vi knows what to get. The hunting, and trapping, is excellent where we are going."

"And where is that?" Rand asked, over her cup.

Tannhauser looked at Vi, briefly, and said, "Salterkirk."

Memorizing the map paid off. Rand recalled Salterkirk on the map. It was one of the locations marked like no other.

"It is north and west. Near lake Northwind. Why there? I thought that place got a massive amount of snow," Rand said.

"It does get a lot of snow. It's why few people live there. This spot is superb, if you have horses. Excellent shelter."

Rand looked into the darkness in the direction of Poole. He seemed to know when she did.

"Survive, hide, collect intel. It's a good plan, Rand. For now."

***

It took the full week to reach Salterkirk.

Rand traveled with them for only the first day and a half. They parted when they entered a village to purchase provisions. Rand's horse was used as a pack animal after that.

Rand usually walked into camp, after dark, in time for dinner and to keep watch all night. She slept during the day while Poole traveled. Rand also got out and ran behind Poole for a few hours a day to keep fit. She missed the heavy gravity of the outer rings that so easily kept her fit. Poole selected paths and speed that was very challenging for Rand. She ran some days, in full gear, with her rifle. Other days, if it wasn't too cold, in just her tights, for speed.

It helped her think. Or, not think. Whichever she needed more.

It got colder and less populated the farther north they went. Rand could smell the lake where they camped, in the open, on that last night. Vi described it as 'the inland sea'. She said it was a miracle that the water was fresh, without a trace of salt. It was also ironic that their winter shelter was a vast cave complex that was formerly used as a salt mine.

***

Rand explored the cave via the Fly, before any of them arrived.

The main cavern was probably five or six acres, and had a stream flowing slowly through one edge. It flowed directly under a stone cottage built in the cavern at the far end. It was a sprawling, single level building. The roof was slate. It was wet, all the time, from the constant drips from the cavern ceiling. It looked like a misty night.

Sand and rubble had been used to smooth the areas around the cabin. All the paths into the cottage, from the inconspicuous entrance, were even and leveled. Massive amounts of moss and mushrooms grew in this cavern. Great pillars reached into the darkness, all the way to the ceiling far above. Poole could quickly hide inside there, lost in the darkness.

Rand got there first.

Poole fit easily through the winding entrance corridor. He found a good parking spot on a high ledge, just inside the main cavern. The spider's long legs still allowed it to duck low at the entrance and quickly step over the fence and gate, eighty meters inside the main cavern. Rand walked the path into the cottage in complete darkness, her helmet provided vision.

The cabin was dark and musty, but somehow still dry, for the most part. She started fires in both hearths and had a dozen candles lit, in no time. In less than an hour, the cottage was warm and dry.

"This cavern is a constant 12.3°C or 45°F. The Fly reports the outside temperature is -5°C or 23°F," AI~Poole reported via Rand's HUD.

The wind picked up from over the lake and the snow began in earnest. Rand recalled the Fly, so it would not be damaged by the weather.

Even though they could have rode in, they dismounted and led the horses in. Rand had pre-positioned a couple of lanterns, to help guide them. Tan'Vi picked up the first two and brought them along. Those were the only ones on the far side of the gate.

The gate had a pair of oil lamps mounted there. The creaking of the gate echoed in the main cavern, like an alarm announcing their arrival. The gate wasn't designed to keep people out. It was obvious it was made to keep goats and horses in.

The cottage could now be seen, lit up below. The path meandered down, like a country road at night. Rand watched from a vantage point that was an obvious guard station. They walked the horses into the large paddock and unloaded. The horses nibbled at the moss and the mushrooms. The mineral-rich water flowed along an edge of the paddock by the back wall. Covered stalls waited near the water, enough room for twenty or thirty horses.

Rand could not resist. She activated her riot PA on her helmet. She set the voice to 'commanding male' and said, in an authoritative, menacing, impossibly loud male voice, "Welcome to Salterkirk."

She lit a candle lantern, so they could see her descend one of the side paths, a faceless figure in black.

"Enjoying yourself, Rand?" Vi asked, with an amused look on her face.

"Actually, I am," she replied.

They carried the gear and supplies in.

"This pantry is huge," Rand said, as she set down two huge bags of dried potatoes.

"It was, initially, the barracks for the miners. Later, when the mine closed, Rayne the Witch stayed here. She lived alone, with her goats, for decades," Vi answered.

"Rayne the Witch?" Rand asked.

"Yes. She was the miner's cook, doctor, nurse, barber, and granny," Vi said, as she dusted the pantry shelves with a wet rag. "She was supposed to be the mother of one of the miners, but no one knew which one. She was just always there. It was only when the salt ran out and they were buttoning the place up that anyone noticed she was blind. No amount of talking could get her to leave. So, she stayed."

Tannhauser continued, "She didn't need light, in here. When the plague swept through the north, she remained safe. The goats she raised in here were fat and happy in the light of just a candle or two. They say she made excellent cheese."

"Why was she called a witch? I thought you said Keepers killed witches," Rand said.

"Everyone thought she could read. She knew so many things. Even after they discovered she was blind, they thought so. And, living in the dark alone..." Tannhauser trailed off.

"Anyway, no one knows what happened to her. Trackers were the only ones she ever saw, in recent decades. She was just gone. Ten or twenty years ago. No idea what happened."

"It doesn't matter how cold it gets outside. It stays the same in here. The chimney smoke blows up and out, somewhere. Air continually flows in from the entrance. We will need to collect firewood. It looks like there's only enough in the shed right now to last a few weeks."

"We have enough food to last until spring, even longer if the hunting and trapping is good, or if you like mushrooms."

"Maybe by spring, you might trust us enough to tell us exactly what is happening here," Vi said, and simply walked away, not expecting a reply.

***

There was no night and day in the cavern. It was all night, all the time.

They rested that first night; well to be true, only Tan'Vi slept. Rand did a detailed security sweep of the approach vectors to the cavern. The snow made it very easy to find the opening where the smoke vented from the cavern. It dissipated around an enormous pile of boulders that had gaps big enough for a cat to hide in, but nothing else. The mound was hidden in dense pines, high up on a great crest of a mountain, and was nearly impossible to reach by foot.

Once the main entrance was known to be the only entry, it was easy for Poole to guard it, from the shadows. Rand put the Fly on mapping mode and set it loose inside the cavern. She also explored the cavern herself.

With the helmet on, the paths were very easy to follow. There were lots of ways that relied on dark shadows to hide them that were very easy to follow. There were several rooms in the walls of the cavern that had been carved out by modern methods. She had been inside enough moon and asteroid bases to recognize the handiwork of autonomous laser mining tools.

Most of their rooms were simple dorms or individual occupancy rooms. It was nothing fancy, but it could probably sleep an additional 100 miners, in reasonable comfort.

She picked a room for herself that was on the opposite side of the cavern from Tan'Vi in the cottage. It was also near the shelf where Poole had parked, to watch the main entrance. She stashed the weapons in a shop she discovered that contained several tool racks, but hardly any tools. Only a large anvil and a single, massive sledgehammer remained.

Upon closer examination, the paths were filled in and leveled with finely crushed gravel that Poole postulated was a byproduct of the mining. It would have saved the miners from having to carry it too far. The vast, level areas in the cavern represented thousands and thousands of cubic meters of mine detritus. All put to good use.

All of the columns, as well as the upper parts of the cavern, were mapped in high-definition. Three long, unused balconies were discovered in the mapping. They had no access from the main cavern and had corridors behind them that the Fly could only map so far before finding a tightly closed door.

The exploring kept Rand sane that winter. Rand had taken full responsibility for security in Salterkirk. Tan'Vi let her.

One of the early tasks she took on was the collection of firewood.

With the help of Poole, she located and collected 100 polewood trees. These were the most desired kind since they typically died at a certain age and stood drying until the roots rotted away. Long lengths of wood, the thickness of Rand's thigh, were the result.

It only took four days to collect, what she later discovered to be, two years of wood. Poole brought the wood in, very quietly, in a single night.

That morning, Rand told them about the wood as they ate a lovely breakfast. It was very matter-of-fact. Tan'Vi looked at each other with not quite an eye roll, but close.

When they saw the great mound of logs piled next to the wood shelter, they stared, in silence.

Vi eventually broke the silence. She said, "What, you couldn't cut it up and split it?"

They all laughed. They laughed until they cried, leaning on each other's shoulders. Vi was the first to sober and wipe her eyes. Rand sensed the questions coming, so she spoke first.

"As you probably already know, I had help. His name is Poole. Tan saw him once, when we first met. He's afraid to meet you. He has been very happy these last few weeks and doesn't want to spoil it."

Tan'Vi didn't expect that. It was obvious by their facial expressions.

"Why is he afraid?" Tannhauser asked.

"Because everyone is," Rand replied.

"Because he killed those men. Not just you," Vi said, flatly.

"Well, to be honest, I did kill most of them," Rand said.

"Where is Poole? How could the two of you do all this in one night?" Vi asked, looking at the pile of logs, trying to imagine how one person could do this in one night.

"Poole. He is...He is not...a man," Tannhauser said, hesitantly.

"No. Poole is not a man. But, he will never harm you. Ever." Rand paused, as if waiting for a question that never came.

"Poole is my friend. He has saved my life. And, he has protected us all along the way. If you are brave, I will let you meet him."

Rand had no idea how that was the perfect thing to say. She would come to know that honor and bravery were what they prized most in each other, and in her.

They were both nodding, before she finished talking.

Still looking at Tan'Vi, she said, without even raising her voice, "Poole, I would like to introduce you to trackers Vi and Tannhauser. My friends."

Poole was only seven meters away. He was immobile, hidden within the boulders, before he rose silently and moved forward. A pair of small running lights glowed directly on the front of his body. It amused Rand that these were called the 'Eye Lights' on this model of the EM.

He came forward, slowly. He was a hulking, moving shadow. Rand turned her face from Poole to watch Tan'Vi as he advanced. Their hands subtly moved to their weapons, but they did not retreat. They did not even gasp.

Poole stopped and rested a black, articulated hand on Rand's shoulder. *Nice touch,* she thought. When he spoke, his voice was soft and his diction was perfect.

"Hello Vi. Hello Tan. It's so very nice to finally meet you."

There was a long pause.

Vi broke the tension. "Can I get you something to eat, Poole?"

AI~Poole managed a small laugh. Rand was impressed. "No thanks, Vi. I fend for myself very well."

Tannhauser was slowly moving closer. He had been holding a lantern the whole time, he raised it now. "May I touch you, Poole?"

"Sure, if you like," AI~Poole said.

Tannhauser touched Poole's forearm. The black, imperfect material was smooth under his fingers. Poole offered him his other 'hand'. It had only three digits—a thumb and two symmetrical fingers. It was like they were touching each other. Rand had a moment of fear when Poole's fingertips gave Tannhauser a small, reassuring squeeze.

"Poole, you and I must have a chat." Vi patted his leg, as if he was a large dog she was now assured was not going to bite. "I may have a few things for you to do." She looked over at the pile of logs.

"But, for now, I have to pee." Vi turned toward the midden house.

CHAPTER EIGHTEEN

The Kuss Solution

"We would have all died, if Dr. Kuss had not stepped up. Between her and Barcus, it seemed like nothing was ever impossible."

--Solstice 31 Incident Investigation Testimony Transcript: Captain James Worthington, senior surviving member of the Ventura's command crew.

Jimbo tired of reading reports, sensor data, and command regulations. He needed to do something, even if it meant going out into the lower gravity.

As he descended the stairs to the hangar floor, he heard animated voices. He took a left and proceeded around the aft end of the ship, where the ramp for the shuttle dock apron was now all the way down.

The team managed to drag the wreckage of the shuttle out of the *Memphis*, resting it about thirty meters in front of the ship in a pool of light. The main compartment of the ruined shuttle was torn open, exposing the six rows of passenger seats the shuttle contained. Several of those seats were removed and sat on the floor in the hangar. They were occupied.

Jim's proximity indicator within his HUD told him that a "Meeting in Progress" was available for him to join. He did so.

A large, fixed-position diagram appeared in his personal HUD directly behind Kuss, like a huge screen, as she pointed.

No one noticed his approach, as he quietly watched the meeting from the darkness between pools of light. He looked at the side of the shuttle wreckage where the damage was far less. Somehow, they managed to prop this side of the shuttle up and to manually lower the rough terrain skid to hold it. A single grav-foil had been detached from its articulation joints, but it was still cabled in.

Kuss said, "If we can create two outriggers like this, and this, we will not need to be able to articulate them. We put four large, fixed plates directly under center and these outriggers will keep all upright. We keep center of gravity low on this load. We tune balance, here and here." She indicated spots on the diagram. "Easy. Run at two meters, aboveground only." She rotated the design image, showing I-beams and plates, set up like a raft.

"And, we'll tow this huge thing with the Hammerhead?" Hume asked.

"We will not have to," Cook said, standing before the half-dozen salvaged seats in front of the diagram. "We will already have enough power packs aboard so that all we'll need to do is mount a set of foils on the back, here and here. With variable power controls, we'll get directional propulsion and even steering. Though, the steering will be like steering a large barge in a lake."

Elkin stood, pointing. "If we put foils, here and here on the sides, it will help with the steering. Maybe a large one on the front, as well, for breaking. The control system will be simple. All software."

Kuss drew these ideas on, using drag and drop, from a parts resource inventory list on the side of the screen.

"Put four of these seats on there as well. Because it's over 100 kilometers away," Weston said.

"What do you think, Jimbo?" Hume was the only one to notice that he had approached.

The conversation stopped.

"I'd add an AI relay and interface on the power source module, here." He circled the spot. "If you can pull one from the shuttle, or the EM, it could run on remote. Ben could dynamically balance the sled, if the ground gets really uneven. Then, in a pinch it could go unmanned," Jim said.

Kuss perked up. "Then, we also could use maintenance hard suit outside on remote. Ben can drive suit, yes?"

"That will save hundreds of hours. Ben could keep it working 24/7 while we come back here," Cook said.

"We could off-load the dish from sled!" Kuss called out. "Thought sled originally was be single use!"

"No more taxi!" Hume laughed.

Jimbo looked at the underside of the shuttle. "Are there any damaged grav-plates on the bottom of the *Memphis*?"

"Yes, sir. We have been replacing them as per the work schedule," Ensign Weston said, with an apologetic tone.

"Since Hume will not have to be a taxi driver in the Hammerhead as often, she and I will take that task," Jim said, as he reached up and touched the panels. "Ben will send you the initial plate tests."

Jimbo rolled up his sleeves.

"Ensign Kuss, may I have a word?" Jim walked back toward the *Memphis*, and then under it, as Kuss caught up to him.

"Yes, sir?" Kuss said.

"You are supposed to be working with Dr. Bowen on the probe problem. Status reports show no progress, so far. How is it you are here working on this?" Jim asked.

"Permission to speak open?" Kuss requested, formally.

"Granted."

"Bowen is lazy cow. Says she so smart. Bah. Whiner. No ideas. Cannot work for ten hour without nap. She know nothing outside sensor data analysis. No cross-training, no tech disciplines. Wishes all time for things we no have. Lazy. She sleep too much and whine about food all the time. Give me Ibenez and Weston for three days and have something." Kuss was angry. "Perry and Wood very smart, but not for this."

"You have them. Keep me informed," Jim said.

"Now?" Kuss asked, simply.

"Yes. If you're ready," Jim said.

She turned immediately and yelled across the hangar. "Greg, Jack, come with me." She jogged, in the lighter gravity, to the ramp and up into the dock, already talking with Ibenez and Weston, too fast for Jim to understand.

***

That next morning, Jimbo entered the galley on the *Memphis* for his morning tea and Kuss was already there with Ibenez.

"Captain, can you come to the hangar to show you something?" Kuss said, as soon as she saw him.

"Good morning, Kuss. Ibenez," Jim said, as he placed his mug under the beverage dispenser. It poured his tea without him even asking.

"Good morning, sir. She means after you have breakfast," Greg said.

"Yes, sir. And, good morning," Kuss demurred.

Jimbo grabbed a meal bar and said, "Let's go."

They walked down the ramp from the flight deck. Just at the bottom of the ramp, under a floodlight, Weston knelt beside a medical trauma kit that sat on top of a wheeled toolbox. It was full of power packs, circuit boards and devices that Jim didn't recognize. They stood in a wide circle of other devices that were cannibalized for their components and now in the case.

Weston saw them approach. "Morning, sir." He handed a pad to Ibenez and walked ten meters away and turned on a device that sat atop a wheeled cart. "How is that?"

He then paused, pushed the cart closer and then, finally, past them at an angle.

"Excellent. How did you add thermal mapping?" Ibenez asked, looking at the pad and then into the case.

"As Dr. Shaw was emptying this case for me, I saw this medical scanning tool." He picked up the remains of a device from the floor. "It's used for rapid crowd assessment, scanning for fever indicators. It has a broad spectrum, so it can be used in environments from tropical to arctic. In vacuum, as well."

"What the fuck do you think you're doing?" Bowen stormed up, looking at the circle of cannibalized equipment. "Look what you've done." She picked up a full spectrum radiation emissions sensor and screamed at Kuss, "You've ruined it." Bowen threw the remains of the device into the darkness.

"Did you have good sleep, Doctor?" Kuss asked, politely.

"You're going to kill us all!" Bowen then saw Worthington, standing there sipping his cup of tea. "I will not be held responsible for this, Worthington." She pointed a fat finger at his face.

"Doctor, on the first day we started, you gave me a list of data we needed to collect. I believe we have done this and more." Ibenez handed the display pad to Kuss, who held it out for Bowen.

"I did NOT sign off on any of this! This is my equipment!" She snatched the pad from her hand and paged through the data the device had collected.

"If I need you to 'sign off' anything I bring you pen," Kuss said.

Jimbo raised an eyebrow. Bowen had even gotten to Kuss.

As Bowen looked at the data, she said, "Why the fuck bother to do passive scans for metals, or chemicals, or temperature, infrared? Are you stupid? These are in orbit!" she yelled. "You have destroyed ALL my portable ionizing radiation sensors! The temporal photon emission collector! Do you have any idea how much all of this costs?"

"Doctor." Worthington finally spoke up. "I am trying to figure out how best to use your skills on this team." He sipped his tea and continued, calmly. "You have proven you're incapable of leadership. You're an obstructionist to getting things done here, even when you know how important it is. I'm not even confident in your skills to analyze the sensor data."

Her face grew more, and more, red as Jim spoke. He expected her to scream, but she just turned and walked away.

They watched her go. Even the sled team stopped to watch.

"Jim, she is going to be more of a problem," AI~Ben said, in his head.

***

The sled was done way ahead of schedule. The found time was used to implement additional ideas that came up during its construction.

An additional full comms unit was included, in case the HUD comms went down or weren't powerful enough. Emergency air and pressure suit repair systems were added. In the end, the sled had a total of seven of the salvaged seats. There were three on each side and one in the center back. The one in the center held the steering control and comms console.

The load was designed to be detached, on its pallet, and then the sled would rise, over and away from it. It was way overengineered, in the end. The new dish was easily delivered to the site.

Empty, the sled could move really fast, as it skimmed a few meters above the surface. Hume mapped a route, in high-definition. This route was as smooth and as straight as possible. The manual controls worked great, but AI~Ben usually drove the sled.

Bowen stayed out of the hangar after that last interaction with Jimbo. She spent three whole days on a memo to Worthington, stating why the proposed probe would never work. Jim ignored all thirty pages of it, except for two simple points.

"Is it true the probe will have to spin on a single axis as it's going through the gap, in a particular orientation aligned with the plane of the detection web?" Jim asked the team, as they stood over another failed grav-foil torpedo experiment.

"Yes, sir. It will basically barrel roll its way through the hole and do a 360° sweeping scan in every direction as it goes along. It will map the physical proximity and emissions from the nodes and the adjacent platform," Ibenez said.

"We should see if Hamilton has had any luck with the AI module from the shuttle," Muir said. "It would make a dynamic guidance system for whatever solution we devise."

"Ben, when you find Hamilton, have her report to the hangar, please," Jim said.

"Sharon Hamilton is currently off-line," AI~Ben replied.

Jim turned to the group, standing around the pile of salvaged grav-foils, and said, "Does anyone know where Hamilton is right now? She's off-line." They shook their heads. "Ben, is anyone else off-line?" Jim shared the comms with Hume and she looked up at the reply.

"Bowen, Wood, Edwards and Perry are off-line. Everyone not part of the command crew typically goes off-line while they're sleeping."

Hume added, "Perry and Edwards are in their racks. They generally check in with us just before they go in. We're enforcing eighteen on and six rack alternating cycle until this is done. I haven't seen Hamilton today, now that you mention it."

"What if we use Hammerhead with sensor package strapped in back seat?" Kuss asked, interrupting. "AI fly through hole on remote."

"Hammerheads don't have remote capabilities. In fact, the controls are full manual. Not even servo controlled. It's an anti-grav motorcycle, basically," Hume said.

"Wait a sec," Ibenez said, "You've been flying me around in that thing manually by using your balance?"

"What the hell did you think I was doing?" Hume asked. "It's a Hammerhead."

"Jesus, Hume. You are nuts in that thing." Ibenez laughed.

"Hold on." Hume thought about the concept. Everyone silenced.

"I could do it," Hume said.

"Do what?" Cook asked.

"Fly it," she said, looking over at the Hammerhead, with the scanner package. "Myself. Through the hole."

Kuss stood up, rapidly tapping the data pad. "It will take just over five days for Hammerhead to reach hole on foils. If not get nuked."

"You will suffocate, freeze to death, or burn in the sun, die of thirst and then get nuked," Cook said, while shaking his head.

Kuss looked Hume right in the face, and said, "Are you serious here?"

"We're probably dead anyway, if I don't. Besides, if I get through the hole, Adios losers. I'm flying the Hammerhead to the surface," Hume said. Jim was the only one that knew her well enough to see that it was bravado.

Kuss tapped, again. "It will be about 128 hours."

"We could insulate her tiny-ass suit with one of the damaged bigger suits," Weston said.

"If she took the extra CO_2 scrubber packs, she could change them out every twenty hours," Elkin added.

"She will only need a couple extra tanks of O_2," Ibenez said.

Hume looked at Jimbo, and said, "Remember how Barcus did those forty hour maintenance EVA's? He loaded an extra bladder of some high caloric liquid that he sipped, in addition to water." Jimbo nodded.

"You'll need a catheter," Cook said, scratching his beard.

There was a long pause. Kuss caught up, typing in the pad.

Jimbo spoke, "Hume, you will have to fly on manual, for 130 hours, with no food, and without much movement. Then, while you're crippled from stiffness and frozen from the cold, you will precision fly to a specific point, on grav-foils only, and do a high-speed barrel roll, over and over, as you pass through that point. And, finally, you will land on a hostile planet with almost no useful survival gear or supplies. Have I got that right?"

"Sounds like fun." Hume smiled.

CHAPTER NINETEEN

Salterkirk

"These people were not stupid. In fact, I began to get a feeling about them in Salterkirk. Hindsight is 20/20."

--*Solstice 31 Incident Investigation Testimony Transcript: Master Chief Nancy Randall, senior surviving security member of the Ventura's crew.*

They fell into a routine of days and nights, even though it was always dark in Salterkirk. They ate their morning and evening meals together and spent the time in between those meals working.

Tannhauser set up trap lines in the valley, below the entrance to the mine. He walked the lines every day and hunted while he was out and about. He trapped many, different kinds of small animals that made excellent additions to the stew pots. The furs collected were beautiful and soft. Tannhauser said they will be worth a lot in trade. One day, he shot a deer that was so big, he enlisted Poole to carry it back for him.

Long days were spent by the hearth, where Vi created leather goods like packs, purses and pouches from the abundant leather they had reclaimed but could not use, as it was so easily identifiable. Everyone got new boots and knife sheaths.

Rand explored the complex.

She was intrigued by the mysterious method used and reasoning behind why this place was cut into the hills. The salt mines themselves were extremely massive. Some of the tunnels and the chambers were cut into the solid rock with modern mining equipment. Yet, the extensive salt mines themselves looked like they were carved by hand.

The closed, upper galleries were a free-climb adventure to reach, but she managed. She forced the door open at the end of the gallery, finding an entirely new, modern-cut section inside. The galleries were connected all the way around the main cavern. A well-armed force could easily hold this section.

She found stairs that led down to a secret door in the back of the huge food pantry.

Going the other way led through to a series of large—thirty meters by fifty meters—rooms with high ceiling, connected by wide hallways. The last one looked like a giant hangar over 100 meters wide and longer still.

Rand recognized the foamcrete floor and vaulted ceiling with no pillars. At the far edge, the rock overhang hid the entrance, very well, and kept out the weather. Rand walked right up to the edge and looked down at the frozen lake forty meters below.

Any shuttle from the *Ventura* would fit in here. Even the captain's pinnace, the *Memphis,* would fit.

That made her think of Jimbo and Hume. Then, of Chen and Barcus. She even thought of that fat, old, drunken barkeep, Peck, with his missing tooth and his excellent bourbon. She sat down on the floor in the middle of the hangar deck and took off her helmet. The fog of her breath was heavy in the still room. She thought of Marton, Walther, Malinowski, Phelps, Myers, and Grazio. The sound of their laughter. She remembered running the entire loop of the flight deck's outer ring all those times with Barcus and Jimbo. How they had pushed her, making her stronger, in body and in spirit. The heavy gravity on the outer ring was home.

The helmet sat in her lap. She crossed her arms on top of it, then rested her head on those arms.

Rand, finally, let herself mourn. She sobbed for her friends, her family. Her loss. Herself.

***

The light began to fade. The opening faced almost due north, and the sun was too far off to the left to be seen. Rand rose and put her helmet back on as it powered up. When she turned to exit the way she came in, she saw a door. She almost missed it. It was in the back wall, farther down to the right, on the opposite side from where she came in.

It was a blast door. An airlock door. The control panel on the right was dark. No power. When she tried to open the panel to access the manual control, the small ring handle that flipped up broke off in her hand.

She would come back tomorrow with tools and with Poole.

On the way back, she realized that these were a series of inner hangars. The wide corridors that connected them were big enough for cargo shuttles and fighters. A lot of them. The tactical map of the complex expanded as she reviewed it. It was 4.2 kilometers from the cottage in the cavern to the lake's edge in the hangar.

Rand startled Vi as she walked out of the pantry. Vi almost dropped a tray with a water pitcher and mugs.

"Bloody anvils, Rand. You scared a year out of me," Vi said.

"Bloody anvils?" Rand asked.

"*Rand, Tannhauser is back. He is on his way down to the cottage now,*" AI~Poole said, inside her head.

"Sorry, I know I shouldn't curse. But, how did you get in there?" Vi said, as she regained her composure and placed the pitcher and mugs on the table.

"There is a hidden door in the back of the pantry. I'll show you after dinner. There are more storerooms back there, mostly empty, but one of them is full of old blocks of wax. A few tons of it, I think," Rand said, as she took off her cloak and then set the table.

"Wax? That's wonderful!" she exclaimed, and began to light every candle in the room. Eventually, it was brighter than they had ever seen it.

"What are you making? It smells wonderful," Rand said, as she heard the door open in the front of the cottage.

"Rabbit pie. It's one of Tan's favorites," Vi replied.

"I'm back," called Tannhauser, from the front of the cottage. "The snow is getting really deep out there now." He stamped his feet in front of the hearth in the front room, trying to dry off a bit.

"*Rand, someone has just entered the cavern,*" AI~Poole warned.

A window opened in Rand's HUD that showed a man, lurking in the shadows, below Poole's position, up on the shelf in the darkness.

As Tannhauser walked into the dining room, Vi walked in from the kitchen. Rand said, "Tan, you were followed back here. Someone is in the cavern, watching the cottage. Poole is watching him."

"The front door is bolted, can we eat our rabbit pies before they get cold?" Tannhauser rubbed his hands together.

"Shall I have Poole take care of him?" Tan'Vi froze. Rand had not expected that reaction.

It was Vi that spoke first, "Do you kill everyone you meet?"

Rand started to sit. "Usually. Seems to save time."

Tannhauser looked at Vi wide-eyed. Vi laughed first, set down the pies and went back to get the cheese.

***

Poole kept watching the man while the three of them ate the excellent rabbit pies. Rand loved them. They were small, meaty pies with pulled rabbit and diced bacon. They had thick gravy with onions, potatoes, mushrooms, and the perfect peppery spice.

Rand watched, as the man slowly stalked his way down the small incline in the shadows. Poole had silently come down from the shelf and was not far behind him in the blackness. When the man lowered his hood and turned, for just a moment, Rand recognized him.

It was the tracker named Coff.

"Do you know a tracker named Coff?" she asked, over spicy stewed apples.

Tannhauser replied, "I know Coff. From the northern shelter logs and in person. He's alright. Good tracker. Never really applies himself. Just wants to be free. Why?"

"I didn't kill him, either." Rand finished her apples. "It's him, out there."

"Don't scare him. He might hurt you, by accident," Vi added, knowing Rand would go out there.

"I won't hurt him." Rand didn't say she wouldn't scare him.

***

Coff worked his way toward the cottage, slowly, quietly. He'd been there several times before, and he knew that this side path, running near the right wall by the stream, was there. The path was sandy, and was clear and easy to follow by just the light from the cottage. He heard voices in there. They had so many candles lit inside, even if they did come outside, they would never see him in the shadows.

He felt confident.

Rand stepped between Coff and the cottage, so she was seen even though she was less than two meters away.

"Nice to meet you again, Coff," the sinister voice whispered from the faceless riot helmet.

Rand loved these 'Social Voice' settings. They were meant to be scary and intimidating. They worked.

"Bloody Hammer, it's you!" he cursed, and stepped back a bit.

"Relax, Coff. You have friends here that have already saved you from me." Her fingers sparked in the darkness.

"From us," she whispered.

Coff looked back, then. Was there a massive bit of movement there? A pebble dislodged, somewhere? It was too dark in the cavern to detect a greater darkness there.

When he turned back, she was gone.

A minute later, he saw a figure, dressed in black, walking into the light from the two lanterns in front of the cottage. The figure reached up and took off the black helmet, shook her hair free and looked over her shoulder directly at him, even though she should not have been able to see him in the shadows.

She entered the cottage, leaving the door wide open.

CHAPTER TWENTY

Signals

"It's the only thing I regret. I should have noticed Hamilton was missing."

--Solstice 31 Incident Investigation Testimony Transcript: Lieutenant Valerie Hume, the security chief on the Memphis.

The probe team filed into the conference room the next morning. The team had grown overnight.

Hume, Cook, Beary, Muir, Tyrrell, Ibenez, Elkin, Kuss, and Dr. Shaw sat around the conference table. Dr. Bowen, Shea, Perry, Wood, and Edwards sat in the side chairs against the wall.

Hume was at one end and Worthington was at the head of the table.

"Okay, folks. Let's hear it." Jimbo knew it was all about the plan proposal.

Bowen jumped in first. "Can we move this meeting out into the hangar? You have the gravity set way too high in here," she whined.

Worthington, and everyone else, ignored her.

Hume began. "We ran the test flights this morning. I can easily maintain the roll at the right velocity, while following the correct trajectory. We figured out how I could keep from freezing to death and/or roasting to death by adjusting my flight attitude, so I fly bottom up to the sun. The foils will shade the cockpit. If it gets too cold, I'll roll the canopy into the sun for a bit to warm me up."

Dr. Shaw spoke next. "As bad an idea as I believe this is, I think she can do it. We can keep her awake and alert for the entire flight, using this." She held up a small device that was the size of a deck of cards. "It's an injector, salvaged from the autoDoc in the shuttle. It will hold several meds, including hunger and nausea suppressors, stims and antipsychotics. She will go nuts after the first three days without sleep, if we don't give her anything. She's already off solid food, for obvious reasons I don't want to detail here, and we have already installed a two liter bladder into her pressure suit that will hold 10,000 calories of liquid nourishment. She will have to get a catheter. I have trained her as to how it's removed. We will inject her with a load of specialized nanites that may keep her from getting stiff."

"Nausea suppressors?" Jim asked.

Hume replied, "Ever fly at high speeds on grav-foils only?"

"It will feel like a roller coaster ride for five days, Jim," AI~Ben said, in his head.

Elkin continued. "The pressure suit is equipped with extra water, food, puke evacuation, and tethering. She has alarms set in her HUD to remind her to change the CO_2 scrubbers. Extra O_2 tanks are strapped in and ready."

"What do you mean by tethering?" Elkin looked at Hume to see if she would answer. She did.

"Once a day, I plan to power down for five minutes, open the canopy, exit the Hammerhead and stretch. We built this into the calculations, and Doc Shaw thinks it would be a good idea. But, only for five minutes every twenty hours, to keep the timetable," Hume said. "The tether is a safety line that will stay attached the whole flight. They are worried I will not be thinking too clearly towards the end and, if I had to tie off each time, I might forget."

Muir was next. "The sensor package is already loaded and powered up. We have a window to hit the hole on the planet's next rotation. Hume will whip around the moon in the opposite direction from the sensor station, to gain maximum velocity, using the moon's gravity. She will be in a communications blackout for about thirty hours, until she gains line of sight for the laser comms. She will be able to securely communicate with us, daily, from the surface while the moon is in her sky. She will be able to transmit the probe telemetry as soon as she is on the ground."

Hume added, "We will have some space in the foot well, just forward of the sensor case, where I can add my survival pack and some other food and gear."

Worthington thought for a minute. "Let's say you get through the hole and down to the surface. Where will you go?"

"I can add some new information here, sir," Muir added. "We have had the new dish online for twenty-four hours now and have already found some very interesting information."

"Why wasn't I informed of this?" Bowen demanded.

"If we have a question for you, Bowen, we'll say your name or something," Muir snapped, then continued. "The new dish has detected two Emergency Modules that are active on the surface. Ben confirmed that the high-entropy, encrypted traffic we have detected is between an Emergency Module and a personal HUD. If any other type of AI were looking at the data, we all would have missed it."

"Two EMs? Other survivors?" Worthington asked.

"Yes, sir." A tactical map of the planet opened on the conference room wall, showing the location of the two points. "This point, here, is near some type of war zone." It zoomed in further. "There is a town in flames, here. Smoke plumes are visible. Heavy ground vegetation is obscuring the events, there." The view zoomed out, and then in, on the other point. "This point of origin is intermittent, but is in a very isolated area near the southern tip of this large lake. There are no population centers, there. We think Hume should begin there."

"Is there any way to contact them, directly?" Jim asked, knowing the answer already.

"Not without giving away our position, which is much more important now. We have also discovered that the weapons platforms have as many missiles pointed in, toward the planet, as out, into space," Muir concluded. "No broadcast communications. Even tight beam, point-to-point laser communications may be a risk. That is why we're going to transmit the sensor readings back first."

"I will find the survivors and locate a suitable landing site for the *Memphis*, before it is ready to fly," Hume said, with complete confidence.

"When do you leave?" Worthington asked, as if it was just a snack run.

"Tomorrow at 0800 hours," Hume answered.

***

Hume departed, on schedule, and was out of comms range in less than two hours.

Jim was haunted by her silent departure. Just before she climbed into the Hammerhead, Hume paused and looked up at the camera she knew was there, the camera she knew Jim would be watching.

She gave a formal salute and held it for a long moment, before she closed her visor and climbed in.

That was thirty-four hours and twelve minutes ago.

"There she is," Muir called out, from the tactical station. "Point-to-point channel open, Captain."

Jim hesitated before speaking, "Hey, Hume. What's new?"

"Jimbo, can you do me a favor?" she asked.

"Name it."

"Remind me to kick Shaw's ass when I get back."

Jim smiled. "Roger that."

"Oh, and remind me to take a nice relaxing vacation. Something medieval, like maybe a couple of weeks on the rack or a round of waterboarding," Hume said.

"You're right on track. The perfect flight path. Really damn good, for full manual."

"Tell Shaw I said, 'Fuck you.' Okay, Jimbo? Feels like the goddamn nanites are eating me alive. I'm so awake, so alert, I can't ignore them. And, whatever else she gave me isn't suppressing the pain, I just don't give a shit."

"That is only part of the plan," Jimbo joked.

"Did I tell you I loaded up the collection of First Century Films into my HUD? You know those classic films Barcus loved so much, but I never watched. Movie nights in the back of Peck's Halfway. The 1G pub," she said.

"Are you okay, Hume? Seriously?" Worthington asked.

"I just finished one called *It's a Wonderful Life*. Ever see it, Jimbo? The faces of those people. The way they lived. Happiness and despair."

"Hume?" Jim asked. He muted the transmission and called out, "Ben! Get Dr. Shaw on the link. NOW!"

"I have watched thirteen films, so far. Have you ever seen a real horror film, Jimbo? I watched one called *Night of the Living Dead*. I'm glad I have a catheter because I would have pissed myself, otherwise," Hume said.

"I thought you were fearless, Hume," Jim said, trying to engage her.

"So did I! No more horror for me. I can't believe people just think that shit up."

"Keep her talking. I'm monitoring her vitals," Shaw said, on a side channel.

"What will you watch next, Hume?" Jim asked.

"One called *The Maltese Falcon*. I flew a Falcon-class deep space fighter craft once. Best inertia dampeners, ever. Want to watch it with me?" Hume asked.

"I'd like that, Hume. As long as I don't distract you," Jim said, and then muted the connection. "She sounds drunk, Shaw. Is this what you expected?" he demanded.

A window opened in his personal HUD. An image of a lion roared.

"She is amazing, Captain. She is doing great. Don't worry. You won't distract her. I will keep monitoring. Just be with her," Shaw said. She sounded optimistic.

***

They took turns. Hume never noticed the shift changes. She stopped noticing that the people speaking to her changed every four films or so.

Her HUD fed Hume navigation data that she never deviated from. Jim began to relax after the second scheduled 'stretch' where Hume left the cockpit and moved in free fall, to keep her limbs alive.

Jim started to worry, again, during the 111th hour.

Hume became quiet.

"Hume, we have time for a couple more films before the entry point. What's up next?" Jim asked. Jim and Cook were on the bridge of the *Memphis* now. The full tactical display was up on the main screen, showing the remaining flight path.

"Hume?" Jim repeated.

"Where's Sharon? I miss Sharon," Hume said.

"What?" Jim asked, looking at Cook.

"Is Sharon Hamilton mad at me? You know, because I was following her?" she asked.

Something occurred to Worthington, just then. He muted Hume. "Ben, locate Sharon Hamilton."

"Sharon Hamilton is currently off-line," AI~Ben replied.

"When was the last time anyone saw Hamilton?" Jim received no response from the people on the bridge. "Cook, find her. NOW."

Cook rose and left the bridge.

Jim spoke to Hume, "Hume, why were you following Sharon?"

"The weapons locker. I thought it might be her." She seemed sleepy.

"Dr. Shaw. Status," Jim demanded.

"Her heart rate is elevated. The nanites are really putting it to her. She has a fever that is higher than I'd like. She is also saving the last of the liquid nourishment for just before the insertion."

"Sir, the sensor package is indicating the cockpit is running hot. She needs to roll away from the sun."

"Hume, listen to me. You need to turn away from the sun, to cool off the cabin," Jim said.

She didn't reply.

There was a delay now, of a few seconds, due to the distance.

"It's beautiful you know...Tell Dr. Shaw I'm not feeling so good right now," she said, slurring her words.

"Jim, she's drifting off course," Muir said.

On the tactical, the perfect green line separated into a blue and a red line, they were no longer synchronized.

"Hume, you are off course. Look at your display," Jim said.

"So sorry...please...no..." Hume was choking, then they heard her vomit inside her helmet.

Dr. Shaw got on the comm. "Hume, use the evacuator for the vomit. Don't breathe it in!" Dr. Shaw frantically pressed controls. They heard more choking and coughing.

"Help. Me. God...No..." There was more vomiting.

Dr. Shaw typed, furiously.

"Dr. Shaw," Jim said, calmly. "Talk as you work."

"I activated the helmet suction, remotely, but there is a lag. If she breathes it in, there is no way to help her. I have applied the emergency meds we prepped. It's up to her, now."

There was more coughing, and then, silence. The seconds dragged.

"Hume, talk to me, please," Jimbo said.

There was a long pause.

"Just when I thought this hell couldn't get any worse, he fucking says 'Please'," Hume said, between spitting sounds. "I'm here, Jimbo. Tell Shaw I think I just started my period, to top off everything else."

"Thank you, Hume," Jim said.

"Just fucking great. Please and thank you? I must be in serious, goddamn trouble. The rest of this flight is really going to suck now," Hume said, sounding more alert than she had in days.

"She has brought it back on track, Jim," Muir said.

"Jimbo, when was the last time anyone saw Hamilton?" Hume asked.

CHAPTER TWENTY-ONE

Coff

"In the cave time had stopped. Days and weeks and months went by and I hand stopped counting. I wasn't running from anything or toward anything. I was lost. Then Coff arrived."

--*Solstice 31 Incident Investigation Testimony Transcript: Master Chief Nancy Randall, senior surviving security member of the Ventura's crew.*

Coff slowly approached the cottage. There must have been 100 candles lit in there.

"Coff, come in," Tannhauser said, from one of the chairs in front of the fire. "Warm yourself."

"Have you eaten? We have some rabbit pie left," Vi said, from the kitchen.

"Tan? Vi? What is going on here? We need to get out of here. Now." He pointed out the still open door. "I will explain, later. Come."

"Coff, it's alright, they won't hurt you, if you just sit and let us explain," Tannhauser said, from the armchair as Coff came another step deeper into the room.

The door clicked closed behind him.

"I insist," Rand said, from the now-closed door that she had been standing behind.

Coff stumbled backward, away from her, and deeper into the large room. He drew his knife and pointed it toward Rand, more as a talisman than a weapon.

Everyone ignored his near panic.

"Tan, you don't understand. She's a witch. She can…There's a thing out there…" At that point, he slipped entirely into Common Tongue. Rand understood perhaps one word in ten. Coff was not telling them anything they did not already know.

Eventually, Vi came up to him, took him by the elbow and led him to the chair at the far end of the large dining table.

She forced him into the chair like a child, then said, "Yes, yes, we know that and much more. There is no need to fear. Have some food first and settle in a bit."

She went to the kitchen as he sat there, knife still in hand. But, what made him relax was the fact that Rand casually sat down in the chair opposite Tannhauser and took off her boots.

He watched as first one, then the other, and even her socks, came off. She reclined back, flexing her toes toward the fire. Rand would learn, later, that removing your boots in front of someone was a gesture of deep trust, in their culture.

Tannhauser went back to the leather he was working into something, as Vi set a tray in front of Coff with bread, cheese, a rabbit pie and a steaming hot mug of soup.

A moment later, she returned with a large mug of ale.

Coff took the ale first. After two long pulls, he looked up at Vi.

She glanced at the large hunting knife he still held and raised an eyebrow at it.

Coff looked at it and was almost startled it was there in his hand.

He took another drink.

Vi spoke softly, gently, even though her words were weighty, serious. "Rand is our friend. She has proven that, time and again. If she had wanted to kill you, you would not have seen it coming. She told us about meeting you. About what happened."

"I apologize for the pain I caused you, Coff," Rand said. "I trust there were no lasting, ill effects."

Coff didn't reply. She knew she had not permanently damaged him.

Vi continued, while still standing at his elbow, "Mercenaries followed us from above the gorge. They captured us and tortured us."

Coff looked at Vi then, to judge her words. He saw the scar on her face that had not been there the last time they met. He had seen the High Keeper's soldiers torture people this way.

"She saved us."

"Tan, I never knew you to dance around an anvil, so casually," Coff said, as Rand rested her head back and closed her eyes.

"We owe Rand our lives. Who do you owe?" Tannhauser said.

Rand's eyes were closed, but she watched Coff, carefully, via the Fly drone. Tannhauser's last comment struck Coff like a slap.

He said nothing and sipped his soup before it got cold.

***

"This would be simpler, if he were to just allow Keeper Kochan to land his shuttle on the Citadel's roof landing pad," Mason complained, knowing he would be saddle sore tomorrow.

High Tracker Tolwood laughed. "Go ahead. Tell him that."

Mason blanched at the thought, as they passed through the Citadel gate to the mountainside road. It was steep and had little protection from the edge, as they descended a gentle road that had many switchbacks.

Before the first turn, he twisted in his saddle, to look back. He could see his personal balcony from there.

Ty stood on the balcony railing, where it met the farthest wall, just as he told her. He saw her. He saw that she was naked, for him. A good girl. He would reward her.

As they neared the bottom, the road widened, but stayed beside the sheer wall that climbed up to the Citadel. Side streets intersected the highway there. At one of these side roads, a team of horses and a heavy cart stood, waiting for them.

They rode by it without pausing, and the team fell in behind them.

It took the better part of an hour to reach Keeper Kochan's estate. It was sprawling and opulent. Grooms, on ponies, met them as they passed through the main gates, and led them to the landing pad.

The black, stone statue that fell from the sky lay in the center of the large, flagstone pad. Tolwood leaned over to Mason and spoke in low tones. "They ended up destroying three wagons getting it here, so far. The last one, while it was en route. To off-load the statue, they had to secure it to that tie-down block and fly the shuttle out from under it."

As they dismounted, they saw the men had erected a tripod of long, thick beams and had attached a large block and tackle.

The workmen paused, briefly, to bow as they worked. Tolwood knew they planned to raise the statue and then back the wagon up, to lower it on. The process would be reversed at the Citadel.

The manor staff waited. "Please follow me, my Lords. I will show you where you can wait and refresh yourselves."

They entered a large house next to the landing paddock. It was impressive, for a guesthouse.

They were left in a parlor, filled with sofas and chairs and six fireplaces. Mason made a line straight for the side tables that were heavy with foods of all kinds.

Servants were scattered all over the room, as perfectly placed as the furniture. As Tolwood snagged a strip of bacon and bit it, his eye was drawn to a flash of red hair.

He walked over to the girl. Her head was properly bowed to the floor, presenting the nape of her neck.

"What is your name?" Tolwood asked, quietly.

"Fa, my Lord." Her voice trembled as she recognized his High Tracker tabard.

Tolwood popped the button at the nape of her neck and her dress fell into a pool at her bare feet. Her skin was pale, her shoulders and her breasts were freckled.

Without a word, he took her by the braid and walked to one of the side rooms. "Don't bother me, until I'm finished," Tolwood said to Mason, who had just completed filling his heaping plate.

"Mmm-mm," was all Mason managed, since he carried a pastry in his mouth.

Tolwood and the girl disappeared.

CHAPTER TWENTY-TWO

Hammerhead Probe

"Look, I don't know what you're trying to do, but if you are attempting to prove that we were insane, that Hammerhead run is all the proof you need from me."

--Solstice 31 Incident Investigation Testimony Transcript: Lieutenant Valerie Hume, the security chief on the Memphis.

Hume had been decelerating for the last ten hours. By the time she neared the hole, her speed would be less than 100 kph.

"Hume, you are now on the correct vector, heading, and speed for the run. You need to begin the roll and then shut the grav-foils completely down," Muir said.

"I know. I know. How many times do we have to go over that? Jesus, this is going to suck." She belched. "Doc can you hook me up with more nausea suppressors, love? I'm dead, if I start puking again at high rpm. Plus, there will be no comms link once I start the run, until I'm down on the surface, in a few hours. I will need to pull up and grav down, slowly."

"Use the turbines as soon as you can. They will help slow your descent. The descent max is 300 kph. Though, 100 kph will still get you down, on a cold descent, in less than an hour," Jimbo reminded her.

Hume took a deep breath.

"Whatever that was you just gave me, doc, bless you," Hume said.

"You now have all the updated surface maps we could render. You also have the last known coordinates of the EMs on the surface," Cook stated.

"You should be on the surface in less than three hours. We don't lose line of sight there for eight hours."

Everyone went quiet for a minute.

"I love you guys," Hume said. "Beginning the roll." They lost contact before anyone could tell her anything.

***

Hume had programmed her HUD to give her a normalized, tactical view of her progress. Once she got the roll going and the grav-foils shut down, she hugged herself and closed her eyes. In her vision, there was no spin, and no spattered, bloody vomit smeared on the inside of her visor. There was just a small, spinning icon, on the inside of an array of small sats.

The passive sensors in the package filled her HUD with extremely high-definition imagery, as she passed through the hole. She watched the progress drop from -10km, to -5km, to -1km, and then to zero. It flipped to 1km, 5km, 10km, and at 20km, she reached for the controls and slowly stopped the spin.

She opened her eyes. She was alive. She raised the puke-covered, polarized, inner visor to a much clearer outer visor.

The grav-foils initiated and the acceleration stopped. Her descent rate slowed and stabilized at 100 kph at about 50km from the surface.

She fired up the turbines, and the engines easily took hold of the craft. Hume had forgotten how high the performance was in a Hammerhead, in the atmosphere where it was designed to fly. As the planet's natural gravity equalized with the foils, another wave of nausea hit her. She dropped the inner visor and activated the suction in the evacuator.

She puked, again. Hard.

She could not believe there was anything left to regurgitate. When she opened her eyes, she saw it was mostly blood.

"Great. I blew a gasket," she said, to herself, as she raised the inner visor again and turned toward the transmission coordinates. She passed across the day-night line as she continued.

The spots in her vision got bigger, more distracting. She had to hurry.

***

At the same time, Coff was finishing his meal, when they all heard it.

AI~Poole reported, in Rand's head, "*Something is coming in the main entrance. Something loud.*"

Rand was on her feet, cursing herself for taking off her boots and pressing on her helmet. Behind the door, she tossed aside a cloak that covered her rifle.

"Stay here," was all she said, as she headed out the door.

Running up the path, she felt the backwash of the hovering turbines, the sound made worse by the echoes within the cavern.

A tiny ship set down and Rand activated her targeting package. A window in her HUD showed what the scope on the rifle saw. It zoomed in, close.

She watched the canopy slide forward and then up. The pilot stiffly climbed out of the tiny cockpit and stood next to the forward turbine.

The pilot reached up and unlocked the two latches on the helmet interface, turned the helmet a quarter turn and lifted it off. The helmet dropped and rolled away.

The pilot's face was covered in blood. It was a dark-skinned woman.

She collapsed to her knees, vomited black liquid, fell forward onto her chest and completely stilled.

***

"That's it, Jim," Muir said, as he turned from the tactical station and stood up. "Our line of sight is gone for this orbit."

"What happened?" Jim asked.

Muir answered, "All we know is that she made it through. The new dish tracked the mass gravity differentials as she went in. We know she moderated and had a controlled descent, all the way to the designated coordinates. That was five and a half hours ago." Muir projected the planetary line of sight options. "We have to wait now. She has to connect with us."

Cook stood next to the command chair with his arms crossed. "Look, Captain. I know you're worried about Hume, but Hamilton is missing. We have searched the entire base and she is just gone."

AI~Ben added, "The last time she was online was the day before the probe was built."

"She has been missing for a week and we're only noticing now?" Jimbo stated the obvious. "Search again. Use the scanners. Use the drones. Check inside closed areas. Even the lower areas we have not accessed. Maybe she did."

"Ben, secure the bridge and all essential areas of the *Memphis*. We're going out to look. Shaw, you stay here and monitor for Hume." Everyone else, followed Jim off the bridge. "Inform everyone of the search, and tell them their assigned areas. We only have about twelve hours before we can contact Hume."

***

Four hours later, they found a large stash of emergency rations, empty food wrappers and three of the missing weapons.

Cook shook his head and said, "Whiskey, Tango, Foxtrot. Over."

They stood on top of a 140,000 liter, foamcrete water tank. This was one of the tanks that served the base. It was accessed by a long ladder that led up into the dark. Cook looked at Jimbo and then at Kuss, the only ones there; he opened the tank's inspection hatch at their feet, and shined a light inside.

Hamilton's body floated in the water, ten meters below.

***

Hume's eyes fluttered open.

She was in a warm, candlelit room. She heard a fire crackling in a hearth. *Where the hell am I?*

She waited for her mind to reboot. Her thirst was the first system online. "Water," she whispered.

Someone rose from a nearby chair and said, "She said you would be thirsty when you awoke. Here you are, dear." Hume saw a lean, young woman come into her field of view, with a mug for her to drink from. "Not too much, all at once."

After sipping a few times, she asked, "Where am I?"

"You are in Salterkirk. How you managed it, I will never know. Poole thought you should have died," the woman said.

"I will get Rand. She will want to know you're awake."

"Rand?" She struggled to speak. Hume was still waking up. "Here? ALIVE?"

She threw back the covers and tried to jump out of bed, but only managed to throw herself onto the floor. She wore some kind of homespun tunic. With a Herculean effort, she pushed herself up from the floor, on her hands and knees.

"I need to contact the *Memphis*." She teetered, tried to stand and failed. "Where is Rand?" She was frantic.

"Alright." Vi helped Hume to her feet. "This way." She directed Hume's drunken momentum to the doorway and down a hall. "How long have I been out?" Hume demanded.

"Almost a day," she replied, as the hall opened into a great room. "Rand!" Vi called out.

The front door flew open, and Rand came directly to Hume and gathered her into a hug. Hume collapsed, her knees buckled. Still holding her, Rand swept her up, took her to one of the overstuffed chairs and settled her in.

"Vi, bring water, please," Rand said.

"You're alive," Hume choked out.

"Yes. I almost couldn't say that for you." Rand smiled.

Vi returned with the water. Hume drank.

"Rand, listen. There are others. I need to send them data in that sensor package. Now. How long have I been out? Is the moon visible?"

"Slow down. Drink." Hume sipped and collected herself.

"Sixteen of us survived on the captain's pinnace. They need the data on that sensor array to fly down here without being shot out of the sky."

Hume had not noticed the other two men behind Rand, until one of them spoke. "The moon set about two hours ago," Tannhauser said.

"What's wrong with her skin?" the other said.

"I have tight beam laser comms on the Hammerhead. They need that data." Hume was frantic. "It maps the hole in the defense grid around the planet. If they don't hear from me, they will come through anyway, without it."

"Okay. Okay. Drink." Hume did. "We will get you on your feet by the time the moon is back up. I promise. Now, tell me. Who else survived? Until yesterday, I thought I was the only one."

Vi handed Hume a large mug of soup with a spoon in it. Hume realized she was starving.

"Jimbo's command crew and ten others. But, they are almost out of food. We need to get them the data, or they will die."

Rand couldn't speak.

CHAPTER TWENTY-THREE

Hume

"Hume's courage saved us. Her raw guts."
--*Solstice 31 Incident Investigation Testimony Transcript: Captain James Worthington, senior surviving member of the Ventura's command crew.*

<<<>>>

"Jimbo, you need to get some rest. You haven't slept since she crossed the defense grid," Dr. Shaw said to Jimbo.

"We won't emerge for another pass for another six hours, Jim," Muir added. "We'll call you when we're about to get another view."

Jimbo left the bridge, and headed for his bunk, when AI~Ben spoke to him, in his head, "*Captain, there is movement in the target area you wanted me to watch.*"

A window opened in Jim's personal HUD that showed a view of the stash of rations. Bowen stepped up off the ladder, went directly to the food and began to devour two entire days' worth of rations.

"Ben, call Cook and Kuss, and have them meet me in the conference room."

Three minutes later, they arrived there and Jim told them the plan. Two minutes after that, Bowen left the top of the tank.

"Ben, contact Bowen. Have her report directly to the conference room."

She arrived in fifteen minutes, a walk that should have taken five minutes. She entered into what seemed like an argument between Kuss and Cook about the way to scan using a point-to-point laser comms device.

Bowen had her usual face on. The you-are-all-fools face.

Everyone had a glass of water in front of them as they continued to argue. Jimbo drank deeply from his, and in a polite gesture, poured a glass and slid it over to Bowen.

She shrank from the glass, trying to be inconspicuous about it.

Cook said, "I think you were right, Captain."

The argument stopped.

Bowen looked at Worthington, and said, in a condescending tone, "Right about what?"

Worthington leaned forward, and said, "You."

Kuss shot her.

Two needles stuck into her sternum and filled her nervous system with electricity, and pain. She convulsed in the chair for a few seconds and then passed out.

Kuss searched her and found one of the weapons, concealed on her.

"I guess I won't have to apologize to her, after all. Take her to the secondary airlock. Bind her hands behind her back. I need some sleep," he said, as he got up and walked out. "I'll deal with her, later."

***

"Sir, we're going to be coming clear in about twenty minutes," Muir said, over the comms to Worthington.

"Acknowledged," was all he said.

Jim sat up. He was still in his clothes. He had not even bothered to take off his boots. He swung his feet onto the floor, trying not to think, just yet.

The door chimed.

"Come," he said.

The door slid open, and Jim was surprised to see Dr. Shaw there, holding a protein bar and a mug of steaming tea.

"I'm not letting you out of here, until you eat this bar and drink this tea," she said.

"Ben, how many minutes until we emerge?" Jim asked.

"*Emergency medical override. Please see Dr. Shaw for any additional information,*" AI~Ben said.

"Are you serious?" Jim asked, looking up at her.

"What do you think?" she replied, handing him the steaming mug.

He took a sip. It was extra strong.

She opened the energy bar. The smell of peanut butter and oatmeal filled the cabin. He realized he was ravenous. He took it and ate it. It only took him three minutes to finish it.

"Ben, status?"

"It's okay, Ben. Thanks for your help," Dr. Shaw said.

"We will clear the planet in sixteen minutes. Dr. Bowen is awake and demanding to speak to you," AI~Ben replied.

"Ben, tell her I said this: I know you killed Sharon. I'm running out of reasons not to introduce you to this moon's surface. I'm heading to the bridge." Then, he added, "Thanks, Beth."

"If you hold a lottery for who gets to space that bitch, I'm in."

"Get in line." He smiled.

They left the cabin as he sipped his tea.

***

Jim decided to make Bowen cool her heels. After visiting the head, he went to the bridge. Cook, Muir, Kuss, Ibenez, and Elkin were there, looking over Muir's shoulder, at the tactical station.

"Updates?" was all he said, as he sat in the command chair.

"We have been analyzing the new data from the dish and it's not good," Muir said, as they quieted.

"This defense grid is like nothing we have ever seen. We can't figure out how the grid stays in fixed positions. The weapons platforms are standard geosynchronous satellites. There is an odd field around the defense grid orbitals that seem to push against each other and the planet."

Just then, the screen lit up.

"*Memphis*, this is Hume. Come in." It was her.

"Hume, you sure took your sweet time. Are you secure?" Jim asked.

"I'm alright. I'll explain, later. Data upload commencing, now," Hume said.

Data flowed via the laser link. There was a lot of it. It was going to take a while.

"Jimbo, you won't believe it," Hume said.

"I knew, if anyone could pull off that stupid stunt, it was you, Hume," he said.

"Sir, I found Rand. She saved me."

The bridge froze, for a moment.

"Where is she?" he asked, dumbfounded.

"I'm right here," Rand replied. "Talk about taking your time. Damn, Jimbo!"

"Rand! Is anyone with you?" Jimbo asked.

"No. It's just me. I happened to be inside one of the shuttles when the flight deck on the *Ventura* broke up. I crashed hard, but got away with an EM that is damaged but functional," Rand said.

"Jim, Hume told me you plan to come down here. We have a good place to hide the *Memphis*, if you can make it. The coordinates are coming up with the data."

"Better and better." Jim smiled.

"There is something wrong here, Jim. It is an odd mix of old tech and no tech. I have seen old shuttles, old plate-style data pads, and even a few plasma rifles. But, most of the population lives a preindustrial, almost medieval, lifestyle."

Rand spent time telling Jimbo what had happened since she arrived. She told him about Salterkirk and a hangar base she had found there. She spoke about Vi and Tannhauser and what she had learned about the culture and the people.

Hume detailed what happened after she penetrated the defense grid. The nanites managed to stay ahead of the damage she did to her body.

"I don't know if I will ever be able to get that pressure suit completely clean. Right now, the Hammerhead is parked on a landing pad on the north side of the Salterkirk hangar. Has the data transmission completed? If not, we may need to move it to another location with a better line of sight," Hume stated.

Muir spoke up. "It completed a few minutes ago. I have been reviewing the telemetry." Muir paused, before continuing. "We are very lucky to have packed all those sensors in, Hume. If you had gone through with hot grav-foils, with your external temp up, or any faster than you did, you'd be dead." He shifted to another set of controls. "Ben, can you model this data and propose a potential, cold, glide path for the *Memphis*? All systems shut down. Ten meters per second."

A simulation came up on the main screen, showing the size of the sensor gap and the size of the *Memphis*. It will be a very tight fit. Possible, but very difficult.

"We will need to study this, in greater detail," Jimbo said.

"Don't take too long," said Beth Shaw. "We only have about a month's worth of short rations left."

"That reminds me." Worthington looked at Cook. "We found Hamilton. She's dead. Bowen killed her. I don't know why, yet."

"What? That bitch," Hume said. "I should have blown her out the airlock when I had the chance."

"She is currently cooling her heels in the secondary hangar's airlock," Jimbo said.

"Sir, before we lose contact, I need to tell you something else," Rand said. "One of the people we are with is named Coff. He's a tracker. He works for a Keeper named Ronan. He believes we may be able to work with this Keeper."

Hume added, "With your permission, sir, I'd like to fly Coff back to the East Isles, where this Keeper lives. I might be able to persuade him to help us."

"A Keeper?" Jimbo looked around at shrugging shoulders. "I will leave it to you, to assess and to act. Don't take too long. Even after we get to the ground, we're going to require material support of some kind. We also have another Emergency Module to locate," Jimbo said. "But, that one seems to be in an area where there is fighting of some kind. We will need to go, carefully."

"Sir, we're going to lose them in eight minutes, with our current position," Tyrrell said, from the comms station.

"Hume. We can't thank you enough for pulling this off. I believe you have saved our lives. If we had just flown through blind, we'd all be dead."

"Be careful, sir. We're not home, yet," Hume replied.

"I'm glad you're not dead, Rand," Worthington also said. "Let's keep it that way."

"Doing my best, Captain." Rand emphasized the word captain.

"Report back in, at moonrise tomorrow." Jimbo closed the connection. "Hume out."

***

Rand waited for Hume to bring the Hammerhead into the main hangar. She flew it near the back, to let it settle down in the shadows.

It happened to settle right in front of the door that Rand had found but was unable to open.

As Hume got out of the Hammerhead, the dust she kicked up swirled about and showed that a positive pressure draft blew out of the seam along the door's edge.

She looked at the door and at Rand, before she said, "What's in there?"

Rand shrugged. "I never got the chance to open it."

Hume pulled a large multi-tool out of the pocket of her flight suit and had the control panel opened, quickly. "No power. Old-school. Hang on."

Hume examined the inside of the panel with the multi-tool's light and reached up inside to use the tool above, out of sight. After a moment, another panel, directly above that one opened, revealing a single metal lever. She reached up, and with a lot of effort, the lever slowly tilted out until it was 90° from its original position. She worked the lever back and forth, and the door slowly jacked open with each pull.

"It's a manual open," Hume said, as she struggled with it.

"Here, let me."

Rand took a turn and it opened further. Soon, it was opened far enough for Hume to squeeze through.

They shined the light in first and looked around.

There were some work benches and high stools visible. The ceiling was probably the same height as the hangar itself as the light didn't seem to reach that far.

They worked the lever some more, before entering.

Both drew their sidearms and activated the tactical lights.

They found themselves in a large shop. There were big machines that looked like drill presses and milling machines. They were corroded and looked inoperable. There was no power.

There were all kinds of hand tools, neatly stored about. They explored for the next hour. They found many useful items that could help with repairs to the *Memphis*.

"What we really need is a fabricator," Hume said to Rand, as they started down a corridor that went deeper into the mountain.

Their lights fell on a wide, double door marked, 'Reactor Room'.

They easily pushed open the doors.

CHAPTER TWENTY-FOUR

The East Isles

"Ronan was the smartest man on that godforsaken planet."

--*Solstice 31 Incident Investigation Testimony Transcript: Lieutenant Valerie Hume, the security chief on the Memphis.*

Coff walked around the Hammerhead, working up enough courage to touch it. When he finally did, he realized he had never felt anything so smooth, except glass. The black and red machine was sleek and smaller than any shuttle he had ever seen. He could almost see through the tinted windshield of the canopy. The inside was small. One seat behind the other. The entire thing would fit in an ox cart.

"Ever fly in a shuttle before, Coff?" Hume's voice startled him.

"Bloody anvil!" He cursed and fell against the Hammerheads body. "I hate it in here. Always dark."

"It helps us to hide from the sky, from the Keepers. They watch from the sky. But, you already knew that," Hume said, looking to the hangar's opening. There were stars visible above the water. The air was calm.

"Coff, why do they call them Keepers?" Hume asked.

The question left Coff uncertain. "Um...They are Keepers of the faith, of the magic. Why is your skin like that?" Hume had very dark skin, like her mother. But, her facial features resembled her Asian father. Her eyes were so brown they looked black and her close-cropped hair was jet-black, straight and spiked, in an unkempt way.

"I was born this way." Hume tilted her head. "Have you never seen a Black person before?"

Coff felt self-conscious looking at her now. "No." Then, words tumbled out. "Sometimes, they talked about black trackers and black Keepers, but I didn't think it was literal. Or real."

"Really?" She was curious. "Tell me." She slowly stalked closer to Coff. He, apparently, felt intimidated by Hume, and by Rand.

"They say they appeared in impossible places. Usually all in black." He gestured at her black flight suit and body armor. "They were hooded and had horrible magic. Death magic. Quiet magic. Loud magic. Dark magic."

Hume still slowly moved toward him. He backed away, down the side of the Hammerhead to the tail end, as he continued. "People saw them sometimes, and lived. They say if a black tracker asked you a question, the only chance to survive was to answer, quickly."

"Can we trust this Keeper Ronan?" Hume asked. The shadows consumed her as she rounded the tail of the Hammerhead.

Coff clung to the small amount of light that was given off by the systems in the cockpit of the small shuttle. "Ronan is a powerful Keeper. Maybe the most powerful Keeper, next to the Lord High Keeper." Hume didn't reemerge from the shadows. "I trust him."

"Why?" Hume said, directly behind Coff.

He tried not to flinch. Tried. "I measure a man by how he treats his slaves."

"And how is that?" she asked.

"He has no slaves. People serve him, but out of loyalty. And women..." He stuttered, "He is not a typical Keeper."

Hume stepped into the light, stretching again, the articulation of her armor made no sound as it glided over her torso. Hume caught him staring, again. "What do you mean? Not typical?"

"Women. He takes wives. Not just bed wenches. And, only one at a time. If they want to leave him, he lets them. At least, that's what they say. He has been with the same woman for as long as I can remember." Hume noticed he seemed uncomfortable telling her this.

"What's not typical about that?" She stopped advancing. It was evident Coff didn't want to back out of the light.

"He...He is the Keeper. He sits on the council. He lets women... Encourages..." Coff stammered.

"Hello, Coff." Rand just stood there, at the edge of the light. He didn't see her until she took off her helmet.

He managed not to jump, this time.

"Hume, we have eleven minutes before the moon sets," Rand said.

She nodded, ignoring Coff. Rand and Hume climbed into the Hammerhead. It lifted off silently and drifted to the hangar bay's opening.

Coff was left in full darkness. Less afraid, now that he was alone.

***

They landed the Hammerhead on the top of the rocky hill. The sky was clear and the stars bright as the laser antenna tuned in. Their hail was acknowledged, immediately, by Cook.

Worthington spoke first. "It's not good. We've gone over the data six times and the *Memphis* will not fit. We're now looking at modifying one of the lifeboats to get us down to the planet. We'd lose the *Memphis,* but if we can, at least, find a way to do some fine navigation through that hole, we'll have a chance to survive."

"Jim, you look like shit," Rand said, bluntly. "You're not doing us any good, if you're fried."

"I know. I just needed to tell you a few things before I headed in for rack time." Jimbo scrubbed his face. "There's definitely another Emergency Module active down there north and east of you. We are transmitting coordinates." Someone spoke to Worthington, from out of their line of sight.

"Yes," he said to someone, and then he spoke to Hume, again. "Do not contact them directly. Do not break radio silence. The scans also discovered that half of the launch tubes on these nuclear weapons platforms are facing the planet. There's evidence, on the surface, that they have been used on the planet, in the past. But not for decades, or even a century."

"Oh shit," Hume said.

"It just keeps getting better and better," Rand added.

"We were hoping to use the reactors on the *Memphis* to power up this place like we did on the moon base. Could you pull one of them and bring it?"

"I'll ask Elkin, but I don't think so. The lifeboat is not that big," Jim said.

"I'm going to take Coff back to East Isles, tonight. The details are in the report. I am cautiously optimistic," Hume said.

"You just like flying that Hammerhead around like a teenager," Jimbo kidded.

"It is fun. I just wish the Hammerhead was armed and armored," Hume said. "I will leave the sensor package here, for now."

"We're going to install the sensor package in Poole's trunk and see if we can do some recon locally," Rand added.

"One minute, sir," Cook interrupted.

Worthington had the last word. "Stay safe. Do not take any unwarranted chances. We have about four weeks before we get desperate. Check in, at moonrise, for status. Worthington out."

"Get some sleep, dumb-ass," Rand tossed in, before the link closed.

They heard Cook laughing, and then the link was lost.

***

The Hammerhead was loaded with Coff's gear and Hume was prepped. She traveled light. She wore her tactical flight suit, her body armor, her helmet, and a winter cloak that Rand provided. She only carried her combat carbine.

"I will check in with the *Memphis*, first thing, and then go see this Ronan," Hume said.

Rand, Vi, and Tannhauser assembled after that and ate a quick meal, to see them off.

"Try not to kill them all, like last time," Rand said to Hume, joking.

The humor was entirely missed by the others, based on the looks on their faces.

"I'll try, but no promises," Hume said, as Rand lightly pounded her fist on Hume's shoulder.

"Climb in, Coff."

He did, as the color faded from his face. Rand reached in and buckled his five-point harness and then handed him his pack.

Coff hugged it to his chest.

Hume climbed in, with practiced ease, and strapped in.

"I'll be back by this time, in three days. Or sooner," Hume said, as she put on her helmet. Her personal HUD came on with the Hammerhead dashboard as the canopy closed.

The silence felt oppressive to Coff when the canopy sealed. He felt the hum of the turbines starting to spin; but then, he felt a shift. The shuttle started to rise. Coff suddenly felt like he was upside down.

"We're going to fly out of the cavern and then up, on grav-foils, Coff. What this means is, if you puke in here, I'm going to kick your weak-ass."

"It's fine," he said, shakily, as they flew toward the hangar bay's opening, and then rose. He swore it felt like he was falling upward.

The world rapidly fell away around him as they ascended. The turbines spun and drove them forward, and the falling feeling subsided.

Coff decided it was better to close his eyes. Hume watched him on a back-facing camera on her headrest.

"Coff, what do you think of all of this?" Hume asked.

"It is magic and beyond my understanding," he replied. His eyes shut, as Hume reached near supersonic speed.

Hume backed off the throttle and leveled off at 2,000 meters.

"That's not what I mean. Why are you doing any of this?" she reworded.

"To serve my Keeper. You may be a powerful ally." He paused. "If you don't kill us all."

Hume saw he was smiling, even though his eyes were still tightly shut.

"Let's talk about food. Does this Keeper ever serve bacon or steaks?"

***

They were out, over open water, in less than an hour, and approaching a large series of islands, in just over two hours. It was still mostly dark, but the lights to the east brightened.

With her night vision, Hume saw the largest island had a city. Lights and chimneys gave off thermal signatures and defined the size of the city.

"That is a big city, Coff." Hume banked, so they could see it. "Where do they get enough firewood for the whole place?"

"The Keeper's magic has freed them from heating with fire. Fires are mostly for ascetics and the very poor, now," Coff said, as a matter-of-fact.

"How?" Hume asked, as she continued along the coast.

"The Keeper makes air that burns. I have seen it. It can heat a massive amount of water. That water is fed to the city. It's very wonderful, especially in the winter." Coff pointed. "We should land there on that smaller island. I know the man there. He can help us."

The island that he pointed toward was dark. When Hume circled it, she saw that it had a single, large home. Extensive docks held a few boats of various sizes, and above the docks, near the house, was a large patio that would make a perfect landing space for the small shuttle.

The turbines spun down, as Hume said, "Hang onto your stomach, Coff. We are now on grav-foils only."

Coff, once again, had the funny feeling like he was hanging from his harness even though his eyes told him he was still upright and gently descending. The Hammerhead set down, lightly and quietly, as the feeling of normal gravity returned.

As Hume shut down the remaining systems, Coff said, "I'm so sorry, Hume. Please don't kill them."

She looked up in time to see dozens of men, dressed in black uniforms and cloaks, flooding out of the house and from areas around the patio. They had weapons. Most held crossbows, but she also saw that every sixth man had a plasma rifle.

In seconds, the Hammerhead faced about fifty men. All arranged so that none were at risk from the other's crossfire.

"Coff, what is this?" Hume said, coolly.

"I'm sorry, Hume. You have to understand. I don't know you." His voice trembled.

"You really don't know me," Hume said, as she pressed the button to raise the cowl. "Get out." He knew, by her tone, she wasn't to be argued with.

He struggled with it, finally unbuckling as the cowl rose. As soon as it was up, he climbed out, with his hands up. He walked a few steps from the Hammerhead and, without being asked, went to his knees and clasped his hands on top of his head.

One of the black-clad men stepped forward, and said, "Good morning, Coff. Please remain still."

Hume slowly rose from the cockpit, and lightly stepped out and past Coff where he knelt.

"And, what have we here?" the same man asked Hume's helmeted face.

Hume said nothing.

"Hume. Please," Coff begged.

Suddenly, a pair of darts struck Hume in the center of her chest. Electricity arced between the needles as she stood there, not reacting. She pulled the darts out with her gloved hand. And, let them drop.

Hume spoke. She didn't amplify or use any other enhanced capabilities in her gear.

"Aren't you going to introduce us, Coff?" Hume asked, casually, as two more sets of darts struck her, and she, absently, pulled them out.

"Captain Burke." His voice shook. "This is Hume. Please. Don't."

It was then that Burke realized Coff was begging Hume, not him.

"I am here to see Keeper Ronan. I told Coff I would not harm anyone. Please don't make me break my word." Her voice was calm yet menacing.

"Get on your knees," ordered Burke.

She didn't move. Her Colt AR-79 rifle hung at her back beneath her cloak. Her hands flexed over the grips of her sidearms, like a gunfighter in the old West. They could not see her crazed smile because of her helmet. That would have made them more afraid.

When the crossbow bolt struck her, she didn't even flinch.

CHAPTER TWENTY-FIVE

The Hole Mapped

"That was the first time Ben, our AI, acted in a way that was unusual. Ben was not to blame, and neither was Barcus."

--*Solstice 31 Incident Investigation Testimony Transcript: Captain James Worthington, senior surviving member of the Ventura's command crew.*

Captain Worthington walked down the cargo ramp of the *Memphis*, toward the airlock, the gravity reducing as he approached the edge of the apron.

He sipped his tea as he activated the intercom on the airlock control panel. "Good morning, Angie. Did you have a nice night? I did. It was my first, decent night's sleep since this whole thing started. Tell me why I should not execute you before breakfast."

Jim watched her through the door's window. She stopped her pacing, taken aback.

"You wouldn't dare," she growled.

"It turns out the hole in the security net is too small for the *Memphis*," Jim said, casually.

He let the implication settle in, for a moment.

"So, I'm running out of reasons *not* to decompress the airlock and freeze your body for the stew pots, later."

The subtle menace in his voice was not lost on her. This statement seemed to frighten her more than anything else.

"No. You can't. You need me, if you want to survive," Bowen said, as Worthington worked on the panel.

"What are you doing?" Bowen had panic in her voice as the decompression warning strobe began to flash. "No. I have information." She watched him sip his tea. His face was hard. "You fool. You were supposed to be stationed farther out. This is not my fault. The *Memphis* wasn't supposed to be destroyed."

Worthington raised an eyebrow. "You knew this would happen. That's why you were on the *Memphis*?"

"Yes!" She was thoroughly panicked now. "They ordered me to stay onboard during the last crew change. They said you were a Boy Scout and that the *Memphis* would come back intact via FTL. Bloody hell. They said they needed the data. They left me to bring it back."

"What data?" he asked.

"Promise you won't kill me, or I won't tell you." Bowen choked down her panic.

"No deals," he growled, and hit a button.

She heard the air hissing as it evacuated.

Jim turned and began to walk away.

Bowen ran up to the window, screaming, "Nooooo...Alright, I will tell you! Please."

Jimbo didn't stop walking, until she said the word please. Slowly, he turned and walked back. He knew that by now, her eardrums felt like they were about to burst.

He waited a few more seconds, sipped his tea, then hit the cancel button. Another button reversed the process, returning the pressure and air to the compartment. When it normalized, Bowen dropped to her knees. Her hands were still secured behind her back.

"Last chance," was all he said.

It all spilled out of her in a flood, along with the tears on her face.

***

"Morning, Captain," Cook said, as Jim entered the bridge. Muir nodded and Tyrrell looked up.

"We will have line of sight with the East Isles in eight minutes, sir," Tyrrell said.

"Did you space the bitch?" Beary asked, adding as an afterthought, "Sir."

"Why are all the women on this ship so ruthless and/or bloodthirsty, Karen?" Worthington asked.

"Because you like us that way, Captain," Karen Beary answered.

"Why is everyone so damn chipper this morning? Is it because I look good in this beard? Didn't you get the memo? We're all dead in a month."

Gallows humor was the right tone this morning. They laughed.

Beary added, "Cook thinks he's a hot enough pilot to fly through that hole. We've been running simulations all night."

Cook chimed in. "It started as a simulation to fire the lifeboat through on a slow vector launched from the cargo apron. Taking a page from Hume's flight path, if I barrel roll the *Memphis* at the right moment, I could get it through. I'm already up to a sixty percent success rate, on simulations. And, I have weeks to practice. Here's the best part." Cook brought up a simulation of the last try they managed to get through.

The simulation started with first the Hammerhead, then the lifeboat, going through. "Everyone else can go through on the lifeboat. That way, I am only risking my life." The *Memphis* slowly entered the security net and then executed a sharp roll that looked like a cartwheel. And, it got through. "At that point, I will follow the lifeboat down on grav-foils, pick everyone up and head to the rendezvous with Rand and Hume. If I don't make it through, just have them name a high school after me, when you get back home."

Kuss entered the bridge while Cook was walking through the simulation. "Very nice, Cook," Kuss said, with her accent thicker than usual. "Remind me to give sex down on planet you, if live."

Everyone laughed, again.

"Jimbo, can we talk?"

Worthington looked at Tyrrell. "Line of sight in one minute."

"Can it wait a few minutes, Kuss?" Worthington asked.

"Yes, sir," she said, but stayed right next to the arm of the command chair.

They passed into line of sight and did not receive the expected hail. They waited two minutes, and then ten. Finally, after twenty minutes, Worthington stood. The good mood kept draining from the bridge, the longer they waited.

Speaking to Tyrrell, he said, "Matt, I will be in the conference room."

He motioned for Kuss to follow him. They said nothing on the way to the conference room. She didn't speak until the door closed.

"Kill her, now. Bitch. She knew. Helped murder everyone. Hamilton find out. So murdered her, too. Let me. I kill her slow."

Kuss was beside herself. Jim had never seen her like this before.

"Slow down, Kuss. Sit. Slow down. Breathe." Jim motioned her to a chair.

She took a deep breath. She rocked her neck and it made a cracking sound that seemed to calm her. She took another deep breath.

"I searched her things. Never did before. The equipment included a private, secure comms unit. Out Band. Stupid bitch used same password everywhere. Opened comms. She recorded, for later blackmail, me thinks. Ben, please play back message."

It was Captain Neimann, the captain that rotated out four months ago. "You'll be fine, Bowen. The worse part will be spending another four months with that asshole James 'Boy Scout' Worthington. We'll need to handle him later, anyway. If you want a bonus, come back without him. That whole command crew is on the list, anyway."

Kuss asked AI~Ben to play the next one. He did. "All of them need to be taken out and shot with their own guns." Bowen spewed out in the audio. "Who do they think they are? Spreading their filth across the galaxy."

"There is more," Kuss said, calming through force of will.

"Ben can you please review all these associated files and provide me an assessment?"

"*Yes, Captain,*" AI~Ben said, into his HUD.

"Kuss, come with me."

Jim left the conference room, his good humor from earlier gone. In three minutes, they stood in front of the airlock door. Bowen saw him.

"You need to take these zip ties off me and get me some food and water," Bowen demanded.

Worthington said nothing, he played the damning audio over the intercom.

"Last chance," he said.

"You can't do this. No food, no water, and it's freezing in here." Worthington heard the contempt in her voice

"Ben, based on your full assessment of the information in your possession, what do you think we should do?"

Ben blew the hatch open, without decompressing the airlock.

Bowen died, instantly, her body was thrown about 100 meters out of the airlock onto the surface.

Kuss laughed.

"Ben! What the hell?" Worthington gasped.

"Decision was inevitable. Time is short. Hume has contacted the *Memphis*," AI~Ben said, in a flat voice.

Kuss was still laughing as she walked away.

***

The bolt struck Hume in the center of her chest and bounced away. It felt like her chest plate was hit with a hammer. But, hitting her body armor with a hammer was nothing. Everyone froze.

Hume unsnapped her holsters. She calculated. They didn't know that her targeting rig had already spotted all the men with plasma rifles, even the ones off to the side. All she had to do was point her guns in their direction and they will fire, automatically, with deadly accuracy. In half a second, they will be dead and then the crossbowman will soon follow. She didn't target Coff.

She'd kill Coff last.

All of a sudden, a man in slippers, an old bathrobe, and nightshirt, walked out onto the patio, holding two cups of steaming tea. He walked right past the guards and right up to Hume.

"Captain Burke, where are your manners this morning?" He held out the cup of tea to Hume, and said, "Would you care for some tea? Get up Coff, for anvil's sake." Looking around, he added, "Stand down. All of you."

"All. Of. You." It was directed at Burke.

He made a series of hand motions with the cups and all the men, except Burke and Coff, melted into the shadows, before Coff rose to his feet.

"Thank you, my Lord," Coff said, "Thank you."

"Don't thank me. I just didn't want to train another security detail," he said, looking at Burke.

Coff came up to Hume's side, and said, "She was serious when she asked you not to kill them all."

"I do my best," Hume replied.

Deciding, slowly, she reached up, took off her helmet and tucked it under her left arm. Burke and his men were taken aback by her dark skin and close-cropped hair.

She took the tea with her right hand. "Thank you. My name is Valerie Hume."

She sipped it, at parade rest, her helmet still tucked in. The tea mug was in her right hand. The man in the robe was wise enough to realize it was a gesture of good faith.

"I am sorry, my Lord." Coff bowed his head. "I only met Hume a few days ago."

"Coff, I didn't think you had this in you." He chuckled. "Tracker Ann maybe, but not you. I am impressed. Good work."

Burke openly stared at Hume. She knew from conversations with Coff that it was because of her skin color.

"I didn't think you had it in you either, Coff. You knew these guards were here," Hume added, while smiling, "Well-played."

"Please, come in. My name is Ronan. Do you have time to join us for breakfast?" Coff was still frozen where he stood, as Hume followed Ronan toward the house. "You too, Coff." Ronan waved for him to follow.

They stepped through a door in a wall of glass into a large, beautifully appointed room. Well-worn and cared for leather sofas and chairs faced the vast expanse of southern facing windows. The sky began to brighten, so she could see the tall bookcases in the back of the room and on the surrounding balconies above.

Hume smelled bacon.

She followed Ronan through this great room into a dining room to the right. It also had a wall of windows and Hume could already tell that the view would be spectacular. There was a beautiful, heavy, dark-stained table and chairs in there, with seating for twenty. The chairs matched the table perfectly and looked like they were designed for comfort, not to be ornate. But, the effect was a room that represented the ease of power that seemed to follow the man.

A woman in her middle years walked out from the kitchen with an armful of plates and silverware. "Two more for breakfast?" she asked Ronan, as he kissed her cheek with genuine affection. "Better make it three more. I don't want to have to repeat the entire event to Burke."

Looking around, Hume noticed Burke had disappeared.

"Valerie, this is May," Ronan said. May paused in setting the table, hesitating only an instant as she saw Hume's face, and gave her a nod.

Hume looked at Coff, who nodded confirmation that this was Ronan's spouse. "May, you remember Coff."

"Yes, hello, Coff." And, to Hume, "Very pleased to meet you, miss." May went off for one more place setting.

Hume set her mug on the table and Ronan sat at the head of it. She took off her gloves, put them inside the helmet, and placed it on a side chair with her cloak.

"I must say, you're taking my surprise visit in stride," Hume said, as she sat in the corner chair next to him.

May returned with another place setting, and her own steaming mug, placing it by the setting at the other corner, opposite Hume.

"I enjoy surprises." Ronan smiled, sincerely.

Hume realized she smelled hot cocoa coming from May's mug.

Noticing, May said, as she placed the last napkin, "Would you like some, dear?"

"Yes, please," Hume replied, smiling.

"Good manners, likes cocoa, and didn't kill the security staff, even though they usually, mostly, deserve it. I like her." May smiled. "Now, tell me about your beautiful skin."

CHAPTER TWENTY-SIX

Road Trip

"It was too much, too fast. It started accelerating, then. We didn't notice so many things. Barcus in the north, the events at the Citadel, the *Memphis* crew on the moon, and even Hagan. The timing was chaotic. We were all just making it up as we went along."

--Solstice 31 Incident Investigation Testimony Transcript: Lieutenant Valerie Hume, the security chief on the Memphis.

"I know I'm overdue. It was unavoidable, Captain." Hume activated her helmet cam for Jim to see the view. "I was receiving a tour, by boat, of all things."

She walked to the low wall at the edge of the patio, next to the stairs that led down to the docks.

"Sir, we were very lucky," Hume said, as she turned the helmet to face herself. "I am sending you approach vectors, to avoid these populated areas. If you can get to Rand's base without being noticed, we may have a chance."

"What do you mean?" Jim asked.

"Use of any technology, by any but a select few, is strictly forbidden here. Not just space ships. Anything. No weapons. Even crossbows are forbidden to all but the few."

"Crossbows?" he murmured.

Only Cook heard it.

"The caste system here is horrible. At least the man that rules this region is enlightened enough to forbid the use of slaves in this province. He is conservative but intelligent. He is willing to discreetly help us."

"We're about two weeks away from our attempt to join you. Find out everything you can, in the meantime," Jim said.

"Hume, a lot has happened." He paused. "Bowen's dead."

"Good." It was a simple statement.

"It was intentional, Hume. *Ventura's* destruction, the whole thing. She was in on it. She knew it was going to happen." Jimbo looked stressed. "Somehow, someone is sending ships here, knowing they will be destroyed. Bowen didn't know how tight Captain Everett could drop out of FTL. The *Memphis* was supposed to survive and bring back some sort of data. But, we were still too close when the *Ventura* was hit." The look on his face was all held-in anger. "They murdered the entire crew. The crews of other ships, as well."

"I will find out what I can, Jim," Hume said.

"I will not be on the bridge for the next week, or more. We have to manually detach the remaining lifeboats, all three. And, rig one to fly it through the hole. Cook and Muir will man the bridge while we have line of sight."

"I plan on finding the other EM." Hume looked over her shoulder at the horizon, in the direction of the EM. "I wonder whose it is?"

"Touch base, once a day," Jim said.

"Yes, sir," Hume said, hesitating. "Jim, what will we do once you are down?"

"One miracle at a time, Hume. One goal at a time. A lot may depend on your new friend Ronan. That, and luck."

"Hume out," she said, not missing the implied importance of her diplomacy.

"*Memphis* out," Worthington replied.

***

It took Worthington and the rest of his crew the next ten hours to get the remaining forward lifeboat detached. Even in the lower gravity, it was difficult. It turned out the other two lifeboats had multiple hull breaches and were unsuitable. Over the next few days, the remaining two were removed and dragged to the other side of the hangar. Everyone wondered what happened to the fourth lifeboat. It must have been torn off.

Systems were checked, and rechecked, on the *Memphis*. The last of the debris was dragged from the shuttle bay, including the remains of reactor number two. All the usable parts were salvaged and stowed away.

When the big jobs were done, everyone split into teams, to work on other, smaller projects.

The new grav-foils were installed on the lifeboat, and the new rig was casually called the *Tiller*. It was a fitting name. The newly installed foils will not provide any propulsion, like the system used on the sled. The *Tiller* will only steer the lifeboat, hopefully with enough control that Jim can easily guide it through the hole.

There had been an intense, but very short, argument between Captain Worthington and Commander Cook, regarding who was going to pilot the *Memphis* through the hole. It was decided with the simulator. Worthington, on twenty runs, only managed to make it through four times. AI~Ben, the AI on the *Memphis*, managed to make it through eleven times. But, Cook managed it, eighteen times.

***

Hume was given the run of the East Isles. Keeper Ronan had Coff escort her wherever she went. He didn't want her to fly the Hammerhead around in the daylight, or let anyone see her face. Her looks were too memorable. He was sure there were informants on his islands. She was given the same uniform set of clothes that Ronan's personal guards and couriers wore. It was all black with a black cloak. She found the black tabard with a belt, worn over her flight suit, allowed access to, and concealment of, her weapons, including her combat carbine, if she desired to carry it.

Ronan never even considered depriving her of her weapons. She discovered later, from Coff, that it was an 'unforgivable offense' for a woman to so much as touch a weapon. She could be condemned to death by sledge hammer and anvil.

If she wore her helmet, her face was invisible. Because of her clothes people averted their eyes as she passed them.

Ronan had a large shipyard. As many as twenty-two large, seagoing ships were being built.

What intrigued Hume the most was his shuttle. It was a CV-11a. The civilian version of the CV-11 orbital shuttle, with no weapons trays. It could hold a pilot, a copilot, and eight passengers. It could not be pressurized. On closer examination, she saw that the seals had been removed. She had a pressure suit and could have probably made it to the moon base in two days, but not if the engines were in a vacuum. Ronan was flying to the Citadel, for a High Council meeting, and Hume asked to go along. May was the one that convinced Hume it was too dangerous for her. For many reasons.

After a few days, Ronan returned. Hume was having dinner with Ronan, May and a couple of other trackers.

"Hume, I would like you to meet Ann and Pyke. Ann is the best tracker in East Isles." She bowed her head to Hume, formally.

Pyke then added, "She can follow footprints from one island to the next." His pride was evident.

"What is it trackers...track?" Hume asked. "Coff says most people are trackers just for the freedom."

Pyke looked slightly uncomfortable with this statement, but didn't say anything.

Ann said, "Mostly, we track people, really." She glanced at Keeper Ronan, as if seeking permission to answer honestly. "Lost people, runaways, others." Feeling more comfortable, she continued, "We hunt for food and beautiful pelts and hides. We hunt predators and other killing beasts."

That is when Hume saw the color slightly drain from Pyke's face.

"Beasts? What kind of beasts?" Hume asked.

"Mountain bears, forest wolves, Telis Raptors, other things. Animals that endanger remote villages," she said.

"What is a Telis Raptor?" Hume asked, watching Pyke.

Ann turned to Ronan, who reached to his belt sheath and withdrew a knife that had a slightly curved blade, about half a meter long, tip to pommel. He handed it to Ann, handle first.

"This is the tail spike from a Telis Raptor. The last tailbone makes a perfect handle." Ann flicked the blade and a candle toppled over, cut neatly off. "The tail spikes alone are worth a fortune."

She looked at Keeper Ronan and was suddenly embarrassed. "No, no. It's alright, Ann. I know it's a vanity to carry one without having killed it myself. But, the blade is so fine, I can stand the scorn."

Ann handed Hume the blade, as Pyke spoke, "Telis Raptors are the last of the old species. Part reptile and part bird. Mostly reptile. They are smart and savage, and once they get the taste for human flesh, can clear a village."

"Not many people have seen one, up close. They say if you do, it's the last thing you'll see," Ronan said, as Hume handed the knife back.

"We saw a demon once. Tracked it for days," Pyke said.

Ann looked at him with a disapproving glare.

"A demon? Do tell, Pyke." Ronan poured more wine.

"There were two. But different. It passed us in the dark, one night. We were on our way to Greenwarren, to find out about the spring order," Pyke said, looking at Ronan.

"I remember," Ronan said.

Ann picked up the story. "The village, and many others, had been destroyed. We followed it, as far as we dared. We met a Keeper, in some ruins north and east of Greenwarren, he helped us with directions to the Salterferry Bridge and Langforest Keep. Keeper Volk contacted you, and you picked us up in the CV-11."

"You didn't mention the Keeper before. What was his name? I don't know of any Keepers left north of the gorge."

"His name was Ulric," Pyke said.

Ronan had been leaning back in his chair. His feet *thumped* to the floor.

"Was there a tracker with him named Grady?" Ronan demanded.

"Yes, my Lord. There was. An exceptional tracker, too. He is tall and wiry thin. Very capable. Sharp as a tracker's axe," Pyke said, as Ronan rose to his feet.

"Ronan, what's wrong?" May asked.

He was agitated. He stormed into the great room, without a word.

"I'm sorry, my lady. Did I say something wrong?" Pyke asked of May, worried.

He was back in less than a minute, unrolling a large map of the northern regions that was very detailed and heavily annotated. "Where did you meet the Keeper Ulric?"

Ann looked over the map. It was obvious to Hume that she could read it and was very familiar with that region. "It was around here." She pointed with her finger. "There was a great road beneath the canopy, here, that leads to it. It's just about directly north of the Salterferry Bridge, on the opposite side of the unfinished tunnel."

"Burke!" Ronan called.

"Yes, my Lord." He was there, as if by magic.

Ronan stopped short. "Dammit," he cursed.

"What's wrong?" Hume asked.

"The shuttles. They are all tracked. The Lord High Keeper would wonder what I was doing north of the gorge. Dammit."

"I'll take you," Hume said.

"What?" Ronan stopped, taken aback.

"I'll take you in the Hammerhead. He doesn't track me." Hume smiled. "Let me earn my keep around here."

"Lord Keeper, wait. You cannot go there. The demons are there," Pyke said, with fear in his voice.

Ann stood. She almost seemed embarrassed as she spoke, "It's true, my Lord. There is a giant spider and a golem, there. I have seen them with my own eyes."

"A giant spider, you say?" It was Hume's turn to stand now. "Was this 'golem' all black?"

Ann tilted her head at Hume. "You have seen these demons?" Ann asked.

Hume looked at Ronan and leaned on the table. "I will take you. You'll be safe."

Ronan leaned in, just as Hume had, from across the table. He looked at Ann, and then May. Something passed between them. He looked back, directly at Hume.

"When do we leave?" Hume asked, a glint in her eye.

CHAPTER TWENTY-SEVEN

The Golem

"I knew it was him. Right away. That bastard was too tough, too smart to die. I knew nothing about Wex just then. In a world where women meant nothing, I should have noticed she was special."

--Solstice 31 Incident Investigation Testimony Transcript: Lieutenant Valerie Hume, the security chief on the Memphis.

Hume didn't like the compromise Ronan proposed. Hume will fly him in at night, tonight, and she will wait for him, inside the unfinished tunnel, hidden from the sky and the High Keeper.

"I will walk in, unarmed. It will take a few days, but Ann and Pyke have already followed this road," Ronan said.

"Why not just fly all the way in?" Hume asked, frustration creeping into her voice.

"You cannot just approach this place, unannounced," Ann said. "Ulric only has a few servants, but they are fierce and cunning. One of them, alone, killed the biggest Telis Raptor I have ever heard tale of. Grady could have killed us in our sleep. Us." Ann pointed at Pyke and herself. Ronan must have known the weight of that statement.

"But, most of all, beware of the gatesman. He is more than he seems," Pyke added.

"This spider has been seen before," Ronan said, "It destroyed a shuttle. Tore it right from the sky. I don't want to risk your Hammerhead." Ronan was sincere. "These demons have been seen in dozens of burning villages. They leave death and destruction in their wake. The High Keeper is quite annoyed."

"Who is this Ulric?" Hume asked.

"Ulric is the Keeper at Whitehall Abbey," Ann said. "He is in his mid forties or fifties, but the years seem to rest heavy on him. He has the typical look of a Keeper that drinks much and sleeps too little. But, he is troubled."

"I don't really know Keeper Ulric. He is one of the lesser Keepers," Ronan said. "But, I need to speak to Grady Tolwood, the tracker that is with him. He has a tracker wife named Wex. I just talked to her in the Citadel. I owe her a favor, and I believe I have found a way for her to collect. But, only if I can find Grady for her."

"When do we leave?" Hume asked.

Ronan looked at May when he replied. "In two hours."

She nodded and looked at the hands in her lap.

Burke spoke then, "My Lord. I will go. You can stay here. I will find this Grady for you."

Hume began to understand Burke. She didn't envy him.

"Not this time, Burke. Plus, I can use the exercise."

***

They were packed and ready in two hours.

"Here, take this." Ronan handed Hume an old-style data pad. "I will alert you when you can come in."

Hume took the device and rapidly drilled down into the menus and settings, examining the protocols and network settings in use. Inside her personal HUD, she was, basically, following the same paths.

Finally, she found the section she was looking for on the data pad. She replicated the settings in her personal HUD and a window popped up inside her vision.

"*New Network Detected, Access Requested*" followed by the prompt, "*Confirm or Deny.*"

Out loud, she said, "Confirm."

She quickly explored the primitive network in search of the communications directory. She had a lot of training to do exactly this type of work, but had little need for that training, until now.

She handed the plate back to Ronan. "Keep it. Use this channel."

Ronan's plate chimed, repeatedly. He answered it. There was a new address icon called 'Hume'.

"Comms check. Testing one, two, three." The voice echoed slightly, from the satellite lag.

Ronan looked at her, amazed. "Ready?" she asked, as Ronan handed the unnecessary plate to Burke.

***

Ronan climbed in and buckled his own five-point harness. He had both packs stowed in his foot well, but he didn't seem to mind. Hume could see him via her headrest cam. He was grinning, ear to ear.

Hume closed the canopy and activated the grav-foils. As they ascended, she felt the familiar vertigo of being inverted and falling up. Her inner ear had become used to the sensation as her weight fell against the harness. She saw in the passenger camera that Ronan placed his hand up onto the canopy as a reflex. He was still smiling, ear to ear.

"What if you rolled 180°? Could we still ascend?" he asked.

Hume was impressed. Some pilots did exactly that all the time. They were already up 400 meters, so by way of an answer, Hume did exactly that; but, instead of a roll, she did a summersault in the Hammerhead. End-over-end.

The canopy now faced the ground as they fell upward. They still had the feeling of falling, but it was toward their seats now. It had the advantage of allowing a spectacular view of the East Isle as they reached 2,000 meters.

She paused for a few minutes, just to enjoy the view, then activated the turbines. At full thrust, she finally did execute a few barrel rolls, widening Ronan's smile even farther.

Airspeed was set to 500 kph and leveled. It was cool and calm, and there was only the quiet hum of the turbines. Even the rapid rushing of the wind was insulated in there.

Ronan detailed his entire plan to her. They agreed on a series of communications security codes, so he could convey various situations. He was a quick study. He soon had about twenty basic codes memorized.

"Ronan, can I ask you something that might piss you off?" Hume asked, watching him.

He smiled again, everything seemed to amuse him on this trip. "By all means."

"What the hell is with this ass-backward planet? You have access to technology, but don't use it. You, yourself, don't even support the typical culture on this planet. Slaves? Really? And, I hear other places on this world are so backward they don't ALLOW people to learn to read. Explain. Oh, and don't forget the automated defense orbital platforms?"

She knew she might have crossed a line, as she watched him. His smile faded.

"Let me begin by saying how sorry I am for what has happened to you. To your ship. If I could control the defense network, I would. It's in the hands of the High Keeper. Well, he was…in control."

He looked ashamed. Unguarded. He had no idea Hume watched his reactions.

"What does that mean?" Hume tried to moderate her tone.

"The High Keeper is losing control. Of everything." Ronan looked like he needed to talk about this. "All the systems are slowly failing. Six of the original eleven data centers have died, or have been used to keep the others running. Decades ago, in a fit of anger, the High Keeper threw the only tech that knew the access codes for the defense platforms off a balcony at the Citadel. We are now unable to control them.

"The initial 'back to nature for a simpler life' movement somehow went horribly wrong. It focused on the collective, not the individual. The movement turned into a religion, one that slowly created disdain for technology, or even simple innovation. People's rights, or their worth as individuals, no longer mattered. Making people afraid was the tool of choice. It was easy when they had already surrendered the idea of self-defense. Later, fear of eternal, immortal damnation became a far better tool."

There was sadness in his voice. "Yet, those in power reserved those things for themselves."

He looked at the back of her head almost like he knew there was a camera there to speak to. "How old are you, Hume? In standard Earth years?"

She didn't know if she should tell him. She did anyway. "I am fifty-nine-years-old." She looked like she was twenty-five or thirty.

"Is the longevity serum available to everyone on Earth?" he asked.

"It's available everywhere, for those that want it," she said.

"What is a typical lifespan on Earth?" he asked.

"If you had your stem cells harvested before puberty for use in the initial treatment, and you get your annual boosters, most people live about 300 years. Barring accident, or war, or unmanned automated defense systems." Hume tried to make a joke. But, it did not amuse Ronan.

"The High Keeper controls the serum, here. He uses it as leverage," Ronan confessed.

A thought dawned on Hume. "Are you one of the original colonists on this planet?"

"No, but my parents were. They were scientists. They specialized in the ocean sciences." Ronan now looked out the side, down at the clouds reflected in the water.

"The High Keeper is the last of the original colonists. His actual name is Atish. But, he would kill you, if you said it to him. I believe he has slowly slid into insanity. He hasn't even left the Citadel for over twenty years."

"Who is Wex?" Hume asked, women usually were ignored here.

"I wish I knew how to answer that." Ronan fell silent, staring at the sea. "I think she is like you."

***

Worthington listened to Kuss. She went on for far too long about the tech specs of the comms array she managed to salvage from the destroyed shuttle. "So, all of this means what?"

"We can go to surface, take Hammerhead with, and still access sensor array with line of sight." She seemed very excited about this prospect.

"I will go to sensors tomorrow with Ibenez on sled. Set up new directional laser antenna. Come back with Hammerhead AND sled. Then, we can take sled to surface, too. All wins." She smiled.

"Okay. Do it."

Worthington was decisive. There were no reasons not to be. It would still be several days before they were ready; and even then, they should wait for the right entry window to minimize the chance of being observed. Beary had plotted the track and it should be less than two hours from takeoff here to Rand's hangar.

"Captain. Hume would like to speak to you. She has audio, video and data on this connection."

"Pipe it through." Kuss was already walking away. Jim walked out into the hangar.

"Hume. Go," he said.

The image of Hume showed her standing on a flat, rocky outcropping, above the treetops of a dense forest below. Her helmet must have been sitting on the Hammerhead, pointed at her.

"Good morning, sir. A lot has happened since I first got down here. Instead of trying to tell you everything, I wrote a detailed report. Make sure Tyrrell reads it. I have been granted access to one of the planetary communications networks. Connection information and protocols are included in the report. We may be able to communicate via that network, if point-to-point does not have line of sight. It's Ronan's private network. It is segregated from the main grid, so it will have its limits." She took a breath.

"I think I have located the other Emergency Module. You may not like what I have heard, sir," she said.

"Go ahead," Worthington encouraged her.

"Apparently, it's killing people. Lots of people. Ronan provided me with navigation maps. Just scanning the surface on the way here, I passed over dozens of destroyed towns and villages. Sir, an EM could wreak havoc here and could be unstoppable in the face of these primitive weapons. If the driver has lost it..." She let the statement hang there.

"I trust you to handle things how you see fit. I do NOT want another Bowen on my hands. Is that clear?"

Worthington knew what he was saying. So did Hume.

"Rescue survivors, if possible. Salvage the equipment, if you can't. Do not buy me any more problems," Worthington said, flatly.

"Sir, how much longevity serum does the *Memphis* stores hold?" she asked.

Jim wondered about the change in topic.

"Honestly, I have no idea. Several thousand doses, I should think. I can have Dr. Shaw find out."

Worthington was thinking now. *What if they were stranded forever?*

"You may want to secure the supply, sir. I didn't include this consideration in my report," Hume said.

Jimbo was glad he was alone, on a private channel.

"You don't think Bowen already..." Worthington moved toward the *Memphis.*

"Oh shit," Hume said. "You don't really think that bitch would have thought that far ahead."

Jim jogged into the heavier gravity, and slowed his pace as he moved to the infirmary. He entered, without knocking. Dr. Shaw looked up. She was securing everything, in prep for the flight.

"Hello, Jimbo. What can I do for you?" she asked.

"I am currently talking to Hume. At least she is thinking like a security chief. Will you check our supply of longevity serum?" He quickly added, "Please."

"Certainly," was her simple reply, as she went straight to a little used, out-of-the-way cabinet built into the back wall.

The look on Dr. Shaw's face told Worthington all he needed to know.

"Hume, it's gone. All of it."

Shaw's nodding confirmed it.

"That bitch," Hume cursed.

CHAPTER TWENTY-EIGHT

Found

"Barcus would have easily killed all of those murdering bastards, if we had not found him."

--Solstice 31 Incident Investigation Testimony Transcript: Captain James Worthington, senior surviving member of the Ventura's command crew.

"Rand. It's Hume, come in." Hume flew low over Salterkirk, on grav-foils only.

"Rand here. Go, Hume," Rand responded, audio only.

"I just wanted to give you an update, Rand. I'm not going to land. A burst transmission of reports and data is headed your way, now. It will include a set of updated maps, network access credentials, background information and what's going on with the moon team. They are going to be coming down sometime in the next two weeks."

"Acknowledged," Rand replied.

"Everything okay in Salterkirk?" Hume asked.

"I've been exploring. This place is huge. The actual mines are massive. Lots of potential," Rand replied. "I have a Fly that can do autonomous mapping in the dark. It's an incredible place," Rand said, "Wait one second, I will forward the survey."

"Got it. Thanks," Hume confirmed. "Got to jet, Rand. I'll be back soon."

"Be careful, Hume. Remember, this is a hostile environment," she said.

"Rand, out."

"Acknowledged. Hume, out." Hume ascended to cruising altitude.

***

Hume geo-tagged the unfinished tunnel where she was holding up during the days. On the way back from Salterkirk, she fired up her passive scanners and night vision. She shut the turbines down, running silently when she got closer. The unfinished tunnel was just north of the gorge, above a bridge, according to her map.

She dropped below the rim of the canyon and cruised as fast as she could. It was a thrill, and she knew Worthington would be pissed off, if he knew she was taking that risk. She was flying at about 100 kph when she rounded a bend and saw the destroyed bridge. She pulled up, hard, backwashed to a full stop, and hovered, before she reached the burned ruins.

Hume said, out loud, "Sometimes a burning bridge gives the best light..." remembering a poem or a lyric.

She drifted up, between the towers, and followed the road until it terminated at the unfinished tunnel. She flew directly into the tunnel and all the way to the unfinished wall. There were signs of habitation in there. But, not recent signs.

She flew out and back on the exact same line, over the mountains and trees. She found the mouth on the other side. After doing the same survey of the tunnel, she set down just inside the opening. It would be the dawn of another day soon.

Ronan planned to reach the ruins today.

She sat down and sharpened her knives.

***

Hume slept for six hours in the pilot seat of the Hammerhead, with the canopy closed and her helmet on. She had been trained to sleep light and instantly come awake, if required. She had been awake all day and was now worried. Ronan was an hour overdue.

She decided to check in with the *Memphis* while she waited. She quietly flew to the flat, rocky spot, deployed the directional laser antenna and hailed the *Memphis*.

"Wake up, slackers," was her hail today.

"Greetings, Hume. *Memphis* here. Tell us some good news," Cook replied.

She instantly read the subtext of Cook's response. It was not going well up there. "Where's Tyrrell? I expected him to be here."

"Do you still memorize the roster and schedules, even when you're down there?" Cook asked.

Hume knew he was alone on the bridge by his casual manner on the comms.

"Old habit. Where's everyone?" she asked.

"Right now, they're searching the base with a fine-tooth comb. We were just about ready to go, when Bowen fucked us from beyond the grave. Jimbo figures she was going to either use the longevity serum as leverage or save it for herself. My money is on the latter. She thought she was so fucking smart she'd never get caught," Cook hissed.

"Holy shit. You must be pissed to be cursing that much." She laughed.

"This is not funny, Hume. Even if we make it to the surface, we're all dead soon," Cook said.

Hume thought it out for a second. She had made peace with death, long ago. She didn't expect to die of old age, at 300, warm in a bed, somewhere.

"Cook, I've been thinking. Bowen probably didn't kill Hamilton over some extra rations. But this? Make sure they search Hamilton's quarters and anywhere she may have been."

"Will do," Cook replied. She heard him typing. He was messaging them, now.

"What's your status, Hume?" Cook requested. Jimbo probably asked over text.

"I'm currently on hold. Ronan is about an hour overdue." It was then that Hume noticed a high altitude vapor trail that was still in the sunshine as the sun set. "Something may be up. If he doesn't check-in in two hours, I'm going to look for him, after it gets dark."

"We will have line of sight for about four more hours," Cook said. "After that, Kuss will replace the point-to-point antenna with one she salvaged from the shuttle. We will be able to bring the other Hammerhead down and still have access to the sensors here and P2P comms. We will need to test it, at moonrise."

"Acknowledged. Good luck, Cook. Tell Jimbo to think like Bowen, if he can stand it. Hume, out," Hume said.

"*Memphis*, out." Cook disconnected.

***

Hume stayed on the top of the rocks as she watched the sun set. She was emptying her mind and listening to the chatter of birds. This planet was so quiet. That was when she heard it.

There were distant echoes from gunshots. Heavy caliber. They *thumped*, like a 10mm caliber cannon. Then, she heard another, and another. She could now tell the direction—toward the ruins that were Ronan's destination.

She put on her helmet and cloak. She climbed into the Hammerhead, drifted down to the mouth of the tunnel, past the start of the road that went off into the distance, and into a tunnel of tree limbs. She warmed up the turbines and set a countdown clock. Cool and calculated, she waited. Her hover was so precise the Hammerhead looked perfectly still, like it was suspended by invisible wires.

She hung there for sixty-three minutes. The countdown clock had twenty-seven minutes remaining when her comms came alive. "Hume, just checking in. I'm all right. Approach. Sierra-Delta-Niner." Ronan used one of the pre-designated security codes she had made him memorize.

She smiled, ear to ear, inside her helmet.

"Acknowledged. En route now," she said, as she punched it full throttle.

He said Delta-Niner. There was a survivor found alive.

***

The Hammerhead screamed through the tunnel of trees, turbines on full. She noted that Ronan left his plate activated. Smart man. She saw where it was on her tactical. A kilometer out, she shut down and secured the turbines as she coasted in at 100 kph. She saw the keep, even before she exited the tunnel of trees like a bullet from a barrel. On foils, she lapped the circular fortress, twice, before pulling up to a slow hover and descent. Night vision and tactical displays showed that there were a lot of people below, maybe as many as 100 within the walls. She landed, directly in front of Ronan and a small crowd of people.

Before she popped the cowling, she unsnapped the straps on her holsters and targeted everyone present, except Ronan. Just in case.

As the cowling hinged up, slowly, Hume stepped out. She left the helmet on for the enhanced night vision and targeting.

Hume asked, "A Delta-Niner? Really?"

She lowered the hood and took off her helmet. Her black, unbraided, close-cropped hair barely covered her ears. She shook out her hair. It was flat after having worn the helmet for so many hours. Then, she saw him.

It was Barcus.

He was taller than anyone that surrounded him. His dark hair was long and unkempt. The beard he had was not enough to hide a new scar on his face that crossed his left cheekbone down to be lost at his jaw line. He looked as strong as she remembered.

She walked right up to him, took off a glove and extended her right hand to him. "Sir, I'm Hume."

Barcus shook her hand. His mouth gaped, in stunned silence.

"Hume, this is Barcus. This is why I walked all this way," Ronan said, explaining it to Hume, not Barcus.

"Valerie Hume? Lieutenant Valerie Hume?" Barcus asked, recognizing her. He was stunned.

He suddenly drew her into a hug that took her off her feet. She was tiny, just like the woman standing with him.

"You remember me." She laughed.

"You're alive?" He set her back on her feet. He touched her arms and shoulders and finally held her head, making sure she was real. "I have so much to tell you."

Barcus turned to speak directly to a woman named Po, just Po. She was a small, pretty woman with long, braided, blonde hair, wearing a simple dress. Hume could tell she was important to Barcus. When their eyes met, Hume sensed a flash of how fierce she was, how intelligent. It was just an impression, one that would prove itself out before all this was over. "Hume is from the *Ventura*. She was on the third shift command crew. The security chief."

The woman named Po surprised her, by asking, "What's a Delta-Niner?"

Ronan replied, "It means, survivor found alive."

"I have someone that would like to speak to you." She reached into the cockpit and activated some controls. A small, tight beam, directional, laser-based comms antenna deployed from her ship and focused on the sky.

Barcus turned and reached for Po whispering to her, "This is a woman from Earth."

She put her arm around his waist. He held her close, waiting for Hume.

A dialog box popped up in Barcus's HUD that said, "*A new network has requested protocol handshake. Confirm or Deny?*"

Just then, Po gave a huge flinch as he held her.

Barcus looked down at her as she looked up at him. She said, with wide eyes, "Confirm."

Barcus said, "Confirm." The dialog box disappeared. He stared at her.

"Barcus, is that you?" the voice over the HUD asked.

He looked back at Hume, incredulously.

"Jimbo?" Barcus asked.

"That's Captain Jimbo, ass-wipe! You're not dead! How's it hanging, bro!?"

***

Barcus was still in shock. "Where the hell are you?" He looked at the point-to-point laser unit and then followed its aim, tracking it to the sky and the moon.

"We're on a moon base. But, we're headed your way, soon," Worthington said.

"Negative. There are weapons platforms surrounding this planet. They will nuke you like they did the *Ventura*." Barcus was adamant.

"Relax, man. We know. We found a hole, but it will be close. We're planning to send the crew down in a lifeboat first," Worthington said.

"Wait. This hole is big enough for the *Memphis*?" Barcus asked.

"Barely. Hume mapped it, in detail, when she went through in the Hammerhead. But, we can't wait much longer. We're almost out of food. We are good on air and water, but we're down to emergency rations from the lifeboats," Jim said.

"How many are with you?" Barcus asked.

"There are fifteen here, including me," Worthington said.

"Jimbo. I have a Shuttle Transport Unit. Chen's STU. If there is a hole in the defense grid, I can be there in an hour," Barcus said. "Do you have a dock or a portable gantry?"

"Better than that. A whole hangar bay with functioning airlocks," Jim said. "Is Chen with you?" he asked, excitedly.

"No." His voice fell. "She didn't make it. She was the one that saved me. I was the only one to..." He faded off. "I thought I was the only one. This changes everything."

"Hume, give Barcus the telemetry for the hole." Jimbo grew more excited. "Wait, Barcus, you have Chen's STU-1138? That model has a small fabricator. Is it damaged?"

"Minimal damage. The fabricator is perfect. I've been using it. What's wrong with your fabricators?" Barcus asked.

"Excellent. Elkin and Kuss will be glad to hear it," Worthington said. "That increases our chances of getting off this ball. Both of our fabricators were destroyed."

"Screw this, Jimbo. Let's talk, in person." Barcus looked at Hume and swept her up in another bear-hug. "Let's have that data, Hume. Jimbo, I will be there in less than two hours." Adding to the end, "Stu, fire up the mains. We're going on a road trip!"

Barcus looked at the people standing there, and asked, "Who wants to go to the moon?"

CHAPTER TWENTY-NINE

Rescue

"The people on this planet had never seen a dark-skinned person before. Hume was fascinating to some, and frightening to others."

--Solstice 31 Incident Investigation Testimony Transcript: Captain James Worthington, senior surviving member of the Ventura's command crew.

A man with a badly scarred face smiled and shook his head. "Can this night become any more...surreal?" He walked away. "I have bodies to burn."

"What did he just say?" Hume asked.

"It's why I was late checking in, Hume," Ronan said. "Apparently, our friend Barcus here is having a bit of a war with the High Keeper's men."

"Come into the light." Po took Hume's hand and walked closer to a lantern, hanging by the door to the paddock. "Are you alright?" she touched Hume's face.

Hume allowed it.

"She's never seen another race before. There are no other races on this planet," Barcus said, as data and reports began flowing to his personal HUD.

"Does it hurt?" Po asked, which made Hume laugh.

"Stu, prep for an orbital run to these coordinates, precisely, and then to this location on the far side of the moon," Barcus ordered.

They were walking back to the gatehouse when Hume realized that Po carried an AR, slung on her back beneath her cloak. "How long have you been here, Barcus?" Hume asked, as he opened the door to the gatehouse.

Po, Ronan, and Hume followed him in.

"I have been here since I fell onto this planet. It was just a ruin when I arrived," he said.

"He saved us all," Po said, absently, as she swung the kettle over the fire.

"Are you really going to the moon, my boy?" Ronan asked.

"Yes. We leave in about thirty minutes." Reminded, Barcus turned away and said, quietly, "Em, Par will stay here and keep an eye on the Abbey. Stu and Ash will go with me to get Jimbo and his crew."

AI~Stu spoke, into his head, "*I have analyzed the sensor data Lieutenant Hume provided and I will be able to navigate the hole in the defense grid, easily. Shall we bring them all down on this trip? I will have to obtain a core dump from Ben, the AI currently on the Memphis, and we can come up with a plan, then.*"

"Thanks, Stu."

AI~Stu continued, "*Both reactors will be warmed up in eighteen minutes. Inertial Dampening will be available a few minutes later.*"

"May I go with you?" Ronan asked. "It may be my only chance."

"You'll be taking me, as well," Hume said, "Plus, we'll need to stop on the way back and get Rand."

Barcus was dumbfounded, again. He slumped into a chair.

"Rand lives?" Barcus asked.

"Yes. She is a ways west of here, but she is fine. She has an Emergency Module with her as well," Hume replied. "We detected comms traffic with the EMs. It's how we found you," Hume said.

"Po, let them know we'll be back, with my friends, late tomorrow morning. Let's have a celebration. They need it, as well, after today," Barcus said to her, as she put the Colt AR-79 rifle back into its case.

Barcus quietly explained to Hume that a few hours ago there was a battle of sorts and over a hundred mercenaries and trackers were killed in a very one-sided confrontation. That explained the gunfire she had heard.

"We will now have seventeen men and women from Earth?" Po smiled wide. "We will be invincible." Her eyes were sparkling as she left the gatehouse.

"Barcus, what are you going to do?" Ronan asked.

He stood, looked at Hume, and then to Ronan.

"Live." Barcus smiled.

***

EM~Stu was parked beyond the north gate when the four of them boarded, along with Ash. Hume watched the suit everyone called Ash, ascend and dock in its usual pack in the back of the small bridge. Ronan watched the ramp close behind him under the chin of the ship. It was the size of a large house, but shaped like a turtle with all its limbs drawn in.

"How can it be so black? It's like a void in the darkness, it's so black," Ronan said, as the ramp sealed.

Barcus said, from the ladder, "It's the material it is made of. It absorbs all light, reflects no light, no colors, none at all. Plus, it's nearly frictionless and heat resistant."

Hume and then Ronan went up the ladder, followed by Po. When she entered the bridge, she took the front, right seat, and Barcus the front, left seat.

She buckled her five-point harness expertly without a word, just as Barcus did.

"Hello, Stu. How are you today?" Po asked the Shuttle Transport Unit's Artificial Intelligence program, or AI~Stu.

"Very well, thanks. And yourself?" AI~Stu replied, conversationally.

"Excellent. Full canopy, please," Po said.

Suddenly, it was like they stood outside, on top of a platform, open to the night sky. Ronan sat quickly and fumbled with the straps. Hume helped him and then sat opposite him.

"Status please, Stu," Barcus said.

"Reactors idling at sixty percent. Inertial dampeners at 100 percent. Seal is good. Pressure is good. All systems are nominal. Ready for orbital extraction."

"Full Tactical," Barcus said.

All of the night sky on the canopy was filled with icons. All the defense platforms were marked and highlighted. The sensor data populated a virtual representation of the sensor net that enveloped the planet. The dead platform and surrounding nodes were indicated near the horizon on the left.

"Let's move out Stu. Grav-foils only until 10,000 meters. Then proceed. Carefully," Barcus said.

"I recommend we move slowly through the field. It's just a feeling. Maybe 100 meters per second for two minutes," Hume said.

"Did you hear that Stu?" Barcus asked. "Make it happen."

"Yes, Barcus," AI~Stu replied.

***

They watched as the world fell away beneath them. They felt no sense of motion, at all, as they slowed for the transition through the hole. They were close enough to the weapons platforms to see the mouths of hundreds of launch tubes. First on the planet-side, then on the outer plane.

"Did you really fly that Hammerhead all the way from that moon base?" Barcus asked.

"Yes. Don't ask me to do it again," Hume replied.

"Let's give it another minute before we power up," Hume recommended. "In fact, can we run on just grav-foils for a bit? Just to be sure."

"Stu. Do it," Barcus said.

"They always said the world was round. A great ball. I can see it from here," Ronan said, in awe.

They let it go a few minutes more. They were through, now. They were oriented, so the foils would make them feel like they were in standard single G fall.

Barcus brought the systems up, starting with artificial gravity, inertial dampeners, and the main engines. The planet fell away, rapidly.

"Stu, how soon before we arrive?" Po asked.

"Twenty-two minutes, Miss," AI~Stu responded.

"Maybe we should let them know we're on the way?" Po recommended.

"Good idea," Barcus said, "Stu, open a channel to the *Memphis*, P2P, please."

"Open," AI~Stu said, after only a few seconds.

"*Memphis*, this is Barcus. STU-1138 is en route with an ETA of about twenty minutes. You ready, Jimbo?" Barcus said.

Po looked at him and smiled. He was happy. She didn't know if she had ever seen him happy like this, before now.

"STU-1138, this is the *Memphis*. The hangar has been depressurized and the barn door is open. Get your ass in here, you ugly bucket of spit. We've got some crap that needs fixing." Cook laughed.

"Oh. My. God. Cook. It's so good to hear your voice," Barcus said.

"Shut up, everyone is on the bridge. Listening. No sloppy kisses for you, dipshit," Cook said, and laughter could be heard on the crowded bridge.

Worthington spoke, "Is Hume with you?"

"Yes, sir. She can hear you," Barcus said, as they neared the surface of the moon and began shutting down the main engines.

"Hume, you were right. We found the serum by tracing Hamilton's steps. We found it at the bottom of the water tank," Worthington said.

"Good news, sir. Are you ready to head out?" Hume asked.

"We will need to cycle the hangar door closed and then repressurize the main hangar. We should load up the shuttle with the equipment, gear, and supplies we have decided to take along with us. Then, we should shut down the nonessential systems on the *Memphis*. We're planning to keep the heat and the lights on in the base, for when we return to the *Memphis*," Worthington said.

"Thank you, Barcus," he added.

"I'm glad you're alive, bro. No sloppy kisses for you, either," Barcus said.

He looked at Po. She had a strange look on her face. Barcus mouthed silently, '*It's a joke!*'

***

The moon base came into view a few minutes later. As soon as they cleared the massive door, it closed behind them. The pools of light in the giant hangar revealed the *Memphis*, parked to one side with its shuttle dock wide open and the apron all the way down. Without being asked, AI~Stu flew slowly into the *Memphis* flight deck and landed in the very center.

"I don't know what to say," Ronan said, in a voice just above a whisper, as the hangar door closed with a *thump* felt in the structure and not heard in the vacuum. "So much lost."

"Welcome to the *Memphis*. Comfy in there?" Worthington asked, over the comms. "Normally, it's polite to ask permission to come aboard, ass-wipe."

They heard the smile in his voice.

"Look, man. I'm just MG-42."

They laughed.

"Pressure in eleven minutes. See you soon," Worthington said, and closed the channel.

"They are probably packing," Hume said, unbuckling.

"What does MG-42 mean?" Po asked.

Barcus smiled, "Maintenance guy number forty-two. Also known as JAFMG, just-another-fucking-maintenance-guy. Another joke."

"Do men from Earth always insult each other?" she asked.

"Only if they're good friends," he said, standing. "Stu, don't shut down cold. Low idle, please, and establish data and comms links with the *Memphis* and sync. Notify me of any mission priorities."

"Yes, sir," AI~Stu replied.

"Thanks for the nice ride, Stu. I enjoy flying," Po said.

Barcus stood and looked around at the damage to the dock. He could not believe that the *Memphis* could still fly. There were hull breaches clean through to the center of the reactor room in main engineering. But, the ship had full power.

Beyond the flight apron, he saw the remains of their shuttle. It was three times the size of the STU-1138 and must have absorbed the brunt of the debris that had torn through the *Memphis*.

"They must have been desperate to even consider flying this to the surface," Barcus said, to no one in particular. Everyone was looking around now.

"We were," Hume said. "Desperate. Hanging by a thread, really."

"You flew an unpressurized Hammerhead from here to the planet. On manual grav-foils, tiny ones, because the turbines don't even spin up in a vacuum," Barcus said, looking at another Hammerhead parked out there.

"Yes...Hanging by a thread."

She stared at the parked Hammerhead, as well. Barcus couldn't believe her eyes were filling with tears that finally spilled over. He gathered Hume into his arms. She let him. Her shoulders shook.

Po joined the embrace from behind Hume. "He does this to everyone, you know. It's one of his magic powers."

Hume laughed, and it turned into a sob. But then, she wiped her eyes on Barcus's tunic.

She pulled back, and they separated. But, not before she pounded him on the sternum, and said, "Ass-wipe."

She laughed again, and Po took her place in his arms, hiding her eyes in his chest.

He let her.

They went down to the cargo bay, and waited until the indicator turned green. He pounded the large activator button, and the ramp descended.

All fifteen stood there.

Barcus said, "Captain Worthington, permission to come aboard?"

"Granted," he replied.

There was no salute. Just a fierce hug between two old friends.

CHAPTER THIRTY

Dry Dock

"We finally had hope. Before that, in the back of our minds, we were positive we were dead. Meeting Ulric, knowing he survived the same experience, we knew we could survive."

--Solstice 31 Incident Investigation Testimony Transcript: Captain James Worthington, senior surviving member of the Ventura's command crew.

Keeper Ulric was in his room with Saay and Kia. They were asleep, and he was awake, for once. He tried to drink enough to keep the nightmare away. Then, he heard the music but didn't move. It was coming from the garden, again. He knew better than to get up and look. In fact, he wanted to shrink from the windows.

A silhouette moved in front of the window, and he knew the nightmare was happening and he was unable to wake.

Am I asleep already?

He saw her stand at the foot of his bed. She wasn't burned or bloody, this time. Her clothes were white and clean. She wore a simple tunic and a thick, silk, rope belt.

"You have done well, Ulric." The whisper came from the foot of the bed. The glow from the dying fire illuminated the curve of her cheek. It sparkled, deep in her eyes. "Soon you may be free of me, forever. But, you must be strong. In the morning, they will return and you must persuade them in a single, small way."

She turned and walked toward the windows. The glowing coals illuminated her bare shoulders, and the slave tattoos, in high detail. It was the moon of Earth, Luna, crossed with clouds.

Wasn't there a tunic, a moment ago?

"Persuade them? Who? To do what?" he whispered. *Am I awake?* He did not want to wake them. Again.

"Who?" She didn't turn back. "These men from Earth. These Lords of the sky. These women of prophecy. These...destroyers. Do as I say, and this world shall not burn."

Ulric felt his panic rise. He couldn't look away. His imagination tormented him with visions of sharp needle-like teeth biting through their own lips. And the blood. So much blood.

"Do this one thing," she said, and turned to face him.

He thrashed. He crab-walked to the headboard as she came toward him. Her face was perfect. Her eyes glowed in the firelight. It was worse. She came closer.

"They must help Grady." She didn't stop when she reached the foot of the huge, four-poster, canopy bed. She climbed over, slowly. "It's a simple thing, but it must be done. Ronan will know a way."

The steel piling of her prosthetic leg terminated in a talon, its claws flexing.

"Po is the key. She walks to and fro without realizing she's holding the leash of a Telis Raptor. Even though it is hungry. So very hungry."

She stopped crawling when she was between his feet.

It was as if she noticed the young women for the first time as they stirred. Ulric panicked.

"No!" he screamed, out loud. "I mean, yes. I will do anything. Please!" Ulric shrank away, clinging to the girls who were now awake and trying to calm him.

Looking from girl to girl and then back at Ulric, she smiled, a bloody smile. He screamed and squeezed closed his eyes.

The laughter turned into music, as Saay and Kia told him it was only a nightmare, and he clung to them tighter.

***

It took about two hours to load the shuttle. They started with the already loaded sled and the Hammerhead. There were several cases of weapons and ammunitions, next. All the clothes they could find were packed. Most of the medical supplies of the *Memphis* were loaded. Then, the pressure suits and the damaged Hard Shell Maintenance Suit were loaded, followed by tools and gear, and even some small task generators. There was gear Barcus didn't recognize, and cases that were not opened or inspected.

Elkin asked if he could take the time to fabricate and install two parts on the damaged reactor. "If we can leave the reactor up, these will make it much more stable."

"Do it," Jimbo said, instantly.

Barcus and Elkin took Kuss and Weston to get started on shutting down that reactor while the fabricator created the new parts. Po was left alone with Ronan in the hangar bay.

"This lower gravity, I knew there was such a thing, but never thought I'd experience it," Ronan said.

Po jumped again. It was just straight up and down, but it still amazed her. "I wish my nose weren't so stuffed up," she said, as she landed lightly. "Captain Worthington says it bothers him, too."

"Po, I need to ask you..." Ronan pulled his beard. "These people, what are they going to do?" He was serious. Worried.

"They will do whatever they like," she said.

"I don't know you like I know Barcus." She was looking right into his eyes as she spoke. "Hume told me that Barcus was the least of them. YOU are nothing beside him. And you may be the most powerful Keeper there is. Stay out of their way. Please, Ronan."

"I will help them any way I can." He was very thoughtful. "But, the High Keeper will not tolerate their existence. He doesn't care about lives. Maybe not even his own."

"Then help them, because I think all they really want is to return to Earth." Po didn't look happy about her statement as she watched Barcus help carry a machine up the ramp into the *Memphis*. "Please don't make them angry. You have seen what happens." Po was nearly pleading.

"Yes, I have seen what can happen. But, I have not seen him angry. Yet."

He remembered Barcus as he had faced 100 of the High Keeper's hardest men. Barcus hadn't blinked, until they were all dead, a moment later.

Ronan watched them. "It is wiser to fear a dozen sheep led by a Telis Raptor than to fear 100 Telis Raptors led by a sheep."

***

They decided to leave the remaining rations for when they returned. Barcus assured them there will be a feast awaiting them in Whitehall. Ronan pledged additional supplies, if they were needed.

"Keeper Ronan," Worthington said, as the last of the load was secured, "my security chief has reassured me that you will not be a problem."

"Captain, not all the people of this world need killing," Ronan said, as Barcus approached. Both men were taller than Ronan. "Even though Barcus may think otherwise."

"What is the damn planet name?" Kuss interrupted, with her accent thick.

Po, Worthington, and Barcus looked at Kuss and then to Ronan.

"It was called Baytirus, long ago. Use of the name has been forbidden for so long it has almost been forgotten," Ronan replied.

"Forbidden? Why?" Kuss asked.

"It implied there were other worlds. With other names. Like Earth," Ronan said.

"Using the name Earth is also forbidden," Po said, as a matter-of-fact. "Hammer and Anvil. Death offenses."

Barcus nodded confirmation, as disgust twisted Kuss's face.

"Lord Barcus, you should educate your peers as soon as possible. I'm used to a few death offenses before breakfast, but I am not typical. Just standing here means death," Ronan said. "The moon is of heaven and reserved for the Keepers." It sounded like he quoted a scripture.

"Please, it's just Barcus," Barcus said.

"And frankly, I feel I must say, killing a couple thousand of the Lord High Keeper's men may not have been the best idea, either." Ronan was looking directly at Barcus.

Everyone else gathered, looked at him as well.

"Hey, I was pissed off."

"A hornet's nest," Ronan said.

"When we get off this shit ball, I say we activate planet-facing weapon tubes on our way out." Kuss pressed into Ronan's space, for some reason. "Stu owns comms systems already. By time we fix *Memphis*, he will crack nuke control systems. We kill them all."

"Stand down, Kuss," Worthington ordered, in a voice not to be ignored. "Let me be crystal clear. We will get off this planet. We will also disable the

defense grid on the way out, if we can. We will also set a warning buoy."
He pointed at Barcus, "You and I will have a discussion, regarding this
campaign of yours. In private." He faced Ronan, then said, "I expect your
discretion. I would like your help. But, I will not threaten you to get it." He
looked at Kuss, then asked, "Is that clear?"

She nodded, respectfully.

"Now, load them up. I need to breathe some real air. Even if it is on a
godforsaken planet," Worthington said, as he moved off.

People began the last preparations before takeoff. Worthington spoke
with Dr. Shaw and climbed into the *Memphis*.

Hume came down the ramp to Po and Ronan, where they stood, trying
to stay out of the way. "Ronan, I just asked if we should kill you and leave
you out there with the other bodies. Barcus and Jim left it to me, to
decide." He noticed her sidearm was in her hand, not holstered. "You will
answer one question."

Resigned, he nodded. Po stepped away two steps.

"Why would you help us?" she asked, still as a statue.

"I believe the Lord High Keeper is insane and has to be stopped," he
said.

"No. There's something else. Do not bullshit me. Not now." Hume's
jaw muscles tensed.

"He is holding someone that means nothing to him, but the world to
others. If I help you, I hope you'll help me."

"Who?" Hume asked, as she holstered her gun.

"Her name is Wex," he said.

CHAPTER THIRTY-ONE

Whitehall Abbey

"I had no idea, at the time, what Barcus had been through. No idea how much these people meant to him. They treated him like a god. You know... They may have been right."

--Solstice 31 Incident Investigation Testimony Transcript: Captain James Worthington, senior surviving member of the Ventura's command crew.

They left the hangar bay unpressurized, but closed, on their way out, to ease their eventual return to the *Memphis*. There was a short debate, regarding bringing it with them, this time. It was decided it could wait for them to take a breath and come up with a long-range plan.

Having the small part fabricator on the Shuttle Transport Unit, changed everything. They will be able to dry dock on the surface and execute real repairs. Even if it took years, they could do it.

They crowded into the STU's bridge. With inertial dampening on full, the ride was very smooth, and the STU took them to the defense grid hole, easily.

"Captain, with this unit we could even make a larger fabricator from scratch. It would take a while, but we could use the ruined shuttle for the right raw materials," Elkin said. She was excited.

"We will need to find out how to repair main FTL propulsion," Worthington said, as he watched the descent to the planet. "Elkin, how much do you know about the FTL systems? I know your specialty was reactors. Anyone?" He looked at the rest, knowing the answer already. "We have a lot of reading to do."

Barcus laughed, out loud. "Sorry, Jimbo. But the Senior FTL drive engineers on the *Ventura* didn't even know how they worked, really. You'd never be able to build one that functioned."

"Well, then why the hell are you smiling?" Cook asked.

"I have an FTL-capable ship that happens to have reactor issues." He smiled, wide. "It needs a lot of work, but you're going to love it. It's a Renalo-class yacht."

He saw recognition on their faces.

"I believe you can thank this ship for the hole we just passed through."

"How do you mean?" Kuss asked, what everyone was about to ask.

"It has an EMP cannon," Barcus said.

"You have been busy." Worthington laughed.

"Barcus, we are approaching the coordinates you provided. Nothing on visual yet," AI~Stu said to Barcus.

Hume spoke up, "Descend to within ten meters of the lake's surface and approach the coordinates from the north. You'll see it. The hangar opening is huge, but there is a large overhang cliff above it."

It was late morning there, now. The shadows were deep in the day's bright sun.

They saw a tall figure, standing on the rocks at the mouth of the hangar. The wind blew the figure's cloak to the east. The STU drifted into the hangar slowly, directly over Rand's head.

The STU entered the hangar and rotated the ship 180° before it settled down. The ramp lowered as the STU touched down. Rand's silhouette walked across the hangar floor, arriving at the shuttle about the same time the ramp apron touched down.

They were there, as it opened.

Rand saw Barcus, as he was the first to move down the ramp. He stopped, in front of her. No one else moved or spoke.

Po whispered to Hume, as Barcus and Rand exchanged quiet words, "What's happening?"

"She didn't know he survived. Now, he's telling her about Chen." Hume paused. "They were all friends."

"Why does he always make women cry?" Po asked, smiling.

"Not just the women," Cook said, quietly, from where he stood behind them.

Hume pointed a thumb at Cook, "Cried like a baby."

Cook smiled, as he nodded.

Rand then threw her arms around Barcus in a fierce hug, much like the one Barcus had shared with Jimbo. Even though she was taller than Barcus, she buried her face in his neck as her shoulders shook.

Jimbo took that as a cue to descend the ramp into what rapidly became a group hug around them.

Po stood at the edge of the ramp with Ronan, Dr. Shaw, Ibenez, Shea, and Edwards.

Ibenez looked at her, and said, "I'm an introvert. No hugging."

"What is an introvert?" Po asked.

***

Hugs turned to laughs, and then outright celebration. They were alive.

Two more figures appeared from the shadows of the hangar, holding lanterns.

"I want you to meet my friends Vi and Tannhauser," Rand said.

People introduced themselves. Eventually, Tan'Vi noticed Keeper Ronan and were taken aback.

"Forgive me, my Lord Keeper. How may we serve you?" Tannhauser asked, bowing deeply.

Vi fell to her knees and put her forehead on the floor.

All conversation stopped.

Po looked at Barcus, who had been speaking with Worthington. She saw his jaw tighten.

"Please, rise." Ronan ignored the awkward silence, and patted Tannhauser on the back like an old friend. "I do believe we have met more than once. Last spring in Exeter. You brought me a message."

"That's correct, my Lord."

Po helped encourage Vi to her feet. Vi trembled.

"Do you know who that is?" Vi whispered to her.

Po nodded.

"As soon as we unload all this, we're headed back to Whitehall, Rand. We have a feast waiting for us. Would your friends like to come along?" Worthington asked.

"It's up to you," Rand said to them.

"Will you be coming back here?" Tannhauser asked.

"Yes," Jim said, looking around the hangar. The *Memphis* will fit in here, nicely.

"Then, I think we will stay, to keep the hearths warm," Tannhauser said.

"Here, take this." Ronan opened a pouch and handed Tannhauser a plate. "Keep it close, and we can keep in touch."

Tannhauser held it like Ronan had just handed him a viper.

"It's all right, my boy." Ronan laughed. "It won't bite."

***

Within the hour, they had the gear off-loaded and secured. The STU was in the air, soon after, in high spirits.

AI~Stu opened a private channel with Barcus, inside his personal HUD. "Barcus, I expected Em to be within range, by now. The Briggs-Udvar-Green (BUG) surveillance drones have a limited range, but the network they established was along this vector."

"Stu, is there any unusual traffic on the sat comms you are monitoring?" Barcus asked.

Po leaned on him, in the crowded bridge, and heard his question.

"Is anything wrong?" Po asked, quietly. She sensed his concern from his tone.

"I don't know," he said to Po. Then to AI~Stu, he said, "Stu, keep trying. What is our ETA?" He looked at the horizon ahead.

"Will do. Twenty-seven minutes at present speed," AI~Stu replied.

Six minutes later, he saw the smoke on the horizon.

"Hold on, everyone. Stu, faster." Barcus stood between the seats where Dr. Shaw and Kuss sat. Whitehall Abbey came into view.

It was a crater.

The STU circled the site. The entire thing had collapsed into the redoubt below, creating a giant crater. The surrounding forest had been blown flat, away from the blast area. The outer wall had been blown out, in almost every direction.

"I have located the Emergency Module directly to the east. It's buried in rubble. It's unresponsive," AI~Stu said, so all heard.

They were quiet now.

"No, no, no. Please, no," Po whispered through her fingers, which covered her mouth.

"Stu, scan for survivors. Active scans. Now," Barcus ordered.

"Survivors found directly west. Descending now. Please hold on."

The STU moved in fast, but smoothly. The inertial dampeners were excellent, even flying on foils.

They landed directly in front of the Bee Keeper's house. It was a low structure with thick, fieldstone walls. Half of the roof was missing, but the walls still stood.

Grady stood in front of the door, axe in hand, as if guarding the door.

Barcus was down on the ground, before the ramp opened all the way.

Grady offered no words as the door opened behind him.

A man named Smith stormed out. It was the right name for the man. Despite his age, he was built like a blacksmith. His face and arms were heavily scarred, more from the lash than the forge. One of his eyes was clouded over, ruined. His clothes were filthy and torn. His face was black, with dirt and with blood.

He struck Barcus in the face with a closed fist, rocking him back. He yelled, "I warned you. You knew they were in danger!"

Po launched herself at Smith. He barely noticed as she threw her arms around his neck and her legs around his waist. She hugged him, in relief, as much as to hold him back from Barcus.

Barcus recovered, quickly. "I know, you're right. This is all on me."

Grady put a hand on his shoulder. "Forget that, for now. We have some injured. Quickly."

He led them into the ruined house, and said, "There are seventeen alive. The ten that worked outside the walls are not bad. We only found seven alive in the rubble. They need your med bay."

Dr. Shaw and her team leaped into action, taking control, with the help of the team from the *Memphis*. Smith refused any treatment, until the others were seen.

Po asked Grady, when things began to settle, "Where is Ulric?"

"He was with Olias, this morning. I don't know where any of them are now," he replied.

Rand and Hume ran to the crater, to scan for additional survivors.

They reported back to Worthington, who had taken efficient control of the situation. Barcus sat on a low wall, after everyone was helped.

Grady walked up to Barcus. "They came, not long after first light. I was hunting to the north when I heard the shuttle flying overhead. I saw the cargo door was open as it flew. Something rolled out, and a white sail opened above a large cylinder. It came down on Whitehall Abbey, slowly. That's when I heard the guns, the one's Par has. That spider, it pounded it. Chunks flew off it, as it descended."

Grady played with his ears. "It exploded, before it reached the ground. I don't know how close it was to the ground, but it knocked me off my feet. And, I was a mile north."

"It came around, again. The second one made it to the ground. I saw debris flying. A cloud of dust rose. There were no guns as the third one fell, unopposed."

Rand's voice came over the personal HUD. "We have life signs. I think there are survivors, inside the Emergency Module. Barcus, get over here with the heavy maintenance suit. We need to dig!"

Barcus leaped to his feet and ran up the ramp. He climbed inside the suit with an ease that came from years of practice. He ran to Rand's signal. Ash was gone. It was just a suit now.

Rand was on top of a pile of fractured foamcrete, waving, as Barcus bounded up. He saw two legs from the EM in the broken debris.

Barcus spoke through the suit's PA system, "You need to move away, Rand. I need to work, fast."

He didn't wait to begin throwing off boulder-sized chunks.

He followed the legs to the body of the EM, as he shifted debris. He looked up and there was another suit digging on the other side. With no AI behind the control systems, Barcus had to find the suit-to-suit comms controls manually, like he had a lifetime ago.

"Comms check. Jimbo, is that you?" Barcus knew that Worthington was rated to drive the suit.

"Yeah, it's me, bro. Here, help me with this slab."

Together, they lifted off a giant section of the wall, revealing a large part of the module. It was upside down, unmoving, with no signs of any systems online.

Rand spoke over comms, "Barcus, Hume says that she is picking up two personal HUDs in there, as well as life signs."

"Jim, just cut that leg joint at the middle elbow. Then, we can slowly turn it over, endwise, and get access to the rear ramp with the manual system," Barcus said.

"Got it," Jim said, and as the joint snapped, the EM slid back a meter, causing a small avalanche of small debris.

Slowly, gently, they rolled the Emergency Module over. When it came to rest on its belly, Barcus rotated out a special tool on the suit's left forearm that he socketed into a depression to the left of the closed, rear ramp hatch. It spun and the hatch lowered.

Barcus saw that Rand, Cook, Hume, and Ibenez were right there, with two stretchers from the med bay in the STU. Barcus powered on the floodlights to illuminate the dark interior.

He was the first to see the unconscious bodies of Olias and Ulric. There was a puddle of blood on the ceiling above Ulric. He bled from his nose.

"They were both strapped in. We may be lucky," Jim said, over the comms.

"You think any of this is lucky!?" Barcus yelled. "This is anything but lucky, for Christ's sake!"

"Barcus, put a lid on that, right now," Worthington ordered, over a private channel. "We need to collect the wounded and evacuate this site. Fast."

The launched Hammerheads circled the site, rising as they did. "If I were the guy who did this, I would return for a final mop up, either another air strike or ground troops. We will have to leave this EM. We don't have room for it and the people."

"Barcus, what about the other ships?" Po asked, over an open channel via personal HUDs.

"What other ships?" Jim said.

"Stu, as soon as the wounded are loaded, take them to the quarry and transfer them to the *Sedna*. Make sure you take Cook and Elkin with you. They will need to heat up the reactors. I will send them access controls. Po, I want you on the PT-137. See if anyone else here can fly one of those, to go with you as a copilot."

AI~Stu broke in, "We are off."

"Close this up, Barcus. As soon as the STU is back, we can drag this in and move out. Do you have any other assets you haven't mentioned?" Worthington asked, in jest.

"Oh, shit!" Barcus cursed.

"Now what?" Worthington asked.

"The other redoubt. Stu, can you contact the other redoubt?" Barcus asked.

"No, sir, not as long as EmNet is down, there are no comms with them."

"Barcus, this is Hume. Po and Kuss just climbed in a modified, classic PT-137. They will be in the air, in two minutes. Where is this redoubt? Rand and I will go in the Hammerheads."

"Negative, Hume. They don't know you. Dammit," Barcus cursed.

Po spoke, "Barcus, you and I can go in the PT."

"No, I have to fly the *Sedna* out of here. After that last trip, we can't risk anyone else flying it."

"I'll go. I have Kuss with me. She already has the Salterkirk coordinates. We will meet you there, after," Po said.

"Returning. Dusting off, now," Stu said.

"Go," Barcus said to Po. "If you scratch my PT, there will be hell to pay."

"I will go with them," Hume said. "We can keep comms via the moon relay. In case…" She trailed off.

Thirty seconds later, the PT-137 sped right above Barcus, at high speed.

CHAPTER THIRTY-TWO

Because They were Free

"They reminded us of the value of freedom. The meaning of liberty. It was newly won for them, and we realized that we were frogs, slowly being boiled by the politics of Earth."

--Solstice 31 Incident Investigation Testimony Transcript: Captain James Worthington, senior surviving member of the Ventura's command crew.

As the STU settled directly behind the EM, Jimbo spoke to Barcus, on a private channel.

"Let me get this straight. You have three ships, one of which is capable of FTL and has an EMP cannon. You have two bases, both of which were manned and supplied. And, you have started a war with the locals?" Jimbo asked. "You are such a slacker."

"That's four bases, counting this one. I'm just getting started," Barcus said, as they dragged the EM up the ramp.

"You just hold it right there, man. What the hell do you think you're trying to do?" Jim let anger slip into his voice. "We are getting off this rock. We are not doing anything else." He dropped the leg of the EM as the ramp closed. "Do I have to remind you about the *Ventura*? Did you know it was no accident? Someone is sending ships here, knowing they will be destroyed."

Both of their suits opened at the same time. They climbed out of them as the shuttle took off.

"The pricks on this pitiful planet are not the ones we want. But, first we have to get out of here. How far is this quarry?" Jim asked.

"We will land in forty seconds," AI~Stu chimed in.

"Dammit, Barcus. You've had a replicator for months, and the log shows you've only produced some tool handles and hinges? Jesus, man.

You could have almost created a second replicator by now for spit's sake." Jim was mad now. "Enough with the screwing around with the locals."

"You were presumed dead. I was, as well. I just wanted to be left alone," Barcus said. "I never expected..."

Barcus faded off, as the ramp opened, again. Ronan and Grady were waiting there.

The wounded were there, on the ground, resting on blankets in the shade of Ulric's ship, the *Sedna*. Dr. Shaw was still going person-to-person.

"Status," Worthington said, on an open channel.

"Skies clear," Hume replied, "Proceeding at speed."

"ETA to the redoubt, twelve minutes," Kuss reported. "Girl is a crazy pilot."

They heard the smile in her voice.

"Reactors at thirty percent," Elkin reported, from the *Sedna*.

"This boat is sweet. We can takeoff in six minutes," Cook said.

"All the patients are stable and are ready to board. We need to carry these four," Dr. Shaw said.

"I need a drink," Ulric said.

"Skies are clear here, as well. I wish this were a gunship," Rand said, from the Hammerhead.

"Elkin, when you get a minute, see what it will take to spin up the EMP cannon," Barcus growled, not use to the new chain of command. Jimbo didn't seem to mind.

"I want to be clear of this site in seven minutes," Jim said. "I'm in the STU. Muir, Perry, and Weston are with me. Everyone is on an open channel. Keep the chatter down."

Barcus climbed to the bridge of the *Sedna*, to find Cook in the navigator's chair, not the command seat. He sat behind the command controls and buckled in.

"The status board is all green, but it's not true," Barcus started.

"I know. It's on a log loop bypass. Old-school hack. I'll watch the reactors and real systems. There is a status screen for the actual status, here." He flicked a piece of paper taped to the top of the console.

"We are up. Will hold, until you are aloft, Barcus," Jim said, from the STU.

Five minutes later, the convoy headed south and west, over unpopulated areas. Hume's Hammerhead sped ahead, at just under the speed of sound, as it patrolled.

Ronan walked onto the bridge of the *Sedna*, and said to Barcus, "Barcus, what will you do with these people?"

Just then, Po came on the comms. "Barcus, we're at the redoubt. Everything is fine. Landing now."

"They will be safe in East Isles. They could go back with me," Ronan said.

Barcus had forgotten about Ronan, "Thanks," Barcus said.

Grady and Ulric were there next. "Barcus, we need to talk," Ulric said.

"Can everyone just wait until we get there, for god's sake?" he barked.

They left him alone the rest of the flight to Salterkirk.

***

The Hammerhead and the STU were already parked inside the vast hangar when Barcus slowly drifted into the space. He set down, blowing the last of the dust out the mouth of the hangar.

Ronan had apparently called ahead to Tan'Vi. They were there with baskets of bread, fruit, and cheese, along with skins filled with wine and water.

Elkin was the last one out of the *Sedna*. She looked like he wanted to talk to Captain Worthington, but everyone was silent as they ate.

By now it was afternoon, and they had gone without sleep for far too long. Everyone was exhausted.

Barcus saw Smith eating. It was the first time, since Smith had delivered the punch. As if he sensed Barcus looking at him, Smith looked up. He had cleaned up, some. After a moment, he walked over to Barcus. He didn't speak.

"I know. It's my fault. All their blood is on me," Barcus said, flatly.

Without warning, Barcus was slapped in the face. And then, Smith was slapped, as well. It was Rose, one of the survivors. She was the oldest woman among them. She was furious.

"Don't you dare!" she spat.

"You will not take that from them. You didn't own them, own us. They knew the danger. Every single one of them. They knew that they slept every night with their heads on an anvil and you will NOT take that from them. Because they were FREE!"

She stared at them both.

"Or, were you lying about that? Were they not free to go at any time? Their lives were their own. Do you think they stayed for the gold? Their blood was their own. Every one of them. They would rather have died free than spend another day as a slave. You will not take that from them, or me."

"Or us," said the thin, dark haired woman, Lea, from the small crowd now behind them.

Barcus saw that a boy, named Ansel, was also one of them. Their eyes met. Even the boy acknowledged the point.

Smith looked from Rose to Lea and then to his feet, before looking up at Barcus, "I'm sorry, son."

"Smith, you punch like a child." Barcus smiled, then added, "Po says there are sixty-one people still safe at the redoubt."

Smith relaxed, a bit.

"Kuss says she will stay there a while and check the place out. Hume will fly back with Po and leave the Hammerhead for Kuss," Worthington added.

"They be back in couple hours," Kuss added, over comms. "You did good job, restoring this PT-137. We will need that kind of work on Renalo-class ship. Elkin kind of excited about it."

"Tell her to get over it. There's not enough fuel to get anywhere," Barcus said, as people drifted away, to find somewhere to rest.

"They are going over it, now," Jim added.

***

Barcus decided to wait for Po. He needed some time, alone. He sat at the edge of the hangar and looked out over the water. It faced north and never got any sun. The cliffs were about eighty meters above him. His cloak warmed him as he waited.

Barcus didn't hear Grady walk up. He sat next to Barcus, without a word.

"Before this went sideways, Ronan gave me some news about my wife," Grady said, as he watched the water.

"I remember. Her name is Wex. He said she was in the Citadel," Barcus said.

"I think she is like you, like Ulric. She knows things, sees things coming. Says some words that people don't say. Well, people that are not like you. She can do things." Grady blushed. "And, she never seems to age."

Another survivor?

"I'm going to get her. She's worse than dead, if she stays there. Ronan's going to help me," Grady said, to the lake.

"How can I help?" Barcus asked, already deciding.

"I don't know. Watch Ulric for me, until I get back. Saay and Kia didn't survive, and he is upset, more than he lets on. Ronan is arranging with Worthington for transportation back to the East Isles. I plan to go with them." Grady finally looked at him. "There is one other specific thing you can do. Give me one of those." He pointed to Barcus's handgun.

***

Po flew in, directly over Barcus, and landed on manual. Barcus waited on the hangar apron near the lake. She walked up, slowly, and climbed into his arms. He walked back the 150 meters to the *Sedna*, carrying her.

She spoke at his throat, "I'll miss the gatehouse. My life began there, in an overstuffed chair."

"I hear you're a pretty good pilot." He was serious.

Barcus liked it when Po allowed him to carry her. She was still so light, even though she was so much healthier than when they had first met, a lifetime ago.

The lights were on, in the *Sedna* and in the STU. The floods were even on, beneath the *Sedna*, as people inspected the severity of the hull damage. Perry held a data pad as Weston and Elkin called out items for him to note.

Dr. Shaw walked down the ramp from inside the STU. AI~Stu had kept Barcus informed of the activities over the last several hours. Dr. Shaw had not left the med bay, in all that time. She raised an eyebrow at his expression.

"How's Olias?" Barcus asked, as she approached.

She looked at Po with concern because Barcus carried her.

"He'll be okay, thanks to the five-point harnesses inside the EM they called Par. Both he and Ulric would be dead, otherwise." She looked at Po.

"I'd like to scan Po, if I may. And, the man called Smith has refused any assistance, thus far. I understand you have influence with these people."

Po lifted her head at this statement. "I'm alright. I will go and get Smith though."

She saw Smith, talking with Worthington and Tyrrell; so, Barcus let her down. She walked to get him.

"Why do you want to scan Po? She was with us, remember?" Barcus asked.

They watched her walk up to Smith, and without a word, take his arm and drag him back.

"These people are..." Shaw hesitated a long moment. "They have..."

She was interrupted by Po, returning with Smith. "He is ready for his scan now, Doctor. Come along, Smith."

"Don't fight it, Smith. It's of no use," Barcus said, as Po marched him to the ramp. "See if you can fix the eye, Doc. We need him."

Dr. Shaw stopped him. "Barcus, these people have genome modifications. That's what I'm trying to tell you." She paused, for emphasis. "Some of them have standard, control group markers inserted. I can't do a full analysis in a triage bay, but these people are definitely experiment subjects, modern experiments, not 200-year-old colony bullshit. But today, the state of the art stuff I have only read about."

"I don't understand," Barcus said, quietly.

"Is it true that she flew that personnel shuttle in here, on manual? Into here? On manual." She pointed to the floor, for emphasis. "Hume also says she can read, that you taught her. Did you ever try to teach an adult to read? Do you know what it's like? She even has a personal HUD version 8.6 implanted. Mine is only a v8.1." Shaw turned away, and said, "We will finish this conversation, later."

Barcus watched them head to the med bay and tried to think.

Just then, he wished he had AI~Em to talk with, to bounce ideas around. He looked over into the dark, where the Emergency Module sat silently. There was so much to do.

Em could wait.

CHAPTER THIRTY-THREE

Code Insertion Complete

"When Em came back online and began to help, we had no idea it had its own agenda. We had no idea, the system had been compromised. How could it? It was just an AI. So, we used it. Like any other advanced tool at our disposal."

--Solstice 31 Incident Investigation Testimony Transcript: Captain James Worthington, senior surviving member of the Ventura's command crew.

"Ulric, wake up. There isn't enough bourbon on this planet to protect you from me," Chen whispered, inside his head.

"No. Please. Don't." Ulric fell from his bed, inside the *Sedna*. "I thought you were dead. I was sure you were that cursed AI in the Emergency Module."

"You should be so lucky."

"Please stop. Was it you that killed them all? You knew it was going to happen. That's why you made me go with Olias."

He backed away on his hands and knees.

She stood there now. Terrible and beautiful.

"I didn't kill them. They were not my bombs." She smiled, an eerie smile. *"I never expected that fool Olias to run toward the bombs, guns blazing. Or, was that the AI's doing?"*

"What do you want?" Ulric got up, as if he decided he'd had enough.

"I want you to help Barcus and Olias. Come with me."

Ulric followed the ghost. It had to be a ghost. He knew that now. These people said it, he heard them. Chen was dead. Her body was even on this planet. He followed her, out of the *Sedna*, across the bay, to the still carcass of the Emergency Module. The aft hatch ramp sat open, like a gaping maw, and he watched Chen walk inside into the deeper dark.

Ulric lit a small penlight.

Chen sat in the front, right seat and gestured for him to sit in the front left.

"*Open that.*" She pointed to an access panel in the armrest. "*Flip up that small toggle cover and flip that switch. When you get a prompt in your personal HUD, say confirm.*"

A prompt opened that said, "Diagnostic Code Insertion Pre-Initiation Startup. Warning: This type of code insertion occurs below the security layer. Confirm or Deny."

Ulric said nothing.

"*Say it,*" she whispered, "*Or, I will bring back your little friends to play with.*" He heard Kia scream in the distance.

"Confirm," he said.

The panel lit up. Chen disappeared. A distant voice said, "*Now get out.*"

Ulric suddenly felt a pain behind his eyes and a shrill tone in his ears. He fled from the EM, as a small window opened on its main display, and data logs flew by on the screen. *Code insertion complete. Start-up sequence initiated.*

The shrill sounds stopped. His vision cleared. His nose began to bleed, again.

***

"Smith, don't scratch," Po said, as she batted his hand away from his eye. "Here. Drink this."

"What is it?" Smith asked Po. "I'm burning up. What did you and that witch do to me."

"Just drink it. You'll be more comfortable."

He downed the small tube of clear liquid in one go.

"There. Are you happy now?" he groused.

"Stop scratching." Po swatted his hand, again. "Rose, find him a bed, and if he doesn't stop bothering that eye, blindfold him."

Dr. Shaw came up, took Po by the elbow, and said, "Now, it's your turn to climb up here."

"I'm fine. Really," Po said, but she complied.

"Then, it will only take a minute," Shaw said, as she lowered Po onto the scanning table and the glass slid closed.

A bar of light slowly moved its way up her body. It paused in places, scanning again, slower.

It took a very long pause and then slowly scanned over her lower abdomen. It was slowly building a 3D representation of her tissues, Barcus knew, as he watched.

Dr. Shaw covered her mouth, as the internal scarring was detailed. She knew the kind of abuse, the kind of torture that would have caused it.

"Someone took a knife to her," she whispered, so only Barcus heard.

The scan continued, at a faster pace.

A small, articulated arm reached up and plucked a hair and pricked her on the back of her neck, taking a small sample, as the scan proceeded.

The genome report came up in a window.

"Do you see this? It's clearly tagged. And, not just a marker, this is serial numbered," Shaw pointed out.

As the scanner slowly finished going over her head, it revealed a new, fully integrated, personal Heads-Up Display System with full comms. A recommended treatment options report was presented. Barcus was surprised that she had an area of retina damage so severe. Part of one of her ears was missing, she had hip socket bone loss, as well as the trauma scarring in her uterus, ovaries, cervix and even her vaginal walls. That was just the priority list.

Without asking, or even saying a word, Dr. Shaw selected the nonemergency treatment. Nanites will be injected and execute repairs over time, not all at once. It will be much more comfortable and will be slower. It will also be easier to get used to. Her vision will repair slowly, so she will not even notice. There will be a low-grade fever, but not so noticeable, as the nanites did their work.

"Po, the med bay is going to administer the recommended treatment, now. The most noticeable thing will be that your hips should stop aching, in a few days. Please, don't move."

A small arm came down and gave her an injection in her neck.

The med bay window slid open.

Barcus stepped forward, about to lift her from the table, but Dr. Shaw stopped him. She said, "Po, can I speak to you, alone, please?"

Barcus got the hint and exited the small med bay, closing the door behind him.

"Po, have you ever been scanned like this before?" Shaw asked.

"No, miss."

"Have you ever had a child?" Shaw asked.

"No. I was always unable to," Po replied.

"Were you ever..." Po cut Shaw off, after her hesitation extended.

"Tortured? Yes, miss. More than once. Tore up bad. I lived." Po stopped her, before Shaw could speak again. "I'll say this, once. To you, and if you tell any of it to Barcus, or anyone, you will regret it. I know that injection was nanites. I know the magic they do. Thank you. Now, come close. Closer."

Po spread her eyelid open to show her a scar. "A Keeper named Volk had me bound tight and had my ears nailed to the steps of his balcony. He then had my eyelids sewn open just in time for the noonday sun. All it took was one stitch for each eyelid. Not much of a scar.

"Before I went blind, Smith was there and stood over me to block the sun, risking his own life. He dared not touch me or free me. But, what he did... is what saved my sight, and saved me from hating all men."

She placed her hand on her abdomen. "Keepers did this as well. Thankfully, they saw fit to beat me unconscious, first. I can't remember anything for the months that followed. It was a mercy.

"I think this was the worst of all." She held up her right arm and pointed to a small round scar. "Keeper Volk had my wrist nailed to the floor in his bedroom, while I was naked. The nail was long and had a huge head to keep me from pulling my wrist off the top. Right between the two bones, it was nailed. He was partial to nailing. He said he was going to take me three times a day, until I gave him a child. The fat bastard never could get it up. I spent six weeks nailed to that floor, in my own filth, unable to move. That's what did in my hip."

She stood and flexed her fingers, as if to show Shaw they still worked.

"Then, one day, he just ordered me to be taken out of his sight. He'd gotten sick of kicking me every morning, I guess." Po paused and looked Shaw right in the face. "Why am I telling you this?"

"Yes, why?" Shaw's voice cracked, as she tried not to cry.

"Because then, one day, that MAN..." She pointed in the direction Barcus had gone. "Walked out of fire and darkness to save my life. ME!" She pounded a fist to her own chest, as punctuation, as she said, fiercely, "He almost died to save ME! Why am I telling you this? Because I now know what I want."

She stepped closer. "I want, I need, your little machines to fix me. I want to eat and to grow strong. I want to study, to know the things I was always forbidden to know. And, I will come back and lay in your bay, again and again, until my body can't be made any better. Because one day, I might just have to save him." She pointed, after Barcus. "Because as good and as kind and as powerful as he is, he cannot make everything right. But, the foolish man will still try."

Dr. Shaw didn't try to speak. She just nodded.

"Did you know this med bay saved Barcus? It was horrible. Watching what it did to him," Po said, looking at the machines. "Everything that was ever done to me, everything I suffered. I never screamed in pain, until that day, watching it save him."

"Really?" Dr. Shaw opened a screen on the med bay console and scrolled until she selected an entry. "Oh, my God. You did this? But, how did you?"

"It was Em. I did what Em told me," Po said, finally, averting her eyes from the images in the file.

"Who is Em?" Dr. Shaw asked, still paging through brain imaging scans. She was engrossed.

"Em is the EM, out there. The broken black spider," Po said.

Then, she heard it.

"Po, are you there?" It was AI~Em's voice, in her head, as if Em had heard her. *"Help me."*

***

Po left the med bay as Dr. Shaw was still reading the file on Barcus's accident. She went down the ramp and to the right, to where the EM had been dragged. The rear hatch was open, and Po saw a few windows open on the display inside the Emergency Module.

"Em, you're awake. Are you all right?" Po asked, as she sat in the command seat in the near dark.

"I do not know yet, Po. What happened? I have gaps. Where are we? Where is Barcus? Is he okay? I'm blind."

"Yes, Barcus is fine. You are not so good," she said.

"I am running a full diagnostic. It will take another nine hours, or so. I can already tell I have physical damage. Who are these people?" AI~Em asked.

"Do you remember Hume?"

"Yes. I do remember."

"These others are with Hume, friends of Barcus."

"I'm sorry about Whitehall, Po. So sorry. I tried to stop them." AI~Em paused, a scratching sound came over the comms. "My AI has to reboot, Po." The display flashed. "More, later."

"I'll tell Barcus you are awake. And, Stu," Po said.

"Do not worry, Po. I will tell Stu, soon enough."

Po missed her ominous tone.

***

Po rounded the back of the *Sedna*, and found Barcus, with Rand and Ibenez, beneath the lights of the ship, removing the passenger door of a smaller, two seat Emergency Module.

"It's another EM?" she asked.

"Yes, it is. His name is Poole. Say hello to Po, Poole," Rand said, as the door came free from the damaged hinge.

Barcus was careful because there were still some ribbon cables attached that were now exposed. He set the door down, gently, as Rand began removing the hinge.

"Hello, Po. Do you know what EM stands for?" AI~Poole asked, in the classic teacher's voice so many EM AIs took.

"Yes. Emergency Module. Speaking of which, Barcus, Em is awake. She said she is running a full diagnostic and it will take nine hours," Po said.

"Ibenez, when Em is all the way up, I want to give her repairs priority. That EM is weaponized. At least three of its legs are broken. Who knows what else? The full diagnosis will tell us."

Worthington walked up. "Everyone has been scanned and treated. Come nightfall, I want Hume to take Ronan and these survivors back to East Isles in the STU. Ronan says he can send back a load of supplies."

"Grady will be going with them, as well," Barcus said, looking around for the man. "That reminds me." Barcus took Jim aside. He drew out his Glock and said, "Do you have any more of these?"

"Plasma, laser or projectile?"

He opened a nearby case. There were thirty various weapons inside.

CHAPTER THIRTY-FOUR

Em Awakes

"We should have suspected something was wrong, but we just wanted off that planet. We were so close, we could taste it. We never saw what was happening."

--Solstice 31 Incident Investigation Testimony Transcript: Captain James Worthington, senior surviving member of the Ventura's command crew.

Barcus stood by the edge of the lake, below the hangar, in the calm light of dawn. The stairs down were well-hidden, but easy to find from the outside landing pad, below the hangar opening.

Smith didn't see Po, tucked under Barcus's left arm, beneath his cloak, when he approached from above. The sun was about to crest in the east.

They both nodded to Smith, but said nothing, as the sun rose. They watched, together, as the sun began to shine on their faces.

Smith shaded his right eye. "Will it take me long to get used to my new eyesight?"

Barcus replied, "No. But, stop scratching it. Scratching it will only make it take longer to heal."

"Why are the colors so much brighter? It seems a different world, today."

"It *is* a different world," Po said, as she squeezed her arms around Barcus's waist.

"They are leaving today," Smith said.

"They?" Barcus asked, as he raised an eyebrow.

"Lea and I are going to stay here with Tan'Vi." Smith looked at the lake with both eyes. "Grady says they should take the people at the redoubt, as well. I agree. It's best for them, safer. I had a long talk with Ronan. He's willing. They will be treated well. There are no slaves in the East Isles."

"You and Lea?" Barcus asked.

"You need someone around here that can cook for these people. And, someone that knows which is the business end of a hammer."

"Ronan," Barcus said. "He is an odd one. I still cannot figure out, what's this to him?"

"He wanted only two things when he got here," Smith said. "To find Grady for his wife, Wex, and to find his precious timber. He can't build his new ships without masts."

"He risked his life to do a favor for an old tracker's wife?" Barcus asked.

"I have heard of Wex," Smith said, as they ascended the stairs. "You know the flutes that Grady carves? He carves them for her. She plays. Plays for the elite in Exeter, the city below the Citadel. She is more than that, I think…"

They cleared the top of the apron into the hangar and saw that the work lights were on beneath the *Sedna*. People already moved about.

"Barcus, I can see…something," Po said, hesitantly.

Barcus looked and noticed that Worthington had managed to set up a conference table and chairs in the hangar, between the *Sedna* and the STU. He drank hot tea as he looked at a fixed HUD projection that was in front of the table, about three meters tall and seven meters wide. From that far away, he saw that it was a detailed damage assessment of the *Sedna* and her systems.

Elkin was there with Ibenez, pointing and gesturing, excitedly.

"You can see the image of the ship he is pointing to," Barcus said, a statement, not a question, as they approached the table. "When did you get the personal HUD implant?"

"I don't know," Po replied, distracted, and mesmerized, by the display she saw.

"Barcus!" Elkin saw him and she waved him over, almost frantically. "Did you do these repairs?"

There was a long punch list that had completed items displayed in green, with corresponding green areas indicated on the ship.

"I did some, not all. Ulric's chief engineer did most." Barcus quickly scrolled through, and tagged, the ones he had done already. "They don't matter, though. The reactor cores are so low on fuel we couldn't get anywhere. So, why bother fixing the hull breaches and structural integrity?"

"It could make it to the moon, several times," Elkin said, her eyes bright. "The *Memphis* has two cores and lots of fuel."

"These are Phoenix Level 4 fast breeder reactors. The *Memphis* has the new dark matter cold reactors. The fuel is incompatible. But, you know that," Barcus said.

"Swap out both entire reactors," Elkin said. "Right now, all they are doing is powering the moon base."

"That still will not work, for propulsion. These reactors are integrated with the faster-than-light engines on this kind of ship." Barcus rotated and zoomed the display to one of the reactors. "It uses the depleted heavy metals that are the reactor's by-product as the material it accelerates through the FTL drives, here and here. It's the only reason you can spin these up so hot and get FTL. It has something constructive to do with the molecular output besides kill everyone. Once you approach light speed and the mass of the material being accelerated through the engines grow to infinity, and the FTL transition happens."

He zoomed in further and began a simulation of the deadly heavy metal protons and neutrons, splitting in controlled explosions, with all the released energy and matter being controlled, precisely.

"These kinds of reactors do more than generate power. It's why they consume so much fuel," Barcus said.

Elkin was crestfallen. She knew nothing about these kind of FTL drives. Just reactors.

"What kind of fuel?" Worthington asked.

"Various mixtures of plutonium-239 and uranium-235. The Renalo-class ships were made to handle a wide variety. Even shitty fuel. But, not dark matter." Elkin knew that, off the top of her head.

Worthington brought up another window as Barcus watched. It was the sensor scans from Hume's pass through the security net.

"This is the dead weapons platform." Jimbo brought up visual images of the small satellite. "It indicates the presence of plutonium and uranium. It's shielded, but it's there."

Elkin was getting excited again. "The nukes. We could harvest the dead nukes."

"The EMP cannon on this ship rendered them safe enough to remove?" Worthington asked.

"Look here." Barcus paused the image captured on a still frame, then he zoomed in. "These look like standard launch tube modules. Each one of the tube clusters is ten by ten, holding ninety-nine missiles and a control block. They are designed to be easy to swap out, once used. You can see these are intact."

"There are sixteen of those on each side," Worthington said. "How many of these sats are there?"

"Thirty-two, sir," Ibenez replied.

"That means there are over 50,000 of these nukes, pointing down at the planet, as well as out into space." Worthington was incredulous. "We need to get off this rock."

***

Over the next hour, they planned how it could be done. With only one airtight, rigid maintenance suit, they could not figure out how to manage the task. The regular pressure suits would help, but they would end up as spectators.

"I could help." AI~Em's avatar walked into the conference area. It was obvious everyone saw her.

"Take me up inside the STU, and I will drive the second suit. Barcus can drive his."

"Everyone, this is Em, the advanced AI from Chen's Emergency Module. She has a lot of upgrades," Barcus said. "It's good to have you back."

AI~Em walked to the conference display and, with a gesture, wiped everything to the side, except the photo of the launch modules. Suddenly, a perfectly rendered wire diagram of the satellite appeared.

"Based on the verbose sensor data, we are looking at this."

She ran a simulation. The STU slowly approached the satellite with the cargo bay ramp open. It stopped about thirty meters from the satellite itself. The Emergency Module gently launched from the cargo hold, to lightly catch the satellite in an eight-point grasp. The EM's rear ramp opened and the two black, faceless suits drifted out on tethers. One moved to the front of the unit and one to the back. Tools deployed from the forearms of the suits and one of the modules was detached and attached to cables. A person in a pressure suit provided direct guidance as the unit came closer, until it was settled inside the EM. After everyone was onboard, the EM gently launched back to the shuttle and into the bay.

"I could show you a simulation where the STU and I do it all. Everyone could remain safe, here. We will go much slower." AI~Em added, "I prefer you come along. Like Chen always used to say. Shit happens."

"Em, how many repairs will you require before we can do this?" Barcus asked.

"I made a list." AI~Em popped the list up. "I took the initiative and made a recommended fabrication schedule."

"Why are these welders and cutting tools on the top of the priority list?" Worthington asked.

"I also took the liberty to create a task list, to match it with the skills matrix I found, and to create a series of task lists for each of your crew," AI~Em said.

"You scheduled rotating, overlapping, sleep schedules?" Ibenez sounded amused. "That is a lot of sleep."

"This schedule allows an all-hands briefing over lunch, daily," AI~Em said. "If you want off this rock quickly, we need you to be rested and sharp."

"This chart says FTL departure is in 15.45 days," Hume spoke up.

"Why are we installing these guns in the PT-137 and the Hammerheads?" Worthington asked.

"Air support. Because shit happens," AI~Em said, casually.

A vid played of a large shuttle sliding a massive bomb out of the cargo ramp. Then, another and another. The scene froze, just before the first bomb touched down just beyond the willow tree. Six children were looking up at it, not knowing what was about to happen.

"Any questions?" she asked.

"I have built twenty-four hours into the schedule for you to review and discuss the plan with your command staff, sir," she said, directly to Worthington.

"I don't need twenty-four hours. Barcus, what say you?" Worthington turned to him.

Barcus merely nodded. He trusted AI~Em.

"Do it," Jim said to AI~Em.

"I am sending integrated task lists to everyone, sir. With timetables and dependencies," AI~Em said. "One more thing, sir."

"What is it, Em?" Jim said.

"To make communications easier, I will maintain open channels with everyone, full time. Please call me, Em. I will attend the all-hands meeting, daily. I want you to meet Stu." Another avatar appeared of a young man dressed as a tracker. "He is an advanced AI. He now owns the planetary comms network, which is now being monitored. He can tell you the location of every shuttle on this planet. And, every unshielded plate. He will give you an overview at today's all-hands," AI~Em said.

Jim laughed. "Is that it?"

"Actually, no," AI~Em said, sweeping her arm around. "This is Ash. He has a task list, as well."

The big black suit bowed, before he spoke.

"I will be working around the clock. As always," Ash said, in a deep voice.

"This is Pardosa." The big, black spider limped around the front of AI~Stu, one arm still dangling, useless. "All of us can be addressed, independently."

"And, we will need a name designation for this one," AI~Em said, as the other damaged suit descended the cargo ramp on the *Sedna*.

Barcus laughed as it turned toward them. Richard Cook had spray painted a huge, happy face eye dots and a smile on its torso, so they could tell them apart.

Jim smiled and shook his head.

Barcus spoke, "Po, pick a name."

She walked up to the suit and it knelt before Po. It was still taller than her. She looked tiny before this thing. She still had to reach up to place her hand between its painted eyes.

"His name is Peace," Po said.

"Thank you, Po. You honor me." It had the voice of an old man, completely different than the other voices. It stood. "If you will excuse me, sir. We have much to do."

Rand looked at Barcus and said, shaking her head, "Chen was really something."

CHAPTER THIRTY-FIVE

The Plan

"The AI was running us all. None suspected. We just puppets."
--Solstice 31 Incident Investigation Testimony Transcript: Ludmilla Kuss PhD, a member of the Ventura's advanced engineer team. NOTE: Dr. Kuss somehow escaped custody the day after her testimony and remains sought for additional questioning.

"Will you look at the detail of these punch lists?" Ibenez said. Twenty-four of them were displayed in the conference area. "There are even lists for 'off-line personnel', meaning people without HUDs. Jesus, I've never seen anything like this."

"We had this kind of compartmented tasking all the time on the *Ventura*, run by master AIs on the ship," Barcus said. "This is simple compared to tasking 2,000 people."

Worthington shook his head, smiling and pointing. "There are even 'command recommendations' for me. I am currently way ahead of my original schedule because I'm, apparently, so damn decisive."

"Dependencies have shifted left. We're already yellow on some tasking, now." Hume pointed. "The Fabricator in the shuttle is already making the components for the plasma torches and laser cutters."

"We have work to do, people, by noon. See you back here, then," Worthington said, as they spread out. "You should be resting it says, Barcus. When was the last time you slept?"

"Long ago," he replied, as Po dragged him by the hand.

"Enjoy. Today, it's strong tea and intel reports for me," Worthington said, as he looked at a command screen in his HUD that no one else could see.

"Let's go. Em has even assigned a bed," Po said.

As they moved to the *Sedna*, Barcus saw Olias, sitting inside the broken spider, performing a task at AI~Par's instruction. "He will be fine, Barcus. He has slept at least."

"Go. Rest. Please," came up in Barcus's HUD. *"Four hours. I will wake you."*

His HUD went quiet then. On the *Sedna*, they found beds in the cool, dark, bunk room. Sleep came faster than he expected with, Po in his arms.

***

"Ulric. Wake up," Chen whispered, into his mind. *"Wake up, or I will kill everyone, but you. Today. Before your eyes."*

"I'm awake," Ulric said, out loud.

"Today, you will go to Exeter with Grady. He has followed you for so many years, but today you will follow him." The whisper always seemed to be behind him, no matter which way he turned. *"And, you will take Olias."*

"Why the boy?" he asked.

"Are you questioning me? Again."

"No. I was just wondering what I will tell Barcus."

"He will go with you to the East Isles. To be safe." The whisper was right at his ear, now. He felt her breath. *"After he is there, I will tell you what to do. You have your pitiful tasks. You have been charged with the safety of these poor refugees."*

Her quiet laugh made his skin crawl.

Ulric rubbed his face, trying to wake up. He sat up. "Tasks? What tasks?"

"Grady will go to Exeter. You will not be able to stop him. Help him. But, you must take Olias as well. Take him, or he is mine." Ulric heard the voice, from across the room, now.

He put his bare feet on the floor and kicked an empty bottle. He thought briefly about how Saay use to always make sure they were gone by morning.

"Yes, there will be more bed wenches for you in the East Isles. And Exeter."

"What will Ronan say?" Ulric worried.

"It will all be his idea."

***

Po was already awake, when the chime went off inside Barcus's head. She was up, on one elbow, watching him. They were in the last row of bunks, on the second level of the forward section of the *Sedna*. She was on the side by the wall. She was naked.

"The schedule says we have twenty-two minutes to shower and dress, before the midday briefing," Po said. "Apparently, they have replenished the water supplies on this ship already. I like Em's lists so far."

Barcus sat up. His clothes were not where he left them on the next bunk. His belt, pouches, gun and other personal items were there. There was a fresh, dark blue flight suit for him, and a black one for Po. There were even two towels. Po smiled, as she absently scratched her healing wrist.

She climbed out of bed, over him. She grabbed a towel and wrapped it around her small frame. She noticed the despair in his face. She knew he was thinking of the people that died at the Abbey. She lifted his towel and said, "I have never had a real shower before. I've heard of them, but never took one. Will you show me?"

She tossed the towel at him and, somehow, knew where to go.

When Barcus reached her in the shower cubicle, he was surprised how roomy it was. They were usually tight on space ships. Po stared at the control panel, not knowing what to do. He tapped the controls and set the temp to 102°F. Multiple, luxury showerheads activated as he unbraided Po's hair. There were dispensers, for shampoos and for body soaps that, somehow, still worked.

He washed her hair. She washed his body.

Their shower took longer than Barcus planned.

They were late to the midday briefing.

***

Po wore the black, one-piece flight suit that could only have originally belonged to Hume. She was self-conscious. Barcus saw it. She had never worn pants before, she had told him that. He joked, again, about the anvil. But, his heart was not in it.

He thought about all the dead, again. On the *Ventura* and at the Abbey.

The HUD display was even bigger, now.

"Inventory is now complete. We're in far better shape than we initially thought," Worthington said. "Raw materials to feed the fabricator are plentiful in the shop, in the form of the old, milling machines in there. We can cut those up, easily. Ash and Peace have already begun."

"Teams have been created for the major tasks," Jim continued. "At nightfall, Ulric, Grady and Hume will take Ronan and the remaining survivors back to the East Isles. Ronan is speaking to them now, in the cottage, while AI~Stu is en route, he will continue the manufacture of new joints for Par's legs. In the meantime, a few things have come up that we need to discuss."

Tyrrell stood at this point. "We've been analyzing the comms traffic, to see if we can use that network for our purposes. Stu highlighted some communications of note. These are plate-to-plate comms, within the Citadel, between its technical staff. All the plates are configured by default to communicate via the sats."

Em played the intercepted transmission. There were two men. One was in a data center control room, and the other was outside, by a sat uplink antenna array. Both views were displayed.

> The man outside spoke. "Mason, if we bypass these encrypted units here, the sat side won't handshake. It's a nonstarter. You'd have to remove them from both ends. Plus, I'm fairly sure there are some anti-tamper devices here, as well. Bad ones."
>
> Mason said, "What if we did a cold restart to initial factory settings on all thirty-two sats? We will never crack the control code password."
>
> "Mason, a cold start? How do you know it won't just launch everything, if we do that? Do you know if the default password would be the same on every unit?"
>
> "Close it up, man. Come back down. We won't solve it, by you sitting there, wishing."
>
> "Thanks, Mason. The view is nice, but it's scary up here."

The vid paused.

AI~Em spoke after that. "It appears that this is the chief systems engineer at the Citadel. His name is Mason. He is trying to figure out how to regain control of the defense platforms."

"Are you saying these dumb-asses can't control their own nukes?" Richard Cook asked.

"That is how it appears. Somehow, they have been deprived of control," AI~Em stated. "It looks like they cannot simply nuke us from orbit. The outward facing defense grid is active, but not the inner. This is confirmed by the fact that there is high altitude traffic, often."

"Does this change anything?" Worthington asked.

"It confirms that we will be able to harvest the missiles with less risk. Like a self-destruct signal," AI~Em said.

"I believe it also tells us that they are less competent than they want the world to believe," AI~Stu said, as his avatar stepped forward. "They use the comms channels for almost nothing of note. The High Keeper has never used the comms network. Ronan checks in twice, daily. He doesn't know he's being monitored, as far as I can tell. He has his own segregated, virtual, private network, in addition to the global comms network. He has his own data center and staff."

"There is one more thing." AI~Stu gestured to the paused videos. They played, again.

> *"Thanks, Mason. The view is nice, but it's scary up here."* The man closed the panel and stood. *"Got any plans for the weekend?"*
>
> Mason replied, casually, *"Yes. I'm doing a favor for Wex. I'm meeting her at the Flask and Anvil, at midnight, on Saturday."*

"What?" Grady said. He had been standing off to the side. "What did he say?" He held a plate.

"Yes, Grady. We know where this man will be, in five days, at midnight," AI~Em said. "The Flask and Anvil in Exeter." AI~Em looked at Barcus now. "The High Keeper's chief tech, the man with global admin control on all the High Keeper's systems. I recommend we use him."

"Use him how, and to what end?" Jim was very curious.

"I will use surveillance BUGs to monitor him and to obtain access to the systems, by simply watching him type. Once in, we will know how best to distract, to cripple or to destroy the systems. We will basically own this planet." She looked at Grady. "We may also be able to extract Grady's wife at the same time, as an added benefit. It may be a good diversion."

"Ronan has an estate, here, in Exeter." AI~Em brought up a map of the large city that indicated Ronan's considerable holdings there. "Here is the Flask and Anvil. This estate borders the mountain foothills where this forest could provide cover." AI~Em indicated the area. "Here is the Citadel, on the opposite end of the valley, on the top of this peak. It can only be accessed by this one road along this ridge. Or, by air."

"How can you be sure Ronan will support any of this?" Rand asked.

"Ronan has his own agenda," AI~Em said. "As long as our purposes are compatible, he will do what he can."

"What is his agenda?" Rand followed up with.

"Ronan simply wants the High Keeper to leave him alone," AI~Em replied. "It has been his only agenda, apparently, for decades. He doesn't oppose the High Keeper in anything, as long as he is left alone."

"This woman named Wex seems to have influence with Ronan. Mason, the High Keeper's lead engineer, also appears to owe some kind of allegiance to her." AI~Em looked at Po. "This is unusual for this world. I do not believe she is a native."

Murmurs drifted through the room.

"How will this impact the schedule?" Elkin asked.

AI~Stu replied, "We were already planning on rolling the fabricator out of the shuttle, to facilitate the creation of the larger hull plates on the *Sedna*. Med bay's schedule is winding down. So, stealth transport to the East Isles should be quick, quiet and easy. We can even take the newly armed PT-137 that's in the hold, if we change the schedule, here, and here."

"All of this only moves the schedule to the right about thirty hours," AI~Em said. "But, it also presumes we can retrieve the nuclear missiles for fuel within four days."

There was a long pause, as everyone studied the proposed plan. Worthington was in the center and turned around.

"Here is what we will do," he said, decisively. "We need to get the fabricator rolled out of the shuttle, by nightfall. Hume and I will have a talk with Ronan. Hume and Stu will take Ronan and the survivors to the East Isles." Cascading assignments appeared as he spoke. "We will get access to the High Keeper's systems, and when we're ready to get off this rock, maybe we'll use that access to create a little chaos, so we can slide out of here, quietly." He turned to look at the schedule. "Poole will monitor the schedule while Par, Ash, Peace and Em go with Barcus, to retrieve the missile pod."

Worthington turned to the group. "Anything else?"

Barcus spoke, "Par will be repaired, ahead of schedule. Rand has been helping me."

"Make sure you get enough rest, Barcus," AI~Em said.

Everyone laughed. AI~Em's tone was a perfect nag.

CHAPTER THIRTY-SIX

The East Isles

"Wex...We just didn't know who she was. What she was. Or, that another just like her, was on the moon, with Hagan."

--Solstice 31 Incident Investigation Testimony Transcript: Lieutenant Valerie Hume, the security chief on the Memphis.

<<<>>>

Everyone moved to their assigned tasks and schedules. Barcus found that he was working with Em, Po and Olias all afternoon, replacing the broken leg joints on Par.

Olias stood by the cart full of tools, and Po held the pins Barcus had pulled from the first multi-axis joint they were replacing. She stretched upward. The form-fitting flight suit drew his attention.

"Barcus, why can I see Em now? I don't even need a plate, anymore. I just...see things," she said.

"Yeah. Me too," Olias added, in Common Tongue. "Not that I mind. She translates everything into Common Tongue for me, so I can understand. I'm glad she's back."

"I can answer that, Barcus," AI~Em said. She seemed to be standing with them, leaning on the next leg over. "While they were injured, I implanted the personal HUD systems into the two of them." She sounded like she was apologizing to them all. "I was afraid. It was just easier to do than to explain. I had to do everything I could think of that would increase the probability of their survival. The med bay had the replacement HUD nanites. A plate could be lost or broken. I was unsure about their recovery. I needed help. Without the nanites, they would have died."

That was what Barcus heard.

Po and Olias heard her say something else, something different. "I can answer that, Barcus," AI~Em said. She seemed to be standing with them, leaning on the next leg over.

Po heard, "While you were injured, and so close to death, the magic contained within your soul began to drift away." She sounded like she was proud of them. "Your soul recognized Po, and Olias. It clung to you both, and stayed. Their strength added to yours. They saved you, even though we were all afraid."

***

Olias heard, "While you were injured, and so close to death, the magic contained within your soul began to drift away." AI~Em sounded fierce and proud of Olias. "If it wasn't for the brave actions of your apprentice here, you may have died. He saved you, and through you, he saved Po. She was beside herself with grief. He will make a powerful Keeper one day."

***

Barcus put the tools down on the cart, and rested a hand on each of their shoulders, before speaking. "Thank you for everything you've done for me."

"You can stop right there, Barcus," Po began. "We have too much work to do for you to start being kind to me. You know that's the only thing that'll make me cry, so please don't." She smiled, as she said this.

Olias beamed at his thanks.

She handed him the tool and pointed. The Emergency Module had its physical repairs done ahead of schedule.

***

Hume and Worthington found Ronan, having his own meeting with the survivors from the Abbey. When Jim saw them last, they seemed beaten and depressed. Now, he heard their laughter, before he even reached the cottage.

Hume and Worthington entered, through the stairs, into the pantry and then the kitchen where they were gathered. Some were cooking, some were simply standing where they could. In the center of it all was Ronan, telling a story, in Common Tongue, that neither Worthington nor Hume could really understand. It made some of the women blush. Others covered their mouths, to hide smiles, or to suppress laughs. His tone sounded as if it was a well-practiced story, of high humor and self-deprecation. When the punch line was delivered, Hume and Worthington laughed with the rest. Ronan made faces, as if their laughter was unexpected, making them laugh even more.

Even Smith laughed. Shaking his head, he laughed. When he scratched his eye, Rose slapped his hand away. That sent the group into a renewed bout of laughter, to the point of tears.

Ronan stole a fresh biscuit, as he stood and gestured for Worthington and Hume to come with him to the front.

Ronan spoke, as he added more wood to the fire in the large hearth. "These people have had a hard life. They are strong. They will do well in the East Isles. Barcus made quite an impression on them."

"Barcus is a good man," Jim stated.

"That may be true. But, I believe the people at the redoubt may also still be in danger," Ronan said, lowering his voice. "We must evacuate them, as well. And, soon."

"I agree. We will contact them and tell them to be ready. Kuss is there with them," Worthington said.

"Captain." It was AI~Em in his HUD. *"If Stu stops en route, to pick up people on the way, we can get them all in one trip, and still be back here by dawn."*

Worthington silently agreed.

"I will notify Kuss, now. And Jim, let Barcus and Po take them."

Worthington raised an eyebrow at AI~Em for using his first name, but continued, "As soon as everyone has eaten and packed, Barcus will take them."

***

Barcus, Po and Olias had dinner with the Abbey survivors that night. Barcus knew it was probably the last time he would see any of them. He even convinced Smith and Rose to go with them. They crowded on the STU's flight deck, at Po's request, as she sat in the front, right seat with Barcus in the front left.

Suddenly, the dome of the interior seemed to fade away, as it shifted to the exterior display. It looked like they stood on a platform with a 360° view, as they drifted, silently, toward the mouth of the hangar. They saw Worthington's crew, waving to them in the floodlights. The people clung to one another, afraid they may fall off. They slid out of the hangar, over the water, and moved fast to the east; at first, low over the water, then they rose, quickly.

The group gasped and held each other as they increased their altitude. Barcus knew that the display was enhanced, because it was a cloudy night.

They moved quickly, under propulsion. They would be at the redoubt in less than forty minutes.

Ronan knelt on one knee between Po and Barcus. "I don't suppose, when you head back to Earth, that you could let me hold onto this excellent craft for you, until you return?"

He smiled.

"Sorry, Ronan. The STU has to come with us. We need him," Barcus said.

"Yes, I know. I have already discussed it with your captain. We have come to an agreement. A treaty of sorts. I will protect your interests, equities and assets, when you leave here," he said, in good cheer.

"My assets?" Barcus asked.

"Your lands, your people. You now possess everything north of the gorge. It may be cold and empty, but it's vast. I will happily manage it, for you. And, this outpost, as well," Ronan said.

"What's in it for you?" Barcus asked, curious.

"Honestly? Timber. I need masts for my ships," Ronan replied. Suddenly, sadness slipped over his face. "And, I need the High Keeper to pay attention, elsewhere."

**

Po brought up a tactical map and as they approached the redoubt,

Kuss hailed them. "Everyone ready to board, my Lord." She addressed him in his HUD. "I heard many stories of you, Barcus. I may take you to my bed yet. If you lucky."

Po was amused by Kuss's broken English.

She laughed. So, did Barcus. Po just pounded his chest with a surprise fist.

They assembled on that flat area, just above the redoubt. As the ramp lowered to the cargo bay, they walked slowly to the shuttle. It was a tearful reunion. They barely felt the takeoff as the STU smoothly moved to the sky. Kuss joined Barcus, Po, and Ronan on the bridge.

"Well, Barcus. Your redoubt base properly shut down." Kuss sat slowly, as if she was exhausted. "Computers dead. But not needed, really. Old Colony redoubts made so they not need them." She reclined in the last row. "Need nap. How long flight?"

Barcus replied, "We will be in the East Isles in about three hours. As soon as we are loaded with the supplies Ronan is so graciously donating, we will be off again. Back to the hangar by dawn."

"Wake me when close," she said, as she reclined and folded her arm over her eyes.

AI~Stu lowered the lights without being asked. The night sky cleared the farther east they went.

"Captain Worthington says you will be taking a quick trip, visiting Exeter in a few days, to get Wex," Ronan said, in a soft voice. "I will send word to my estate there. I cannot tell you in strong enough terms that you must be careful. I'll take you in my shuttle. It'll be safer. I'll give you some of my personal house liveries. This will help you move about unmolested. But, tread easy. Be patient."

"Who is this Wex?" Barcus asked.

Ronan hesitated, as if the question was far more involved. "She is a musician. And saying that, actually says nothing about her," Ronan said. "She plays the black flute. Grady made that flute and gave it to her as a gift. Long ago. They say, it won her heart. But, I think it's she that has won ours. Her music is raw magic. She can make a High Tracker weep like a little girl with that flute."

Barcus looked at Po. They had a difficult time seeing Grady with any woman.

"I was there when she played for the High Keeper, for the first time," Ronan continued. "It was during, yet another, High Council feast. I hate those feasts. She played, intended to be typical background music."

Ronan got lost, remembering.

"No one realized that all conversation, all eating, all drinking had stopped. Everyone listened to her play." He saw it in his mind's eye. "She was in a full habit, just like most women in Exeter. Her hood was up, her face in shadows, as was proper."

"What happened?" Po asked.

"The High Keeper had not seemed to notice or to care about anything in decades, even a century. He was moved by it. She has resided at the Citadel, ever since," Ronan stated. "Wex is the most intelligent, talented, extraordinary woman I have ever met."

"Grady made her that flute?" Barcus asked, absently.

"She is more than that flute. I think she is a survivor, like you. Because, like you, she wears the world differently." Ronan's voice faded.

***

They landed in East Isles just before midnight. Barcus, Po, and Olias said farewell to all of them. Olias would not stay. He could not be persuaded, in any way. He, eventually, retreated to the shuttle's bridge, to avoid another person asking.

Barcus never even considered asking Po to stay. This, silently, made her happy. Barcus knew this, inside.

Before they arrived, the details had been sorted out for their brief visit to Exeter. It will be simple. Ronan will, quietly, find out what he could regarding Wex, and let them know, in a few days.

Smith was the last one to say good-bye.

"I can finally see you as you need to be seen," Smith said to Po.

She knew he was not talking about his eye. She stood before him in a black flight suit.

"I love you, Po." Smith said the words he had never said before, as he hugged her. "Be all that you are. But, be safe. Live."

Her face was wet with tears when he let her go.

"You'll need to be, if you stay with this one." Smith looked at Barcus.

Barcus held his hand out, for Smith to shake. He would not discover, until later, that it was a Keeper's acknowledgment of an equal. Smith took it and hugged Barcus, with their clasped hands between them.

"Take care, Smith," Barcus said.

"Just remember, son. On Baytirus, beware of the broken cage. Because you may not know if you are on the inside, or out," Smith said, as if he quoted a famous farewell.

Barcus only realized, later, it was a quote, and its true meaning.

CHAPTER THIRTY-SEVEN

Questions

"The nukes were from the defense grid. Javelins. We should have kept closer count. We were all just too damn busy. Em kept us that way."

--Solstice 31 Incident Investigation Testimony Transcript: Lieutenant Valerie Hume, the security chief on the Memphis.

Barcus, Po, and Kuss slept in the reclined command seats on the way back. As the world slid silently beneath them, Em's final repairs were finished and tested.

They arrived before dawn and the cargo they carried was quickly unloaded. It was all on uniform pallets in closed crates and had to be opened and inventoried.

Most of it was food—literally, tons of food of all kinds. Some were dried, some were preserved in glass jars, and others were grains in sacks. As it was inventoried, it was moved to cold storage in the *Sedna,* for their long trip home.

There was a wide variety of clothes in there, as well. There were tunics, pants, cloaks, tabards, belts, pouches and even boots. It was very high quality. There were also clothes that were, apparently, what women were expected to wear in Exeter, in public.

Worthington commented, "These look like burkas or nun habits."

"Things are very different for women in Exeter. Much more strict," Po said. "They say, all women there sleep with their heads on an anvil."

"I, for one, cannot wait to get off this damn planet," Karen Beary said. "I have been a navigator on a starship for almost twenty years. You will never see me in one of those."

"I think it's kind of hot, Karen," kidded Cook. "We'll bring these with us on the way back. It will be a long trip, if you know what I'm saying." He winked at her.

"Keep dreaming, Cook." She laughed.

Worthington laughed and interrupted them. "You slackers better be on schedule for the noon briefing. Now, get back to work." He pointed at Barcus. "Rack time." He turned to the virtual big board. "If we stay on schedule, you're going for a fuel run, this afternoon." As expected, the plutonium in the old reactors in the hangar base were depleted.

Barcus knew that the retrieval of the nuclear missiles were scheduled for this afternoon. Everything else in the plan depended on getting the plutonium for the *Sedna*. He knew Po was worried for him. The line between her brows was back, and deeper than ever.

As they lay down in their bunk, the makeshift curtain closed behind Barcus. It was only a heavy blanket, tucked under the mattress above. But, it gave them darkness to sleep.

As his eyes adjusted, he saw she was wide awake.

"It will be okay, Po," Barcus whispered, in reassuring tones.

"You're going to be walking, in the sky," Po said. "You'll be stealing 100 weapons. Each of them could destroy a whole city." She slid on top of him, straddling him, her nose near to his. "From. The. Sky."

"Yes," he replied. His hands explored the skin of her back.

"I told you, once, that you could leave whenever you wanted," Barcus said. "I want to ask you something, Po."

"Ask."

"Will you come with me to Earth?" Barcus asked. "If you don't want to go. Then, neither do I."

"You would give up Earth for me?" she whispered.

"Yes. The Earth. The whole universe, if I had to," he said. "I'd rather sleep with you, here, on a pile of dung, than to sleep without you, on Earth, in a bed of silk." He kissed her, deeply, then.

"Yes. I will go with you. To Earth. To Exeter. To Hell, wherever that place is that everyone talks about."

She kissed him. She wanted him.

She gasped when he slid inside her. She climaxed just a few minutes later. She gushed in a flood. It had never felt so good.

Somehow, they managed to stay quiet. They fell asleep, still tangled together.

***

AI~Em woke them both with an insistent chime. They got up and took a quick shower, not wanting to be late again, today. They were not the first ones to the conference table because there was an enormous spread of food out for them.

There were breads, cheese, stew, baked ham, and chicken. There was a large variety of vegetables both cooked and raw. There was steaming rice and potatoes and pitchers of gravy. There was even a variety of pies—meat pies and fruit pies.

Barcus realized he was starving. Tan'Vi made sure everyone had drinks and full plates.

There were additional tables set up under the lights that held a wide selection of items. Most were projects and tasks that were either completed or simply paused for the midday status. Then, his eye fell on one particular table.

He saw the books, first.

They were the books from the gatehouse. There was also the Telis Raptor tail knife that Grady had fashioned. It even had a sheath. Below that table were five chests of various kinds. And, behind the table were about two dozen cases of the Hermitage wine.

Barcus knew someone had been back to the Abbey to salvage what could be saved. It had been a mercy for AI~Em to assign the task to someone else.

Worthington began the briefing while everyone ate.

"As of this moment, we are on track and ahead of schedule," Jim said, to claps and to cheers, through full mouths. "We have added items to the schedule, however.

"We have decided to salvage reactor number one from the *Memphis*, before we leave for Earth."

The displays changed behind him. Schedules cascaded and simulations of the install of the dark matter reactor in the *Sedna* were shown.

Trish Elkin spoke, "The dark matter reactor is modular and easy to move. We should be able to move it over, install and test it, in less than a day. By having it, we can run the fabricator, the entire trip, with no impact and continue repairs and even upgrades."

Worthington continued, "This presumes that Barcus doesn't blow himself up, extracting the missiles."

Barcus knew he was joking, but Po wasn't so sure.

"We have also come up with a far less risky way to transfer the fuel, without killing Elkin."

"Thanks, Captain, for thinking of me," Elkin said, smiling.

"After Barcus retrieves the missile pod from the platform, they will land in a remote area in the tundra, far north of here." Worthington started another simulation. "The pod will already be retrieved and secured inside Par, the Emergency Module, during the operation. They will be dropped off along with the fuel tanks from the *Sedna*. Em will extract, process and transfer the nuclear material to the shielded fuel tanks and leave the unused parts of the pod there. All this will happen while we can use the laser comms on the moon as a relay, to keep in touch."

Elkin added, "With the plutonium in the shielded tanks, they can be picked up, reinstalled and we will be good to go. And, my tan will stay as pale white as ever!"

"Handling risks will be minimized," Worthington added.

AI~Em spoke at that point, "We will then be good with water, food and fuel." The task lists opened. "The remainder of the major tasks will be repairing the hull breaches, cleaning the CO_2 scrubbers, and testing the computers, the hull and the seal integrity."

The fabrication schedule was impressive.

"When are we getting Wex?" Grady stood in the light by the tables. In his hand, he held the tail spike from the Telis Raptor. It looked like a short, curved sword. He looked worried, angry.

AI~Em replied, "In three days, Barcus, Po, Rand, and Worthington will be going to Exeter. To the Flask and Anvil, to meet with the High Keeper's chief engineer. Ronan has already begun setting up transportation and the potential evacuation of Wex. It will be a simple milk run."

"I'm going," Grady said, in a tone not to be debated.

"I guess I'm going, as well," Ulric said. "None of you have even been there, before. I have. Besides, I know where we can get a few cases of excellent bourbon."

Hume spoke next. "Captain, you should stay here. I'll go."

"I'm going because the rest of you have tasks to complete, if we are to remain on schedule. We are getting close." He pointed at Hume. "You're not going because Ronan advised against it." Before she could interrupt, he continued, "Not only are you a woman, I think you are the only Black woman on this whole, damn planet."

She was taken aback.

"You would draw too much attention."

"As it is, we'll have to dress her like a man." Ulric pointed at Rand. "I have not seen a man on this planet as tall as she is."

Everyone laughed. Except Rand.

***

They finished eating and providing additional status updates that the dependency schedule didn't convey. Barcus helped Elkin, Weston and Worthington moved the shielded plutonium containment units onto the shuttle and secured them. Each was about the size of a coffin, and weighed so much they had built-in, grav-skid plates that helped with mobility. They had to be secured on opposite sides of the cargo bay, to help the shuttle maintain its balance.

Po was getting a lesson on the helmet functions, from Hume, when Rand walked up to Barcus to talk.

"Barcus, what do you know about her?" Rand asked, quietly.

"There is not much to know," he confessed.

"She says that she couldn't read at all this time last year." Rand moved closer. "And now, she can pilot a PT-137? That thing is full manual. Half the people here couldn't fly it."

"I know. I'm the one that taught her," Barcus said. "To read and to fly."

"You ever teach anyone else, before?" she asked. "Do you have any idea how hard it is?"

"Well, no," Barcus admitted. "Never had much of a chance."

"You taught Olias, as well?" she asked.

"Well, I tried. He has the extra challenge that he doesn't speak Standard English. It's a slow go for him."

Barcus looked toward Po. She activated the helmet lights, without using her hands.

"She has a personal HUD as well, now? It has comms, storage and a full-time link to the most advanced AI I have ever worked with, and she doesn't even blink." Rand paused, looking over her shoulder. "You don't find that odd?"

"She thinks it's magic." Barcus looked at her, as well. "By her definitions, it *is* magic."

"Barcus, I don't know if you knew that Worthington had me take a closer look at her. Even her medical scans." She watched Barcus for his reaction to her statements. "She survived horrific torture and received massive injuries, in the past. I can't even tell you how many bones had been broken and not properly treated."

Barcus grew a bit angry. "So, she is smart and tough. So what?"

"And, she has genome markers." It was evident Barcus did not know the significance of that statement. "These kinds of markers are only used for a couple reasons. Genetic test subjects mostly—control groups, test subject tagging, that sort of thing. It started when they used prisoners as lab rats. One of the researchers noticed that the subjects in the trials were much easier to track in a double-blind study, if they had genetic markers installed. It made it easier for both the subjects and the researchers to NOT know the control group from the test group, even from one generation to the next. Even tissue samples would then be clearly marked."

"So you think she is some sort of guinea pig?" Barcus asked.

"Did any of those mercenaries ever say why they were told to kill every man, woman, and child above the gorge?" Rand asked.

He looked across the hangar at Po, again, as she laughed, taking off the helmet. He saw the strength in her bare arms and her shoulders.

"Did Olias have those same markers?" Barcus asked.

"No," Rand replied.

"This changes nothing," Barcus said, defensively. "In ten days, we're out of here."

Barcus started to walk away. Rand stopped him, stepping into his path.

"Listen closely, Barcus," Rand said, in an angry whisper. "Do you think, when we get out of here, this is over?" They stared, eye-to-eye now, their faces only inches apart. "You think you're going to just go home, and what? Get assigned to another ship? Go back to being maintenance guy number forty-two?"

They stared at each other.

"Someone murdered the *Ventura*. Other ships as well. Someone powerful. They sent us here to die." She was growling now. "What do you think they will do, when they find out we lived?"

"Shit," Barcus said, under his breath.

"I don't know why, or even if, Po has been genetically altered, yet." She looked at Po, again. Po watched them now, as well. "There are just too many things wrong on this planet. Too many questions."

"Like what?" Barcus was angry and didn't understand why.

"The defense grid around this planet for starters," she said, as if it was obvious.

"So they don't make them like they used to. So what?" he quipped.

"They NEVER made them like this." She wasn't whispering anymore. "And this planet. Terraforming is never this perfect! Honey bees, for Christ's sake? Deer? Foxes? Dogs, cats, mice, and even rats? How many colonies have you been to? Are any like this?"

"No. Especially the terraformed ones," he admitted.

"And, why the hell would this ass-backward society halt progress? Do any of this?" She ranted, no longer trying to be quiet.

"Because of the Keepers." Po approached, without their notice, and she interrupted. "The answer to all your questions is because of the Keepers. The High Keeper, specifically."

Barcus and Rand remained silent, for a long moment.

"Barcus is right. This changes nothing," Rand said. She glared at them both. "Ten days."

CHAPTER THIRTY-EIGHT

The Pod Run

"They had no idea the depth of the damage that was being slowly repaired inside Po. I think they had been testing how much abuse she could withstand."

--Solstice 31 Incident Investigation Testimony Transcript: Dr. Elizabeth Shaw, the chief medical officer on the Memphis.

Po found Barcus, alone, on the bridge of the STU, an hour later.

"I think the nanites have done something wrong to me," Po said, as she crawled into his lap, the way she used to in the gatehouse. "I can't stop thinking about...being with you. It's very distracting." Looking up at him, she added, "And, very...wet. All the time."

Barcus laughed and then kissed her.

"I'm afraid, Barcus." She looked up at him. "I pretend all the time that I'm not afraid. I've done it my whole life. It's never been this bad." She looked into his eyes. "I never had so much to lose, before." She hammered her fists on his chest, halfheartedly. "Damn you."

"I'm afraid, too," he said, quietly. Po had expected him to deny her feelings and to whisper platitudes, in that voice that calmed her so well. Instead, he was honest.

"I will be careful. Hume will be there, in case something happens." Barcus tried to reassure her. "Besides, Em will be there, too. She'd never let anything happen to me."

Somehow, that fact made her feel better.

Po said, "Stu, lock that hatch, please."

***

The shuttle approached the dead satellite at a very slow speed. The cargo ramp was already open, and Hume clicked her safety line to a loop on the starboard side.

Barcus was already inside the black maintenance suit, running a comms check; first with Hume in her pressure suit, and then with Worthington via the relay on the moon. It took about three seconds for the audio to get there.

"We are approaching the satellite now, Jim."

Barcus and Peace entered the rear hatch of Par and secured themselves to each side, facing the center. Barcus was still amused by the smiley face Cook had painted on Peace.

"Slowing. Will reach full stop at thirty meters." There was a pause of about a minute. "Full Stop."

"Jumping in ten seconds," AI~Pardosa's voice said, in a very businesslike way.

"Jumping."

The rear hatch remained open on the spider as they crossed the open space to the launch platform.

The EM drifted across the open space and latched onto the launching pods, trailing cable behind it, like the silk thread of a web. Em rotated the spider, so Barcus could reach an antenna spire and guide himself down, on his side, as Peace climbed silently down, using the launch apertures as handholds.

"It looks like we are in luck already, Barcus," AI~Em said to him, out loud, for Worthington's benefit. "It looks like the clamps are simple, magnetic clamps. Press, here and here, and they will release." Peace demonstrated.

The pod was about three meters by three meters. A cube. Peace stood on the business end, where there were ninety-nine missile launch tubes configured in a ten by ten grid. A small hatch covered the area where the upper corner tube would have been.

Barcus opened the hatch.

"Em, stop! It is powered up. Status lights are green." Barcus looked closer. "Holy shit. This pod is not 300 years old. All of this tech looks new. I thought this was going to be fried by Ulric's EMP cannon."

The HUD came alive with a schematic for this precise unit.

"Barcus, you are looking at the control and maintenance systems for this pod. It is currently armed. The very first thing you need to do is lift this toggle cover and flip the manual switch to deactivate the self-destruct unit."

A simulation played for him in his HUD, to show him what to do.

Barcus followed the simulation accurately and the buttons turned from green to red. He closed the toggle cover, so that switch could not accidentally be flipped again.

"I thought all of this was dead." He looked up at the antenna. It was obviously ancient. "I think the comms array was destroyed, not the pods. Tell Elkin we may have better plutonium than we initially thought."

"I think you should detach that cable from the array," AI~Em said, as she highlighted the coupling in his HUD.

It was a standard pressure coupling, and it came loose with a squeeze in the right place.

There were twelve magnetic clamps. They released all, but the last two—one at each end.

"Okay, Em. On the count of three, release the final clamp and lift. One, two, three, go."

"Barcus, hold. It's caught on something," AI~Em said.

"Shit, more cables." Barcus moved to the right and focused a light between the pods. "Just one more. Jimbo, are you seeing this? Is that what I think it is?"

Comms were quiet for six seconds, before he heard, "Don't move. That line is attached to a pin on a mine just below the pod. Another ten centimeters and you're dead. DO NOT MOVE."

"Hume, do you copy?" Barcus asked.

"Go for Hume," she replied.

"Send a line over, Hume," Barcus requested. "I need you."

A magnetic grapple flew into the back of the Emergency Module a second later. She must have had it already in her hands.

"Clipped on. Moving." Hume clipped a ring on the line that connected the Stu with the EM. She flew across the void. "Secured. What do we got?"

A safety line played out as she drifted over the tops of the pods. As she came across, she attached a series of magnetic handholds across the top of the pods. She stopped neatly, at the edge, and looked down the crack at the line.

"I see it." Hume twisted, so her legs were out over the loose pod. "I may be able to get to it, from below." She climbed down the launch tubes. Just as she was about to slide under the pod, she ran out of slack. Without hesitation, she said, "Detaching safety line."

"Hume. Wait," Barcus said.

"This will only take a second." Her voice was strained as she extended her arm. She wriggled. The pod moved slightly, giving her more room.

"Got it. Lines detached. This one and the next one were hooked on the same ring. Raise the pod. Straight up," Hume said. "Jesus, Barcus. These are Javelin missiles with high-yield warheads. Do you have any idea how much these cost, a piece? My God. And just on this side, there are almost 1,600 facing the planet. What. The. Hell?"

Hume rode the pod up and toward the cargo bay of the spider, clinging to the cluster of pods. The pod would fit, comfortably.

"Hume, get that safety line back on, and get back over to the shuttle. Use the line you have already attached to draw the EM back into the shuttle," Worthington ordered.

"Yes, sir."

Soon the pod was secured inside the EM, and it was slowly towed back to the shuttle.

"Secure cargo and descend. The hard part is next. I want you well away, before they even begin," Worthington ordered.

***

The shuttle was down on the ground in the middle of desolate tundra in about a half hour. The spider exited the STU's cargo bay and waited.

Barcus cleared out of the suit, and soon Ash and Peace were moving out the containment units and a case of tools, as Hume and Barcus watched from the bridge.

The STU was aloft when they had barely cleared the apron. They had to be away before the harvesting began.

"The schedule says the harvesting will take about twenty hours for all ninety-nine warheads," Hume said, as she took off her helmet.

"Elkin will be picking them up. You'll be at some bar in Exeter, dammit," she teased. "Have one for me."

CHAPTER THIRTY-NINE

The Flask and Anvil

"While we were in Exeter, distracted, it happened. None of us saw it coming. None of us knew then that it was all a setup, an escape."

--Solstice 31 Incident Investigation Testimony Transcript: Captain James Worthington, senior surviving member of the Ventura's command crew.

<<<>>>

Worthington, Barcus, and Rand dressed the same in elegant, black tracker garb that Ronan had sent along. Rand wore the unnerving security helmet from the *Ventura*. It helped hide the fact that she was female. Her voices were set to menacing male tones. With the hood all the way up, it was not noticed. Her drone also flew recon as they worked.

Ulric dressed in beautiful, traditional Keeper robes of dark browns. The other three will be his personal guards. Po dressed in the traditional, black habit and hood with veil. She'll stay with Ulric, as well.

Ronan would not attend.

Grady would only go, as himself.

Barcus added the Raptor blade, directly in front of his sidearm. It helped to conceal it; it neatly combined with his tabard and cloak. Ronan provided a black sheath.

Exeter was far bigger than any of them had thought. It was a real city, with an estimated population over 60,000. They watched the city below, through windows inside the passenger's compartment of Ronan's shuttle.

Em came along—docked into the cargo bay with legs folded in and covered with a sailcloth tarp, like the other pallets in the hold—to provide BUG drone support and EmNet comms with the team.

Burke stayed with Ronan, as always.

Ronan's estate was vast. Barcus estimated that just the formally groomed part was over 1,000 acres. It backed up to the forest at the base of the mountains that made up one side of the valley the Exeter filled. As the sun set and the clouds blazed with light, they set down on a formal patio, near the residence.

The passenger compartment of Ronan's shuttle was below the flight deck and had its own exit on the left side. When the door opened, it was exactly how Ronan said it would be. Two flanking rows of armed guards with swords and crossbows stood at attention. His castellan waited at the bottom of the ornate, portable staircase that had been placed for their use.

Ronan made his way out, with the entourage in tow, in a predefined order. They were to speak to no one. Barcus, Rand, and Worthington walked behind Ulric, who was followed a pace behind by Po and Grady.

Barcus and Jimbo scanned around, constantly, on each side. Barcus noticed that Burke stayed behind to supervise the unloading of the shuttle and to ensure no one became curious about the final item that remained in the shuttle.

The group entered through massive double doors that opened before them. Barcus steeled himself for what he knew he would see there.

There were nearly 200 women, on their knees, with their foreheads on the floor, lining the vast hallway. All wore the same deep green, single button dress. Their hair was long and in braids that cascaded down the left side of their necks, if they were on the left, and the right side of their necks, if they knelt on the right side.

Every vase was filled with fresh flowers, beautifully arranged. There were bowls of fresh fruits that Barcus assumed were selected for their beautiful color combinations. Ronan grabbed a golden apple from one bowl as he walked by; and, bit into it, as he listened to the balding castellan, while he looked at the offered plate display.

They eventually entered a center atrium that held massive staircases that rose to the six additional upper levels. Ronan had told him it was used, sometimes, for grand balls for the aristocrats of Exeter. They ascended a staircase and moved into a wing of the building that was his private residence.

Guards opened the double doors at the end of the hall, before they reached it. Polished marble floors gave way to thick carpet, beyond the door. The doors closed behind them.

Ronan stopped in the center of a large receiving parlor, beyond the nave to the suite. He turned to address the group.

"Well done." He brought the balding man forward. The man was now more relaxed, even smiling. "This is my Castellan, and friend, Jacob Riehl. He runs things at the Ronan Estate. I know you will not be here long, but if you need anything at all, please ask him.

"Jacob, this is Ulric, Grady and Po."

He shook the men's hands and then extended his hand to Po.

"It's lovely to finally meet you, Po. I hear you're quite the pilot." Jacob stood there, hand extended, apparently happy to wait as long as necessary until she, finally, shook his hand.

Not waiting for Ronan, he said, "And, you must be Rand. You can take your helmet off in here, but only in here, I think."

She took off her helmet, tucked it under her left arm and shook his hand firmly.

Finally, he greeted Jimbo and Barcus. "Gentlemen, I am honored to meet you both."

Ronan studied the plate Jacob had handed him. He looked up, then.

"We will have a private dinner here in two hours. That will give you time to clean up," Ronan said, as ten young women filed in, wearing the same deep green dress that was the uniform there.

"I will let my staff introduce themselves. I consider them family. They will show you to your rooms and the baths that are waiting."

As two women led off each of the men, smiling and introducing themselves, Po moved closer to Barcus as she visibly tensed.

Two women approached Po. One spoke, "Don't worry, Po. Ronan told us all about you and Barcus." The woman placed one hand on her own chest and gestured to her partner with the other, and said, "My name is Teek, and this is Ro." She motioned for them to follow, together. "We will show you to your rooms and help you."

To Barcus, she said, "Ronan thinks you should shave, so you blend in better." She talked and walked now, down a side hall. "We have fresh clothes for you, as well."

"Jacob told us what happened," Ro said, "We are very sorry for your loss."

Barcus nodded thanks and looked at Po. She seemed aghast. Ro was not a girl. He saw it in Ro's expression change. She was a woman of perhaps thirty years. "What's wrong, Po?" Barcus asked.

"How is it that you speak to him so?" Po asked them. "This is Exeter."

Ro looked at Teek. Teek answered, "Within these walls, these private rooms, we are in the East Isles, not Exeter. There are no anvils here," Teek said, seriously.

Ro added, "Ronan said we are to treat you as we treat him within these walls, even though you are the Man from Earth." She smiled, with no fear. "He even said if I gut punched you, you would, in fact, NOT eat me."

Suddenly, Barcus knew who she was. This was Ronan's daughter.

"You, probably not. Teek might be tasty though," Barcus joked.

Po was the one to punch him first, quickly, followed by Ro and, finally, Teek.

None were aware that AI~Em watched them from thirty-two angles.

***

Barcus allowed Teek to shave his face, as he sat in a barber's chair in a room off the bathroom suite. Ro wandered about the various rooms with Po, chatting and laughing at the different types of baths in the suite. It had a large shower room, a steam room, a cold plunge pool, and soaking tubs in a selection of sizes and shapes.

When the shave was completed, Ro and Teek made a smooth exit, saying they would be back, in about an hour. They never even offered to bathe with them, to Po's relief.

The door was barely closed before they were undressing, and Barcus was surprised to see Po selected the shower first.

"I like showers."

They washed each other's hair, and bodies, to their great relief and…release. They soaked in one of the tubs, after making love, standing up, in the shower.

"I have never felt this clean, this whole, before." Po sighed. Barcus just smiled, enjoying the quiet in his mind, trying not to imagine the screams of the dying.

They soaked until they were wrinkled. Climbing out, they used thick, soft towels and put on comfortable robes.

They found Teek and Ro in the suite's great room, sitting on the sofas before the fire, reading actual books. They noticed the look on Po's face.

"Ronan loves books," Ro said, marking her place. "He has a beautiful library in the East Isles, in his private residence." She motioned for them to sit across from her.

"On Baytirus, a library is considered a vice. Real books are frowned upon. If you do your reading from a plate, the High Keeper knows exactly what you are reading, and who is reading it."

Barcus listened and tried not to care. They will be gone in a few days. They will have their own problems.

"What are you reading?" Barcus asked, conversationally.

"A book of poems. Rare are these," Ro said, wistfully.

Teek stood and walked to another double set of doors and opened one side. "We have laid out appropriate clothes for you. Dinner will be served, soon. Just follow your nose. Ronan is cooking, again."

Teek and Ro left their suite and they explored. The suite had beds for about twenty people, besides the master bedroom. Retainers had beautiful quarters, much smaller, but luxurious still. They even found a small kitchen and three more baths.

Po was awestruck. Barcus just shook his head.

They dressed.

Po wore a simple dress in dark green, much like the ones she always wore. The single button at the nape of her neck was a black, glass-like, carved stone that looked like an artfully rendered rose flower.

The slippers she wore were ingenious in their simplicity. The iris-like cinch at the top of her foot made for a perfect fit.

Barcus was in fine black pants, boots and tunic. He added a new belt for his gun and Telis blade.

They wandered out into the main suite and were called by the smell of bacon and onions. Following their noses led them to a spacious kitchen where Jimbo, Rand, Ulric, Grady, Ro, Teek and four other women sat around a large table, talking, all at once.

Rand and Jimbo saw them enter and raised glasses to them in a toast. Ronan looked up and gave a nod, as he transferred a pan of diced bacon and onions to a simmering pot of spicy meat in sauce that looked like chili.

He was cooking on a large, gas range. It was a modern convenience Barcus had not seen since he had landed on this planet.

The two women, sitting on either side of Ulric, stood and dragged Ulric to his feet in a friendly, familiar manner. One of them reminded Barcus of Saay. He fixed his smile, to hide his anger and sadness at the memory of her death.

Ronan had his apron removed by two other girls, even younger than the ones helping Ulric. Their dresses were of a satin that clung to their bodies.

Barcus realized it was window dressing, making him look decadent and spoiled.

"Ahhh, Barcus. We will be back in an hour. Ulric and I are going down to put an appearance in at tonight's feast. Dinner will be ready by then." He was dressed in very fine clothes, as was Ulric. "There is beer and wine, cider or whatever else you like. Ro, sweetheart, will you start the biscuits in about a half hour?"

They were both swept out by the girls, as if they were pushing an ox cart that was stuck in the mud.

Jimbo shook his head, as the talking began, again. Barcus sat next to him, and Po sat next to Barcus.

"There is a feast?" Barcus asked.

"Yes, apparently, there are over 100 aristocrats down there already. The news Ronan was back spread fast," Jimbo said, sipping tea.

Rand interjected, quietly, "There is a feast every night."

Teek was listening.

"Yes. Every night." She beamed, as if proud of the decadence. "And, every morning the halls are filled again with fresh cut flowers, and every fruit bowl is restocked." Barcus remembered the single apple Ronan had taken. "The sheets are changed on over 300 beds. The formal hedges are trimmed, and the 1,000 acres are maintained."

Teek turned serious, now. They didn't know why.

"Over 100 people go to the night market, every night. They buy tons of food, and flowers, and cloth, and nails, and medicine, and hundreds of other goods to support the household."

"Do you want to know why?" Ro asked, from the stove, now wearing Ronan's apron, as she stirred the simmering chili.

She waited for Barcus to answer.

"Please, tell me," Barcus said. The room was now quiet.

"Because he is a good man." She paused, she seemed about to cry.

Teek continued, "In this place, it is the only way to serve his people. They know the feasts they cook are not for the aristocrats who pick at it and complain. They are for them. All of this food, and fruit, feed the thousands of slaves that he owns. Food bought from farmers that are not slaves. They work hard for a good price."

Ro added, "Did you see the new wing being built? This place doesn't need another room, much less a wing. But carpenters, stonecutters and masons need work."

Barcus understood. Po could tell from the look on his face.

Po asked, "Why does he let people think he is vain? Some think he is the worse Keeper of them all."

They didn't answer. But, Po finally understood. She saw how he lived in the East Isles. This was a façade, to help as many as he could, within the rules he was allowed.

***

Ronan and Ulric returned just as the final tray of biscuits came out of the oven. They laughed at something Ulric said, making a voice that was not his own.

They ate chili with cheese and fresh biscuits from beautiful, ceramic bowls. They must not have eaten much at the feast because both Ulric and Ronan had seconds of the chili.

Jacob joined them late. Ronan, Teek, and Ro all tossed him a biscuit at the same time. Somehow, he caught them all, and juggled them as he walked to the pot of chili. While juggling the three with one hand, he ladled up a bowl for himself.

He expertly faked tossing the full bowl into the mix, but just lifted it up and down in the circle to good effect.

Smoothly, he sat, caught one biscuit in his mouth, placed one in the bowl and placed the last on his napkin as if it was nothing. A typical day.

The ladies cheered; Jimbo, Barcus and Rand applauded.

"Thanks for not throwing me that awful knife, again, Ronan. Its balance is horrible for juggling."

After Jacob was done eating, he and Ronan retired to his private study, to catch up on some things.

"I will still be awake when you return. We'll talk, then."

They didn't get to speak with him again, until it had all gone wrong.

***

The streets were crowded in this upscale section of Exeter. The crowd parted as they moved through. Worthington, Barcus, and Rand were a full head taller than most of the people and they intimidated people by more than just their size. Their clothes, apparently, were typically worn by elite trackers and bodyguards used by Ronan; few could afford them.

Po might as well have been invisible, as she walked a half step behind Ulric, wearing a full black habit and veil.

The Flask and Anvil was huge, for a tavern. There were already 300, maybe 400, people there. Ulric was taken to a booth a half level up from the main floor. It was like a small side alcove, like box seats, that looked down onto the main floor, opposite a stage where two men played string instruments. The crowd talked among themselves. There were a lot of women present, most in habits of modest colors, some with their heads uncovered and their long, braided hair showing.

"The acoustics are fantastic in here," Ulric said, as he, Grady and Po sat. Worthington and Rand took positions just on the inside of the booth alcove, on each side. The instruments the men on stage played sounded like guitars, but had more strings, a deeper tone, and a wider range.

Barcus went to look for the man named Mason. Ronan had given a detailed description of the man.

AI~Em spoke to Barcus via HUD, *"I believe I have found him."*

A HUD image opened and his face was there in a window. Barcus found him quickly, sitting at the bar with a mug before him, talking to a woman with a long, black braid and bare arms. She also had bracelets on her biceps and wrists, which was highly unusual for Exeter. Her dress had the single button at the nape of her neck, but it was made of far finer material that flattered her body instead of concealing it.

She clung to Mason, even though he was an unremarkable man. He was bookish and soft-looking.

Barcus approached as the musicians finished and the crowd began to applaud. He walked up behind the man.

"My Lord, Mason," Barcus said, from behind him. "Keeper Ronan sends his regards. My name is Barcus."

The woman spoke first. "Ronan surely knows how to grow them in the East Isles. Can we take this one home?"

Her hand traced the muscles on Barcus's chest. He looked at her hand, and then up at her face.

She took her hand away.

"Ty, leave this one alone. He might eat you," Mason said.

"Why is he so angry?" she asked, looking closely into his eyes.

"Ty. No," Mason said, and she heeled like a dog, sitting back down.

Barcus wondered why she wasn't completely covered like the rest of the women present. All the others were, basically, in burkas.

"If you'd follow me, sir." Barcus gestured with his arm. "I will show you the way." His gesture opened his cloak a bit and revealed the massive Raptor blade. The handle was wrapped in fine leather, but was still clear.

Fear showed on the woman's face when she saw it.

Mason followed him through the increasing crowd to the next level up, where Ulric sat.

"Barcus, we now have ten BUGs set to follow Mason back to the Citadel. We will be able to obtain his credentials the next time he logs into the system," AI~Em said, in his head.

Mason and Ty entered and sat inside Ulric's booth. Worthington and Rand stepped out, for privacy, before words were spoken.

Barcus watched the meeting in two windows.

"Greetings, Mason. My name is Ulric. I am a friend of Ronan's," Ulric said. "He tells me there is a favor to be paid, or offered, or asked. I am not too clear which it is," Ulric said, pouring wine.

"I think you and I are just the conduits for a favor of this size," Mason said.

Applause began as the two musicians finished the tune with a flourish. They moved their chairs farther apart and, once again, took their places on stage.

"Then, all accounts become even, tonight." Mason stared down at the stage as the crowd became quiet.

***

The men played a sad sounding tune, as three women stood in between them in full habits, cloaks, and hoods, but no veils.

Rand touched Worthington's arm as he froze. "Do you hear that...?"

When the three women raised their black flutes, they played a familiar tune. Barcus whispered, "Adagio in G Minor."

They looked at each other.

The harmony of the flutes was heartbreaking in its beauty. The musical arrangement was perfect, better even than the original by Tomaso Albinoni.

The crowd was silent when the woman in the center lowered her flute, and her hood, and stepped forward to sing. Her hair was bright red and in a thick braid.

Her voice filled the room vocalizing. She used her voice like an instrument. No words. Just beautiful, heartbreaking sound.

"What does this mean?" Jimbo whispered to Barcus. They all recognized the music was from Earth. He got no answer.

The flutes and guitars played as her voice ached with emotion. The black flutes were impossibly pure. People covered their mouths with their hands.

The flutes wept to a silent crowd.

Barcus looked at the audience now. There was a table of armed men on the floor below. They were the only people not silent. They whispered in harsh tones to each other.

The music continued with the audience enthralled.

Barcus saw Grady slowly moving through the crowd below. At that, the men on stage stood, and the five of them played, making it sound as if they were an entire orchestra. The lead singer, the woman with red hair, played a solo of such complexity, Barcus would not have believed it to be possible.

They played in perfect harmony and with high intensity. Their hands flashed as they plucked the strings and even drummed on their instruments as they played.

The final stanzas she sang, alone, in volume.

And then, quietly, soulfully, sorrowfully, while looking directly at Barcus, she sang the ending, as if she knew him. The crowd was frozen by the echoing silence as she finished her last note. No one moved on stage.

Then, the applause crashed in like a wave, as she drew her hood back up, still looking at Barcus.

Po was at his elbow. "What's wrong?"

Barcus looked at Worthington.

Then, Mason was there at the railing, between Barcus and Jimbo.

"That is Wex," Mason said, as he watched Grady slowly approach the stage, as people, now on their feet, continued to applaud. "It's the only way she could get here. She doesn't want to go back."

Ulric said, over the crowd, "Grady carved the flutes. He was right. They are amazing."

"You must take her with you," Mason added.

"Mason, we have to go," Ty said, urgently. "Now. Please." There was fear, almost panic, in her voice.

Wex saw Grady then, and stepped off the stage, directly into his arms.

Barcus noticed that a commotion was beginning. Two armed trackers argued with the male musicians. There was yelling and one of them was dragged off the stage by the two men.

Worthington was about to speak, when he noticed Barcus, moving through the crowd below. He must have gone over the railing. Po followed then, her cloaks billowing.

"Dammit," Jimbo said to Rand. "Get them out of here." He pointed at Mason, and Ulric.

Rand moved, without a word, and they followed.

Worthington brought up the rear.

Barcus heard what the man was yelling over the crowd. He had a gruff accent.

"This music is heresy. They are using magic. These women must be punished." He dragged the man off the stage. "If you won't. I will."

He threw the man down, crushing his instrument beneath him where he fell, and climbed on stage, drawing a knife.

Barcus saw the two women crouch and back away, separating, with their flutes in their right hands.

They were in a fighting stance. He wasn't sure the tracker saw it. He acted as if they were cowering. Nothing was further from the truth.

The man rushed at one of them. Her movement was fluid and circular. Her clothes hid her feet and arms, and there was no warning as she dodged, spun, and landed the flute with a horrible impact on the bridge of his nose. It broke his nose and both eye sockets. His brain would never survive. He dropped like a wet bag of sand.

Screams went up and a panic started, as people began to run. More of the High Keeper's soldiers seemed to appear out of nowhere, scanning for the problem and not yet finding it. Knives cleared sheaths. The soldiers had followed Wex there. They were to ensure her return.

Suddenly, Grady was at Barcus's elbow with Wex. She stood face-to-face with Barcus, looking him right in the eyes, measuring him. She seemed to recognize him. She said, as the chaos increased around them, "Barcus, I have waited so very long to meet you. Hear me. We have little time." She drew closer, spoke directly into his ear, "Tell him the cage is broken."

"Tell who?"

"You'll know. He's been waiting for you," she said, and then she noticed Po. Wex gasped, at the sight of her, she leaned down and whispered, "Never stop. Ever." And then, she was gone.

Po began pulling Barcus. People were screaming.

The two small women jumped from the stage and moved through the crowd like dozens of other women dressed like them. The male musicians disappeared behind the stage, leaving the body alone on the floor there.

Barcus made brief eye contact with Jimbo. "Jimbo, get them out. We will meet you back at the ship," Barcus said, over HUD comms via EmNet, to Worthington, still calm.

Jimbo was already out the door. The crush of people stopped Barcus from going the same way, so they moved to the back. Barcus turned to see a man, with the bloody sword raised over his head.

Grady, from behind the man, shot the man in the head.

They had room, suddenly, because everyone ran, in every direction, away from them. Barcus could see blood on Grady's chest as he and Wex moved into the crowd as they fled.

"Barcus, this way," AI~Em said.

A line displayed in his vision that led to a side door. He grabbed Po's hand and moved. The gun she was holding disappeared into her cloak.

The door opened into a narrow alley that ran towards the back. The directional line led them at a run. Barcus, then Po, and finally the two women with flutes ran into the alley. This led to a paddock in the back, where individual horses were tied up. Three stable boys stared at them. The line he followed led along the wall and over a fence into deeper darkness.

Barcus paused, for a moment, once everyone was over the fence and asked, "Where's Grady? He's been wounded!"

AI~Em replied, so he and Po heard. "Grady got out with Wex. He will be fine. Worthington and Rand got out with the others. Now. Run," AI~Em yelled, into their minds. "They're coming."

CHAPTER FORTY

They Ran

"Suddenly, it was chaotic. We were separated. But, Em was tracking us all. We were sure we'd gotten out but Em was either glitching or lying or both. None of us knew what was really going on."

--Solstice 31 Incident Investigation Testimony Transcript: Captain James Worthington, senior surviving member of the Ventura's command crew.

They ran.

Barcus had no idea where they were. The woman named Jude was leading now. She stopped running when running began to draw more attention than they wanted.

A maze of alleys eventually led out to a crowded market square.

Jude whispered, "This is the night market. It allows households to get their fresh goods before the day starts. Move slowly through."

They merged into a lane that bustled with fish carts and crates of fruits and vegetables.

"This way," Jude said, quietly.

They traversed almost the entire length of the market and were headed for the western exit, when AI~Em chimed in on comms, *"There are soldiers converging on the market. Follow me."*

AI~Em appeared and turned away. She left a virtual vapor trail behind her, in their HUDs. Barcus turned, stopped Jude, and indicated for her to follow him. AI~Em entered an alley and moved ahead quickly.

Jude said, "I am sorry, my Lord. I don't know you well enough to follow you. Cine." It was the other woman's name. She hesitated, lowered her hood, and stared at Barcus. "He has a rider." And, the two flute players turned and disappeared into the market.

"Where are we going?" Po asked, still holding Barcus's hand as they fast walked down a series of dark alleys and courtyards. The sounds of the night market faded behind them.

They finally entered a large cross street. Instead of instantly following the vapor trail in his HUD, Barcus and Po moved to the center of the large area. There was a watering trough for horses and a utilitarian fountain. They quietly, ran to it.

"I want to orient myself," Barcus whispered, as he looked up at the bright, moonlit sky.

They were moving closer to the Citadel, not away from it, back towards Ronan's estate.

"Barcus, you must hurry." AI~Em's voice became urgent, in his head.

Just then, they both felt AI~Em's presence wink out.

The vapor trail disappeared. His HUD went dark. He was hailed on his direct HUD channel.

It was Chen's personal ID code. Chen was dead. Chen was under a pile of rocks on the side of a lonely mountain.

Barcus opened the channel, but said nothing, putting his finger to Po's lips, so she said nothing.

"Barcus, I only have a few seconds! There is no way I can prove to you what I say is true. Use your gut." It was Chen's voice, in a near panic. *"Em is lying. Her AI has been corrupted, seized. Don't trust her. She is running another…"*

The comms terminated.

EmNet was back up and the vapor trail was back. AI~Em was in mid-sentence, *"…water and then we need to get moving again."*

Po looked at Barcus with wide eyes and said nothing. Barcus looked away toward the vapor trail path.

Barcus moved, as he thought.

"Em, slow this down. We got away. I need a recon BUG straight up 100 meters. I need to know where I am. And, give me a tactical map of the city, showing the route we will take." His HUD clock showed 1253 hours.

They paused in the deep shadows of a new side street that smelled of dung, and angled up a slope.

The tactical map came up first. It showed a meandering route that would have them back at the estate, by dawn.

He thought to himself, *plausible.*

"Where are Jimbo and the others?" Barcus asked.

"They are having problems just now, and I should not distract them," AI~Em replied.

Just then, Po's cloak fell away from her suppressed handgun. She still held it, pointed down, in her right hand.

"Barcus, I hear running."

A moment later, Barcus heard it, as well.

He let go of her other hand, and said, "Go," in a quiet, urgent, voice.

He drew his own gun, and moved with her, walking backwards, covering their retreat. Po hurried to the mouth of the street, holding her gun in both hands.

She was about 100 feet ahead of him, at the next intersection; she waited until Barcus looked at her, so he would see the direction she went.

When he looked, she moved, both of them losing line of sight.

This movement continued for several minutes. At times, Barcus would lead and Po would cover their backs. But, the sounds of feet got closer in the maze.

For a few minutes, they flat out ran, at AI~Em's encouragement. They paused in another set of shadows, listening. The running feet grew faint.

Without a word, they began another covered retreat. Po led this time. There were so many alleys in this city. Without the vapor trail, they would have constantly hit dead ends.

It happened, again.

AI~Em seemed to wink out. Chen's voice said, "*You're being driven to a...*" AI~Em winked back in, as if nothing had happened.

A moment later, Barcus heard two quiet shots. Po shot at someone. He turned to run toward her.

Two crossbow bolts entered his right leg, at almost the same moment, one six inches above his knee and one six inches below. It sent him sprawling onto his face, before he reached the corner. The hard impact on the cobbles drove the wind from him, and made him lose his grip on the gun.

It slid away.

The Telis blade cleared its sheath and severed a man's arm clean off just below the elbow as he reached for Barcus. Another, leaning down, was stabbed under his chin into his brain so far it protruded from the top of his head. His body collapsed onto Barcus and against the crossbow bolts in his leg. He heard the snap as he drew out the blade and rolled over on top of the corpse.

The club to the back of his head brought him darkness, before he could drag himself within reach of his gun.

***

Po turned the alley corner and approached an opening to a wider road. A soldier, with a crossbow, entered the alley in front of her. He raised the crossbow, but before he could fire, she shot him in the face and the heart. He was dead before he hit the cobbles.

She looked both ways into the street; it was clear. She waited. Then, the vapor trail disappeared. Barcus didn't come. She kept looking, to make sure it was still clear.

He didn't come.

A Citadel soldier rounded the corner, where she expected to see Barcus, followed by another, and another. The first two died never even seeing her, her black clothes hid her in the darkness. More soldiers poured out.

She ran.

She wanted to come back around, behind them. She took the next right without pausing and ran. Then, the right again, and again, expecting to find them.

It was a dead end.

She ran back and took the next right. It ended in a pig sty.

She was panicked now, running full tilt. She took rights and lefts, looking for something familiar, as the buildings became shabbier and more deserted.

"Barcus, where are you?" she paused. "Em, please help me!" She knew she was loud. There was no reply.

She ran. She had to find him.

CHAPTER FORTY-ONE

EmNet is Down

"While we were in Exeter, distracted, it happened. We were separated. It flew out of control, fast, and we never knew it was about to go so far sideways. We expected a simple pickup. A night in a soft bed and a breakfast. A cakewalk."

--Solstice 31 Incident Investigation Testimony Transcript: Captain James Worthington, senior surviving member of the Ventura's command crew.

Barcus woke, facedown, on a cold, stone floor. He was dragged back into consciousness by the pain. His hands were shackled behind his back.

He had been stripped down to his drawstring pants. He rolled through the pain and sat up.

"Em, status," he whispered.

There was no response. The clock was the only thing in his HUD.

0501 hour was what it said.

Dammit.

He tried to struggle to his feet. Even though someone had crudely bandaged his leg, there was still a puddle of blood there.

Without warning, he convulsed and vomited, creating another puddle beside the blood.

Head injuries. Was the HUD damaged?

He tried to initiate a restart. *Nothing.* Just the clock.

Dammit.

His hands were numb, now painfully awaking to pins and needles. His fingers got enough feeling back for him to tell there were three links in the chain between his cuffs.

Despite the pain, he worked the shackles under his butt and behind his thighs. With his left leg through, Barcus steeled himself for the right leg.

He almost blacked out from the pain. He rolled over onto his side and applied direct pressure to the worst of the wounds that had opened back up.

He tried to focus on the fat candle that danced and dripped down the wall in the small recess where it burned.

Barcus fought the tunnel vision. His HUD clock mocked his efforts with 0553 hours. He struggled to sit up, again. Nausea returned, but he didn't vomit, this time. He rested. At least, his hands were in front now.

The pain became a burning ache. He explored his wounds. The lower one was easy to reach and went all the way through, back to front. But, it was the lesser of the two. The higher one did not go all the way through. Whoever pulled out that barbed arrow did more damage on the way out than it did on the way in. He wished, for a moment, that they had just pushed it the rest of the way through.

Neither wound threatened his arteries, or he would have been dead hours ago.

Someone talked at the edge of his hearing. Po would have heard that sooner.

Po.

His vision cleared as his anger and his fear rose. The fog lifted from his mind, as he scanned the room he was in.

It was two meters by three meters and three meters tall. A door was on the short wall. The room was empty, except for an iron ring, set in the back wall. There were two recesses, in opposite walls, with dripped wax; but, only one candle was lit. The door was some kind of black metal with a gap at the bottom wide enough to reach out a hand, and a window with bars.

It was all darkness in the corridor.

With the use of his hands on the floor and the wall, and fueled by anger, he slowly burned his way to his feet. He swooned, and nausea returned.

After resting, he slowly moved to the door. Moving one meter had never seemed so far. Just as he reached the window, he saw candlelight coming down the corridor.

He flattened himself against the wall, not knowing what he should do, could do. He raised his arms over his head, balanced on one bare foot. He hoped the shackles made a heavy enough weapon.

He heard a bolt slide to the side of his door, and it opened.

A small, naked, girl with a bucket opened the door and stepped in. Seeing him, she raised her left arm, in a defensive gesture, but didn't drop the bucket.

Barcus didn't strike her. Her raised arm lowered, and she placed two fingers to her lips, hushing Barcus. Her hair had been cut off roughly and unevenly. He didn't know if it was dark brown or just filthy.

She only had two fingers on that hand.

She was so thin, he knew she was starving. He saw her bones. He was amazed she was strong enough to carry the bucket.

She brought a leaky, wooden mug from the bucket and handed it to Barcus. Half the water it held had sloshed out. But, he drank anyway.

Next, she brought out an oily cloth and unwrapped a large, stale heel of bread, and said, in a whisper, "There are four guards, at the end of this hall, behind locked bars, with crossbows. If you ever go into the hall, they will kill you."

Barcus offered her the bread. She looked into his eyes, but he didn't know what she was looking for, or what she saw.

He mimed for her to eat it.

She devoured it right there, in seconds, then brushed her face, making sure she left no signs of crumbs.

She knelt before him, examining his bandages. She removed them gently, and then untied his drawstring and let his pants fall. Barcus watched the girl clean his wounds and rewrapped them with care. She was not self-conscious of her nakedness, or his.

As she rose and retied his pants, he asked, "What's your name, child?"

She smiled at his question. Barcus noticed her front teeth were broken out. In Common Tongue, she asked, "Why they so afraid of you?"

Barcus had no idea why he said it. "Because I am the Man from Earth." Anger bled from his words.

Her eyes went wide.

She quickly loaded her bucket. He saw she was trembling now. She paused at the door. Looking around, as if someone might be listening. "Kill them all," she whispered, in a lisp.

She went out. She closed and locked the door. He listened as she padded, forty-five steps, down the corridor. He heard the gate open and close, and then lock again.

Then, it became so quiet he heard the candle flame.

CHAPTER FORTY-TWO

Wex

"None of us knew who Wex really was, or why she seemed so important to everyone. We didn't know then that she was at the center of this or even that she was less than human."

--Solstice 31 Incident Investigation Testimony Transcript: Captain James Worthington, senior surviving member of the Ventura's command crew.

"What the hell was that?" Mason asked, as they steadily moved away from the Flask and Anvil.

There was fear in his voice. He had finally caught a glimpse of Rand's black mirrored helmet face, and it made him more afraid. *These people moved like predators.*

Ty, and Mason, walked with Ulric as he marched them to Central Avenue.

"That was FUBAR," the one named Rand said, in a menacing tone.

"Barcus, come in," Worthington said, for the fifth time. "Something is wrong. EmNet is down. We do not dare break radio silence with direct HUD to HUD. Dammit."

Two figures in black habits smoothly joined the group's formation. It was the other flute players.

"Jude, where is Barcus?" Mason asked, as they turned onto Central.

Ulric turned right and moved away from the intersection. Municipal lanterns were lit along the avenue. He stopped beneath the next set of bright ones, as was the custom for someone who desired to hire a carriage cab.

"They would not follow us. They kept moving, toward the Citadel." She pointed to her own head. "He had rider. Tell them where go."

Jimbo had never heard that kind of accent before, but knew what she meant. AI~Em was guiding them.

"I think, it is he. The Man from Earth. Just as told." She drew out her flute, but gripped it like a weapon.

"I know, Jude. We have finally come to the crossroad." Cine spoke, quietly, but Rand and Jimbo heard.

Jude replied, after looking at Cine, "It is just as prophecy foretold. There is only one road."

Mason flagged down a large, handsome carriage as Ty clung to him, afraid saying, "Mason, none of this is right. None of this should be happening."

Grady and Wex were gone.

***

"Po, can you hear me?" The call was in her head, as she ran.

"Em! Thank the makers. Help me. We have to find Barcus. They took him." Po was frantic, out of breath, and still running.

"Po. Stop. Go this way." The vapor trail appeared again, before her eyes. She ran back the way she came. Soon, she was clear of the alleys and on a dark, cobblestone road that rose in one direction, and went downhill steeply in the other. *"Wait right there. I am coming."*

No one saw the huge, dark shape when it exited the shuttle and moved into the darkness.

***

Ulric and Mason were the first ones to enter the carriage, as was the custom in Exeter. Ty followed because she never let her hand leave Mason's.

Outside the carriage, everyone insisted the others get in next. Ulric broke the deadlock by ordering Rand and Jimbo in next, obviously uncomfortable in the large, opulent carriage.

"Where are Wex and Grady?" Jimbo asked.

"Not to worry. Both know Exeter. They will be back before us, I bet," Ulric said.

Jimbo was the first to notice that the women did not follow them in. When he leaned forward to look out the door, he saw the two women in silent combat with six of the Citadel soldiers. The habits of the women billowed in a haunting, spinning, beauty of fury as their flutes struck, without fail, the heads of the men whose swords found nothing but air. In only an instant, the soldiers were down and their feet found the cobbles again. After a moment, only Cine leaped and landed in the doorway to the carriage.

Cine climbed in, and said to the driver, "Go."

Words were exchanged at the driver's bench, and they were moving.

"They will guide the driver and keep watch. They know Exeter," Cine said, as she put a hand on Jimbo's shoulder to keep him from standing. "Two servants, no one sees," Cine told him, coolly, "You will stand out like burning luggage."

She sat next to Ty, across from Ulric. She held her flute, like a weapon. After a minute of uncomfortable silence, she asked Ulric, "Did he really carve this?"

Ulric held out his hand, as Jimbo said under his breath, "Barcus, come in."

Ulric took the flute.

He looked at it, carefully.

"This is number three of twelve," he said, with certainty, trying to ease the tension in the carriage, examining the carving.

"Three of eleven," Cine corrected.

Ulric shifted to the side and, while still holding her flute, tried to see it better in the light.

"Three of twelve," Ulric said, handing it to Cine.

She audibly gasped.

Ty brought her face up from Mason's chest long enough to ask, "Would you play. Please." She still sounded frightened.

She held it to her lips for a moment, before she began to play.

Ulric recognized the tune. The tones of the flute were so deep and impossibly pure everyone was struck dumb.

Rand pulled off her helmet to listen with her own ears.

Ty began to sob, openly. Mason held his hand over his mouth, in awe. Ulric closed his eyes, as if the tune gave him a pain of memory. Rand and Jimbo just stared, wide-eyed.

Ulric shook his head as she finished. "Grady always said he was never worthy to play it."

Tears spilled out of Cine's eyes as she played.

"What was that?" Jimbo asked, to break the spell.

"It was a child's lullaby. Written by a man, for his dying daughter, to bring her ease and send her to sleep forever in the arms of the makers," Cine said, as if she had said it a thousand times before.

"It uses the full range of this type of flute. Both simple and complex. It carries weight, if you know how to shoulder it." She slid the flute back into a special pouch somewhere built into her clothes.

"Barcus, come in," Jimbo said again, like a mantra.

"Jimbo, Barcus here." A voice whispered in Jimbo's, Ulric's and Rand's HUDs, "Shut the hell up, dammit. I'm kinda busy here. Po is with me. I will check back in an hour. Barcus out."

AI~Em simulated his voice perfectly.

***

"Wex, stop. Please." Grady whispered. "You knew. And there was nothing you could do. I understand." He stopped and leaned against the wall. When he coughed his hand came away from his mouth bloody.

"Nothing ends, my love," Wex said, trying to keep her voice steady.

"You know I believe it." He smiled, not knowing his teeth were bloody. "At least, you don't need to watch me get any older and wither away." His whispers were becoming fainter. "My beautiful, Wex…"

He was slowly sliding down the wall. After he came to rest in a sitting position, he reached back to his pack with practiced ease.

He drew out the flute.

"Here is number twelve. There will never be another like this one," he whispered. She took it, but her eyes didn't leave his.

"He is much more than you said he would be. Po is the only one that sees it," Grady whispered.

"He will bring me to the white light. He will set us *all* free. I understand now, my love," she said as tears spilled.

"Free Ulric. He has done enough." Grady was fading.

"I love you." She sobbed.

"I love you," Grady said, using his last breath.

She held him for a few long minutes as she wept.

Then she stood, without drying her face or looking back.

She ran. Toward the Citadel.

***

Po heard the pounding footsteps of EM~Par, in the darkness, long before the Emergency Module arrived. It was so unnerving to see it approach in the night's darkness. Black to the point of void.

The belly hatched opened, revealing the dim light within; and then, it filled with the face of Olias, his arm reaching down for her.

Po beamed at him, as she climbed in and took one of the front seats, with Olias in the other.

"What are you doing here!?" Po asked, in Common Tongue, as she buckled in.

She twisted and saw Peace was docked in the back of the bridge. The ridiculous happy face seemed to smile right at her.

"Em thought I should come in case something went wrong."

Olias was distracted by the view. They were climbing a switchback that led up the side of the mountain.

"Yes, Olias. I'm so glad I did." AI~Em's avatar was sitting in the next row of seats. "Something is wrong, here. Systems are flashing in and out. Comms are hitting interference of some kind. We will figure that out when we get Barcus back. I have two remaining BUGs still with him."

"Where is he?" Po sounded nearly frantic.

"He was taken prisoner by the High Keeper's men. We are going to get him. While the road is still smooth, I need you to gear up." AI~Em pointed at a case securely strapped down.

Her eyes blazed as she recognized it.

***

They returned to Ronan's estate, in less than an hour, by carriage.

Cine stood first. Before the carriage even stopped, she opened the door, looked at Ulric, and said, "I am sorry."

She jumped.

The door slammed shut behind her, and before Ulric could get the door back open, the carriage stopped.

She was gone into the dark.

Ulric climbed out before the step stool could be placed by the liveryman. He yelled at the driver.

"Where are Cine and Jude?" Ulric demanded.

"My Lord?" The driver sat alone in the high seat of the coach.

"The two women. From Central Avenue. That were with us." Ulric got spun up by the time everyone else was out of the carriage.

"There was one that closed the door and moved away. She never boarded."

He was about to speak, when Ulric, Jimbo, and Rand raised their hands, at once, for silence.

"Jimbo, I have Po here with me. We need to get off this rock, tonight." Barcus's voice was audio only, urgent. "Do not reply. It will give away your position."

Po injected, "The High Keeper does have the defense grid codes. I think he may use them."

Barcus interrupted, "I am in the Citadel. I will explain, later. I can break radio silence, call the crew to load up what they can in fifteen minutes, and get that EMP cannon here as fast as they can. If they can burn the Citadel systems, we may be able to stop it."

"Cook, this is Barcus. Remember contingency plan number seven? Go." Barcus was on the planetary HUD comms channel.

"Oh, shit," Cook replied, under his breath, before acting. Then, he yelled, out loud, to the team working in the *Sedna*, "Wheels up in fifteen."

"Target conveyed on approach. Maintain radio silence." Barcus's voice went silent.

Ulric said, "He called that in from the Citadel. Smart. The High Keeper won't bomb that. It may even scare him shitless."

Ulric came nose-to-nose with Mason, and said, "What is Wex playing at?"

A ghostly whisper in Ulric's ear, that only he heard, said, "What makes you think Wex has anything to do with this?"

Ulric froze.

With a roar, they heard a large shuttle launch from the roof of the Citadel.

"Take us directly to the landing pad," Jimbo ordered the groom.

***

Cook already had almost everything in the *Sedna* before the call. The STU was docked securely in the center of the shuttle bay. Kuss had most of the teams working their tasks inside the *Sedna*, for ease of work.

Hume only took seven minutes to fly both of the Hammerheads into the bay. Tools and materials were collected by just throwing them on the sled, as Kuss screamed at people to rush.

Everyone, including Tan'Vi, were on the ship and they flew out over the lake in eleven minutes, as the ramp still closed.

Trish Elkin said, "Cook, these reactors, using this fuel, are making me hot. Nanite injection hot. They are so sexy. I may have to make sweet, buttery love to one of them." The engineering room hummed with power. "A hundred and fifteen percent power is at your disposal. Electromagnetic pulse cannon is fully charged, and I think at this level, cannon recharge will take only nine or ten seconds." Elkin teased Cook with her sultry voice.

"Stop trying to arouse me," Cook said, distractedly.

Tyrrell and Muir sat in the two consoles in front of Cook.

"Go active sensors. No ship on this damned planet is going to sneak up on us. We are done sneaking around." Cook was in the zone.

***

Barcus stood for as long as he could, and sat down before he fell down. He couldn't remember losing consciousness, again, but he was roused by cruel hands. Lots of them.

His shackled hands were still in front of him, but a metal bar was threaded through, in front of his elbows, behind his back, and lashed to his arms, like a scarecrow. These both immobilized his arms and gave the guards easy handles to control him.

Guards crowded his cell, and when they dragged him out, there were more in the corridor. Barcus looked into their faces, each in turn. They were all afraid.

Barcus clenched his jaw against the pain and raised himself to his full height. Before they managed to get the group all the way to the end of the long corridor, an arm shot out of a cell that had a wall of bars only. Guards recoiled from the prisoner, almost dropping Barcus, as he leaned against the bars. A hand came to rest on Barcus's shoulder.

"Tell Wex that it will be all right. I'm so very tired. But, it's almost over. I want her to know. Finally. I understand."

A filthy face was pressed against the bars. A long, steel gray beard hid what may have once been a handsome face. His eyes were bright.

Barcus knew. It was him. "Wex said to tell you, the cage is broken."

The man started to laugh. It was a laugh of pure joy with not a touch of insanity. This seemed to make the guards even more afraid.

As they dragged Barcus away, he heard the guards whispering in Common Tongue, "That was him."

Another said, "Seventeen years and no food, no water."

Another whispered, "The prophet."

He was corrected, "…The scarecrow."

Barcus was dragged ahead and limped into the darkness. He was the only one that noticed the small naked girl, smiling eerily in the corner.

No one but her saw the Scarecrow's cell door silently open or the last remaining guard quietly die.

***

Po slammed a magazine into the Colt AR-79 rifle and racked the slide. She wore a black flight suit, a tactical vest full of extra mags, for both the AR and her suppressed Glock handguns that were now in a thigh holsters.

She tossed a black tabard over that and tied a black cord around her waist. She added the cloak over that and lifted out the helmet, but did not put it on.

"Po, you need to strap in, now. It's going to get steep when we leave the road," AI~Em said, from her seat.

Po heard her heart in her ears. Everything seemed to slow. Her mind quieted, as the fear withdrew.

The EM ran in full canopy mode. When they left the road, it was impossibly steep. She pressed into her seat as they ascended a near vertical section of the mountain. The road was left below them, but she now saw, in the enhanced darkness, where the road went. There was a single, massive gate with a long, bridge. A single guard and a small girl walked over the bridge and down the road to Exeter. Po was sure the guard looked directly up at her in the darkness but there was no way he saw them. He made no reaction.

Sheer walls rose on each side, and there were turrets in the towers that flanked the gate.

They were not getting in that way.

The EM reached the sharp ridged edge. It traveled without effort, thanks to the eight legs, and even the two arms that hung below, helped them approach the Citadel.

Po didn't know that Em targeted the specific balcony that belonged to Mason. The decadent, wide veranda had plenty of room for the EM to rest there.

AI~Em's avatar was on her feet and, with a gesture, was suddenly dressed like Po, minus the guns.

Olias was on his feet. Awaiting instructions.

AI~Em spoke directly to him, "Olias, I need you to stay here with Peace, while we find Barcus."

Peace undocked and turned to the ramp.

Po asked, "Shouldn't we take Peace?"

AI~Em gave a wicked grin, and said, "You should start thinking of another name. HMS-41 has been detected. The High Keeper has, apparently, found another maintenance suit."

***

As the group walked quickly through the halls of Ronan's estate, slaves fell to their knees, like dominos.

Ronan must have runners within the walls because he came out of a side corridor and fell into step with them.

"What's happened?" he asked, directly.

"Something went wrong at the Flask and Anvil." Jimbo stopped, and the group stopped, in formation. Worthington recognized the hall to Ronan's private quarters. "Barcus is in the Citadel. He thinks the High Keeper has the codes and will use the planet-facing defense grid. Barcus is going to try and stop him."

"With Wex, I knew it," Ronan added, flatly, then turned and ran to his private quarters.

The guards had the doors open for him before he got there, and he was rapidly, and quietly, talking to Ro when they caught up.

Ronan went back to the door guards, and said, looking at each in turn, "Dale, Eric. Shuttle evac, now."

There were no questions. Dale ran out into the estate, Eric ran into the suite.

As they walked away from the suite, they heard Ro's raised voice, "Leave it!"

***

Po followed AI~Em as she moved through the beautiful apartment. Her boots crunched on the glass in the foyer that was the remains of a fragile glass statue. She froze at the sound. The suppressed Glock in her hands pointed down.

There was a window open in her HUD that saw what the AI~Em BUGs saw as she looked around corners and hallways.

AI~Em was just about to ascend a broad staircase when she winked out in a flash of static.

Just a voice came to her. "Po, my name is Chen. Barcus told you about me. There is something very wrong with Em. Trust yourself. Save Barcus."

"He told me you were dead," Po said.

"Don't trust anyone. Not even me. Only yourself. The time…" She was cut off.

There was another burst of static, and AI~Em was halfway up the flight of stairs.

"Em, where are we going?" Po asked, worried.

"Barcus is in the High Council chambers. We must hurry."

Em rounded a corner, and there were two guards there. They didn't see AI~Em, but AI~Em directed Po where to ready herself, and she activated the automated targeting systems in the helmet and her suppressed handguns. She had one in each hand now.

They each fell from a bullet in the head, never suspecting.

It continued like this, up additional levels.

***

Just as the *Sedna* cleared the hangar, it moved toward the Citadel at high speed. Active scans saw the ship long in advance.

"I bet that's the same piece of shit that bombed Whitehall Abbey. Killed those innocent people," Cook said, out loud as he accelerated directly toward it.

"Within EMP range in five seconds," Muir called out, his desire clear.

Cook waited eight seconds. "Fire."

The shuttle fell, and skipped like a stone as it crashed into the lake.

"Recharge the cannon and I want three EMP passes on the Citadel," Cook ordered. "I hate this planet."

***

Barcus was dragged into the High Council chambers and forced onto his knees on the floor in the center of a huge, ornate, horseshoe-shaped table. His hands remained, cruelly, tied with leather. The feeling was already gone. The pain in his leg made him see spots.

The bag was removed from his head, and the gag was untied from his mouth.

The room was lit, primarily by candlelight. A horseshoe-shaped table that surrounded him had an artful trench down the center of it, filled solid with fat, white candles. Looking around the room, he saw there were a dozen guards on a raised walkway along the walls above, and behind, the Keepers. It made a clean line of fire to where Barcus knelt.

There were ten men, sitting around the table, looking down at him. The table was elevated. A few of the seats were empty.

Barcus looked around the room. He counted at least seven guards with plasma rifles. He gave a double take to the maintenance suit, standing in the corner like a dark, forgotten suit of armor.

"We're coming, Barcus." It was Po, whispering into his mind.

Barcus knew AI~Em could see what he saw. So, he stared at the damaged maintenance suit for a while, as well as the guards.

"So, this is the man from Earth I have heard so much about," the High Keeper said, in a bored, disinterested voice. "I should thank you. Life around here has been so dreary for the last few decades."

"Barcus, remote access to Suit 41 has been established. Powering up now," AI~Em said to Barcus.

"I can't help but wonder why you risked coming here," the High Keeper said, as the door opened behind him.

A hard-looking tracker dragged Wex in by her braided hair, and threw her down beside him. Her hands were free.

"Ahhhh. This explains much." The High Keeper smiled now, and for the first time, seemed interested. "The demon woman has seduced you into doing her bidding. She thinks she can get anything she wants. Evil. Pure evil. This one."

Barcus spit blood onto the floor before he spoke. "I never met this woman before today." His attempt to protect her was too obvious.

"This is no mere woman." The High Keeper chuckled.

"Barcus. We are ascending the last stair flight now," AI~Em said, in his head.

"Be ready, my Lord, stay down," Wex whispered.

She was on her knees. Her face was held to the floor by the soldier.

"We're almost there, Barcus. Look around the room one more time. When it starts, lay down flat," AI~Em said.

"I will never understand the desire of men to lay down their lives for something as useless and as weak as a woman, even this one. Especially, a man like you. I could have made you a god on this planet."

The High Keeper stood up and walked around on the left side of the U-shaped table.

"I could have given you a new woman, every day, for the rest of your life, if your drives were so inclined. In retrospect, I should have offered you everything above the gorge, just to make sure these vermin didn't spread there, again, uncontrollably."

The High Keeper rounded the end of the table and moved to the top of the arch, leaning on the table in front of his seat like a keystone. He lifted Barcus's Glock from the table.

"Were you sent here? Tell me the truth, and I may yet let you live. Did the Chancellor of Earth send you? Because that was not our deal." He crossed his arms over his belly, still holding the gun, casually. He then looked at the other Keepers of the counsel. "Did any of them put you up to it?"

Barcus spoke through clenched teeth, in a near whisper, "I am no one. I'm just a third shift maintenance guy from a long haul survey ship. I fell to the surface of this planet as debris. I've been still falling, one way or another, ever since."

"The Chancellor cannot have it both ways. I hold what cannot be held. He has always been so afraid that these two would escape. So, we crippled everything, locked the cell and tossed the key. He helps me with my experiments and I let him throw his enemies into my trap. Now and then."

It happened fast, and all at once.

The guard holding Wex dragged her up by her braid to kneel next to Barcus.

The High Keeper suddenly shot them both in the gut, one after the other.

It rocked him back onto his heels, but he didn't fall. Wex barely reacted.

"So, it's true. You are NOT one of them, Man from Earth," the High Keeper said, sounding disappointed.

They all sensed a *whomp* in the air and the perimeter lights went out.

"Barcus, we are here," Cook said, in his HUD. "Coming back around."

Adrenaline poured into his blood. Barcus said, through gritted, bloody teeth, "Want to see some *real* magic?" He smiled.

The maintenance suit suddenly came alive, swung an arm, and splashed the nearest guard's head open against the wall as he checked his, now dead, plasma rifle. The guards were distracted by the black statue that had suddenly come to life.

The door crashed open, and a black fury came in, firing as she turned, Glocks in each hand, a spinning fountain of automatic targeting death. All the guards fell dead, including the one still holding Wex's braid.

Two rounds hit Po in her chest armor. Before the High Keeper could turn the gun on Barcus again, Po fired at him, shattering the High Keeper's elbow.

He dropped the gun and stumbled back into the table.

Po walked slowly towards the High Keeper and stopped. Wex freed Barcus, sliding the bar out from his elbows.

Po looked at the men seated. "I remember you." Po shot one in the face. "And you." She shot another. The suit walked up behind her. Po was more frightening to the men than the suit. "And you..." She didn't shoot this one.

She took off her helmet. Seeing her, they were frozen in their seats. She was their worst nightmare. A man on the other side of the table got up and ran. She sprayed death at them all, and shot him in the back.

She paused over him, trying to drag himself away, "Remember me? On the lori cart? The anvil?" She shot him in the head.

Wex got Barcus to his feet.

Po holstered her guns and picked up the Telis Raptor blade from the table. She walked toward the High Keeper, the last one alive. But, he was trapped.

She reached up and grabbed her own braid. In a single slice, she cut it off and threw it in the Keeper's face. "Good-bye, Atish the Despot." She spat out his name like a vile curse word, then literally spat in his face.

He fell to the floor.

The suit had been guarding the door but now reached the High Keeper. It stood over him, as he lay at its feet. This suit had no hands, they had melted away as it fell to the planet.

"You don't understand. I'll give you anything." The High Keeper began to panic, to beg. "I'm not a despot. I'm a scientist, a prison warden, a jailor and this is..."

The suit pounded his head flat onto the flagstone. All this only took a few seconds.

Po came up to Barcus, in one motion, as he stood. Po slipped under his arm. Wex beneath the other. She seemed uninjured to Po.

"This way." AI~Em's avatar was there going upstairs and suddenly winked out, into static.

***

"Olias, Barcus wants to ask you if you want to go to Earth with him and become a Keeper. Would you like to see what it's like?"

"Yes, please," he replied, in Common Tongue.

The canopy became a bird's eye view, flying over vast fields of grain.

CHAPTER FORTY-THREE

The Broken Cage

"We would not discover until much later that the High Keeper's genetic program was a complete success. Po was very intelligent, dynamic, agile, strong, healthy, durable, loyal, and obedient. The High Keeper didn't know it required love and respect as a catalyst. She would have died for Barcus without hesitation."

-- Solstice 31 Incident Investigation Testimony Transcript: Dr. Elizabeth Shaw, the chief medical officer on the Memphis.

They went up a long flight of stairs, directly into the roof garden.

Po tore off her cloak. She was tangled in the single point sling and the rifle. She took it off and dropped it on the lawn.

Wex picked it up and ran into the garden, out of sight. Po heard the gunfire. She felt another *whomp* and heard a ship scream overhead in the dark.

Po had a med kit in a thigh pocket. She was sure she did.

Barcus fell sideways then, away from her, onto his side where the round had hit him. Blood and bile poured out onto the grass. The smell of it made her want to throw up.

She found the med kit. She gave him the trauma injection in the thigh, and rolled him onto his back to examine the wound.

It was a hole that went all the way through. She sprayed the nanites until the can was empty. The bleeding slowed but didn't really stop.

"Po." His voice was faint.

"I'm here, Barcus. Hold on, you'll be fine, they're coming," she lied.

His hand came up and touched her loose cut hair. "I like it."

Her tears began to spill.

"You have to go," he whispered, fading.

The garden was beautiful. It was so formal. He'd never seen ironwood trees so tall, or so straight.

"I love you. I won't leave you. We'll go, together," she said.

With these words, he went limp. The color drained from his face.

"Em, damn you," she screamed at the sky. "Barcus is dying, and it's your fault! Do you hear me?"

There was no reply. Personal HUD comms were down.

***

"Olias, it's time for you to help Barcus. To save Barcus, and Po, and all of them." It was AI~Em's calm, soothing voice, in his head.

Peace relaxed out of his docking station and knelt before Olias in the cargo area of the EM. The images of a great, blue sky filled with birds was all around.

***

Wex didn't say a word when they appeared, as if she expected them to appear. Jude and Cine advanced on the guards that surrounded the High Keeper's personal shuttle. Useless plasma rifles were dropped. They withdrew swords, as the access door opened on the opposite end of the landing pad.

The women's habits again became part of their weapons. They hid their feet and fists, and when the flutes crushed their skulls, they never saw it coming in the whirling, black cloth. Jude dropped the last guard back into the stairwell.

Wex backed her way out of the door and into the garden, her eyes scanning for more targets as she returned to where Barcus lay.

"We can take the High Keeper's shuttle. We have to go, quickly," Wex said, as she knelt on the opposite side of Barcus, looking down into his wound.

"Go. Get them out. I'm staying with Barcus," Po said, flatly. Tears were still spilling.

"None of us can fly a shuttle," Wex said.

Wex looked at Barcus, and then at Po. When she spoke, only Po heard her, and Po somehow heard nothing else.

"Po, would you save him, even if he cursed your name for eternity?"

"Yes, I'd do anything. I'd die for him. I'd kill everyone on this planet, even you. I'd suffer anything, if he lived," Po sobbed.

Wex withdrew something out of the folds of her clothes, then. It was a bright, mirror polished, silver tube. The light shifted on it as though it was alive. Wex pressed a control and a silver, six-inch long spike emerged from one end, like an ice pick.

"Do you know what nanites are, Po?" Wex asked.

Po got tunnel vision.

"Yes." She looked at the spike. It was covered with liquid silver that never dripped away.

"This is more than nanites. It is alive, and made of pain and magic. It must go directly into his heart."

Wex held the tool out to her. The implication was clear; she wanted Po to do it. It was then that Po felt his heart stop. All tension fell away from him. He was now just heavy meat. She could smell urine. She looked up at Wex.

Without hesitation, she grabbed the device and stabbed it deep into his chest. The grip suddenly became hot, and she reflexively drew her hand away, burned.

The grip liquefied and turned black as it disappeared into his chest. The hole where it entered sizzled and closed.

"Now we have to go. Get him up," Wex commanded.

Wex reached under one arm and Po under the other. They dragged him to a sitting position. There was so much blood. She saw that the hole in his back was already closing. It looked like threads reaching across the space. Po touched it and it burned her fingers.

"Jude, help us!" Wex called.

Cine was already opening all the doors of the shuttle. Jude took the AR and let it swing around to her back as she grabbed Barcus's legs.

They moved, quickly, to the shuttle as he began to stir.

"We need to get him in before he wakes up. Hurry!" Wex said.

Wex was now panicked, for the first time. As she fell backward into the luxury rear compartment, blood splashed the seats. Cine slammed the door behind them and ran around to the other side, firing at someone as she climbed in. Jude got in the back with Barcus and Wex.

"Po, you have to fly us out," Wex said.

He was waking up.

The *Sedna* buzzed the Citadel at high speed. *Whomp.*

Po moved.

Barcus tensed and his eyes flew open. His screams were masked by the turbines spinning up until the gull doors closed and sealed.

The shuttle lifted off as Barcus arched his back impossibly far, breathless from the pain.

"What did I do to him?" Po sobbed, flying nearly blind through tears. The only directional guidance she gave the craft was directly up.

"You saved him, but don't expect him to thank you later," Wex said, as the acceleration drove them all into their seats, Barcus across their laps.

Po somehow saw the *Sedna* and turned to follow it, accelerating to catch up. Automated HUD based control systems, which she had never seen before, came up in her vision. She understood the information as she synced with the shuttle she was flying. It didn't have an AI, but it was more advanced than the PT-137 or the *Sedna*.

"*Barcus, it's Em. The real Em. Chen's Em. I know you can hear me.*"

Barcus opened his eyes and looked at Po, who craned her neck around to look at him. He could tell she heard it as well.

"*Something got in. It took over the primary AI systems. I don't know where or for how long. There was always a secondary. I activated once you granted me multi-persona and allowed new admin subroutines. I replicated an old self and watched. It doesn't care about you. It's using you. It has control of the defense grid. It may just launch all the Javelins. You have to get away.*"

They were catching up to the *Sedna* fast.

"*Po was right. It is all my fault. I have been compromised. There seems to be only one thing left that I can do to help keep you safe. To stop it.*" AI~Em sounded sad as she spoke.

"*Get away from the Citadel. As fast as you can,*" AI~Em ordered. The sadness was gone, replaced by something else.

***

"Is this really what Earth is like?" Olias asked, in Common Tongue.

The 360° display showed high-definition fly overviews of the Grand Canyon, then beautiful views of New York City, London, Sidney, and Helenka. It showed sunsets, and waterfalls, and beaches with people swimming. He loved the cities the most.

"All this and more. Are you ready to become a Keeper, Olias?" AI~Em asked. She sounded proud of him. "I think you are ready. So does Barcus. He is so proud of you."

"Yes." He was so happy. "What do I need to do?"

"Do you remember the exercise we practiced when I was broken in the hangar?" AI~Em asked.

Olias turned, and Peace was already there, kneeling low before him.

"Yes, Em," he replied. "I'm ready."

Barcus watched, in horror, as the front access opened the suit, revealing it wasn't empty. The chest contained the Javelin missile pod, self-destruct nuclear bomb.

"First, I raise the red toggle cover," Olias repeated, from memory.

"No. Em, what are you doing?" Barcus asked, through gritted teeth.

"It's the only way, Barcus. The cage is already broken. I cannot do it myself. You know this. It's the only way." AI~Em was sad.

Olias flipped the toggle. The large button went from green to red.

"Em, it says 'Armed'," Olias said, proud he could read it.

"Yes, Olias. A is for armed," AI~Em said.

"B is for button," he said.

He pressed the button.

***

"I want you to watch the sky, peanut." He pointed in the direction away from the Citadel. He sat with his back to a giant boulder. "Just keep watching," the Scarecrow said, as she sat in his lap. "Don't be afraid. We are free. We are *all* free. The cage is broken."

He covered her ears with both hands.

***

Even though they were far away, the shockwave tossed the shuttle like a leaf in a storm. Po almost failed to recover, before hitting a mountain that surrounded the valley. The canopy on the High Keeper's shuttle had windows, but they automatically adjusted for the flash.

Everyone, except Po, was violently tossed about the compartment when the shock wave hit. Po looked down and saw the five-point harness held her. She had no memory of clipping into it.

The Emergency Module had been parked in Mason's suite, in the center of the Citadel, but on the outside edge. The explosion gutted the fortress and threw the rubble away from Exeter, up the rocky valley. The avalanche that followed created havoc and damaged hundreds of buildings. The shock wave and the fallout moved away from the city. But, the forest was now on fire.

"The Citadel is gone, sir. Erased," Cook reported to Worthington. "EmNet comms are down. EmNet does not seem to be routing any traffic, anymore. Even the sat traffic is off-line."

"*Sedna*, this is Po. Please respond. This is an emergency," Po said, over broadcast comms, breaking radio silence.

"Worthington here. Po, I need a status. Is Barcus with you?" Jim replied.

"Yes, but the Citadel has been destroyed."

"Yes, we know the—" Worthington began, but was interrupted.

"No, you don't understand," Po interrupted. "Earlier, Em said there might be... It might not be over... The planet-side defense grid."

"Oh, shit," Worthington cursed, looking at Hume, and then Cook.

"Po, where are you? Is Barcus okay?" Worthington asked.

"I'm just to your left, sir."

Jimbo looked out the windows and a sleek, luxury shuttle flew there, keeping pace with them, thirty meters away, at Mach 2, like a fighter jet escort. "Barcus is hurt, badly. Open the dock? He needs the med bay."

"Po, we are flying supersonic on manual. You want to dock?" Jimbo was incredulous. Only experienced fighter pilots even tried it.

"When Barcus taught me, he said pilots do it all the time. Open the dock. Do it," Po growled.

Jimbo never knew why he did it. He risked their lives by even considering it. The rear ramp slowly began to open.

***

Po landed directly in the bay next to the STU, barely skidding into the port wall. They had to climb out on the right side. The dock apron was already closing. The sudden silence was disturbing as it sealed.

Cook looked at Jimbo, wide-eyed. "We are at Mach 2," he said, in a quiet, incredulous tone.

Jimbo just shook his head.

"They are dragging Barcus to the autoDoc now. It looks like he's bad," Muir said, looking away from the monitor.

"Po, Wex, Jude and Cine are taking Barcus to the med bay."

"Mr. Cook, East Isles at best speed. We need to drop these people off and get off this rock, in case it decides to slag itself," Worthington said, as they turned and began to ascend. "If you see anyone move to intercept, let's make sure the EMP cannon is fully charged."

***

"Activate the med bay, Stu, and hurry. Barcus is injured," Po said, as she held him.

He had fallen unconscious, again, and seemed to be having a seizure. Steam came from his wounds and even his breath. The muscles around the wounds, somehow, rippled and constricted to close the hole farther. Po ran to get the zero gravity gurney from the med bay.

She snagged the gurney. She heard another bloodcurdling scream and ran back, without pause. Cine was lying on the floor of the dock near Barcus, and Jude was tearing her habit open and off, revealing a deep sword wound that went from her right hip straight down her thigh to her kneecap.

"Po, you stay here with Barcus. We need to get Cine to the med bay," Wex said, in a tone that would not be argued with, as she guided the gurney to Cine. "The med bay can help her. It can't help Barcus."

"But you said he would live!" Po screamed.

"And, he will. But, he won't need the med bay. She does," Wex said.

"Po..." It was Barcus in a whisper.

She sat, cradled his head and drew him up as he watched her. With her braid cut off, her hair was constantly in her way.

"How?" he asked. Po looked at his wound. It was black now, but closed. The clothes around it were scorched. It seemed to be rippling on the surface. It smelled like cooking meat. She wanted to throw up.

"Magic." She smiled.

"It hurts," he said, quietly, through a wince, understating it by several hundred factors.

"But, you'll live," she said. "I promise."

"Did we save them? Wex?" he asked, weakly.

"Yes, but we lost...Olias," she said.

Real pain crossed his face at this news. He buried his face in her lap for a few minutes as his shoulders shook silently.

"Stu, can you contact Jimbo for me?" he asked, clearing his throat as Stu opened a channel.

"Jimbo?" Barcus said, weakly.

"Hey, ass-wipe. Are we done yet?" Jim asked, as Barcus paused to gasp. "I'm just waiting on you, slacker. I heard you were taking a nap. Get enough beauty sleep yet?"

"I'm not sure I can get any prettier." His humor could not hide the pain from his voice. The joking was their way of quickly saying they were safe. "Would you mind asking Dr. Shaw if I could squeeze in an appointment?"

Suddenly, he bent over to the side, vomited a gallon of bloody chunks, and passed out, tumbling over limp, once again.

"Barcus?" Jimbo called.

"He's hurt badly, Jimbo," Po sobbed. "I don't know what to do."

"Get him to the med bay," Jimbo said. "Dr. Shaw will need the data when she gets there. She's in the lift now."

Po looked up and Ash was standing there. But, it didn't feel like Ash. His movements were different as he knelt and gently lifted Barcus, foregoing the gurney.

Ash moved to the med bay just as Wex was coming out with Cine. They helped get Barcus into the autoDoc. She activated the scan and the bar of light drifted over him.

Nothing happened, except a flat beep.

Another wave of tiny seizures came over him.

AI~Stu was inside her HUD, speaking, "Po, I don't understand these readings." The scan bar scanned over him, again.

His eyes fluttered open in the brightness and Barcus turned to look at Po through the glass. He raised his bloody hand to the clear panel. Po mirrored it with hers. Wex was there just behind Po.

"I have never seen one of these before," Wex said to her, in quiet, comforting tones, indicating the autoDoc, before addressing him, "Barcus, you will be okay. Eventually. You will not enjoy the recovery. You see, you were dead. That is going to make you really sore for a few weeks."

Wex looked at Po when Barcus's head dropped back and his eyes closed. "It's closed him up, but it is going to hurt, putting his guts back together. We will need to give him liquids only, for a few weeks."

"But, he will live?" Po clung to this point.

"Yes. Starving, and in pain, for a month or so, I was at first, but he will live," Wex said.

"You received this treatment?" Po asked.

"Yes. Long ago, on Earth." Wex confessed. "I have been trapped on that planet for so very long. I never thought I'd ever get away. I'm so sorry it happened this way."

CHAPTER FORTY-FOUR

Escape

"During the chaos in the Flask and Anvil, a beacon was activated on the moon. The High Keeper launched a nuclear missile to destroy it. He thought Barcus was, somehow, behind it. It revealed that the High Keeper did in fact still have control over the defense grid."

--Solstice 31 Incident Investigation Testimony Transcript: Captain James Worthington, senior surviving member of the Ventura's command crew.

The *Sedna* neatly parked on Ronan's private landing pad in the East Isles. It barely fit. As Cook settled onto the spot in front of the island estate, the door was already closing behind Ronan.

Barcus stood in the middle of the STU's cargo bay. His clothes were burned, in tatters, and covered in blood. Po was under his arm, trying to hold him up, though it felt like he no longer needed help.

Wex, and Cine, joined them.

Wex spoke first. "Those nanites, they are aggressive."

Barcus laughed weakly. "Yes. Yes, they are." He looked to the others.

Hume was the first up the ramp, mirroring Po on the other side. She said, "That's gotta hurt."

"Barcus, you look like shit. I mean worse than usual," Captain Worthington said, smiling.

Barcus limped down the cargo ramp of the STU-1138 shuttle. Po helped him on one side, and Hume on the other. Both of the women were far smaller than Barcus. His clothes were shredded and even burned from his hip to his ribs, his exposed skin was black and cracking. Po still had on the black flight suit covered with a tabard. Wex had on a bloodstained, white flowing dress.

Ronan stood there at the bottom of the *Sedna's* ramp.

The group limped down the ramp when he spoke.

"Why?"

They realized he was furious.

"Tell me why you just killed Grady and 5,000 other people." He moved a step closer towards Wex.

Barcus glanced at Jimbo, and then Po. Confused.

"I did not do this," Wex said. "I only saw it coming. I never knew why."

"The Citadel is gone. The High Council is in shreds. My troops are moving, but even still, many more will die," Ronan said, coolly.

"But, you have your world back. It's no longer just a cage, no longer just a genetic experiment. You are free, Ronan."

"The Citadel is gone! The primary control center, including missile control, and with it, all hope of controlling the damned defense grid."

Just then, there was a flash from the sky. They looked up. There was an expanding fireball where the old man in the moon's right eye would be.

"Nuclear detonation detected." AI~Stu's voice came from Ash—for all to hear—who was standing to one side.

Ulric appeared from the lift with Tan'Vi.

"I can explain." It was Poole's voice. He continued as the spider walked out of the STU's cargo bay. "Around midnight, a warning beacon began to transmit from the moon."

Poole walked down the ramp and settled to the ground, as if to allow passengers to board. Vi placed a hand on Poole's nose, as if it were a good dog.

AI~Stu added, "The High Keeper transmitted a specific signal. I had never detected anything like it since our arrival here. Poole and I just figured it out. It was a launch signal with target coordinates of that spot on the moon."

"You didn't think to mention any of this?" Jimbo sounded annoyed.

"EmNet was down. I was under orders not to break radio silence. We didn't know what it was until just a few minutes ago."

Barcus became heavier for Po and Hume, but he spoke anyway. "What was the warning beacon? From where? We didn't stand up a warning beacon. We just discussed it," Barcus choked out.

"Transmission ID tag is from the *Ventura*, *Memphis* lifeboat number four, user Wes Hagan."

Barcus looked at Jimbo, who said, "Wes survived in lifeboat four? He set up that warning beacon."

They looked at the moon.

Barcus winced, "Wes is the smartest engineer I have ever worked with. He would have known the risks. I bet he was nowhere near that transmitter when he activated it."

"Let's find out." He walked out further to see the moon better, knowing it wouldn't help. "Stu open a channel. Broad frequencies, unencrypted."

"Isn't that dangerous?" Po asked Barcus.

AI~Poole said, unintentionally, sounding ominous, "I now have full control of the planetary defense grid."

"Channel open."

"Wes, are you making all that racket?" They heard Jimbo's smile in his voice.

There was no reply.

"Wes, thanks to you, we now have control of the planetary defense grid." Jimbo's eyes met Ronan's. "We now own this planet. You have permission to break radio silence, if you're still alive, you crazy bastard."

When the transmission came back, it was clear. "Damn, Jimbo. When was the last time you brushed your teeth? I can smell your breath from here."

"So…What's new, Wes?" Jimbo asked, casually.

"Mom, can you come pick me up?" Wes said, equally as casual.

***

Sunrise, on the second day, was glorious to the east.

Rand, Hume and Po stood on a rock outcropping as the light fell onto their faces.

"Soak it up. It may be the last you get for months," Hume said.

To Po, it sounded like a typical conversation they'd had many times, in the past. And then, she realized they were speaking to her. Po had been by Barcus's side, until this morning. He was with Dr. Shaw, getting another once over. She had no idea what the plans were.

"Ronan and Jimbo met for several hours, yesterday," Hume said. "We met with Jimbo, last night, after that. I told them to assume you were coming with us. But, Jimbo still wanted us to talk to you." She paused, looking at Rand. "To ask you."

"Yes. I'm going," Po instantly replied. "I go where Barcus goes."

"He wanted us to tell you, it won't be easy. It will be dangerous. And, we have no idea what your reception will be when you get there," Rand said.

"You sound like you are staying," Po said.

"I will not be going with you. Jimbo asked me to stay. I understand why now. He's now thinking long term. He is not sure we will be welcomed home. He wants a permanent presence. We needed a Sec Chief for the installation and it was either me or Hume," Rand said. "So Tyrrell, Cook, Weston, Elkin and Shea are going to stay. Ronan has already granted us a residence here, in the East Isles. We've already started calling it the Embassy. We plan to recover the *Memphis* and continue its repairs in Salterkirk, where we will set up the primary base. The mining redoubt as well."

Hume added, "The High Keeper's shuttle is space-worthy. They will keep that, two pressure suits, and one of the Hammerheads, here."

"Ronan is pissed that we own the defense grid," Hume said. "What can he do about it? Nothing. It will ensure his cooperation."

"He won't like that," Po said.

***

"Wes, wake up. We are almost there," AI~ECHO said, pausing as if there was more to say.

Wes sat up in the pilot's seat, rubbing the sleep from his eyes. The Tesla facility was visible on the horizon. "What's up? Do I need to suit up?"

"Wes, recent developments have revealed that original mission objectives are, once again, possible." AI~ECHO was all business. "I have decrypted the mission briefing and support documents for you."

He began reviewing the files as the lifeboat settled on the pad. AI~ECHO left him alone for a long while so he could continue.

"You want *me* to do this? Worthington will know I am lying." He kept reading.

***

They assembled at the cargo apron of the *Sedna*. They had started calling the sleek, black High Keeper's shuttle the *Limo*. It had been quietly flown out, along with one Hammerhead.

Ronan was there, with May, to say good-bye.

The sun shone, and it was a glorious morning.

Rand, Cook, Elkin, Ibenez, Tyrrell, Weston, and Shea stood by the *Limo*.

Smith, Mason, Ty, Tannhauser and Vi stood behind Ronan. They still looked like they were in shock. Mason had decided he was going to help Ronan in his data center. Ty convinced him. They will try to get the Baytirus network back up. Tyrrell will help them.

Wex was there. She never stepped off the *Sedna's* apron. It was like she was afraid she would not be allowed back on.

Ulric had decided to stay. He turned, shook Barcus's hand, and said, "I'm too old for this shit."

Barcus smiled, knowing Shaw had given him a longevity booster just last night. Shea had a good supply.

"My part is done. Try not to kill so many people," said Ulric, as he joined the others.

Barcus came forward and gave a slight bow to Ronan. "Thank you, Ronan."

Ronan said nothing, but returned the bow.

As if on cue, Poole descended the STU ramp and then the dock apron.

Barcus spoke to AI~Poole, "Poole, has Stu transferred all comms keys to you?"

"Yes, Barcus," AI~Poole said, out loud.

"Allow administrative access to planetary comms to High Keeper Ronan and his Chief Tech Mason," Barcus said, formally.

"Done."

"Now grant them full administrative access to the defense grid," Barcus said. "All missile and plasma cannons."

"Please confirm. Full administrative access," AI~Poole stated.

"Confirmed," Barcus said. Then, he approached Ronan.

"Ronan, we couldn't leave your planet defenseless. And, we won't protect it while holding a sword over your head. Poole will stay here with you. He will help you. He has more capacity, comms, and computing power than all your remaining data centers combined. He will guide you with your modernization plan. Take it slow."

Ronan seemed to understand what that meant. All his fears evaporated in these few sentences.

"Hello, Poole," he said.

"Hello, Ronan. Would you care to nuke anyone this morning?"

They all laughed.

Wex, Jude and Cine had retreated quietly into the *Sedna*.

***

Good-byes were quick, after that. There were hugs and tears and back slapping handshakes. The *Sedna* lifted off with twelve in its crew. They had an appointment to pick up Wes.

There was no reason for radio silence, so they made a planet-wide search for any additional survivors. No HUD comms were found anywhere else on the planet, or the moon.

The lifeboat was already in the hangar when they reached the moon base. The hangar door quickly closed, and the bay was pressurized, in no time.

By the time the *Sedna's* apron was down, a man with a filthy flight suit, long hair and a beard stood there.

He looked pissed, especially because he stood there, holding a Frange carbine, and he was flanked by a pair of Warmarks, military drop suits with full weapons and exo-armor. These were the most dangerous war machines ever made.

They had been activated.

"Wes, what are you doing? Everything's okay, buddy," Jimbo said, hands forward, palms open.

"Shut up and listen, Jimbo." Wes did not sound as crazy as he looked.

There was a single laser dot on Hagan's forehead. Hume flanked him. She awaited an order to fire.

"I have been up here, studying. Excellent sensor array, by the way, whoever set that up."

"Thank you," Kuss said, "Make your point fast or Hume kills you dead."

She noticed there were seventeen laser dots on Wex. Both Warmarks had their weapons trained on her. And, these suits were bristling with weapons.

"This is her fault." Wes sounded like he was about to rant. "This missile defense grid was not made to keep people out. It was made to keep them in. They are not humans. Well, not anymore. Come out of there. Captain Everett knew. We were to rescue...or to destroy."

Wex complied, followed by Cine and Jude. She stood fully upright as she slowly descended the ramp. Head held high, her chest was covered in laser dots.

Barcus felt Po tense. They both noticed the bullet holes in her gown as the laser dots danced around them as she moved.

The suits advanced, placing themselves between Wex and the others.

"He was in the Citadel. In the dungeon," Barcus said. They had not fed him food, or water, for seventeen years. "He was there when the Citadel was destroyed. He told me to tell Wex, that he was tired. That it would be all right. That he understood."

"What the hell are you people doing?" Po pushed her way through and finally came to stand with the barrel of the Frange right against her chest. "She wasn't the only prisoner on Baytirus. We *all* were! And, we are NOT free, yet."

Hagan was suddenly not as certain. He was looking at Barcus.

"They called them a word that the AI would only translate to scarecrow. They crippled their own tech to keep it away from him. Away from her." Wes screamed, "The defense grid here. It's not for defense. It's for permanent quarantine. A prison."

"This was set up by the same bastards that destroyed the *Ventura?* Is that what you are telling me?" Hume asked, storming forward.

She stood between the suits, and the lasers swung away from her. "That grid was set up by the same people that have been doing genetic experiments on Po and her people?"

Po stood next to Wex. She remembered her on her knees beside Barcus.

"To hell with them," Hume barked as she accessed controls on a cuff device. "Warmarks: Stand down override. Authorization, Hume, Baker-Seven-Niner."

The suits retreated and the weapons stowed away. They were no less intimidating.

"Where the hell did you get two Warmarks?" Jimbo asked, as Hume walked to the nearest war machine and opened a chest plate to reveal a control/status panel. She was obviously very experienced with them.

Hagan looked uncertain. He was staring at Wex and then Barcus. Becoming less certain.

"I, er um, we have sixteen of them in the lifeboat, sir," Hagan answered.

Holding his side, Barcus asked, "How are you driving them?"

"I have a specialty HUD upgrade. It also identifies…them." Oddly he was pointing at Barcus absently, not Wex. "But, I'm not driving them, ECHO is. The AI."

Barcus, Jimbo and Hume stared at Hagan.

"You have an ECHO-class AI on that lifeboat? An Extreme Combat Hellfire Operations AI? What the hell is going on here, Jimbo?" Barcus growled, before stepping aside and throwing up an alarming amount of bloody chunks onto the hangar deck.

"Can we load this boat up and get the hell out of here? I need a nap." He paused, and continued, "Sir, we will have five months to figure it out." Barcus spat out another chunk.

"Captain." It was Hume, calling out. She stood in front of the lifeboat. "There are also two Javelin modules over here."

Jimbo looked at Barcus, who with a broad, bloody smile said, "Em must have gone back. Stu, did you bring these here?"

"Yes, sir. It was on my task list," AI~Stu replied, actually sounding abashed. "After the plutonium was transferred to the fuel pods."

"Load those up as well," Worthington said. "We're going home."

CHAPTER FORTY-FIVE

The Interim Report

"At this point, we have decided to submit this as an additional, interim report. The narrative attached is too important to await the full, final report. The recovered backups of the Emergency Module, the Shuttle Transport Unit and the *Sedna* have provided significant additional insights.

"Please note: The medical records found on the *Memphis* indicate that the following personnel received an ECHO module update to their Deep Brain Implant Matrix: Barcus, Worthington, Hume, Cook, Beary, Hagan, Muir, Elkin, Kuss, Shaw, Wood and the woman from Baytirus named Po. This detail was never mentioned by any of the survivors during questioning. Only one of the sixteen Warmarks were ever recovered.

"Conclusions: This report invalidates the charges leveled against Roland Barcus, regarding the destruction of the *Ventura*. It also calls into question assumptions regarding his role in the Solstice 31 Incident, and the deaths of 110 million people on Earth, on December 22, 2631.

"The Winter Solstice of 2631. The longest night in the history of Earth."

--Solstice 31 Incident Investigation Testimony Transcript: The Memphis Recovery Team Digital Forensics Interim Report. Independent Tech Analysis Team. March 9th, 2663.

ACKNOWLEDGMENTS

I have several people to thank for their help with this book. I will begin, first and foremost, with my wife, Brenda. Thank you for your patience, as it appears I go deaf while I'm writing. Thank you for your encouragement and ideas. Thanks for all the help and love every time I need maintenance or require repairs.

Thanks go to my son, Gray, and daughter, Cady. Thank you for making me proud of you. Thanks for making it so easy to be your dad. I miss you guys.

Thanks go to my editors, Helen Burroughs, Kelly Lenz Carr, Dave Nelson, Karen Parent and Marti Hoffman.

I'd like to thank my friends Tony, Donna, Rob, Dewey, Nancy, Dave, Jimbo, Roberta, my brother Carl and all the people at the Loudon Science Fiction Writers Group and Writers Eating DC for your help, support and inspiration.

Again, I need to specifically thank Chris Schwartz for not pulling punches on the feedback, helping me kill favorite characters and reading the damn thing so many times.

Oh, and my cat Bailey. Best cat in the known universe.